RUN FROM THE DEVIL

BOOK ONE OF THE BLACK CHRONICLES

John Whelan

One Magpie Media

Thank you to my family for putting up with me during the writing of this book.

CONTENTS

PROLOGUE

She was so cold. It was dark. Where were her clothes? The pain in her neck was gone, but her limbs were so heavy. No strength to lift them. She could see the sky. The stars and a sharp edged crescent moon. She had fallen. Something was sticking into her back. Several somethings. Didn't hurt though. The drugs were numbing. Good Hash. Better Coke. Making her tired. So tired. So cold.

Her killer looked down at her from above. Her pale body splayed out. Displayed on the heaped branches at the bottom. Long lines of blood streaked from the red crescent slashed into her throat. A terrible mirror of the moon above. Radiating down over her breasts and her belly, the thin red lines looked like they were alive as the blood oozed along her white flesh. Then she was alone, dying. Dead. Waiting to tell her tale.

CHAPTER ONE

A magpie landed on the window of a large auditorium and looked in. Nothing shiny or edible in there really. A massive screen at the head of the room flashed different colours and briefly attracted the magpie's attention. A tall, good looking man was standing in front of it as the screen settled on a vivid red colour with the words "THE DARKNET" centred in large pulsing black letters. His name was Tiberius Frost, Tiber to his friends. He glanced at his notes and said in a soft Californian accent.

"So, to conclude this Presentation on Digital Security, I would like to end by saying that if you are tempted to explore the Darknet, please be aware you may be confronted with unsavoury content and you may encounter some of the equally unsavoury people who inhabit this space.

It is like wandering into a bad part of town for the first time. You stand out as a visitor and run the risk of being mugged. So don't just click a link without first considering who you might bump into and what you might encounter. It is not possible to unsee something. It may stay with you for the rest of your life. Thank you very much."

The man gathered his notes and acknowledging the enthusiastic applause of his audience with the briefest of nods, walked from the podium and exited behind the screen. Startled by the burst of noise the magpie flew away just as quickly.

A short while later Tiberius and his host were standing in a well-appointed reception room elsewhere in the Institute of

Criminology in University College Dublin enjoying tea and sandwiches. Although Tiberius was not so much enjoying it as wondering when he could escape without giving offence.

"Thank you so much for your excellent presentation, DI Frost. Very useful and timely in view of the upcoming Web Summit," said Professor O'Connell, the Director of the Institute.

"You're welcome."

"Not at all, Tiberius. Great ending. Very dramatic! I rather think you might have a future as a lecturer if you ever were to consider a change of career." The academic enthused. "Yes. Yes, indeed. Not a word wasted. Everything precise and yet quite illuminating. As a retired barrister, I enjoy listening to someone who understands the real value of a word."

"Call me Tiber," he replied automatically as he thought that if he had to endure the horror of standing in front of a large group of students every working day for the next ten years he would undoubtedly shoot himself.

He was saved by an older man and an attractive, slightly younger woman, in her late forties or fifties with short, spiky cut grey hair, joining them, carrying glasses of red wine.

"Tiber, this lovely lady is Jessica Plenderleith, whose hubby we are honoured to have sojourning with us on campus for a few months. Fortunately, she and her lucky consort, James have just returned to Dublin this morning. Jessica, James, this is Detective Inspector Frost previously of Los Angeles and currently working with our Irish Police."

The woman slid up to him and standing very close, put her hand on his forearm saying in an elegant English accent, "I thought it was a wonderful presentation. Very illuminating. Paul was so persuasive that I postponed a little soiree with my husband and our houseguest in order to attend. You must come to dinner with us some night soon."

Before Tiberius could thank her the Professor threw his arm around him and said "I feel Tiber has definite potential as a lecturer. Definite potential. Persuade him for me Jessica? Use your feminine wiles on him?"

"Not going to happen Paul," She retorted. "I can think of much better uses of Mr Frost's potential." She squeezed his arm softly. She was a sultry woman with a curvaceous figure, which contrasted with her somewhat severe, short grey hair. Standing so close with her hand still resting on his forearm, he could feel the heat from her body. Tiberius was feeling increasingly uncomfortable and wondering how to disengage from this situation. He was effectively trapped between the Professor on one side and this provocative woman on the other.

Suddenly, a girl said loudly, "Someone turn on the news quick! There's something happening in Shannon." After a few moments, a large flat screen on one side of the room, flickered to life, showing images of smoke pouring from the terminal building at Shannon Airport, a small airport in the Mid-West of Ireland. A plane was on fire near the terminal. The room quietened, punctuated by gasps and exclamations.

An excited reporter was saying "At this point in time, it is unclear how many are dead. Early reports say that initial shots were heard on the first floor at the US immigration and customs pre-clearance facility. At least one United Airlines flight had just landed and was taxiing towards the western end of the Terminal Building when it was hit by a missile fired from the golf course adjacent to the airport.

Several US military personnel travelling through Shannon were simultaneously attacked by unknown assailants inside the terminal building. There have been exchanges of gunfire. As you can see from our cameras, all approaches to the airport have been sealed off and at present the attackers are still inside the terminal building as are police and airport security. It is not known whether or not they have taken hostages and, Oh My God!"

Three large explosions separated by milliseconds, shredded the roof of the Terminal building. Uniformed figures could be seen racing inside and some sporadic shooting could be heard. By this point, Tiberius was standing to one side of the crowd with his phone to his ear.

"Where the hell are you Frost?" roared his boss the moment the phone connected.

"UCD. Giving the lecture you told me to do."

"Get back in here ASAP. We're going to need everyone."

"On my way."

Tiberius put the phone in his pocket and turned to the Professor saying "Gotta go, Paul. Sorry. Thanks for your hospitality."

The Professor was staring at the TV with a bleak look on his face. "Yes. Yes, of course. You go."

As Tiberius left, he could see some people holding each other, crying, while others were frantically making calls and texting on their phones.

CHAPTER TWO

Tiberius sipped a takeaway coffee. Thank God, he had diverted via the 3FE Café on his way back to the University. Their coffee was so good, it almost made this unpleasant duty palatable. Almost.

He was still annoyed at his superior for refusing to allow him to get involved in the Shannon Investigation. When he arrived at Garda Headquarters in Harcourt Street the place was in uproar. Tiberius spent three hours waiting to speak with his boss who was locked into a succession of crisis meetings. Eventually, he was called in by his secretary, handed a slim manilla file and told he was to head back to the University to take over the investigation of a murder which had taken place on the grounds earlier that morning.

No point in arguing about it, he was told, when he suggested that as an American he might be of more use at Shannon Airport. It was a case of all hands on deck, although she did admit, sympathetically, not using him in Shannon was "a bit Irish."

Tiberius was standing inside a roped off area within a wide belt of trees and undergrowth running between a busy road called the Stillorgan Dual Carriageway and the University campus.

"You, Frost?" A technician came over to him dressed in a white hooded jumpsuit.

"Yes." Tiberius never used two words where one would do.

"You can come view the site now, we've finished around the boundary, so you can look in at the body before we move it."

"Look in?"

The technician looked at him. "You'll see."

"What's your name?" Tiberius asked.

"Jonathan. Everyone calls me Jon," the technician called over his shoulder without looking back.

They walked along a grit path used by walkers and joggers and turned right into the trees. Tiberius could see flashes of light ahead. They stopped at a large hole in the ground. It was manmade, rectangular, about thirty five feet wide by fifty feet long and quite deep with smooth walls. The bottom was cluttered with rubbish and undergrowth. People passed by this tank-like hole every day and didn't even know it was there.

A bit like an amphitheatre, and we are in the Gods, thought Tiberius to himself.

Lying on the bottom was a female body with the head thrown back and a gaping wound in her throat. She had long fair hair with vivid pink streaks. The lower half of her body was covered in a brown and white covering which reached just below her vagina. Two other technicians were carefully removing and bagging pieces of debris resting on the cloth. A camera on a tripod was standing unattended at the edge. Her body was stark white with red stripes running from her sliced neck over her breasts and down her stomach.

Tiberius scanned the hole and the body, then asked: "what's she wearing?"

"Looks like a fancy dress costume. We think it's a cow. Someone said there was a fancy dress party on campus last night"

"Was the body was thrown in, or?"

"Not sure yet. Someone may have thrown her in or she could have fallen. She was found by a guy out walking his dog. It was still darkish. The dog went nuts, barking at the edge and fell in. He got a ladder from a security guard and climbed in to get the dog. When he saw her, he grabbed the dog and got out of there. The security guard rang it in."

"We need to eliminate both of their prints and material"

"Already doing it." The technician was lapsing into the same laconic style as Tiberius. Everyone did after a while.

"Time of death?"

"Dunno. Forensic Pathologist is on her way."

"Right." Tiberius handed the technician a card and said, "can you give this to her and ask her to call me when she's ready?"

Tiberius pulled out his phone and took a photo of the general area. Then he pointed it into the hole and took one of the body.

"We've taken plenty of pics," said the technician in a defensive tone.

"I know," answered Tiberius. "Just helps me."

He walked around the hole and climbed down a ladder into the hole. The sound of the nearby traffic dropped to almost nothing. The air in the hole was still and heavy. He stood about ten feet from the technicians and studied the body and face for a few minutes. Then he stood in the centre of the area and turned slowly in a full circle scanning the area. He climbed back out. The other technician was standing near the top of the ladder. Tiberius looked at him.

"You sample the blood on the wall over there?" He pointed at darkened stains on the wall near where the body lay.

"Yes. Got two sets of footprints too."

"Well done. She's late teens - early twenties?"

The technician nodded. "We found a wristband from the party so we reckon she's at the college here."

"Wristband?" queried Tiberius.

"When they have a party, instead of giving you a ticket they give you a wristband so you can go in and out during the event."

"That's smart," said Tiberius.

"Yeah. They make sure you have to cut it off with a scissors or whatever to get rid of it, so there's less likelihood of it being given to someone else to get in for free. It's used at most concerts and festivals now."

"OK. Get the Pathologist to give me a call?" said Tiberius turning away.

"Sure," said the technician beginning to climb down the ladder.

"I suppose, the post-mortem will take some time?"

"You have no idea mate. We still don't have final figures from Shannon and the bloody US Army want to repatriate the bodies to the States to do their own autopsies. How stupid is that?" He paused, realising who he was mouthing off to. "Oh sorry."

"That's OK" smiled Tiberius. "Army folk are the same all the world over"

"Yeah. Anyway"

"OK." Tiberius began walking away and then turned back to the technician and called, "thanks for your help, Jon."

"You're welcome." The technician continued on down and Tiberius slowly meandered back to the path, deep in thought.

"Who was that Jon?" One of the other technicians asked.

"The Yank in the NBCI," replied Jon. "He didn't seem as stuck up as I've heard. Just a bit quiet."

"Apparently, he's a bit of a genius too. Had a great success rate in California or wherever, but then some sort of scandal happened hence his transfer to the land of the bogs and the little people."

"He probably got plenty of practice in a mad place like that," Jon grinned.

"Yep, we only get boring murders in Dublin, excluding that lunacy in Shannon."

The third technician, who was crouching over the body, stood and said "could you two morons just focus on your work please? We need to get as much done as possible before the boss arrives so we can head to Shannon Airport."

"How many dead now?" asked Jon quietly.

"You'll find out when we get there," came back the brusque

reply.

It had started raining again. Tiberius headed back along the path and climbed over the tape blocking it. He approached a uniformed officer standing beside a police car.

"Hi," said Tiberius.

"What can I do for you?" asked the young officer with a pale, expressionless face marred only by a large wart growing out of his left eyebrow.

Tiberius fumbled for his ID and showed it. "Sorry, I'm NBCI. Just wanted to find out who's in charge here and where I can find them?"

The officer's demeanour changed immediately and he replied, "Oh right. No problem. We're all out of Donnybrook Station. DI Kellett is in charge. She went over to the Security Guard's place to talk to them."

"Thanks," said Tiberius. "Uh. Where's that?"

"Hang on a sec. They might be back at the University Community Garda Office instead. I'll check." He thumbed his radio and spoke into it, "DI Kellett?"

"Yes?" a woman's voice answered.

"NBCI Detective looking for you."

"Oh great."

"Are you in the Security office or the Community Garda office?"

"In the Campus Garda Office, just where you left us Garda Sweeney. You warty pillock!" came back the increasingly irritated voice.

Sweeney's hand moved involuntarily to his forehead. Then, realising what he was doing, he lowered it abruptly and turning slightly away from Tiberius, pointed towards the cluster of buildings in the distance.

"Head over that way, until you come to a pond and the Campus Garda Office is in the smaller building at the far corner."

"Thanks" said Tiberius, turning to go. He stopped, turned back and looked at Sweeney, who sheepishly looked at him, still side on. "She's a bit unpleasant?" he said sympathetically.

Sweeney turned fully away, presenting his back to Tiberius and muttered "you have no idea mate. You have no idea."

CHAPTER THREE

The morning before, on Grafton Street, someone was saved and someone was killed.

Grafton Street is more than just a pedestrianised city thoroughfare. It is a social hub. People come to promenade, to busk, to meet friends, to shop, to eat and drink. It's always full and lively. At the bottom end it intersects Nassau Street and Suffolk Street with the ancient buildings of Trinity College Dublin across the way. The traffic is busy at that junction and with droves of pedestrians trying to cross there is always a chance of an accident.

Beth didn't believe in luck or fate, karma or God. It was all just random to her. So to her mind it was just a random event that she was standing near a tall, handsome, well-dressed man when he stepped off the footpath in a crowded Grafton Street and into the path of a fast moving truck. Beth instinctively grabbed him and pulled him back out of the way of the lorry. She overbalanced and he fell on top of Beth. He sprang back to his feet. Another man who had also stepped off the footpath a millisecond after him was not so lucky. The lorry ploughed into him, hurling his body into the air. He landed with a sickening thud on the unforgiving road. People were shouting and a young girl screamed. A bystander, grabbed the man's arm asking him "are you OK? My God, she saved you. She saved your life!"

Beth had banged the back of her head on the pavement and was a little groggy. She had a sensation of being picked up by other people, while this gorgeous guy stared at her, showing no expression whatsoever. Nearby, she heard someone shout "get an ambulance" but someone else said "no point. he's dead." Beth and the man she saved both turned to look at the people clustered around the front corner of the lorry where a pair of legs could be seen sticking out. "You're lucky pal. If she hadn't grabbed you back, you'd have been killed too," said an elderly man.

"Yes," replied Mr Black. He turned to Beth. "Thank you............ ah?" He looked at her inquiringly.

"Beth," she smiled weakly. "Beth Frontemont" she said. Everything rotated and her last thought before she fainted was that he was dangerously good looking.

*   *   *

Later that day, three girls were sitting at a table in a café in University College Dublin eyeing up a tall, well-built, young man in his twenties, standing at the counter waiting for his coffee.

"Dear God, would you look at him? He's gorgeous! Who is he?

"Dane something or other." Another girl sitting at a neighbouring table leaned back towards them whispered theatrically "and you can forget about him. He's like, not into girls."

"Gay?" asked one of her audience.

"Noooooooooooo, don't think so. But he's as weird as anything, and just like blanks you if you try and talk to him? We've all tried but he only hangs out with one girl and she's deffo not his girlfriend, because I saw her score a different guy on Black Monday. So?"

"Weird."

"Yup"

"You said it"

"Even his name is cool!"

Dane was watching the TV coverage of the Shannon terrorist attack while waiting for his order. He paid and brought two coffees past the groups of other students; his eyes fixed on the window table where his friend was sitting. He studiously ignored his mini fan club, who tracked his progress from till to table.

"Still………. ," groaned one girl

"I know"

"Deffo would"

"Oh God! In a second"

Dane plonked the two coffees on the table and sat opposite a petite girl in a hoodie who was staring out the window at the rain pouring down.

"I think you have new additions to the fan club," smirked his companion without taking her eyes from the deluge outside.

"Huh?" Dane looked up with a frothy moustache of coffee foam surrounding his mouth. Beth glanced over at him, laughed and said "Dane, you really need to look over at those girls near the till, right now!"

"Why?"

"Because I think your cappuccino moustache might just put them off for ever."

"Give me a break Beth. I was up all night re-doing the code on the predictor engine," he answered grumpily, but in this low deep purring voice which Beth always said would charm the knickers off a duchess.

"More importantly" he asked. "How are you feeling?"

"Oh much better. The headache has almost gone and I don't feel as nauseous."

"Did that guy thank you for saving him?"

"Dunno really, can't remember. It's odd but I remember walking down Grafton Street and then nothing until I woke up in the Hospital. I do remember he was good looking. Like a male model but didn't show up at the hospital and then cruelly forgot to give me his number. Story of my life." She sighed, "thanks for coming to get me by the way."

"I suppose I'll always be there for you……………..well, until I can get rid of you!" He laughed softly.

Beth thought to herself. *Thank God I never fancied him. The poor guy doesn't know what an effect he has on the opposite sex. On all sexes come to think of it. Even my Mum's rabid, psycho-bitch dog adores him.* Then what he had said penetrated her headache.

"You re-did the code for the predictor engine." And?"

"Sorry?" Dane wiped his mouth, managing to smear the foam and chocolate topping across his chin. "Oh. Yeah. It works. Quite pleased with it actually."

"You're quite pleased. Quite? Pleased?"

Dane looked at her, picking up on the tone in her voice. Suddenly wary.

"Well yeah. I mean, like. I tested it to see if it would work and it does. Y'know?"

"And it didn't occur to you to text or WhatsApp me? Even to phone me? I mean we've only been slaving on this for two and a half years solid. You finished it last night and it works and you kept it to yourself?"

"Jeez Beth! Take it easy. I was wrecked." Dane scrambled to dig himself out of the hole he had just created with his partner. "Seriously. As soon as I saw it worked, I crashed. Slept from four thirty am until I got your text and went to the hospital to pick you up. Sorry."

"You're right, Dane. I shouldn't have snapped. So my suggestion worked?"

"Absolutely. I used two US serial killers and one UK guy for the test and it predicted them with an average of 98% accuracy from the total sample of one thousand. I need to tweak a few things to get it to 100%, but I reckon the fact that their childhoods predate the internet and social media reduced the volume of publicly available information about them, which accounted for the 2% deviation."

"This is great. Dane. You did it. Well done!"

"No Beth." He corrected her quietly. "We did it. It was your idea to try it on famous criminals. The amount of data on them was just huge. I would never have come up with the strategic plan that underpinned the development of the application or come up with half the changes. I just wouldn't have gotten here on my own." He paused, then added, "you created the roadmap and I followed it. We make a good team, I guess."

"OK well, let's celebrate and get dressed up and go to the Party tonight, yeah?" Beth grinned.

"On one condition. I want to wear something that covers my face and people can't recognise me. It gets annoying otherwise."

"People? You mean girls."

"And gay guys. It's really annoying."

"It must be dreadful to be beautiful!" Beth did a grandiose sigh and then brightened. "I have just the solution for you! Unless you want to continue wearing your cappuccino face mask?"

*   *   *

Hours later, two human shaped cows complete with udders and cow masks were walking through the campus towards a building that was throbbing with music. They were passing a large bottle of watery looking Coke between them.

"I think you put too much vodka into it Beth. It's like drinking petrol" said Dane as he handed her over the fast diminishing bottle.

"Nonsense, fellow Unicorn," said Beth, staggering as she tripped over her tail for the umpteenth time since picking up the costumes in town.

"Stop calling us that. We only have an app not a billion-euro company. We're a long, long way from making any money out of the software."

"Ahhhh," said Beth, tapping the side of her cow nose, "but we will be. This is going to be huge, Daney-bubbles, old pal. Absobubbly huge-y-mento! Trust me." She stopped and looked further along the queue ahead of them.

"Dane! Plagiarism Alert! Do my eyes deceive me? Is that not another moo-cow identical to ourselves further up there?"

Dane straightened to his full, considerable height and looked along the queue at a blonde girl about thirty people ahead, wearing the same outfit with the headpiece tipped back off her head. She was chatting animatedly to a guy wearing a Devil Costume. "Yep" he said.

"Yep? Yep? There's no Yep about it! We must either entreat her to join in the safety of our herd or cast her adrift to suffer loneliness and possibly a one-way trip to the McDonalds supply chain!" Beth was in full flow and made to move out of the queue.

Dane grabbed her arm and whispered urgently, "Beth, you start any messing and I'm going home!"

"Oh Dane. Sorry"

"Just remember and don't ruin it."

"Okeydokey." Beth's cow lowered her head, chastened. She leaned against her much taller friend. And then she mooed. A very realistic moo.

Dane stared straight ahead.

Beth mooed again.

She gave a final moo accompanied by a snort of laughter and elbowed him. Suddenly the two of them were giggling.

The queue shuffled forward at a snail's pace and they with it, heading for a night of dancing and fun. The girl in the cow suit ahead popped her mask on as she entered the hall.

Dane and Beth finished the bottle of doctored Coca Cola and were about four metres from the door when Beth said, "Oh God! Dane?

"What?"

"Oh Dane. I feel sick."

"You are joking me."

"Oh God, Dane. No. I feel really bad. I think I'm gonna throw up."

"Well if you puke on your costume we'll lose the deposit so we need to get you out of it. Fast."

"Whatever." Beth was already struggling out of the cow costume. She shimmied it down over her hips and Dane knelt to pull it off her feet. Freed, Beth bolted across the road and leant over the railings at the other side. She retched loudly and long, to the cheers of the other costume clad members of the queue. Dane folded her costume and walked across the road to her.

"Finished?" he asked.

"Not sure. Maybe. Oh God, no!"

Beth vomited again, this time a little less copiously.

When she finished she asked weakly, "got a tissue?" Silently, Dane fished in the pockets of his cow costume and handed her a wad of tissues.

Beth wiped her face and slowly straightened up, holding onto the rail with a desperate strength.

"Better?" Asked Dane

"Yeah, but I feel a bit weak."

"Too weak to go to the party?"

"Oh God yeah. Sorry Dane."

"No. That's fine. Let's head back to mine. It's closer and you can crash."

"Thanks."

Dane tucked his arm around her tiny waist and half carried her to the student accommodation block where he lived on Campus.

Inside the venue, the other cow costumed student was having a great time. She had ditched her brother and was dancing with a very dashing looking masked Pirate. She was so drunk and stoned that she couldn't quite make out whether the Pirate was a man or a woman but was determined to enjoy finding out.

CHAPTER FOUR

Tiberius wandered through the collection of ugly modern buildings that comprised the UCD main Campus until he came to a large desolate looking, expanse of water unrelieved but for a limp cluster of water jets in the centre. As he made his way to the Agricultural building, Tiberius decided that modern architecture was a high risk business, and when it got it wrong. Boy was it an insult to one's senses. The Campus Garda office shared its home in a three storey concrete and glass building with the Agriculture School and Campus Services.

He entered, found the office, knocked and went in. Two female police officers in uniform and a familiar looking plainclothes male turned to look at him.

"You NBCI?" asked the taller of the two women.

"Yes," Tiberius smiled at her. She didn't return it.

The man standing beside her looked familiar. Someone on TV. An actor in some series? Tiberius's mind compared the dour face in front of him to images he had seen and then it clicked. The stocky, short haired guy was the spitting image of an actor called Gerard McSorley a.k.a. Father Todd Unctuous in the Father Ted TV programmes. Tiberius discovered it on Amazon Prime some months back and had become addicted to the comedy series.

The tall woman walked towards him and gave him a perfunctory handshake. "So you got stuck with this gig due to all your buddies prancing around Shannon Airport chasing terrorists eh? Right. I'm D.I. Kellett. She's Detective Prendergast and that lovely man is D.S. Doyle. God love him."

Tiberius said "hi" and then asked, "can you bring me up to speed?"

Kellett stepped backwards to a table and rested her buttocks and hands on it. "Victim is a female. Jo Anne Sutherland. Early twenties. Died sometime after ten pm. We have confirmed she attended the Students Fancy Dress Bash here on Campus and was still wearing a wristband ticket on her left wrist. The pathologist will probably give us death due to massive blood loss arising from a sharp implement cutting her throat. Poor bitch." Kellett spoke in a low grinding monotone and stared coldly at Tiberius. She stopped speaking.

After a few moments of uncomfortable silence, Tiberius, now realising he wasn't going to get anything else without working for it, asked "anything else?" Kellett just continued staring at him and after a few more moments D.S. Doyle cleared his throat and said, "there was very little blood on her fancy dress outfit."

"Yeah, I noticed." said Tiberius. "What do you make of that?"

Kellett interjected in a venomous tone "Oh D.S. Unctuous here has a doozy of a sex angle on this one. Don't you Toddy?"

Doyle ignored Kellett and addressed Tiberius directly. "We found massive blood stains and spatters along the inside wall of the tank near a barrier, so it's possible she was leaning over the barrier when her throat was cut. We have also taken plaster casts of two sets of prints from two different sets of shoes. One set is positioned just behind the other with both facing the barrier."

"Basically he thinks the murderer was shagging her from behind when he cut her throat. Lovely." Kellett interrupted again.

"Then what?" Tiberius asked.

"He waited until she bled out," Doyle continued, "partially pulled up her costume and threw her into the hole. This morning she was found by a guy walking his dog."

Tiberius had moved to the window while he listened and looked out. Then he saw them, walking along. A tall guy dressed all in black and a girl dressed in a Cow Costume.

"Gee whiz, I hope we haven't bored you," Kellett said to his back.

"Do we have somewhere to interview people?" Tiberius asked as he moved quickly from the window towards the door.

"Yes, why?" asked Kellett, but Tiberius was gone. Kellett looked at her colleagues and muttered, "what the hell? Should we test that nutbag for drugs?"

Ignoring her, Doyle had moved to the window and was looking out. He watched as moments later Tiberius walked towards the couple and spoke with them. The three of them walked back towards the building. "Lucky bastard" muttered Doyle, "he's only on the case five minutes and he catches a break."

"What the hell are you on about?" asked Kellett.

Doyle turned back to her and grinned. "You'll see."

Tiberius re-entered the office, ushering in a pale, slightly built, diminutive young woman wearing a Cow Costume and a tall, broad shouldered, very handsome young man.

"Well, well," said Kellett. "How do you want to do this?" she asked Tiberius in a more accommodating tone.

Tiberius ignored her and asked Doyle, "can you get a private room somewhere and have a chat with this gentleman who has kindly offered to help us? His name's Dane."

After they left the room he asked the young woman to sit and took the chair opposite her.

"It's Beth isn't it? That's what you said your name is?"

"Yes, Beth. Look, do you want to tell me what's going on? Are we in some sort of trouble?"

"No, not at all," said Tiberius.

"Not yet," interjected Kellett.

Tiberius paused and turned to face Kellett. Just locked eyes without saying anything. Silence stretched out, until Kellett finally glanced away. Tiberius turned back to Beth and asked her if she wanted a coffee or water.

"Both, please. I'm dying of a hangover here." She smiled at him.

Tiberius turned to the other Detective. "Detective Prendergast, would you mind getting this lady a coffee and a glass of water?"

"No problem" said Prendergast and asked Beth "Milk and Sugar?"

"God yes. Three sugars and lots of milk. Thank you." Prendergast left the room.

"Do you want to wait for the drinks or can I ask you a few questions now?"

"Fire away, Boss. Are you American?" said Beth

"Yes Beth. Did you attend the costume party here on Campus last night?"

"Almost."

"Sorry? What do you mean almost?"

"Well, I was pre-drinking with Dane and had too much so when we got to the queue for the party, I got sick and he brought me back to his place. Anyway, I never got to the party. Bit of a waste, huh?"

"What's pre-drinking?"

"Doesn't everyone pre-drink these days?" Beth looked over at Kellett for support.

"Pre-drinking is where kids get pissed on cheap alcohol before going out so they don't have to pay the expensive prices for drinks at whatever venue they are attending," Kellett stated in a matter-of-fact tone.

"Yup! You can save serious money on your social life through pre-drinking, Boss!" Beth grinned at Tiberius. "Not that I'll have to worry too much about the cost of a few drinks soon."

"Why? "asked Tiberius.

"Why what?"

"Why won't you have to worry about the cost of your social life soon?

"Oh God! I think I'm still half pissed. I just meant that if everything goes according to plan, Dane and me will make some serious money with the predictor software we've written. That's all."

"OK" Tiberius said with a smile. He liked this elfin, young woman's pleasant, open manner.

Just then Kellett leaned on the table, giving the girl a hostile stare and said "Look this isn't a funny situation. We've a dead body to investigate. Quite frankly, we don't give a toss about your software pipe dreams. Did you know a girl called Jo Anne Sutherland?"

Beth was visibly shocked. Both from the vehemence of Kellett's tone and the news that someone had died.

"No. I mean. No, I didn't. Know her, that is. Sorry. I didn't mean to make light of it. I just didn't know." She stammered and dropped her head.

"That's OK Beth." said Tiberius quickly. "We realise you weren't aware of the nature of the investigation." He stared coldly over Beth's head at Kellett before looking back at the young woman. "So, you didn't know her. Can you tell me where you got the cow costume from?" He moved things on quickly, hoping to rebuild the relationship he had been working on before Kellett derailed everything.

"Oh. I hired it in town from The Fun Place on South King Street."

Tiberius asked Kellett, "can you contact them and find out how many of this type of costume they rented to people attending the Party here and who rented them?"

"What? Now?" Kellett glared at him.

"Yes. Immediately please. They should still be open." Tiberius stared back, unmoved.

Kellett walked to the other end of the room and began speaking into a phone.

Tiberius turned back to Beth but before either of them

could say anything more, Prendergast returned with Beth's drinks. Tiberius pulled up a chair for Prendergast, effectively sealing Beth off from Kellett.

Beth downed the water in one go. Then she asked Tiberius "Is that why you want to speak to us? The person who died was wearing the same outfit as me?"

She's quick thought Tiberius.

"We're going to be speaking with a lot of people on Campus. Don't worry about it," Prendergast replied with a warm smile.

Beth sipped her coffee.

Tiberius asked "can you tell us roughly what time you got to the Party at? Sorry," he corrected himself, "to the queue?"

"God, I'm never going to live that down. I just hughied all over the place. In front of everyone!"

Prendergast's grin widened and she leaned forward, "don't worry about it. We've all been there. But if you could remember the time it would be very helpful. Or anything else."

"Well I reckon it was about nine thirty, ten-ish 'cos the doors were open when we arrived and the queue was quite long and.......Oh!" She stopped.

"Go on" encouraged Prendergast.

"No. I've just realised that I saw someone ahead of us in the queue wearing the same outfit as me. A girl. Wow! Could she have been who you're talking about?"

Prendergast glanced sideways at Tiberius. He asked quietly "do you remember anything else about her, Beth? Anything that stood out, who she was with?"

Beth stared down at her coffee cup, concentrating.

"OK." After a few moments, she said, "blonde hair with pink streaks. Maybe five foot five-ish? She was standing beside someone wearing a Devil costume, all red and black and with horns and a pitchfork. I don't know if she was with him or not. Sorry I can't help any more. I was pretty pissed."

"No. That's great help, Beth. Thanks. Can you give Detective

Prendergast your contact details and we'll be in touch if we need to clarify anything." Tiberius stood and walked over to Kellett. She said, "Hang on" into the phone and looked at him, "yes?"

"Can you ask if they have records of renting out Devil costumes to men for the same event?" Without waiting for a reply Tiberius turned and walked back.

He brought Beth out into the corridor to find Dane and Doyle standing there talking. They said goodbye to the two students and went back inside. Kellett got off the phone and said "they rented out eight cow costumes, and they're the only people in Dublin who carry them. They rented out fifteen Devil costumes. They're going to email us the details."

"Good." Tiberius turned to Doyle and asked, "what did you find out from the guy?"

"Well. They're not a couple, just best buddies. And they're collaborating on some project together which he was reluctant to talk about.

"What project?"

"I didn't press him on it as it didn't sound too relevant at this point in time. "

"OK. I'll be following up in the next few days with them and I can clear it up then. I've got to get back into Harcourt Street," said Tiberius, referring to the Police Headquarters building where the NBCI were based. "I'll be in touch over the next few days."

"Why?" asked Kellett. "Surely NBCI are taking over from us now?"

"We're very shorthanded due to the Terrorist Attack in Shannon. So I was thinking of requesting you guys to stay on board and work on this with me?"

"Don't do us any favours." Kellett said tight-lipped.

Doyle, on the other hand, seemed pleased and his dour expression lightened. "Well it does have all the hallmarks of an interesting case, but DI Kellett's right I won't get my hopes up. The powers that be will probably refuse your request."

"We'll see," said Tiberius and he turned to go.

As he walked down the hallway Tiberius got out his cellphone and keyed in a U.S. phone number. A number in Silicon Valley, California.

*   *   *

The following morning found Tiberius in a large cafeteria back on Campus about to share a most unhealthy fried breakfast with Detective Prendergast and DS Doyle.

"So when did Kellett hear she was seconded to the investigative team in Shannon?" Tiberius asked.

"Sometime last night" answered Prendergast.

"It means a bit more work for the three of us. You guys OK with that?" Tiberius queried his two new partners.

"No problem" answered Doyle "I just don't understand how you managed to get them to let us stay on the case. Not that I'm complaining, mind you."

"My boss needs this sorted in a hurry and he outranked your boss. Basically," grinned Tiberius.

"Fair enough, Sir."

"Call me Tiber."

"Tiber?" Doyle replied, "how are you spelling that?"

"It's short for Tiberius."

"Right." Doyle's face was immobile. "What about some grub?" he suggested.

They ordered breakfast and while they waited, they went over the case notes, discussing the next steps and deciding who was doing what. Prendergast would deal with the crime scene, techs and any evidence collection and analysis. Doyle would check known criminals with relevant form, known to be in or near the area and also research any and all CCTV cameras on campus and on any of the roads around the university. Tiberius would concentrate on Beth and Dane and all three would divide up interviewing the remaining students and staff who attended the party that night. Unfortunately, there were three other events on at the same time so there were thousands of students moving in and out of the campus.

A waitress arrived at their table with three large plates full of various fried foods and they suspended their conversation briefly to attack their cholesterol infused breakfasts. Tiberius had succumbed to the lure of the "Irish Breakfast" after his first few months in Harcourt Street. He reckoned the entire Irish police force ran on them.

"Interesting," said Doyle around a mouthful of sausage. "Look who's heading our way." The other two looked around to see the tall figure of Dane Wilson walking towards them. Tiberius was amused to see every female student in the café eyeing the tall young man as he strode towards them.

Dane stopped beside Prendergast and asked if he could join them for a moment. Tiberius motioned him to sit beside Doyle. Dane plonked himself down and hunched forward, silent.

"What can we do for you Mr Wilson?" Tiberius said with a smile.

"Well, I figured I should tell you about some stuff, but now I'm here, I'm thinking that I'm probably wasting your time, so I'll go" and he made to rise.

"That's OK," said Prendergast quickly. "As you can see we're sort of on a break so we don't mind listening to you and we might see something in whatever you want to talk about, so just fire away," she smiled at him.

Doyle grinned and raised his eyebrows at Tiberius, who ignored him and said to Dane, "what's on your mind?"

Dane seemed to come to a decision and sitting back in his chair said "well, it's like this and it may not have anything to do with what you're investigating but there was a break-in at my office, a few days ago."

"We thought you were a student? How come you've an office? Where is it?" asked Prendergast.

"It's in the Nova-UCD facility," answered Dane.

"What's that?" asked Tiberius.

Doyle answered, "they provide office space and facilities to academics and students in return for a small piece of equity in whatever company is created from the research and development they carry out."

"Yeah," nodded Dane, "except for ours, 'cos we don't have a company yet and I'm just using my pal's office while he's stuck in Greenland for a year doing research. Look," he continued "it was clearly an attempt to steal our software. I checked my security logs and whoever it was tried to access my computers and also our servers and when they couldn't get in that way, they ripped out the hard disks and took them."

"Did they get what they were looking for?" asked Tiberius quietly.

"Nope." Said Dane

"Are you sure?" Tiberius probed.

"Absolutely."

"Explain, please."

"I created a secure virtual workplace elsewhere on the Net, which is well protected. It's where everything we are working on relating to the software is kept. All physical systems in the office are wiped whenever work is finished and also at pre-set daily intervals. I doubt even a top level Black Hat could hack us."

"OK." Said Doyle. "What's the software they were after?"

"I don't want to get into that right now." Dane stared at Tiberius.

Prendergast picked up on Dane's reluctance and stood saying she needed the loo. As she did so, Doyle said that he was getting a refill and did Dane want a coffee? Dane said no and Doyle headed for the counter.

"Dane, I can see you are concerned about the security of your software and you appear to have put serious measures in place so I assume whatever it does will create significant value for you and your colleagues." Tiberius said softly. "I guess I can understand you being reluctant to talk about it to us. But I do need to know a little more about it, if only to determine whether or not it has a bearing on the murder we are investigating here."

Dane looked uneasy. "I know. I know, but you don't understand. It's our life's work. It's ground-breaking stuff. Seriously."

"Dane, I'm a police officer and if I give you my word, I won't discuss it with anyone until I've determined whether or not it's relevant to this case, then that's going to have to suffice. I'm sorry but that's the way this works."

"I don't have a lot of faith in the word of cops, man. Sorry." Dane said obstinately.

Tiberius just stared at him quietly. Waiting.

After a few moments of uncomfortable silence, Dane leant forward and said, "look. I'm not going into what it does but I can tell you this. It's a new application of Artificial Intelligence and Big Data. OK?"

"Fair enough. Let me tell you what I already know." Tiberius replied gently. "Beth informed me during our discussions yesterday that it's a form of predictor app? I guess it's based on analysing large amounts of behavioural data?"

Dane threw his eyes up to heaven.

"Don't blame her. I think she was still a bit drunk. You reckon it will be worth a lot of money?" asked Tiberius.

"Dunno really. Beth is the one you want to ask about that. She says we're going to be a Unicorn company."

"A Unicorn company?"

"A tech company worth over a Billion. It's a Silicon Valley thing."

"Anything else?" asked Tiberius.

"No, that's it really. I just thought you should know about it cos it happened so close to the day that girl was murdered and I was worried."

Tiberius looked at Dane for a few moments and then said "why?"

"Why what?"

"Why do you think the break in might be related to the murder?"

"Beth told me the girl was wearing the same costume as us and I just thought............" He tailed off.

"Go on Dane. Follow it through," Tiberius encouraged him.

"Well, it just occurred to me that maybe whoever killed her might have screwed up and got the wrong person? Being a bit over-dramatic here aren't I" he added sheepishly.

"Well it's a bit of a stretch but I see your line of reasoning." Tiberius smiled.

"And I was wondering if you could provide some kind of protection for Beth?" asked Dane. "But you can't tell her I said any of this," he rushed on. "I mean she'd kill me. Well not literally," he grinned sheepishly, " but you know what I mean. She may be tiny but she'd be really pissed that I was looking for some kind of, y'know, security for her?"

"I know what you mean. Right now, I can't do much about that. Unfortunately, in the absence of greater clarity about the value of the software my hands are tied." Tiberius probed again. "If it is as valuable as you say then it may be relevant. You might also be correct about the mistaken identity issue, but even then it's a long shot. I will check it out further. I promise. Protective custody is not something we would offer lightly but if it is merited going forward, we'll consider it. Just bear in mind we're seriously stretched in light of the Terrorist attack at Shannon Airport. Anything else?"

"No man. I figured you wouldn't do anything." Angry, Dane jumped up and strode away. He was so annoyed, he had forgotten to mention that despite his security paranoia, he was also a member of a small online collaborative forum for techies like him, where he has been discussing the app with other developers and programmers and that he had been posting progress updates and problems encountered and solved on the forum.

As he watched Dane storm off, Tiberius sat back. He was surprised the young man had just voiced what he had suspected from the time he had discovered the existence of the extra costumes and now Tiberius was beginning to wonder about the software. Certainly if it was as valuable as Dane had suggested then it would constitute a powerful motive. Doyle and Prendergast returned to the table.

Doyle asked "what's the story on his software then? Why's he so edgy about it?"

Tiberius said, "They believe that their software may be worth hundreds of millions."

"If it's true, that's a bloody serious motive," stated Prendergast thoughtfully. "Are you beginning to think the victim may have been murdered in error?"

"Not sure." Then Tiberius's phone rang and he answered it. "Hey babes" boomed out a loud woman's voice with a strong West Coast accent before he could get it to his ear. The other two smiled knowingly, until Tiberius mouthed "My sister." He stood and walked away.

"Hey Raynie. Thanks for calling back. How are you?" he asked as he moved outside the cafeteria.

"I'm great Tiber! Looking forward to hooking up when I come to Dublin for the Web Summit gig!"

"Me too." Tiberius paused for a second, thinking about the advisability of what he was about to do. "Rayne, I'm in the middle of an unusual case here and there may be a digital angle to it. If that proves correct, can I pick your brains?"

"Oh wow! Absolutely. I'll be like an expert witness right? Like someone in The Good Wife on TV. I'm totally into that."

"No Rayne. Not quite," said Tiberius trying desperately to backtrack and reduce his sister's expectations.

"It's OK, Tiber. I'm just teasing ya! God! You've gotten so serious since you moved back to the Ould Sod! So what's the angle?"

"Not sure right now but am I correct in assuming that Artificial Intelligence and Big Data are hot areas right now?"

"Hot? They're so hot, Babes. They are the future. Everyone's piling into them. The creatives and the money men. Now, I'm intrigued Tiber. What gives?"

"I'll tell you when you get here, Rayne."

"Ring me or whatever and I'll try and help. OK? Gotta go. See ya in Dubs," and the phone went dead.

Tiberius shook his head smiling at his infuriating, brilliant, funny, younger sister for whom he had a massive soft spot and let get away with so much over the years. Rayne had survived a tragic boating accident which had taken the life of their youngest sibling, Godiva and it had made them very close. As a result, Tiberius had been over-protective of Rayne, growing up. Now, he was very proud of her high profile achievements in Silicon Valley and further afield. She was one of the best known entrepreneurs and investors in the US Technology sector and had even advised the Obama administration.

He had been delighted when she rang a month ago telling him she had accepted an invitation to deliver a keynote address at the upcoming Web Summit in Dublin. It was a technology conference which had grown into a global event and which would bring twenty or thirty thousand of the cream of technology entrepreneurs, workers and investors together in Dublin over three frenetic days of talks, meetings and general wheeling and dealing.

And my little sis is one of the top honchos. He shook his head, heading back into his two colleagues.

He was still smiling as he walked back inside and headed towards his two colleagues when Doyle answered a call on his mobile, stood and walked away. Prendergast glanced towards Doyle and then out the window. As Tiberius sat, she waved towards the window and said, "one for sorrow."

"Excuse me?" asked Tiberius, bewildered by this behaviour.

"Oh, it's an Irish superstition. Silly really."

"Explain"

"There's a magpie outside the window."

Tiberius turned and noticed a cocky little bird with striking black and white plumage standing on the window ledge looking in.

"OK, and?"

"Well it's a rhyme you say when you see a single magpie."

"Go on," grinned Tiberius, encouraging her.

"Well. It's
One for Sorrow,
Two for Joy,
Three for a Girl and
Four for a Boy,
Five for Silver,
Six for Gold,
Seven for a secret yet untold."

"So, when you see one Magpie, there's going to be Sorrow," said Tiberius.

"Yes, and that's why I waved. Part of the tradition is that you wave at the magpie and you wave the bad luck away," she smiled.

"There seems to be lots of them on this Campus."

"Oh, they're a very successful little scavenger and they thrive in urban environments." Prendergast looked up as Doyle came back to the table.

"That was Donnybrook Station. They've found two more bodies." Said Doyle.

"And?" said Prendergast.

"They're here. On campus."

"Didn't work did it?" Tiberius said to Prendergast as they headed for the door.

"What?"

"Waving away the sorrow."

*   *   *

The three police officers were walking across the campus,

heading west.

"Any other information?" Tiberius asked Doyle.

"Two bodies, one male and one female were found in the upstairs bedroom of The Glebe House. It's a small two bedroom stone cottage. It's rented to an English lecturer and his wife for six months. They've been there about a month. The cleaning staff visit once a week and they went in about an hour ago to discover the bodies. One of them lost the plot and is pretty hysterical, but the other was more together and called it in. Whoever was on despatch in Donnybrook was very efficient. Sent out a car immediately. The area's been roped off. The cleaners are in an office at the nearest building waiting for us to come and interview them. Then the girl on despatch remembered we were already on campus, got approval for it and contacted me on the mobile."

"It's not like we weren't doing much is it?" complained Prendergast.

"Well at this point. We don't know it isn't related," replied Tiberius reasonably.

"Actually, what are the odds that three murders would occur within two days of each other on a University Campus which has never seen a murder in its hundred odd years of existence? Pretty slim chance that they're not related, especially if these two died of anything other than natural causes, I'd say." Doyle mused aloud as they walked along.

Tiberius's phone rang and a brief conversation ensued with his end consisting of monosyllables and OK's. He put the phone in his pocket and said "that was the Pathology lab. The victim had significant amounts of alcohol, cannabis and cocaine in her blood stream and you were right, well partially" he said to Doyle. "Her body showed signs of vigorous sexual activity, the bruising suggests that it occurred just prior to death, but interestingly there is no DNA in or near her genitals or even signs of condom usage?"

"So how?" began Prendergast.

"Sex Toy?" interrupted Doyle.

"That's what I was thinking" replied Tiberius. "Therefore we still don't know the sex of the perpetrator."

"Well why would a man use a sex toy? He would get no pleasure from it? Neither would a woman for that matter?" added Prendergast.

"Unless she was trying to make it look like it was a sex crime committed by a man?" threw in Doyle.

"Or a man was trying to achieve something similar?"

"It's all a bit convoluted at this point. The absence of useful evidence is leading us to tie ourselves in knots. Let's park this and just focus on what's immediately ahead of us." said Tiberius. He wanted the team and the conversation focussed on the crime scene they were heading for.

They passed by a large old Victorian House adorned with beautiful sandstone arches, coats of arms and various other embellishments which Tiberius recognised.

"Roebuck House or Roebuck Castle," said Doyle. "This grand old lady, for you philistines and yanks, was rebuilt in the mid-1800s in what was called Gothic Revival style. The original building dates back to the 1300s."

Tiberius decided not to mention that he'd been there the day before.

"And you know this because.............?" Asked Prendergast.

"It's the home of the Law School of the University and the Institute of Criminology," answered Doyle as though he was surprised that every Dublin police officer didn't possess this knowledge.

"And you know that because.............?" Persisted Prendergast, grinning.

Doyle took a deep breath, "because I'm doing a bloody PhD there, alright?"

"So where's The Glebe House?" asked Tiberius, ignoring the banter but taking note of Doyle's course and thinking that he may have lucked out with the partners he had recently acquired.

"It's around the back. Bit isolated, especially now that

they're digging up the pathway behind it which leads off Campus to Roebuck Road at the back." Doyle pointed as they rounded the corner and walked along a narrow roadway. After about a hundred metres the road opened onto a small square area with parking and they could see construction works blocking the road which continued on.

Facing them to the right of the construction works was a wooden, ivy-covered fence with a gateway in the far right hand corner. There was a black sign on the left hand pillar with gold lettering which said "*Glebe*" and underneath "PRIVATE RESIDENCE". A police car was parked to the left of the gateway and the narrow part of the road had large plastic red and white tape securing it. A uniformed officer was standing watching them walk towards him.

"Morning Garda Sweeney." Tiberius greeted him with a grin. "You're a bit busy these days?"

Sweeney looked surprised that Tiberius had remembered him. "I get all the fun gigs. DI Frost," he said laconically as he held up the tape to allow them to walk under it.

"Hope you haven't had a big brekkie," said Sweeney, as they passed him. "Cos you're about to lose it."

Tiberius turned back to him and asked, "you've been in to have a look?"

"Yes. Looks like whoever did it is a right nasty bastard and he took his time. I reckon they took a long time to die. Very staged, it seemed to me."

"Thanks Sweeney" said Tiberius thoughtfully.

They went past and through the large wooden gates. A short tarmacadam driveway weaved up to the front door of a picturesque granite cottage with a slate roof and dormer windows. The area around it was set to grass and a variety of trees bounded by mixed granite and old brick walls and ivy clad wooden fencing.

How peaceful and idyllic it all seems, thought Tiberius.

"It's very secluded and private" said Prendergast. "No reason for anyone to come down here, especially as the walkway out to the road beyond is all dug up."

Doyle said quietly, "it'll be interesting to see how observant Mr Sweeney back there was. Hopefully, he was overstating it."

"Or how accurate," added Prendergast tartly.

Doyle stopped at the doorway and said over his shoulder "hate this bit." He took a deep breath and went in. Tiberius looked at Prendergast quizzically. She said nothing, just mimed throwing up and followed Doyle inside.

Who knew? thought Tiberius.

CHAPTER FIVE

Some days earlier, Mr Black was sitting in the front row watching everyone else board an EasyJet flight from London Gatwick to Dublin. He was very organised when it came to air travel. He was always at the airport in plenty of time. Always one of the first to check in and always located himself in the seats nearest the gate and nearest the door of the plane. Though not a snob, he did despair of the democratic effect which the low cost airlines had brought to air travel. The mad rushing for seats and interminable queuing annoyed him. He always felt it was safer to be merged into the herd from a surveillance and security perspective. He just didn't have to behave like them.

As usual, he played one of his little games. This one involved stripping each person, regardless of age, and assessing their suitability for indulging in sexual activity with him or perhaps in a little blood sport, as he liked to call it. Well, excluding kids, for some reason the young didn't float his boat. He didn't know why and didn't care. They simply weren't on the menu, as it were.

His phone binged and he checked the screen. He had just received a sizable payment from a client. He insisted on being paid in Bitcoin, a crypto-currency he favoured. He wondered, as he often did, if he were the only human disposal service, as he liked to call his little business, which was paid in Bitcoin? *Hopefully,* he thought. *Don't want too many idiots attracting attention to the Darknet and the anonymous payment benefits that virtual currencies offer naughty chappies like me.* Years before, he had convinced himself that he possessed a richly irreverent sense of humour.

He watched a voluptuous mature woman step into the cabin. *Good posture,* he decided. *Large breasts, which would droop delightfully and swing around. Mmmm.* She had a curvy bottom with slim ankles, all topped off by a strong, attractive face and short, close cropped grey hair. She reminded him of his Aunt Grace, and his mind went back to how Grace provided some of the only pleasant memories of an otherwise horrific childhood. In retrospect, he reckoned dear old Aunt Grace would be locked up today for introducing an eleven year old to sexual activities, but he had never felt abused by her, not when he compared it to other demons which had figured to a much greater extent in his young life.

It would be interesting to take her roughly from behind, he thought, looking up at the woman's blue eyes as she turned towards him to pass by and move along the cabin. She caught his gaze and locked eyes with him for a moment. Then he smiled. More a tweak at the corner of his mouth than a smile, but enough for her to return it and then feeling the passenger behind her moving into her space, she moved on and passed by him.

I wonder does she like Anal? he mused.

An hour and a half later, the plane's engines turned off in a lowering whine. The cabin lights flickered and all of the impatient passengers rushed to be first off. Standing. Stupidly squeezing into each other's personal space.

No. He decided. *Not doing that. Let's wait until this bunch of bovines has stumbled off the plane and we have a tad more space and time to alight.*

He bent his head to place his novel into his coat pocket and turn on his mobile phone. It was a sleek dark grey iPhone, which delivered his email, allowed him to browse the internet, kept his diary up to date and tracked his costs and revenues. And he made the occasional telephone call on it.

After a good one hundred or so people had passed, he began to stand up and realised he was facing his mature Odalisque, who was just passing. She stopped with a smile to allow him to step into the aisle.

"Thank you, kind lady," he smiled at her and locked eyes again. Then turning, he walked off the plane. He moved a little slower than normal along the corridors of the airport to allow her to catch up, but she either couldn't or decided not to. By the time he went through Passport security into the baggage area, he had not had the opportunity to exchange any further conversation with her. He went to a section with trolleys, slipped one out of the stack and smoothly swung it around to find her facing him. He moved it sideways and manoeuvred it so the handles faced her and said "there you go. All yours."

"Thank you, kind sir." She was full on flirting with him now. As he followed her over to the luggage belt his gaze slipped to her rounded buttocks moving delightfully beneath her skirt

He moved to where she was standing, slipping in beside her. Before he could say anything, his bag came around in front of him and he deftly lifted it from the carousel and plonked it onto his trolley.

"Lucky you," she said softly, "getting it so quickly. I always seem to wait ages for mine to come." She looked past him and said, "Speak of the Devil, here's mine." He turned and pointed at a revolting pink bag and asked, "this one?"

"Yes thanks."

It weighed a ton. As he lifted it onto her trolley, she grabbed for it as though to help him and her hand closed over his, then moved backwards, skin rubbing against skin, as he put the bag on her trolley.

Someone banged into him from behind and he pivoted to encounter a large crew-cut man in a Manchester United tee-shirt, with a big belly, which would feed a small nation, facing him. The man apologised in a broad Northern Ireland accent. Mr Black blanked him and moved his trolley. He turned to find her heading towards the Exit, so he began to follow. There were too many flights being disgorged from the Baggage Reclaim area at the same time and now several bodies and trolleys were between them. As she vanished through the Exit doors, she glanced back at him and raising her eyebrows, smiled ruefully.

By the time he went through the doors he couldn't see her anywhere. Then, off to the left, on the edge of the crowd around the Arrivals Exit, she was standing, arms around an older man, ending a kiss and talking. She looked around and then noticing Mr Black, said something to her companion. He looked over at Mr Black and smiled. Which was somewhat surprising, and he wondered what she had said about the mild flirting that had been going on. Then the white haired man walked over to Mr Black with a pleasant open smile on his face and said, "my name is James Plenderleith and my wife and I would like to offer you a lift into Dublin."

Mr Black stared at him blankly and asked "why?"

"Perhaps you might like to join us for dinner? Maybe even stay the night?" The man's smile became broader. "I guarantee you'll enjoy it." He paused and added "and her."

Mr Black's smiled back, baring his perfect white teeth and said, "I'd be delighted."

As they walked towards the woman, a thought struck him and he asked the man, "James, how would you describe yourself?"

"Oh, I'm a cuckold." Came back the breezy reply. "Bisexual and loving it. Jessica is utterly voracious sexually and I'm just unable to satisfy her"

They joined the woman and she smiled slowly in anticipation. She linked arms with both of them as they walked towards the car park.

Forty eight hours later, Jessica began screaming, but the ball gag he had playfully asked her to wear kept the noise at what Mr Black regarded as an acceptable level, while James struggled futilely against his bonds watching in total horror what was happening to his wife.

*   *   *

"Your pilot called while you were in that meeting, Mr Lee" a fit, tall black girl with crewcut hair said to a smaller, well-built man with Asian features in jeans and a white shirt walking beside her. They moved along a glass walk-way which curved above a soaring atrium in a modern office building.

"Your jet is ready for your flight to Dublin. Your London driver will be waiting for you at the airport. I've also booked a second residence just south of the city as you requested."

"What about the presentation at the Web Summit, Shaylene? Did you get me out of it?"

It was a sore point. She had accepted an invitation for him to give a keynote speech at the Web Summit think-ing it would dovetail nicely with a PR campaign they were conducting aimed at improving his profile and erasing the otherwise extremely accurate perception that he was a backstabbing, ruthless business pirate, whom you invited to invest in your company at your absolute peril. He had ver-bally eviscerated her, reducing her to tears for the first time in her career. It was not an experience she wanted to repeat. Nervously, she started "well, I rang the head guy and"

"Did. You. Cancel. It?" He said in his quiet voice but with a controlled ferocity.

"Yes sir." She answered, "I was just trying to explain that I…"

"Never mind." He cut across her again. "Pack a bag. I want you in Dublin," he said brusquely as he turned left at an inter-section in the glass walkway and walked away from her. The door to the office he entered was open and the smell of oranges was noticeable. He walked past an industrial sized juicing machine with a massive basket of oranges beside it and stood behind a seated young man facing a wall of com-puter screens.

"Hey Deng. How're they hanging ol' buddy?" said the slight

young man without turning around. His voice sounded like that of a child, soft and high.

"Did Wilson post anything new on the forum?"

"Nope. Just that his partner can't drink" the young man giggled.

"Are you sure you don't have enough information to replicate what they've done?"

"Nope. He's naïve but not stupid."

"Are you certain the software can do what he claims, Kent?"

"Yep. Deffo. It's amazing. The keys to the kingdom. Bring it back Deng ol' buddy. Bring it to me and it'll be like printing money."

"I am flying to Ireland to buy it. Also I have put in place an alternative method of securing it, just in case."

"Ahh, OK." Kent didn't want to know what that meant and knew Deng well enough not to ask. And to be honest he didn't care. He just wanted to get hold of it so he could figure it out. He adored good software and this looked like it could be some of the best he had ever encountered. Kent finished typing a sequence of keys and said as he swivelled his chair, "so when do you think you'll get...?" *Gone*, he shook his head. *Like a ghost. Creeps me out every time.*

Deng had arrived at Kent Gulbenkian's high school when they were both fifteen. At first glance he looked like a Eurasian geek. Unfashionable haircut. Slacks not jeans. Collared, short sleeved shirt, not the obligatory Superdry t-shirt everyone was wearing at the time. Of course, a pair of spectacles and massive rucksack chock full of books. He was short and appeared slight of build. Totally deceiving. Kent reckoned he had bundles of steel wires under his skin, not muscles.

One day, Deng walked into a toilet in the school where three big guys were cleaning a toilet bowl using Kent's head. It was straight out of a Hollywood movie. The primary instigator of this bit of ad-hoc bullying turned to see Deng looking at them.

"Whaddaya want, Chink?" He growled.

Deng just stood there. He turned to his two friends who were busy holding Kent over the toilet and putting his arms around their shoulders, said "fresh nerd meat boys!"

They dropped Kent on the ground and advanced towards Deng. Kent still couldn't say for sure because it all happened so fast but all three ended up whimpering on the floor. He did recall Deng leaning over each of them and whispering something in their ears, with which they clearly agreed. No, fervently agreed. Then Deng walked over to Kent and said "get cleaned up. What did you see?"

"You were great! How did you do that? Wow! I jus…"

Deng interrupted Kent, saying softly "you saw nothing. OK?"

"But"

"Nothing, you unnerstan?

Kent wasn't stupid and knew his future survival in this school meant staying on the right side of this kid so he said, "I don't know what you're talking about. I just came in here to go to the toilet."

Deng looked at him again, appraising him and nodded. He walked over to the nearest prostrate, whimpering boy, unzipped his trousers and urinated on him. He repeated the process with the other two. Sometime later Kent asked him why he had pissed on them and Deng replied, as though surprised to be asked "I went in there to urinate. Why else does one go into a toilet? And I needed them to be sufficiently humiliated so there would be no necessity for further violence."

Emboldened, Kent asked "how did you learn to fight like that?" Deng didn't answer and Kent figured that he wasn't going to. Then he said slowly in that soft voice.

"Careful. Structured. Unpleasant. Constant. Training."

"Wow," Kent believed him and then Deng added, "from the age of three."

*   *   *

At the same time as Mr Black was ogling his fellow passengers on an EasyJet flight out of Gatwick, Rayne Frost settled back into her seat in the first class cabin of a British Airways plane bound for Heathrow, from where she would transfer to an Aer Lingus plane for the short hop to Dublin. It was going to be a total of about fourteen hours of flying. However, the only direct flight from LAX to Dublin was with Ethiopian Airways who didn't offer a First Class Option and Rayne was determined that when it came to travel, she turned left at the door of the plane and not right, even if things weren't great financially.

A handsome air steward brought her a glass of champagne and she felt a flicker of interest until she realised he plucked his eyebrows. "Dead giveaway" she told herself. Rayne stretched, shrugging the stiffness from her limbs. Earlier that morning, she had gone for a long run along the beach where she lived and had pushed herself hard. She was almost as tall as Tiberius, very lean and surprisingly strong. She had always been a bit of a tomboy and hadn't changed. With her long auburn hair she attracted a lot of attention, which she had used to great effect in networking her business in the early days.

Now if you were in the digital world or a Silicon Valley head, you knew who Rayne Frost was and she didn't need to push so hard anymore.

As long as I stay on top, she thought. *This has to work. I'm not going to claw my way up the damn ladder again!* A shiver gripped her and she looked out the window.

Rayne had invested heavily in some tech plays which were now in serious trouble. She was in danger of losing most of her fortune. Maybe all of it. She had put forty-one million bucks into a UK mobile payments start up. Now, it was worth about four percent of that valuation and she had lost over thirty-nine million. Unfortunately, she had also made other stock market investments using a leveraged method of buying shares and they were going to fall due in the next six months. She no longer had sufficient funds to meet those debts.

She needed a magic bullet and when she noticed Dane's postings in an esoteric little programmers group online, she persuaded a friend who worked for the online site to download every conversation Dane had contributed to since he joined. After a few days of sifting through a mixture of nerdy silliness, macho bull and technical programmer jargon she began to understand what Dane and his partner Beth were working on. When she saw how close they were to achieving their goal, Rayne realised that this could be the solution to her financial problems.

It will be good to see Tiber again too, she thought. She was fond of her older brother. He had always been there for her and she felt a little guilty she had not been able to reciprocate when he had gone through a tough time a few years back. Unfortunately, it coincided with launching the stock of her company on the NASDAQ. She had built the company up from nothing and knew that to successfully IPO the business, she needed to maintain a laser-like focus on the process and ignore everything else. She lost nine pounds during the process without even noticing. When it was over and she came up for air to discover the media storm and resulting career meltdown that Tiberius had endured, she was astounded. She felt bad about it, and the fact that he was very understanding and nice when she had raised it with him, just made her feel worse.

What's worse is that there's really no way I can make it up to him she grumbled mentally *he has absolutely no interest in money or things. Even guy stuff like cars or whatever.*

Rayne liked money and how it eased the wheels of life in L.A. and had gotten used to solving problems by just paying them away. The best way she could redress this perceived imbalance in her relationship with Tiberius was to be there when he needed her at some point in time in the future. That was like, how long is a piece of string? Who knows? He might have his gotten his act together so well that he might never need her again and she'd be stuck with this bad karma for good. What was worse was that he was in Dublin and while she wanted to see him and spend some quality time with him, she did have a crucial objective in Dublin and wasn't going to allow anything to impact on it, even Tiberius.

"Is your champagne OK?" the cute steward was bending over her with a friendly smile.

"No" she said coldly. "I would prefer some chilled still water please." She handed him back the glass and turned to look out the window.

After a few moments, Rayne opened her briefcase and took out a mobile phone and an envelope with a SIM card in it which she swapped for the one in the phone. She turned on the Wi-Fi and connected to the airplane's Wi-Fi service. Then she logged into a website which offered a variety of voice over internet services. She selected one and entered her Los Angeles mobile number and then the mobile number of the SIM she had just inserted.

Now she would be able to have incoming calls to her L.A. mobile instantly and seamlessly re-routed to the mobile number of the phone in her hand, no matter where in the world she was. All calls made from the mobile would be routed to her L.A. mobile and would appear to those being called as though they were receiving a call from that phone, which in fact was what was happening. It's just that she would be elsewhere.

This proved its value a day or so later when Tiberius rang her from Dublin and she answered sitting in the lounge of a Dublin apartment she had booked via Airbnb using a false name, email address and some untraceable Bitcoin for payment.

CHAPTER SIX

Tiberius and Prendergast stood outside Glebe Cottage breathing in the fresh air. Doyle could be heard around the corner getting sick.

"Still think Sweeney was being melodramatic?" Tiberius asked his colleague who was leaning against the wall of the house.

"I'd say his description fairly nailed it" she answered quietly. Her voice was low and displayed a slight tremor.

"Never saw anything like that before" she added "have you?"

"Yes, unfortunately. Back in the States. I think Sweeney's assessment of it being staged was also quite accurate."

"The way they were posed facing each other? Yeah. Seemed that way. What was the thing on the poor guys penis?"

"It's called a chastity cage," said Doyle as he came around the corner, wiping his mouth with some tissues. "I worked a case where a guy died due to sexual asphyxiation a few years ago. He was wearing one of those yokes. It turned out he and his wife were into cuckolding and it went wrong. Death by misadventure was the coroner's verdict"

"Cuckolding? Asked Tiberius.

"Yeah. We had to do a pile of research into it at the time just to rule out the possibility of a sexually motivated attack. It's where a couple operate an open relationship where she has sex with other men. Sometimes it happens because he's unable to satisfy her and they see this as a solution and sometimes it's a lifestyle choice. Often the husband or cuckold will arrange the meetings, attend them, video or photograph the activities and even get involved.

In the case I was investigating, yer man had looped his belt around a hook on the wall and tied it around his neck to induce an element of slight asphyxiation to increase his sexual arousal."

"Jesus Christ! Give me strength." Prendergast sounded disgusted.

"Different strokes for different folks," Doyle replied in a mildly reproving tone. Then he continued, "unfortunately the hubby slipped, banged his head and passed out. His wife and her lover were too busy on the bed to notice and by the time they did, he was dead. I suspect what we saw upstairs was a similar situation. However, in this case a third party killed them both."

"Try slaughtered them," said Prendergast.

"I didn't notice any sign of a break in. So, either the murderer had a key or was invited in, which would further support your theory," speculated Tiberius.

"Sweeney was the first of our people on the scene and he checked right around the outside. He said there's no obvious sign of anyone breaking in," said Prendergast.

They were silent for a minute, all still processing the horrific scene they had just witnessed.

"Sorry for puking," Doyle said. "Happened on my first murder and happens almost every time since. Just can't help it. We see some horrible things in this job eh?"

"You're right" Prendergast agreed. "Sometimes it's really hard to take. Like that was really weird up there. Lots of cuts and gashes but nothing frenzied about it. It all looked very measured and............I don't know.........focussed?"

"Measured and focussed is as good a way of describing the killer's methodology as any," said Tiberius. "And he was a neat and tidy boy. The smell of bleach and detergent in there was significant."

"I reckon we'll be lucky to get any prints or DNA" added Doyle.

"Well, I don't think we'll do much more here," said Tiberius. "Get someone to check out if anyone saw them arrive, alone or with someone else? It's a long shot because it's so isolated but you never know. Also, did the perpetrator have a separate car? If so, where did he park it? Maybe someone saw the vehicle?" Tiberius stopped and looked over at Garda Sweeney and said "ask Sweeney to get someone to replace him and have him do it. He seems pretty smart."

"Sure" said Doyle.

Tiberius stopped suddenly and ran back inside the house, leaving his two colleagues staring after him. He bounded up the stairs and asked one of the techs if would be possible to lift up the woman's head and he stared at her.

"Can you clean the blood off? And the make-up maybe? Would that be OK or too soon?" He asked.

"Why"

"I think I might know her."

"Oh," the tech looked over his shoulder and asked his boss if it was OK.

"Sure go ahead. We've finished and we got good photos."

The tech carefully dabbed at her face. As he slowly cleaned her, it occurred to Tiberius that he did so in a gentle manner and with great respect.

"Can you push the flaps of skin down so I can get a better sense of her" asked Tiberius.

"Yes. How's that?" the tech lifted and tilted her head towards Tiberius, whose stomach fell.

"Do you recognise her?"

"Yes. Met her yesterday."

"You're joking me."

"Unfortunately not." Tiberius left without another word.

Doyle and Prendergast were waiting outside the front door.

"What's the story?" asked Prendergast.

"I met her briefly yesterday after a presentation I gave here on campus."

"What the?"

"What's her name?" interrupted Doyle

"Jessica Plenderleith. I think her husband's name is James."

CHAPTER SEVEN

Jocelyn Fanthwaite-Gibson looked and sounded like the typical old buffer. A classic Whitehall mandarin. He inhabited the shadows of the corridors of power. To those who encountered him, his brief seemed to traverse a wide variety of areas but was best described as covert. His tall, lean, tweedy appearance, however, belied a deep-rooted humanity and rock solid sense of right and wrong, something which had caused him no end of problems throughout his long and eventful career.

It was a miracle to his wife how Joss could reconcile his work with who he was. He told her next to nothing but she was an intelligent and perceptive woman. Over time she grew more and more impressed at how he had managed to deal with his career and the impact it had on his conscience. Oh, he did have sleepless nights and difficult periods when he wrestled with his demons and with the ramifications and morality of his work, but by and large he was still roughly the same person he had been at twenty seven when she married him. Just a little singed and battered around the edges. The ultimate realist, Joss knew he enjoyed a privileged upbringing and a wonderful lifestyle. He lived inside of one of the most exclusive tents in the world, the British aristocracy. Ultimately however, his love for his country was at the core of who he was and was what informed his decisions.

Joss was deep in thought as he walked along Pall Mall, heading for a rendezvous he wasn't looking forward to with a colleague he no longer trusted at a rather discreet little hotel. He was probing a memory. Thinking through a chain of events which stretched all the way back to 1986, to Belfast, to one, one................ he didn't want to give the bastard the title of *man*, because to Joss he was more animal than man. *Minimal humanity and maximum beast,* he thought. An animate machine really. Utterly devoid of morality, empathy or any feeling for human beings. Joss knew him as the most effective operative he had ever worked with and the most dangerous predator he had ever encountered.

"And he bloody well works for us!" he muttered to himself savagely as he strode along.

He headed into the hotel and took a lift which brought him out on the top floor where he walked down a corridor and nodded at the dapper young men sitting in chairs on either side of a door at the end. As he approached, one of them stood, knocked and opened the door for him. He walked through into the living area of a very well-appointed suite of rooms. An overweight man sat on the arm of a couch with his profile facing Joss as he looked out the window over the roofs of the buildings opposite towards the river.

"Wonderful view, Joss, ain't it?" He drawled in a cut glass English accent.

"Damn the view, Barty. That bastard's popped up in Dublin and there's corpses popping up too!" snarled Joss.

The other man, Sir Bartholomew Stubbs, swivelled his not inconsiderate bulk and plopped down onto the couch. It was an odd trait of his, to bounce around like a young teenager. It belied his advanced years and suggested there was a good deal of power and strength left beneath the layers of fat.

"Well, he's not there on an assignment Joss. I'm fairly sure of that," he smiled up at his taller colleague.

"I thought he was not supposed to leave Belfast except with permission. And as I recall you were the one who was to handle that. So, did you give him permission Barty?"

"No"

"Bugger! So, he's AWOL?"

"Not quite."

"Not quite, Barty?" Joss growled.

"He contacted us to say he wanted to come to London briefly and then travel to Dublin for some silly event called the Web Summit. A bunch of boffins all chatting about the Internet and techie stuff."

"Go on."

"Well, we were going to tell him to just fly or drive straight to Dublin, when one of our chaps in Asset Surveillance said he was already there"

"Airport pictures?"

"Indeed, courtesy of your little friend Bourke. So, he's not really AWOL. He's just sort of AWOL and sort of observing the terms of our agreement."

"Hmmm. That's not going to fly Barty."

"Well, what do you suggest?"

"It depends on what he is really up to. I recall he was very tech literate and into the whole area but I remain to be convinced he's just attending this Summit thing."

"Ditto"

"Ditto? What the hell do you mean ditto? What else is going on Barty?"

"Well. There has been a development, which may or may not be related. Apparently two young Paddy Techies, students in one of the Dublin Universities, have developed this very nice piece of software, which is going to be a bit of a game-changer. Certainly, in our game anyway." Barty sat back, shifting his buttocks on the couch for all the world like a big dog trying to find a comfortable spot to sleep in.

"What does this software do?"

Barty stared at the ceiling and recited in a monotone, "The best way to describe it is to call it Behaviour Prediction Software. Basically, you feed in every bit of info you can find on someone or a group of someones. Doesn't matter how trivial the data is and it will predict whether or not they will ever commit a crime and what sort of crime they are most likely to commit."

"The yanks have that. It's called profiling."

"Not really Joss. Their approach tends to operate after the fact. This bit of kit can predict the future likelihood of a crime being committed" he paused and added "with close to 100% accuracy."

Joss sat on the opposite couch and stared at Barty for a long time silently.

"What else?" he finally said.

"Sorry?"

"Come on Barty. I know you too long."

"I'm not following you Joss. What are you asking here?"

"What are you not telling me about this software?"

"Well, from what I understand and it's just the opinion of some of the Cheltenham chaps so please bear in mind it might just be a steaming pile of bull doodie."

"Barty." Joss's tone turned menacing.

"All right. Dear me, so aggressive! Anyway, what our chaps are saying is that whoever possesses this software will have a tremendous advantage as it will give them the ability not just to prevent crime but also to identify and build accurate profiles of all sorts of people and all sorts of behaviour. For example, to determine the most likely reaction of large groups of stockbrokers to different types of events and to profit handsomely from predicting the resulting movement in global markets. Or how the members of a government might behave given a specific set of circumstances and what their resulting actions or legislative response might be.

It may even be capable of determining whether or not a country will invade another. When and what are the tipping points which could cause them to do so. The possibilities are endless for a software program that can accurately predict people's behaviour and the wealth and power which will accrue to the possessor of such software would be unimaginable." Barty had sat forward gesticulating, punctuating each sentence with his meaty manicured hands. He sat back as though exhausted.

"How seriously do they take this piece of software?"

"Joss, I was there when the software was discussed and I've never seen those techy types get so excited. Granted they kept saying it would need to be tested and lots of caveats, but the bottom line is that if the software works, it genuinely changes everything."

Joss stared at Barty, thinking. Then, as the gears clicked into place in his thought process, he let out a long breath and said "So although the Asset is in technical breach of his agreement, you're going to let him get away with it provided he locates the software and acquires its exclusive use on behalf of Her Majesty's Government?"

"Something like that" Barty grudgingly agreed.

"Does he understand what it's worth?"

"Dunno that dear boy. Don't think so."

"I'll lay odds he does."

Joss fell silent again. After a few moments, he got up and walked towards the floor to ceiling window and stood looking out.

Barty reached for his teacup, sipped it slowly and sighed contentedly.

"Are you aware of the Asset's freelance activities?" Joss asked after a lengthy pause, still staring out the window.

"Yes. He's a very naughty boy. Let's hope he never moves to dear old England eh?" replied Barty flippantly.

"I don't mean that Barty" responded Joss in an annoyed tone. He laid his forehead against the cold pane of glass momentarily then straightened. "He ought to be taken to the Tower, hung, drawn and quartered for those pursuits. No, I'm talking about the fact that time to time he takes on work from third parties and gets rather well paid."

"Why ever would he need to do that?" asked Barty, whose surprised tone indicated that for once Joss had provided him with information which he wasn't already in possession of. "Our agreement leaves him very well paid, as I recall."

"Well, he's bloody doing it. Communicates with clients via

the internet and gets paid in a sort of virtual currency called Bitcoin which he then converts into hard cash and transfers to a bank in one of the Baltic States"

"Sneaky little sod, ain't he? How did you...?"

"We have always monitored him. Every aspect of his life including all of his IP addresses and any tech he acquires or uses. So, although his method of communication and payment are via this dreadful Internet marketplace known as the Darknet, we harvest his screen data and all of his mobile data."

"Very thorough Joss. Good stuff. We can all sleep better at night."

"Thorough my backside, Barty." Joss turned to face him. "If I had my way he'd be six feet under. At best, he's a double edged sword, with the keenest edge facing us and at worse, he could represent the gravest threat to our international reputation. If word ever got out we utilised and indeed tolerated the continued existence of a psychopath like him................ perish the thought. He's nothing more than a bloody killing machine. You never want to be alone with him Barty. Never. It would be far better for the world if he didn't exist."

"I always thought that's what James Bond was like y'know!" said Barty flippantly, unfazed by Joss's unsettling demeanour. "A complete psychopath, but firmly under the leash of Her Majesty's Government, of course." He grinned.

"He's no agent. He's a barely tolerated Asset and his life hangs on a thread very much from moment to moment. The minute I get the right set of buttocks on the right seat down the street, his tenure on this planet will be abruptly ended. But to return to his activities in Dublin. Did it occur to you he may be operating on a private contract? Attempting to acquire the software for a third party? Have you briefed him yet? Is he aware of your requirements and has he confirmed he will acquire the software? And if so when will he have it in his possession? When and where will he deliver it to you?"

Joss fired out questions to Barty's still smiling face.

"This particular Asset worries you Joss, doesn't he?" grinned Barty. "Look, we are contacting him again in the next twenty four hours. We're using his usual point of contact. Dempsey. He's well used to dealing with him and will give him the full S.P. on everything."

Joss walked towards the door, stopped and turned. "Just make bloody sure he's not playing a double game Barty. We need the software on an exclusive basis. I don't want him providing it to any third party. If there is the faintest possibility that someone else is going to get it I want it and him destroyed. Apparently the Chinese fellow we've been looking into is going to be in Dublin at the same time."

"Umm remind me?"

"Deng Holman Lee. Chinese American tech Billionaire. Born in China and moved to the U.S. with his parents when he was sixteen. American father lectured in Beijing University. A rather good Mathematician as I recall. A Chinese mother who was a Physicist. Rumour is Deng disappeared from the family home in Beijing aged three or four and wasn't seen until he arrived in the US with his parents. By this time, the father had experienced a stroke and was paralysed. The father went into a highly specialised facility in California and the family lived locally. The story regarding Deng's time in China was that he had been put into a school for gifted children."

"From the age of four?"

"Indeed. Our people in Beijing suspect it was somewhat more than a school, more of a training facility for agents."

"Nice idea," suggested Barty. "Take a long term view, yes? Get 'em young, brainwash 'em. Train them to within an inch of their young lives and you could end up with a very useful bunch of Assets. I won't ask how you know about all of this, but rather will content myself with saying that it's a pity we can't emulate the Chinese."

"What do you think your friend from Belfast is Barty?" replied Joss sarcastically. "He is just a naturally occurring version of the products of that Chinese training facility. A genetic screw up, trained and nurtured in what was the most brutal and violent training location in Europe, until they all came to their bloody senses and stopped killing each other. Don't mess this up Barty." Joss warned. "Make sure he's on-side. On our side. Exclusively. If he isn't, I'll happily sign the termination order myself and deal with the consequences." Joss left without giving Barty the opportunity to reply.

Barty looked at the closed door and wished his old school friend didn't have such a bloody conscience. It was his only flaw really. Joss would have been Head of something or other by now if he hadn't made decisions along the way which, while they didn't conflict with Her Majesty's Government's best interests, didn't quite accord with them either, but they did satisfy Joss's damned set of morals.

Imagine a chap with morals in our game, Barty smiled. *It was so bizarre. If Joss wasn't so brilliant and, I suppose, if he didn't know most of HMG's little secrets and indeed, where all of the bodies were buried, he'd have been put out to pasture long ago. Of course having a power base which was unrivalled in British espionage history was rather useful as well. Made him nigh on impregnable. Having said that, if I land this one, I can write my own ticket. Joss could end up answering to me. Interesting thought.*

Right now, however, Barty felt Joss was a perfect trump card to play, should it be required.

Because if there was one thing on earth that the Asset, Mr Black, feared, it was the Right Honourable Jocelyn Fanthwaite-Gibson, Earl of Lansbury, Viscount Baskerville and half a dozen other titles. A silly name but a truly ferocious beast when roused. Barty, stood up and walked to the windows. He sipped his tea.

*   *   *

The Asset in question was strolling through the UCD Campus grounds, happily considering the logistical issues relating to James and Jessica and how he would deal with them or as he now labelled them, the ex-Plenderleiths. He passed the front of Roebuck Castle, turned the corner and stopped. There were police vehicles parked some hundred or so metres up ahead and the roadway was blocked with red and white plastic tape stretched across it. Two men and a uniformed female police officer were walking towards him at the far side of the tape deep in conversation. Another uniformed officer lifted the tape to allow them under and they stopped to talk to him. The uniform dropped the tape and was facing him. Mr Black realised he was looking straight at him.

Oops. Shouldn't have stopped, he thought. He reached into his pocket and lifted his phone to his ear as though he had just received a call, angling his head fractionally away from the line of sight of the policeman's gaze. He walked around in an aimless manner for a few seconds with the phone to his ear until he was comfortable he was no longer under scrutiny and strolled casually back around the corner of the building. He returned the phone to his pocket and moved away rapidly.

Back outside Glebe house, Garda Sweeney, hadn't actually noticed Mr Black. As though to compensate for his facial disfigurement Garda Sweeney was blessed with twenty-twenty vision but unfortunately on this occasion he was actually looking at the top of the pole just behind Mr Black on which he had noticed two CCTV cameras. As Mr Black disappeared around the corner, he pointed them out to Tiberius and the team.

"There's also one behind us on top of a pole in the alley but it's pointing down the alley, presumably to monitor any pedestrians entering onto the campus. So not much use." Sweeney added.

"Can you head over to the Campus Security office. See if they record from these cameras and how far back the recordings go?"

"I'll get copies. Do you want them in Donnybrook Station or here in the Campus Garda Office Sir?"

"Campus Garda Office" replied Tiberius.

Hours later, the team were weary from running and re-running the CCTV footage. They had quickly noticed the navy Range Rover belonging to the Plenderleiths drive past the cameras up the side of Roebuck Castle and park just out-side the cottage gate. It was too dark to make out anything other than three figures get out. Two were male and one fe-male. One of the males who seemed to be pulling along two pieces of luggage, opened the gate and the other two, unen-cumbered by luggage, walked through. One man who looked quite tall in the distance, was wearing dark clothes and it looked like he had his hand on the woman's bottom as they walked up the slight slope to the gates. The other man with the bags, closed the gates, which were about six-foot-high and they disappeared from sight.

Doyle leaned back. "OK. If we assume that's our murderer with them, we now know how he got in. He knew them somehow, but how did he get out?" he asked grumpily. "Is there another exit?"

"Yes. There's a gateway which leads directly from the rear of the house onto Roebuck Road," answered Sweeney quietly, sitting to one side and slightly behind Tiberius, Prendergast and Doyle. "If he climbed over the garden wall to the right of the gate he could easily jump down into a landscaped area at the other side and get to the road that way."

"What's at the other side?" asked Tiberius.

"A housing estate, Sir. Same name. Roebuck Castle." said Sweeney.

"We need to check to see if there's any footprints at that side of the wall. If it's landscaped, it may be soft underfoot," Tiberius addressed the other three, deliberately including Sweeney in the statement. He had decided Sweeney had a lot of potential and could be very useful, so he wanted to get him involved.

"When we first arrived on the scene, I walked around and checked the other side, Sir. After we got the site secured. You're right, the ground along the other side of the wall is quite soft but there aren't any footprints," said Sweeney still in a low, quiet voice.

"Good work," said Tiberius. He stretched and said "OK, well that saves us time and hassle. Now we need to work on what we do know."

Prendergast said, "I reckon he's done it before."

"Why?" said Doyle. "I mean, I have the same feeling, but why do you think so?"

"The scene is so efficiently set up, staged as it were. But I'm not sure he was doing it for us, by the way."

"Go on" said Doyle.

Prendergast continued, "well, the cleaner who found the bodies wasn't supposed to come this week, she was supposed to come last week but she was sick and reported in late. So...."

"Hang on." Tiberius interrupted her. "How do you know all this. We haven't interviewed her yet."

Prendergast nodded towards Sweeney who said, "ah, sorry about that, I brought the cleaner over to the Campus Doctor's office and I just chatted a wee bit with her on the way. Sometimes, I find people look past the uniform, when you're physically assisting them and they open up."

"Don't apologise," smiled Tiberius. "This is all useful."

"So as I was saying," Prendergast interjected with heavy emphasis on the last word, "I don't think he expected to be interrupted and therefore the scene, if it was staged, was done so for his benefit. Not ours. I recall reading that some of these twisted bastards like to set things up to either distract or involve the investigating officers in some way, but my guess is that's not what was going on here."

"Based on the positioning of the chairs he obviously wanted the guy to watch his wife being tortured and murdered?" added Doyle.

"Yes. That was part of the gratification he took from the situation." Prendergast replied, "also, looking at the knife wounds and the way they were both tied up. I think it might be a man who did this. Not just based on the video footage but based on the amount of strength required to utilise those types of knots and to inflict that kind of damage."

"Not so sure I agree about the blade wounds," said Tiberius. "It might be down to the sharpness and nature of the cutting implement. However, the rope work would require strength. Have we found any likely candidates for the murder weapon yet?" he asked, then added "or weapons."

"Nothing in the house or on the grounds" said Sweeney.

"At first glance, I'd suggest these murders and the one over in the pit were so different in nature that they were not committed by the same person. Except for the fact that a sharp cutting implement was used to cause death in both cases and the presence of a strong sexual element also," said Tiberius.

"Seems too much of a coincidence for them not to be related in some way, though," added Doyle thoughtfully. "We just have to find the link. For what it's worth," Doyle faced up to the elephant in the room, "I now feel they could be two separate events. One was staged. Carefully and meticulously carried by someone who was an utter sadist, possibly a psychopath. The other was much more opportunist in nature. Someone met the girl in the fancy dress outfit, chatted her up, lured her to the wooded area, possibly on the pretext of doing some drugs and maybe some sort of sexual activity and killed her. Brutally and quickly."

"Could still be the same person though," argued Prendergast.

"And there is always the possibility that the wrong person was murdered. It would be easy to mistake who was wearing the cow outfit. They were both women and roughly the same size." Said Tiberius.

"The DJ who played the event said that she thought she saw

the girl wearing the cow outfit dancing with someone in a Pirate outfit near the stage in the early part of the night," said Prendergast.

"Not the guy in the Devil outfit, then. Anything else?" asked Tiberius.

"She wasn't sure, but she said she reckoned the person in the Pirate outfit might have been a woman. Quite tall, if it was a woman, but it was more the way she danced."

"The DJ is gay" added Prendergast. "So her Gaydar was probably on overdrive given that the venue was full of pissed and stoned female students."

"All of which means?" Doyle sounded a little confused.

"Sorry, I forgot you were born when Ireland was still Catholic and pure!" retorted Prendergast with a grin. "Gaydar, is a type of social radar which gay people develop in order to sort straights from gays."

"Jesus," Doyle muttered in a world weary voice. "I've heard it all."

"Look it at from their perspective," said Prendergast reasonably. "After you've been involved in a myriad of embarrassing situations where you get the wrong end of the stick with people you encounter and fancy, eventually you develop a sort of sixth sense about who might and who might not be susceptible to your advances."

"Saves you getting a bloody nose. Well, metaphorically speaking," chipped in Sweeney.

"Anyway, you reckon the DJ might have it right? That the person who was with our victim in the queue and later during the night might have been a tall woman rather than a man?" Tiberius was focussed on Sweeney's original comment, wanting to tease it out.

"Why not? It's possible" said Prendergast "and that would account for the use of the sex toy. Make it look like she had penetrative sex with a man. Just to throw us off the scent."

"It would be worth ringing the lab to ask them to check for foreign female DNA in her mouth," suggested Sweeney.

"Come again?" asked Doyle.

There was a brief awkward silence which was broken by Prendergast giggling, followed by Sweeney and then they were all laughing.

"Oh God, sorry. I did not mean that the way it sounded Boss" spluttered Doyle. "What I meant was, what do you mean foreign female DNA and why in her mouth?"

It had been a day of grim discovery and the unintentional double entendre had lightened the mood a little and, Tiberius felt, brought some unity and balance to the group.

Sweeney leant forward and said "I meant she might have kissed the perpetrator. Either at the murder site or beforehand? So we might get some saliva from the perpetrator in her mouth, on her lips or nearby. It's a long shot but might be worth a try?"

"Contact the lab and ask them," instructed Tiberius. "With the exception of the video footage, for which we can thank Garda Sweeney, we have so little hard evidence right now, we need to look at everything."

CHAPTER EIGHT

"There's something about the scene in Glebe House ringing a bell somewhere in the dim recesses of my dopey brain" came Doyle's voice down the phone.

"Uh huh," was all Tiberius could manage having just woken up. "What time is it man?"

"Eight thirty, Boss, on a lovely sunny Saturday morning. Anyway, like I was say…"

"You woke me up on the only morning I get a lie in to tell me about a hunch?" growled Tiberius. "Coffee's on you, buddy."

"Coffee?"

"Yup. Once I wake up, that's it. I can't sleep again. So now I need coffee, and we're going to talk this through. Where are you?"

"Ahmmm, I'm on the back pitches at Stradbrook?"

"Sorry, where?"

"Blackrock Rugby Club, Boss. I coach kids. It's a great way of clearing the head after a fun week like we've just had. We start at nine."

"I'll be there once I get showered and dress," Tiberius turned off the phone.

Tiberius made his way from the car park of the clubhouse along the side of the main pitch where some players were practicing kicking balls down to the far end and turned left to find a large open area sectioned with lines of small plastic cones into about eight small playing areas. There were lots of kids running around and bunches of enthusiastic adults shouting encouragement from the various side-lines. Tiberius stood for a long moment surveying the scene, until he finally located the stocky figure of Doyle standing in the middle of one of the pitches, dressed in a navy tracksuit with a whistle in his mouth and green beanie on his head.

Tiberius approached the pitch and stood between two groups of supporters. There seemed to be no real pattern or system to the game. The kids, all around eight or nine years old, would cluster together around the misfortunate with the ball. After a brief bit of tugging it would squirt out and off would race some delighted player. At one point, the recipient of the ball headed in what must have been the wrong direction as a woman beside Tiberius yelled out "Cian! Wrong way! Wrong way, pet!" At which point the pint-sized speedster turned around and waltzed through both teams to touch down the ball at the opposite end of the pitch. Doyle blew the whistle to signal the score and then stopped to attend to one youngster who was sitting on the ground in the middle of the pitch crying. He beckoned to the side-line and a man moved out quickly, picked out the young boy, gave him a hug and taking his hand walked him back to the side-line.

"Silly, isn't it?" The woman who had redirected the scorer, said to Tiberius.

"Excuse me?" said Tiberius.

"Just that we've gone so politically correct and worried about our children that even his coach can't comfort the little lad. The coach has to get his father out from the side-line to deal with it."

"Oh. Right," Tiberius didn't quite know what to say. He didn't have kids and had little or no experience of them. He turned towards her and realised that she was gorgeous with long dark wavy hair, in a navy puffa jacket and tight blue jeans and boots.

"It's nuts really," she carried on, smiling. "Especially when you consider that the coach is a policeman. So silly." She sighed "Which guy is yours?"

"I'm not a parent. Just here to meet someone," said Tiberius.

"Soooo, not into rugby." She looked sideways at him, still smiling. "Or kids, I take it?"

"Just meeting someone I'm afraid."

Just then Doyle blew a long blast on the whistle. The diminutive boy who had scored what turned out to be the levelling score, sprinted off the pitch and leapt into the arms of the woman beside Tiberius.

"Mum! Mum! Did you see?" He yelled into her face. "Did you see me score my try? Saved the day Mum! We'da lost, if'n I hadn't."

She hugged him close and said quietly. "Well done Cian. Now go back onto the pitch and shake hands with the other team."

"God yeah! I forgot!" He said as she lowered him back down and he dashed back onto the pitch and began shaking hands vigorously with the kids from the other team. Doyle patted him on the head and said something to him as he walked towards Tiberius.

"Hey Boss," he said as he ambled up.

"Hey, yourself," said Tiberius. "Nice job Doyle. Coffee's still on you."

"Sure thing. I'll just get changed. We'll need to go elsewhere though. The coffee in the clubhouse is only instant and tastes like it."

"OK. We'll leave your car here and take mine?"

"Fine. By the way," Doyle turned to the woman standing beside Tiberius, "your lad Cian has the makings of a fine player. Once we fine tune his sense of direction."

She laughed and said, "Just don't tell his father or he'll be arranging for special coaching and all kinds of stuff, OK?"

"Sure thing, Mrs C. My lips are sealed."

Cian ran up and his mother took his hand and walked away.

Both men watched her walk away, unashamedly enjoying the view.

"Like two plump ferrets in a sack," sighed Doyle. "Dear God, she'd give an erection to a dead bishop."

"From what I understand, your Irish bishops didn't need much encouragement in that area," observed Tiberius drily.

"True. True." Said Doyle. "And we're a pair of disgusting misogynists. In our defence though she's the full package. She's not just lovely looking, she's a nice woman, very smart and down to earth. Having said all that, she's not possessed of great taste in men. She is married to one of Ireland's biggest dickheads."

"Oh?" said Tiberius, knowing that Doyle was just looking for a bit of encouragement to talk.

"Robert Brady. Internet millionaire and total plonker. He started a company with two buddies. Then his father, a serious predator in lawyer's clothing, got involved. Next thing Robert's two pals get shafted and a year later the company is sold to a US Venture Capital firm for twenty-three million. RCB swans around as if he knows everything about everything and actually knows nothing about virtually everything, especially Rugby and coaching kids in any fecking sport!"

"OK. I get it. You don't like him" said Tiberius with a hint of amused sarcasm.

"Dislike is such a strong word." Doyle paused considering. "Try, loathe the prick and I'm not alone. OK, I'll get changed. See you in five," said Doyle as they approached the clubhouse. Tiberius wandered in the entrance and turned into a large gymnasium where a melee of kids were being served sandwiches and soft drinks by a bunch of harassed looking adults.

"I'm outta here," he muttered and turned abruptly to leave but instead bumped straight into Cian's attractive mum again.

"Oh! Sorry!" He said.

"No. No. My fault. We're rushing. Cian needed the loo and now he has to get his drink so we were rushing." She stopped. "I said that twice didn't I?" Smiling.

"It's OK, I get it. Anyway, I'm the one wasn't watching where

I was going. No harm done?" He looked down at the little boy staring up at him. Unsure of the correct way of dealing with the situation, Tiberius squatted down on his hunkers and looking at the boy in the eye put out his hand and said "Sorry pardner. Shake?"

"Wow. You're a yank!" an enthusiastic handshake was followed by a complicated fist bumping and hand waggling routine that would have done credit to a homie from an L.A. gang. Then Cian darted off. He got up to find her looking at him with an interested smile.

"Sooo, he's got a little bit to learn about the social niceties? I apologise for him calling you a Yank," she said.

"It's accurate. I'm a Yank."

"Indeed. Well nice meeting you again. Sort of." She flicked a lock of long brown hair out of her face and seemed to glide around him and followed her son to the melee.

Tiberius headed back out to the car park where he was eventually joined by Doyle. They drove to Dun Laoghaire Harbour, bought coffees from a van at the entrance to a long granite pier which they began walking along. After a while, Tiberius looked at Doyle and said "So?"

"Well. This goes back a bit, and it's a bit of a mishmash of anecdotal information and hearsay." Doyle temporized.

"Another long shot?"

"Well let me just tell you and you can make up your own mind Boss. OK?"

"OK."

"Right. Well when I started out in the force, those eejits in the North were still bumping each other off. It was in the height of the Troubles. You know what I mean by the Troubles right?"

"Yeah it's what people call the period from pretty much Bloody Sunday until the Ceasefire in the late 90's."

"Right. Well. Some people reckon that however it started and for whatever reasons, the Troubles gave a wonderful opportunity to the more criminally inclined elements, north and south of the border to further their own interests, and they took full advantage." Doyle paused.

Tiberius encouraged him, "go on."

"Existing gangs were able to recruit more members and ran protection rackets, robbed banks, etc., etc.. People were being murdered every day. As a new recruit, I had the delightful task of border duty. It was one of the single most boring times of my career. In my life, probably. The border was like a Swiss cheese and people were going back and forth with ease. Sure, the British Army blew up and blocked a load of roads on their side but it just wasn't possible to stop cross border movement. So, we just sat there every day doing nothing, but knowing the bastards may have been just two or three fields away heading north or south.

Anyway, I figured out a way of tracking some of the traffic and mentioned it to my Sergeant, who for some unknown reason mentioned it to someone else and the upshot was that I was called back to Headquarters and asked to explain how it could work. Being the times that were in it, they tried it out and it worked. Well, some of the time anyway."

"Well done. Not so dopey after all."

"Now. Now. Faint praise is no praise, but I'll take whatever's on offer." Doyle grinned sheepishly. "So, the next thing I knew, I wasn't in uniform anymore. I was sent to our training facility in Templemore and ended up as a plain clothes detective, part of a team which handled cross border liaison with our brethren in the Royal Ulster Constabulary." Doyle adopted a Northern Irish accent.

"This is turning into a long story," warned Tiberius sidestepping a lady picking up dog faeces in a plastic bag while her large black Labrador barked happily beside her.

"Bear with me" answered Doyle and continued, "for the next several years I worked with the RUC and sometimes the British Police on a variety of cases. The reason I asked to meet you is because the scene in Glebe House reminded me of one of them. As in, precisely one particular case where the modus operandi, layout of the scene, sexual element and number of the victims and perpetrator were pretty much identical."

"OK. It was worth the lost sleep. Go on." Tiberius encouraged.

"Right. Well I was in an RUC police station in Queen Street in Belfast for a meeting with an RUC lad, DS Roger MacAllister. A staunch Orangeman if there ever was one, but we got on. Dunno why, but we did. When he came south, or we met in London, we would have a drink together after work. He came to my place for dinner once or twice and vice versa. So it wasn't strange when he popped his head into the office where I was waiting for our meeting and said 'C'maun ye southern bastarrd! We've an interesting wee Murrderr up the Shankill.' It was a rare hot summer and I was delighted to get out of the sweatbox I had been sitting in, so I followed him into an armoured police Landrover and we headed up to a working-class Protestant housing estate in central Belfast. Think Coronation Street with barbed wire."

"Coronation Street?"

"A TV Soap set in a working class part of East London. Rows of tiny houses, built for workers, packed in tight with no front gardens. Except that on the gable end of each row of houses were painted massive Union Jack flags and mural's glorifying some murdering bunch of terrorists or other. An urban art concept replicated in the Catholic Republican areas too. Fortunately for the RUC, this was home territory, a Protestant Unionist area so we didn't need a British Army escort and there weren't many negative vibes.

We ended up in a slightly nicer part, in that they had gardens front and back and the houses were semi-d's."

"Sorry, Semi-d's?"

"Semi-detached houses. Two houses joined together? On this island at that point in time, homes were not apartments. They were either a row of houses, two houses stuck together with one party wall or fully detached. Very few apartment buildings. So, we went into this neat and tidy semi-detached house at the end of a cul-de-sac. Whoever owned it also owned the house next door and had broken through the party wall in several places to create much larger rooms. So it was quite a large residence for a working class part of Belfast back then. Very impressive inside, very nondescript outside.

We went upstairs and walked into a room where the bodies of a man and a woman were posed facing each other, with identical injuries to the victims in Glebe House. Except he wasn't wearing a chastity cage. His scrotum had been severed and was on the floor, exactly halfway between the two bodies. There was a pattern of lines and measurements drawn on the floor in chalk."

"Was it similar?" asked Tiberius.

"Identical. Then it got interesting."

"Right. Then it got interesting." Tiberius couldn't help a hint of sarcasm at Doyle's exposition.

"Obviously, I wasn't involved, just observing and as usual, trying to keep my breakfast down in front of these RUC boyos. Curiously, I noticed the team working the scene seemed relaxed about the whole thing. I put it down to fatigue and just being used to dealing with this sort of brutal death on an all too regular basis. I was making my way downstairs when I overheard someone ask MacAllister was he sure it was him and MacAllister replied that he was positive. I don't know why but I stopped at the top of the stairway hoping to hear more but a few Techs passed me heading downstairs also. When they got near the bottom, MacAllister and the other guy both clammed up. Anyway as the Techs went past, I stood back against an internal wall which felt a little bit unstable. Not solid.

I moved back to the other side of the corridor and looked at it. It occurred to me the wall was situated where the top of a bannister would normally have been when the house was separate from the other one. It seemed they had just blocked off the small area. They wouldn't have needed it as the other rooms ran through to the other side of the house. So, I called up MacAllister and said that the wall seemed hollow and there might be a room behind it. He looked at it, pushed against it. It moved slightly but didn't open. Then he walked along the corridor to the first room and stood in the doorway looking back towards me and then inside the room. He disappeared and when he returned he paced and counted his steps from the doorway to the top of the stairs. He looked at me and said 'you're right. It's a hidden room.' Then he called the head of the Techs back upstairs. He wasn't best pleased that a southern cop had spotted something they had missed so I said I'd wait outside.

I stood outside for about half an hour waiting for MacAllister to show up and when he did he looked troubled.

'It's a sort of dungeon or torture room, I think,' he said to me.

'MacAllister!' the head Tech called urgently. This time I followed him back up. We stood in the hallway and looked through the doorway into a dark room in which a Tech was standing. He held up a portable UV light. The walls, floor and even the ceiling glowed brightly. They were totally covered in blood spatters.

'Good Lord,' MacAllister muttered.

'Some of the stains are very old and some quite new, from what we can ascertain at this early stage. It's appears to have been in constant use over quite a period of time,' said the Head Tech. No one spoke for a while until MacAllister said quietly 'Bastards.'

That night I went to MacAllister's house outside Belfast for dinner with his missus. After an early dinner he suggested a walk through the fields while it was still bright. After a while he asked me for my analysis of the crime scene. I told him my impressions and he seemed to be thinking hard about it. Then I said I had the feeling that whoever committed the murders had done it before and how it all seemed almost ritualistic and ceremonial.

He agreed and said I was bang on the money. He asked me if I would be surprised to know that the murderer was related to the two victims. I said that they obviously knew who did it and that was great. They just had to locate him and bring him in.

At that point he swore." Doyle paused and then continued, "what you have to understand is that this was a God-fearing, bible hugging Ulster Protestant. He never used bad language. But what he said next surprised me even more. He told me they couldn't touch him."

"Why?" asked Tiberius

Doyle said quietly, "he worked for the British Secret Service."

"No way." Tiberius was stunned.

Both men were silent as they walked along.

"Look, I know it's hard to believe," Doyle continued, "and there was no reason for him to trust me and we had nothing in common but over the years, well, we just clicked. To the extent that as time went on and we dealt with each other more and more, we got to a point where I trusted him completely and he me. I helped him out on numerous occasions and vice versa. Which was why he brought me to the murder scene. The sad thing was, I reckon I was the only person he really trusted, outside of his missus. I was an outsider with no axe to grind and nothing to gain either way. You have to understand what it was like in those days. You never knew who to trust, what side they were on, or had links to. He had decided there would be no benefit to me in this information which he was sharing with me and, as long as I kept quiet about it, no danger to him.

Anyway, he knew who this bastard was and he couldn't touch him. Couldn't arrest him. Couldn't question him and would never be able to bring him to justice for his crimes.

MacAllister was a good cop in a dreadful situation. There are people like him in every police force in every country, thank God."

Tiberius looked at him quizzically "thank God?"

"Sorry." Doyle rushed to clarify, "I mean, it's good that guys like MacAllister exist. The level at which their code of morality operates elevates those around them, yeah?

Doyle's insight into the operation of Police forces on a macro level was a pleasant surprise to Tiberius. He was liking this guy more and more as he got to know him.

"This was eating him up," said Doyle "and he just had to tell someone. I happened to be there at the right time and he trusted me to tell no one. And I didn't. Until today."

"This adds a whole new dimension and an extra level of damn complexity to this case," replied Tiberius who had stopped and was leaning with his arms folded along the top of the harbour wall, looking out to sea. There were lots of tiny sailing craft in the distance, little multicoloured triangles against the deep blue of the sea, but he didn't see them.

"That's a bit of an understatement."

"So, this happened a long time ago right?" Tiberius asked Doyle.

"Just before the end of the Troubles, so between fifteen and twenty years roughly."

"Can we talk to MacAllister?"

"Nope."

"Why not?"

"IRA blew up his car outside his front door. Remote controlled detonation the instant he got inside." Doyle paused for a moment and then added, "well, the story was that it was the IRA, but who knows?"

Tiberius said nothing and they walked along in silence. Eventually he said, "I need to digest this."

"Fair enough. Let's maybe leave it until Monday?"

"Yes."

They started back along the pier moving against the flow of families, walkers, joggers and dog owners, all taking advantage of a pleasant and rare sunny Saturday.

Doyle thought to himself as they meandered along, *'I need to digest this?' Christ, he's a cool one.* He glanced sideways at Tiberius. *No reaction other than 'I need to digest this'. Either he doesn't understand the ramifications or he does and is overwhelmed. On the other hand, he may be just working it out. Let's hope that's it. Or we're all screwed.*

Half an hour later Doyle was driving home when his phone rang. It was Tiberius.

That was quick, thought Doyle.

"Hi, Tiberius here."

"Hi. What's up?"

"I think we shouldn't share this with anyone just yet until we have determined how to deal with it OK?"

"Makes sense Boss."

"Even Prendergast."

"Right."

"We may bring her and any other members of the team in on it when you and I feel we have a better handle on it."

"OK."

"Bye"

Doesn't waste words, does he? Doyle thought. *Still he's on the money.*

*   *   *

Tiberius was sitting at his desk in a large nondescript modern redbrick building, called Harcourt Square, the regional headquarters of the Dublin Police. He had been researching online since he had left Doyle that morning. His eyes were tired after several hours staring at the computer screen and he was annoyed. He was about to make a phone call on his desk phone when he stopped in mid act. Tiberius thought about MacAllister again and wondered at his need to confide. *If he shared such sensitive information with a southern cop like Doyle then maybe, just maybe......*

He dialled a different number and after a few rings Doyle answered. His voice sounded tired.

"Yes Boss?"

"What about his wife?"

"Who, MacAllister's?"

"Yes."

"What about her?"

"How close were they?"

"Very. She devastated when he died. I visited once or twice after. She was in bad shape."

"She might know something. He might have confided in her."

"Yeah. Might."

Doyle was silent, then added "she moved to France some years ago."

"Where?"

"Not sure. Want me to find out?"

"Yes"

"Actually, I might still have her old mobile number but she's probably using a French number by now."

"Find her."

"Will do."

Twenty-four hours later Doyle and Tiberius were sitting together in cramped seats on a Sunday evening Ryanair flight to Nice in Southern France.

Doyle sported a massive bandage on his index finger as a result of trying to clear out the mechanism of a garden strimmer machine belonging to a neighbour which he hadn't turned off correctly. He didn't lose the finger, but as he answered Tiberius's query in a wry manner, he had done a good job of landscaping his fingernail.

Tiberius was dozing but Doyle's grunts of pain caused him to open his eyes and notice Doyle attempts to clumsily trying to type on a laptop with this massively bandaged finger and his elbows tucked in so as not to bother Tiberius or the woman sitting on his left.

"What's so important that you can't give your finger twenty four hours to rest?" he asked.

"Sorry if I woke you. Boss"

"Just call me Tiber OK?"

"Ahhh. OK. My first name is Tiernan but everyone calls me Doyle. Even my ex called me that."

"Fine. So what's so important that you need to attempt the nine-fingered typewriter shuffle?"

Doyle was silent and then he sighed and said "It's my dissertation for my doctorate, but please, keep it to yourself OK? I'm way behind and I need to deliver some content."

"Right. I'm gonna grab some shut-eye" Tiberius tipped his head back against the bulkhead and drifted away.

CHAPTER NINE

Dane liked to work early most mornings but especially on Saturdays. It was the one day he could be sure he wouldn't be disturbed because the Nova UCD facility would be as empty and silent as a morgue. Balancing a Starbucks cup, a laptop case and a portable hard drive, he opened the door to his cubicle office and stopped short. A woman was sitting in his chair with her crossed legs up on his desk, typing rapidly into an Apple Macbook Air Laptop.

"Uh hello?" asked Dane. "Can I help you?"

She didn't look up, just said "Be with you in a minute Dane. Just got to finish this email." Her typing, already fast, seemed to speed up and she tapped the mouse pad and said in a triumphant voice "Done!"

She jumped up and Dane was surprised to find she was looking at him almost directly in the eye. The tall lady offered him her hand and shook his vigorously. "I'm Rayne Frost." She looked at him expectantly as though expecting recognition of who she was.

"Right. Dane Wilson. But hang on. You already know that. Actually how do you know me? And what are you doing in my office, like, uninvited?"

"Oh the receptionist downstairs told me I could wait here. She was very nice," replied Rayne breezily flashing a dazzling smile at Dane. "So, you wanna go get a coffee and have a quick chat?"

Dane looked at the takeaway coffee cup in his hand and back up at her. "Uh, I already have one and I need to........."

"No! No! We're not going there and I'm not gonna let you

destroy your insides with crappy Starbucks coffee, Dane. It would be a terrible start to our relationship." She took the coffee cup from his hand and walked past him, calling back over her shoulder, "coming?"

Dane was totally bemused by this whirlwind and, a little bit intrigued by her. So he followed her out of the building, amused by her dumping his Starbucks coffee in a bin on the way out to a waiting glossy black people carrier with blacked out windows.

As he walked, he texted Beth "Who is Rayne Frost?"

She immediately replied with "Massive Internet Entrepreneur – worth gazillions - a legend to us tech-chickies..... why?"

Dane replied "havin' coffee with her."

Beth came back instantly with "Holy cow, Batperson! Play it cool - could be gud 4 us."

"Will do" texted Dane.

Half an hour later Dane was sitting on a bench on Sandymount Strand looking out at Dublin Bay with Rayne beside him drinking an, admittedly, far superior coffee, still wondering what was going on. They could see the entirety of the shallow bay from where they were sitting. When the tide was out, like today, a broad expanse of sand, stretched way out in front of them, sprinkled here and there with the odd jogger and dog walkers. Further out, the horizon was dotted with little white triangles as one of the yacht clubs based in Dun Laoghaire held a dinghy race.

"So." Rayne swivelled towards him and turned the full intensity of her gaze on Dane. "Bet you're wondering what is going? Eh, Daney?"

"Uhm. Yeah. Kind of." Dane admitted. Rayne didn't answer and the silence between them stretched as she looked at him as though examining him, peering into him.

Dane was becoming uncomfortable and said "good coffee though. Thanks."

"Why, you're welcome." Rayne replied and then finally said

"I know what your app does. I can guess as to how it works. But I'm wondering if you guys know quite how valuable it could prove to be, Dane."

Dane was confused and suddenly very wary. "How did you find out about it?" he asked. "We haven't even launched an alpha version and we haven't told anyone about it."

"We both know that's not quite true Dane." Rayne answered with a grin.

"Sorry. But Beth and me have kept this strictly under wraps for the past two years!" Dane claimed indignantly. "And that's a fact."

"Dane. Chill bro." said Rayne calmly. "I'm a member of Github.com too?"

"Oh." Dane sat back. "Right. Well. Hang on, there's only four of us in our little group on Github and the last time I looked the other three were guys!"

"I know. And one of them is an ex-boyfriend of mine," explained Rayne. "Once I realised what you were doing and how exciting it was, well I just leapt onto a plane in LA and popped over here ahead of my planned arrival, just to meet you guys. I'm sort of speaking at the Web Summit in a few days."

"Right. The Web Summit. You're like giving a speech or something?"

"Yes. A keynote address, they're calling it."

"So you like it then?" Dane asked.

"Not really. I'm not good in front of crowds but hey ya gotta do what ya gotta..." Dane was staring at her with a blank look on his face.

"Sorry Dane. You mean, the App. I love it babe. And I want to help you guys in whatever way you and your partner think I can be of assistance."

A light came into Dane's eyes and he said "OK. Well I think you should meet Beth. She's uh, my partner and like, you really should talk with her too, OK?"

"Absolutely. I met with you first because I knew you operated out of Nova UCD. To be honest I thought your partner would be there too. So let's try and get together this weekend for dinner, just the three of us and see if we can't take things further?"

"Cool. I'll tell Beth. She thinks you're great, by the way."

"OK. That's nice. If you wanna drop these cups into the trashcan over there and I'll take you back to your office yeah?"

Dane got up and headed over to the bin with the cups. Rayne watched him as he walked, thinking "That's a nice butt and an incredibly hot guy, but he's kinda missing something in the ol' wiring. There's a disconnect there. Granted he's a techie and they all seem to be screwed up in one way or another but he didn't check out my boobs once, and God knows, they weren't cheap. Yet there isn't a hint of him being gay. Wonder what's happening with that?"

*   *   *

Beth and Dane got out of a taxi on a lively street in the centre of Dublin called Wexford Street. It was jammed with restaurants, bars, cafés, dance clubs and people.

"Gotta tell you, Dane. I love Dublin when the weather's good," said Beth.

"Not too often then," said Dane as he skirted around a large inebriated group of teenagers marching along singing Coldplay's song Viva la Vida.

They stopped outside a Tapas Restaurant called Las Tapas de Lola, with a large awning and tables outside. Beth noticed a woman with amazing long auburn hair and a thousand kilowatt smile stand up and wave them over to a corner table.

"Hi Dane," she said as they approached "and you must be Beth. I'm so pleased you guys could take the time to have a bite with me."

In truth, Beth was a little intimidated at meeting someone she hero-worshipped and then discovering she was even more impressive in real life, so she just shook the hand that was offered to her, said hi and sat opposite her quietly.

"From what I understand this place does the best tapas in Ireland." Rayne said to Beth. "So let's just dig in. Right?"

"I've never eaten Tapas. How does it work?" asked Dane.

"It's basically just a collection of small dishes rather than one or two big ones. It's a type of cuisine which comes from Spain. In some places, the Basque areas, I think, they call it pintxos. But it's great for just casual dining and you can eat just a little if you're not too hungry or whatever. It kind of frees you from portion sizes really. You know, if you go into an upscale Michelin star type of place and they serve you a tiny bit of food on a huge plate and when you go out you're still hungry?" Rayne said cheerfully.

"Or you go somewhere which loads you up with too much food when what you really want is a snack. It's just a collection of Spanish snacks," added Beth

"Got it in one Beth." Rayne looked up as a slender, very effeminate waiter loomed over her with a cheerful grin and said in a strong Spanish accent "you would like sometheeng to dreenk? Yais?"

They ordered beers all round and started studying and discussing the menu. Beth found Rayne to be disarmingly pleasant. Much more relaxed and down to earth than she had anticipated. There was no talk of the app or business, just a lively and fun discussion about the different dishes.

Rayne proved to be right. The food was exquisite. They laughed as Rayne flirted outrageously with the Spanish waiter, who seemed to be charmed by her and acted up equally outrageously.

They finally finished eating what turned out to be a mountain of food and were relaxing over some Café con Leches, or milky coffees as Beth called them.

"That brings me back" said Dane in a thoughtful voice.

"What does?" asked Beth.

"This coffee. It reminds me of when I walked the Camino in Northern Spain a couple of years ago. You remember? I wanted you to come and you wouldn't." Obviously, Dane hadn't forgotten the argument they had about it.

"Dane. You're six foot four and all legs. I'm what, five foot four with short little legs? You would have killed me within a week because I would have slowed you down soooo much. Seriously. You know it." Beth answered with the hint of an exasperated tone to her voice.

Dane got up saying "well it still woulda been nice. Gotta go to the loo. Sorry."

Rayne looked at Beth as Dane walked away and asked "why didn't you go? Just out of curiosity? I mean, there isn't a woman in here who wouldn't trek sorry crawl on her hands and knees across the North Pole with him if he asked, let alone one of the most romantic landscapes in the world. And carry the bags!"

"We're not a couple, despite what everyone thinks." Beth said with a little asperity. "Dane is," she paused, trying to answer the question but not be indiscreet. "Well, he's complicated and he needed to go on that trip on his own. Just to get away and deal with some stuff. I'm not sure how well it worked really but he was a lot more content when he came back."

"OK. Sorry I didn't mean to intrude."

"No problem. He's a really nice guy and frighteningly bright. Like genius level, y'know."

"Well if the software you two have developed is anything to go by, I'd say there's two of you at that level."

Beth sat up; aware the conversation had moved to the real reason a megastar like Rayne Frost was slumming in Dublin with two students like them. "Thanks for the compliment, but Dane's the one figured out how to actually achieve what I came up with. He put the AI engine together and all of the security."

"He's good at security too? You two make a great combination."

Dane returned and sat down as Rayne asked, "so what are your plans for it? Have you developed a go-to-market strategy or what?"

"Well we were thinking of launching the beta version at the Web Summit and using that to try and attract investors so we can fund finishing it off and doing a full launch in the next year," said Beth carefully.

"Right," said Rayne in a thoughtful voice. "Have you thought of selling it outright? Now?"

"What? Do you want to buy it?" Beth was surprised and it showed.

"Well. I have a few ideas which perhaps you might consider? OK? Can I speak frankly?" asked Rayne, playing the two bright but inexperienced students like violins.

"Sure," urged Dane.

"Go right ahead," added Beth quickly.

"OK. Well the way I see it, you can go down the road you're talking about but you're competing with hundreds of other startups who have paid lots of money to be at the Web Summit and they will all be clamouring loudly for the attention of investors. You could easily get lost in the noise despite the quality and uniqueness of what you've developed." She paused, watch the other two heads nodding as she spoke.

"An alternative approach might be if I was to mention your software in my speech. It will focus on upcoming new disruptive trends in the Digital World? Crap title, I know," Rayne grinned depreciatingly and then continued. "From what I understand, I'm speaking in the main auditorium and it's gonna be full so that's around a thousand people, most of whom will be investors."

"Jesus, what an opportunity," breathed Dane.

"I think it might be worth exploring. So what I propose is that I re-write my speech and use your software as my 'business case'. I can mention that you're looking for funding and then we can watch them all come running. And believe me, by the time I'm finished, they will come running. Announcing it in such a public way should cause a feeding frenzy."

"That would be amazing, but like, these will be high powered people and will just eat us alive. I mean we have no experience of cutting deals like this. We won't know what value to pitch at?" Beth asked Rayne directly. Mentally Rayne was ecstatic, turning cartwheels!

Gotcha! She thought and took a slow breath as though considering Beth's comments.

"OK well, how about I assist on the negotiations with you? I have taken a suite in the Intercontinental Hotel right beside the Web Summit venue and we can meet people there? I've also taken rooms at the Ritz Carlton in Wicklow where we could meet for an update immediately afterwards and use it as kind of base camp? I probably know most of the top people we need to speak with anyway and I have been through this process more than once so I know some of the pitfalls"

"That'd be great" said Dane, "I've never even seen the inside of the place."

Rayne smiled at him and turned to Beth.

"What do you want in return for all this help?" asked Beth.

Rayne was surprised, not by the question, but that it had been asked so bluntly and so early on. Clearly, she had misjudged this girl.

"What do you want to offer me?" She shot back. "I didn't come to you with a specific agenda or price. I was just fired up by what I had discovered about you guys and by the software, of course."

Dane began to speak but Beth kicked him under the table and he subsided.

"Can we talk about it and get back to you?" asked Beth coolly.

"Sure, just remember I need time to rewrite so don't leave me hanging out there too long, OK?"

"Will do. This is a really big deal for us and we just want to talk about it, like we do everything else."

"Cool," said Rayne, "I'm just going to the bathroom" as she stood up and went inside to the toilet, asking for the bill as she passed the woman at the till.

"Beth," said Dane, sounding worried. "Beth don't screw this up. I think she can get us serious dosh. It's everything we dreamed of."

"I know but look Dane, she's not doing this out of the kindness of her heart or because you and I are lovely people. What do we have to give her? We have no money so what's left? Only shares in the business, right? So the question is, how much is it worth to us to get Rayne Frost on board? How much extra will she generate? Once we can put a number on that then we can give her an answer. OK?"

"Fair enough Beth. What you're saying makes sense. So how much do you think we sho…." Beth kicked him again and smiled up at Rayne who had just returned and sat beside Dane.

"So guys, I think you two need to go away and get your heads together y'know. Discuss all of this and get back to me OK?" Rayne said breezily.

"Sure thing" replied Dane.

"Thanks Rayne. We are grateful to you for giving us the time to work this out. Cos, we know how much it would mean to have you on board, helping us. We just want to be sure." Added Beth.

"OK Great. I'll wait to hear from you. We can have lunch, OK? I got the bill so let's boogie, guys." Rayne stood up and they all headed for the door. Outside, Rayne turned before she got into the dark limo style people carrier which was waiting for her and asked, "do you guys want a lift somewhere?"

"No we're fine thanks. We'll contact you tomorrow OK?" replied Beth quickly before Dane could accept.

"OK," Rayne closed the door and the vehicle pulled away.

As they made their way along Wexford Street, Dane asked

Beth what she thought of Rayne.

"She is so impressive. Better than I expected. Maybe, a bit intense perhaps?"

"Right. You reckon we should steer clear then?"

"God, no! Actually the strategy she mapped out makes huge sense. Her involvement would add massive kudos to us. People would take us a lot more seriously and if she actually refers to our software in her speech, well, describing the aftermath as a feeding frenzy could turn out to be a bit of an understatement."

"So why did we walk away from that meal without a deal? I don't get it."

"Well, for starters she was love bombing us."

"What's that?"

"Love bombing is where someone's all over you. Being really nice, buying you meals and stuff, because they want something from you?"

"Beth" Dane said "it doesn't occur to you this is just how multi-millionaires like Rayne Frost do business? Like this is nothing unusual for her? Maybe we're just a little intimidated by her lifestyle and are misinterpreting it?"

"You mean I'm misinterpreting it." Beth retorted hotly. "Dane, I'm just trying to protect us OK? We're so close to our dream becoming a reality that I don't want to see anything or anyone screw it up. We mustn't make a misstep now."

"Point taken. So do you want to offer her some kind of commission or shares or what?"

"How about a percentage commission on the funds she raises? But I don't think she'll go for that" said Beth answering her own question. "She's a Silicon Valley head and it's all about having skin in the game for them. So realistically if we want her on board then we need to offer her equity. A percentage of the company." She fell silent and Dane said nothing as they walked along. Knowing she was working out the different permutations and combinations in her head.

After a while Beth said "OK. We offer her a percentage based on valuation. We have to get her to give us an idea of what she thinks the company is worth. Trust me. Someone like Rayne has already done the numbers and has a good idea of the valuation. So, supposing she says the business is worth twenty million euro, and she can sell twenty percent to someone for four million then we'll give her a commission equivalent to ten percent of the shares but she has to take up a seat on the board and agree to help us and get us more funds later on if we need it? That leaves you with thirty five percent of the company and me with the same. But we have enough money to fund us for the next year or two and for the launch. Does that make sense to you?"

"Yeah. It works. Seems like you're valuing us a little high though, especially when we haven't made a penny of revenue yet."

"People will buy into the future revenues which this software will generate. That's how it works. I'll ring Rayne and ask her if she can give us an idea of where she sees the value of business in the morning."

"Why not do it now? She gave you her number."

"I don't want to seem to desperate."

"You're just asking for a clarification. Nothing more."

"OK." Beth pulled out her phone and rang the number Rayne had given her.

"Hi Beth." Rayne answered on the second ring.

"Hi Rayne. We were just chatting about this and we were wondering if you could give us an idea of where you would see the value of the business, so we can work out the best way to move things forward."

"Valuation." Rayne sounded amused. "Well I guess that's the sixty-four-dollar question ain't it. How much can we raise? I take it you have already worked out how much you need to get the finished product to market?"

"Yes. We have a good idea. About four million euro, we reckon."

"Four?"

"Yes. Do you think it's a bit rich?"

"Honey. Let's get real here. I think I can get you about a hundred million. Anything under that and I'm gonna be disappointed in myself."

Beth swallowed. "So how much equity do you think it'll take to get that much money Rayne?"

"Somewhere between fifteen and twenty five percent. Are you guys OK with that?"

"I don't see a problem but I need to talk to Dane OK? I'll get back to you. Thanks for talking with me."

"Sure thing Beth. See ya."

Beth stopped Dane and dragged him to one side. They stood in a doorway and she looked up at him with tears in her eyes. "Dane." She had difficulty catching her breath. "Dane. She says the company could be worth about five hundred million."

"What the hell?" Dane was dumbfounded. "Wow! Wow! I can't believe it. So soon? I mean, I thought that someday, y'know, it'd be worth absolutely huge amounts of wonga but this? Right now?" He stood back against the door looking over her head at the passing traffic.

He put his hands on her shoulders and looked intently into her face. "Beth, we'll never get a chance like this again in our lives. Never! We have to secure this. We need to tie down a deal with Rayne, OK?"

"Yeah. Yeah. I get it. I mean we can make it contingent right? Like if she sells anything up to twenty five percent for one hundred million euro then she can have ten percent of the shares. She'll deserve it right?"

"Right."

"Decision made. Now let's go and get sozzled!"

The pair linked arms with each other and marched down the street.

As they moved off neither of them noticed the man stepping out of the doorway of the pub they had been standing outside. Mr Black stood looking after them with a thoughtful expression on his face.

Rayne sat back in the car and let out a long low breath. She was sure she had played them wrong when Beth cut everything short. She had noticed Beth kicking her buddy under the table and taking control of their side of the conversation.

At that point Rayne felt she had misjudged the situation and underestimated Beth. Accordingly, she had been barely under control when she left the restaurant, but Beth's call had changed everything.

"Got 'em" she said quietly to herself, smiling out the window. She could smell the money.

CHAPTER TEN

Doyle broke the surface of the water and roared "Jaysus!" Up and down the stony beach on the seafront of Nice, one or two elegantly tanned and skimpily clad French people raised their head. Some inclined eyebrows or merely stared at the pasty Irishman clutching his bulbous finger bandage and tottering unsteadily, barefooted, along the stony bottom. Others, far more elegantly, just ignored the disturbance.

Tiberius swam smoothly in towards him, having previously gone well out to sea. They had borrowed swimsuits from the apartment in which they were staying and headed to the seafront for a quick dip. Doyle had been amazed to see Tiberius slip into the water and head straight out, scything through the waves. He was an average swimmer himself and content to stay close to shore and within his depth at all times.

"You OK?" Tiberius popped up beside him.

"Well. A. it's colder than I expected, bearing in mind it's the Mediterranean and B. the salt water is stinging the crap out of my finger."

"Yeah. It's colder than back home too."

"Have you not had a chance to get into the water since you came to Ireland?"

"Nope."

"You want to try the Atlantic off the West coast. Have a swim in the Pollack Holes in Kilkee sometime. Even in the height of the summer, that water would turn your uncle into your auntie."

"That cold, huh?"

"Yeah. So I suggest we get a bite to eat and then head over to the Sûreté HQ and let them know we're in town out of courtesy, and then meet Gillian MacAllister at her apartment at eleven thirty. Is that OK?"

"Yeah. Fine."

The two policemen dried themselves and got dressed. They walked across the Promenade, dodging cyclists, rollerbladers, skateboarders and tourists and headed through a side road beside the Negresco Hotel, a famous Nice landmark with massive art installations outside and visible through its windows.

"My mate texted me about this little café where he has breakfast when he's in Nice" said Doyle as they walked along.

"Nice of him to lend us the apartment. If it wasn't for that we wouldn't have gotten authorisation to travel."

"They couldn't veto two forty-five euro flights and no accommodation bills. He's a great guy. Done quite well for himself but decent. Generous to a fault and never lost the run of himself, y'know"

"That's kind of rare amongst self-made people in Ireland, if you don't mind me saying so."

"Well during the boom years a lot of people were making so much money they kind of lost their bearings. People don't realise how much Ireland has changed in such a short period. Over the past thirty or forty years our society altered so quickly and so fundamentally that the landmarks which people orient themselves by, the traditional keystones which ground you, were all shattered. No one trusts the politicians anyway but they really let the side down when they were needed and then the clergy came along and completely destroyed the trust which existed between them and the Irish people. They did some awful things while they lived off the fat of the land. Not just the paedophilia and abuse. They were guilty of terrible arrogance and hubris.

So in the absence of traditional values or any kind of moral compass to use, people were lost. It is a generation who grew up and prospered dramatically, almost in a void, in my opinion. So a lot of them mistakenly replaced the old gods with money, material possessions and lifestyle. Bit sad really."

"The Catholic Church messed up in the States too."

Doyle stopped and sat at a shaded table outside a café which ran around the corner of the street they were walking along.

When the waiter came up Tiberius said in accent-perfect French "Deux Café au Laits et deux croissants, s'il veut plait, Monsieur."

"Your French is excellent. Did you ever live here?" Doyle asked.

"No. I picked it up from French friends of my Mom."

"OK." Doyle didn't ask any more as Tiberius's terse reply suggested it wasn't a welcome subject.

After enjoying perfect milky, strong coffee and soft buttery croissants, of which Doyle had seconds. The pair left the café for the French police HQ and then on to Gillian MacAllister's home.

*   *   *

"Come on up. I'm on the fifth floor, the door straight opposite the lift." A soft Northern Irish accent came from the intercom of the nineteen eighties apartment block which Tiberius and Doyle were standing outside. Number thirty one stood on Boulevard Franck Pilatte which ran from the old port in Nice beside and above the sea out towards Villefranche and Monaco.

Tiberius had his back to the Entrance Gate and was looking out over the deep blue Mediterranean sea. In the distance a motorised boat was towing nine or ten tiny white sailing dinghies along like a mother and her ducklings. Below in the port, massive, floating plastic palaces, masquerading as pleasure craft were tied up, side by side.

The buzzer on the gate sounded and Tiberius turned to follow Doyle through to the building. It was a relief to get out of the heat and into the air conditioned foyer. Tiberius could feel his shirt beginning to stick to his back with perspiration. Nice had to be at least fifteen or twenty degrees warmer than Dublin.

They exited the lift into another marble floored modern corridor. The door opposite was being held open by an elegant looking woman with long grey hair. She stepped back and said "Come in. We'll talk on the balcony. There's a nice breeze today."

Doyle introduced everyone and they settled themselves into comfortable chairs around a table set with a jug of iced water and three glasses.

Gillian smiled and poured them some water and then sat back with her glass in her hand and looking at Doyle said, "Been quite a while Tiernan, hasn't it?"

"Yes. Sorry about not keeping in touch but what with one thing and another and you moving away it's been difficult."

"I can imagine. I'm so sorry about your wife. I would have gone to the funeral but I didn't find out about it until some months later."

"No problem Gillian. I totally understand and anyway it all happened so quickly in the end that I was surprised so many actually heard about it, to be honest."

Tiberius took note that Doyle had lost his wife.

Then Gillian swivelled her gaze and turned what had to be the most intense deep brown eyes he had ever seen, on Tiberius.

"So, Mr Frost. Tiernan said you are originally from California? You may have a few wee questions for me? Are you interested in the painful history of our divided little island?"

"Not quite, Mrs MacAllister. I'm just trying to understand if some elements of it may have a bearing on a case we're pursuing at the moment. It is not my intention to upset anyone."

"I'm sure. Unfortunately, the history we all carry with us from those difficult days has more than enough potential to achieve that state in all of us. So merely talking about it brings with it that penalty."

As putdowns went it was elegant and also drew clear cut battle lines. Tiberius sensed it would foolhardy to underestimate this quietly spoken widow. Her fragile appearance belied a sharp-edged intelligence.

"We just wanted to talk about an unresolved case which Roger had discussed briefly with me." Doyle put in. "To see if he had ever mentioned anything about it to you?"

"I suspect I know the one you mean. There was only one unresolved case which bothered Roger."

"Would you mind discussing it with us?" Asked Tiberius.

"Yes." She sighed and looked down at her hands. After a pause she added, "But I will anyway. I was much older than Roger. Fifteen years. People used to look at us like we were freaks. There were plenty of couples where the man was older than the woman but not so many the other way around, but we were very happy. Until they took him away."

"Dreadful things were done by both sides during that time." Said Doyle.

"Yes." Again she paused and then said, "it would be nice to know which side though."

Doyle looked at her, surprised, "Gillian? The word was that it was the Provisional IRA that killed Roger?"

"I'm not so sure. I wasn't then and I'm still not convinced. There were constant army manoeuvres going on in the countryside around where we lived. Even at night I could look out my bedroom window and see soldiers moving across the fields."

Tiberius didn't fully understand where she was going with this and asked, "I'm not clear on the relevance of the army movements to what happened to Mr MacAllister?"

"If the countryside around Roger and Gillian's house was crawling with Army then it is unlikely that the IRA would have been able to mount an operation to attack him. Think about it. They would have to approach the property discreetly, get under the car and set the bomb and then get clear," answered Doyle. "They would have been more likely to pick another time or location."

"I understand from the wife of a friend in the ordnance analysis section that the bomb was remotely detonated," said Gillian with a pained look on her face.

"Which means they had to be able to see him get into the vehicle. There's no way they would have gotten out of the area undetected." Doyle said thoughtfully. "The explosion would have alerted hundreds of soldiers and RUC officers in the vicinity. Every movement would have been scrutinised. There couldn't have been a worse time to carry out this attack. Whatever people thought of the IRA, they weren't dumb. The risk profile of the action would have been too great, bluntly."

Tiberius turned to Gillian and asked, "So who?"

"I don't know and I probably never will." A bitter note underscored her words. "But I can't help but feel it was to do with that case."

"Can we talk a little about that?" Tiberius asked.

"Yes but there's a problem." Gillian answered.

"Oh?"

"I have an appointment with my Doctor now and I'm always very tired afterwards, so I'm not going to be of any use until tomorrow. Would you mind deferring this until then?"

"We're not flying back until Sunday evening so that's no problem Mrs MacAllister."

"Unfortunately, that's only part of it. Tomorrow morning early, I will be driving just over the border to Ventimiglia to the weekly street market. I promised to get some bags for my grandnieces who are coming to visit next week and this is my only chance." She looked from Tiberius to Doyle and back.

Doyle said, "look why don't we accompany you and we can talk in the car or after you've done your shopping?"

"That's fine with me." She sat back. "Is it acceptable to you

D.I. Frost?"

"Sure. Long time since I've seen Italy. It would be better if we talked once we get there rather than in the car on the way though. Might be less distracting for you."

"How thoughtful of you." She sounded amused. "Indeed it will be less distracting and probably safer for all concerned. I will leave at seven am tomorrow morning. Do you want me to collect you at your hotel or whatever?"

"That won't be necessary, we'll be back here at seven tomorrow." Tiberius replied.

Tiberius stood and Doyle followed suit. Gillian showed them to the door and they thanked her for her hospitality.

In the lift, both policemen stood silently looking at their reflections in the mirrored glass walls until Tiberius said quietly, "we're going shopping? Nice one Doyle."

Doyle stepped out of the lift on the ground floor and retorted "it's either that or nothing, Boss. I don't think she'll talk to us again. This is damn hard for her. I know she seems tough but she's been through a lot. We need to keep this conversation going. Sorry."

Tiberius shook his head. "No, you're right. Do we need passports?"

"No, and God bless the EU for it. There's no more border checks between Italy and France and we skirt past Monaco without going into it so no passports necessary. Look it's a just a fifty-minute drive."

Tiberius and Doyle jumped on a bus which took them back to the Promenade des Anglais on the sea front and walked back to their apartment. Doyle broke out his laptop and started transcribing his notes of the meeting with Gillian which he had scribbled down on the bus journey.

Tiberius got changed into running gear and went out for a relaxed run along the sea front heading towards the airport which curiously was also on the sea front. Every now and then his calm was interrupted by the progress of a massive jet taking off or landing on the runway further along the coast.

There were lots of people on the Promenade but it was so large and broad that there was plenty of room for people moving along it. As before it was full of skateboarders, rollerbladers, tourists on Segways, cool dudes on electric Unicycles and even old fashioned joggers like him. Tiberius moved smoothly through a selection of all shapes and sizes of human beings. Old and young, and young looking older people - triumphs and failures of the plastic surgeon's art.

He thought about the conversation they had just had with Gillian MacAllister and how guarded and careful she was. Product of her environment, and life experiences, he felt. He ran on.

*   *   *

After a great meal in a local restaurant recommended by Doyle's friend who had loaned them the apartment, Tiberius and Doyle had gotten an early night. They headed over to Gillian's apartment so they were waiting for her outside when the door to the underground garage opened and Gillian drove a dark grey Renault Captur SUV up the short slipway to the main road. They got in and greeted her as Gillian expertly manoeuvred the car off the sloping entryway and onto the road. Tiberius was pleased he was sitting in the passenger seat as he had a great view of the sea while they drove along.

"Should get there in fifty or sixty minutes," said Gillian as she drove along. "I'll get the shopping done, which shouldn't take too long as I know precisely what I'm looking for and which stalls will have them."

"Actually, I might accompany you while you're shopping if you don't mind?" asked Doyle. "A friend of mine mentioned the market to me and I'd like to check it out while I'm there."

"Fine, Tiernan," said Gillian.

"Uh, I'll take a rain check, if you don't mind" said Tiberius smiling.

"No retail therapy for you DI Frost?" teased Gillian.

"Not my thing. Sorry"

They pulled into the busy little town of Ventimiglia about forty-five minutes later and Gillian parked on a side street near the Train Station. Already the town was lively and Tiberius spotted a café just outside a large permanent food produce market. He stopped there and ordered a Latte and a sweet pastry. His table outside on the pavement was in the shade of the building which housed the café which was a major plus as the temperature had climbed towards thirty degrees plus while they had been driving. The heated air was like a blow in the face when they exited the car.

It has to be fifteen or twenty degrees warmer than Dublin, thought Tiberius, *weird weather for this time of year, I reckon.* He relaxed and watched the people heading past and the traders in the Market hall opposite going about their business, often with much passionate discussion and flamboyant gestures. He was impressed by how smartly dressed everyone was. It occurred to him these people had an innate sense of style which showed not just in how they dressed but in how they lived. They consumed their day with passion and a ferocious appetite. He decided he would have to return to explore this area of the Ligurian coast at some point in the future.

After an hour or two Gillian and Doyle returned with carrier bags in both hands. "Retail therapy huh?" Tiberius grinned at Doyle.

"Actually they're mostly mine" said Gillian. "Tiernan, being the gentleman he is, carried them for me. You only purchased some sunglasses and a pair of shoes yes?" she turned to the red-faced Doyle who had flopped into the chair opposite Tiberius.

The waiter deposited two bottles of water and two coffees which Tiberius had ordered when he spotted the intrepid shoppers in the distance making their way through the crowds towards him.

"How thoughtful of you," commented Gillian.

"Yeah. Cheers Boss," added Doyle as the contents of his bottle of water disappeared rapidly.

Gillian smiled at Tiberius as she drank. He noticed she sat bolt upright always.

"I have a suggestion to make," she said hesitantly. "Rather than head straight back to Nice, whereby I'm trying to answer your questions and drive at the same time, perhaps we could drive back along the coast to a little town called Ospeditiale and have brunch there? I know a nice little place on the seafront and we can have a good chat?"

"Fine with me," answered Tiberius.

"Ditto" added Doyle.

Twenty minutes later Gillian parked outside a little café halfway along a seafront road in the town. They chose not to sit inside. Interestingly, the exterior seating was situated across the sleepy road from the little trattoria where they had a good view of the pebbly beaches running between the breakwaters.

They ordered and looked out at the Italian families enjoying the beach and the warm sea.

After a few minutes, Gillian shivered and remarked "it all seems so far removed from Northern Ireland."

Tiberius flicked a glance at Doyle, warning him not to reply. He wanted her to speak, to begin without prompting if possible. Having spent some time with Gillian, he now felt it would be the best way to move forward, to get the most from this investment of time and effort.

"It was always so cold and damp," she continued. "Either it had just rained or was just about to rain. It's why I came here really. I swapped over three hundred days of rain and low temperatures each year for over three hundred days of sun. I felt I needed the heat of the sun to warm me, heal me." She paused, looking out at the sea. "Or if not heal then at least help. And the distance from that damned madhouse would lend some perspective. Of course I've thought about it a lot. Analysed it. Once I began being able to sleep at night. Once I stopped bloody crying and feeling sorry for myself. Pathetic!" She said angrily.

"You could never be that Gillian." Said Doyle kindly.

"You're sweet to say so, Tiernan" she replied.

"Do you feel Roger's death might have been related to that case?" asked Tiberius, feeling that the time was right for a gentle nudge.

"Undoubtedly" she said firmly.

Tiberius and Doyle sat quietly, expectant.

She sipped her glass of water and then continued, "He believed there was a single common denominator relating to a number of murders, some of which were attributed to sectarian elements and some of which were not."

"Do you know how many?" asked Doyle.

"He felt there were elements in common running through about thirty-nine murders."

"Thirty-Nine?" Tiberius was shocked.

"Yes. He also had come to feel that the perpetrators or rather perpetrator, as he eventually felt that there was only one person doing this, was somehow being protected."

"By whom?" asked Doyle.

"This is what was caused Roger the most anguish really. He came to the belief it was elements within the Security Forces, within the Establishment, as it were. Very senior people."

"Was he able to do anything about it? I mean did anything ever happen about it?" Tiberius pressed.

"Yes and yes. Roger prepared a report on the murders and submitted it to his superiors in the RUC. He had heard nothing back regarding the report and he decided to put some pressure on the senior officers to whom he had submitted the report. He told me he had requested a meeting with his senior officers. However, some spook from the mainland, as Roger called him, also attended. The man refused to give his proper name when Roger asked him to identify himself and his interest in the report. He said to just call him Joss and that he had been asked to try and help. Roger ended up having a row with them all and walking out, which wasn't like him. He was very calm and controlled usually but he said that during the meeting he had felt a real sense of futility, that nothing would come of his efforts and the murders would likely continue. Everyone was stonewalling him and ignoring his concerns. The English chap kept saying that Roger needed to consider the greater good and that no boat could make progress if one member of the crew was rowing in a different direction. That was when Roger lost his temper and stormed out."

She paused and they stayed silent waiting.

"Three days later he was dead, and they would have me believe that an IRA assassination squad managed to get to our house during a time when the surrounding fields were absolutely crawling with military and police personnel. That they had time to place a complicated and sophisticated bomb under his car. Locate a suitable vantage point which had enough cover to hide them from the security forces all around them and then wait for hours or even a day or two for him to get into the car. Then they had to blow it up, alerting all of the surrounding security forces and make their escape. It beggars belief, quite frankly."

The waiter arrived with their food and they all busied themselves with eating and once the waiter left and they were alone again Doyle spoke.

"I was very fond of Roger, as you know." He nodded at Gillian. She smiled. "So I did a little checking of my own into his death. Especially after you rang me that time. What was it? A few months later?"

"More. The following Christmas. I'm sorry for that call. I wasn't really myself and just got it into my head that because you knew him so well and he trusted you, that you too might have been at risk. I had finally gotten around to cleaning up his study and desk and I noticed it had been disturbed and some files were moved around on the desk. All of his filing cabinets were closed and locked except one. Silly really, I was possibly attributing too much significance to it. The product of an overactive imagination but it was a difficult time, so easy to make mistakes"

"No. No," interposed Doyle. "I had no problem with the call and it was good for us to talk, but it did set me to thinking. Now I didn't get very far with my ah, let's call it research, at the time but I did manage to get a little further more recently."

"Go on," encouraged Tiberius.

"OK. Well, I tracked down an ex-member of the IRA I had had some dealings with back in the day and I asked him about Roger's murder and he said, point blank, that they didn't do it. Don't get me wrong, he wasn't sorry about it, in fact his approach was that they were just sorry someone else had done it and not them."

"What about the INLA or some other republican splinter group?" asked Tiberius.

"Good question boss. I asked the same source and he said that the level of sophistication of the operation, as he called it, suggested professionals far more experienced and skilled than them. So who's left?"

"Northern Ireland security forces, UK mainland security forces or Southern security forces, it appears to me" said Gillian.

"Well let's examine that," answered Doyle. "Why would the Southern security forces kill someone who was very helpful to their efforts in dealing with the situation in the North. Roger was noted as someone who was very even-handed and cooperative by us in the South. To be honest his death set relations back quite a bit as his successor was far less helpful to us."

"So that leaves Northern Ireland or British Security Forces? Or possibly some criminal element which was allied to neither?" suggested Tiberius.

"I don't think his colleagues in the RUC would have countenanced colluding in any way with the murder of one of their own" said Gillian. "They were like a band of brothers and loyalty was everything. As far as they were concerned they were fighting a war against an enemy who wanted to change and if possible, eradicate their whole way of life."

"Granted," said Tiberius, "but that doesn't mean they would not adopt a, let's say, more passive approach to something which already happened, i.e. the subsequent investigation into Roger's death, if ordered to. To follow and deliver an officially sanctioned explanation of what had happened. Especially if someone, say from Whitehall or some other more senior part of the British Establishment put it to them that they did not want the boat rocked?"

Gillian sat forward and added "you also have to remember Britain was paying for everything. The Exchequer was pouring billions into the Security Forces in Northern Ireland, which paid for everyone's salaries and everyone's nice lifestyles, such as they were in those terrible days. As you say Mr Frost, no one was going to rock the boat when their paymasters laid down the law, as they saw it."

The waiter reappeared and cleared away their plates. They ordered coffees and Doyle had a slice of Tarte Tatin or "Upside-down Apple cake" as he called it. "I'm a martyr for French Desserts," he laughed.

Suddenly, a young black man laden with designer handbags sprinted past followed by five or six more, also carrying various goods for sale. They all stopped some two or three hundred yards further on, laughing and out of breath. When the waiter arrived with their coffees and Doyle's dessert, Gillian asked him in perfect French about what had happened.

She told Doyle and Tiberius that the market traders who had paid the Town's council for a pitch to sell their goods in the little market, which was going on uptown, had probably called the police to chase them away. "They are all migrants and this is how they make money. They are tolerated but not with any good grace," she said sadly, "and it's getting worse."

"Now, I have answered all of your questions," Gillian said. "You must answer mine. OK?"

"If we can," answered Tiberius warily.

"Why have you raised all of this again after so many years? And what does it have to do with the American Police?"

"Well, firstly Ma'am, I'm here in my capacity as an officer of the police force of the Republic of Ireland and not the U.S.. I was kinda co-opted into the Gardai when I moved to Dublin some time back."

"Ah. I see. What part of the States are you from?"

"California."

"Quite a difference, I would imagine."

"Yep. Back home in the Summer it's sunny all day, pretty much every day, but in Ireland, the only way to tell the difference between the seasons seems to be that in the Summer the rain gets warmer."

"And if you don't like the weather just wait five minutes and it'll change!" Doyle chipped in.

"You're not answering my question." She stared directly at Tiberius.

He looked uncomfortable. "Well it's difficult to get into. Seeing as it's part of an ongoing investigation, Ma'am. We're not really at liberty to.."

"He's killed again hasn't he?" She interrupted Tiberius. He didn't answer and she nodded her head thinking. "You've got some case which is linked to that awful person Roger was investigating?"

"We can't confirm that," began Tiberius.

"But you're not a million miles out," interjected Doyle.

Tiberius threw him a look and said quietly, "let's just say I'm investigating a case which has thrown up several different lines of enquiry and this may be one." She looked at him mutely, pleading.

After a long minute or two of silence, Tiberius came to a

decision. He tossed back his expresso and stood up saying "I'm sorry I can't answer your questions Ma'am, but I can't speak for my garrulous colleague here, especially when I'm not around, so I think I'll take a walk." He smiled at her and walked away down the promenade.

After about twenty minutes, he strolled back along the promenade towards Doyle and Gillian. They stood as he approached and as he got nearer Gillian mouthed the words "thank you."

Doyle asked, "Are we all ready to head back?" They made their way to the car which the sun had baked while they ate and talked, so they waited outside it while the air conditioning worked its magic and cooled the car down enough to travel back to Nice.

The traffic back to Nice on the Motorway was very heavy and the journey took twice or three times as long as it had earlier and by the time they all returned to Gillian's apartment in Nice everyone was wrecked. Doyle and Tiberius refused Gillian's kind offer of dinner on the grounds that if they were tired and only passengers then she must be doubly so. She, in turn, refused their offer of dinner in a restaurant and admitted she needed to rest.

They hailed a passing taxi and went back to their apartment. Doyle began to speak about what they had discovered from Gillian once they closed the door behind them, but Tiberius suggested they take a break and separately consider everything and then discuss it over dinner. So he went out for another run along the promenade and Doyle repaired to his room to work on his thesis, with a notepad beside him on which he jotted random thoughts and ideas in relation to the case as they occurred to him.

A few hours later they were sitting in a little restaurant not far from the apartment and shared a large metal pan of mussels in garlic and wine.

"So," Doyle said munching happily, "do you reckon it's the Brits? She clearly does."

"She ain't a cop," answered Tiberius.

"Granted, but she's got good instincts and she lived with one of the finest police officers, north or south of the border for a long time. Roger had one of, if not, the best arrest and conviction records in the RUC. But what do you think?"

"Look Doyle, I reckon your breakdown of reasons for and against is pretty accurate, and by a process of elimination.............."

"We come to the British or some section of the British Security Forces, possibly British Intelligence, yes?"

"Yes but think it through. What possible rationale would they have for shielding or protecting someone who was either a serial killer or at the very least a psychopath. Remember, not all of the murders Roger looked into were not related to the armed conflict in the North at that time. Some of them were just murders and apparently quite gruesome ones. The British would have been taking a serious risk. Why bother?"

"Point taken. The only reason for protecting a nut job like that would be if either he had some sort of leverage and was blackmailing them or he was useful to them, providing them with something they regarded as very valuable."

"Killing for them?"

"Yes. While you were strolling along the Prom in Ospeditiale, Gillian said Roger had determined that the murders he had classified as sectarian or politically related were not as gruesome as the other murders. The victims were either Republicans or Republican Sympathisers with three exceptions."

"I'm listening."

"Well, Gillian said three members of Loyalist Paramilitary gangs were killed with a similar M.O. shortly after they had caused problems for the authorities. One threatened to kill Tony Blair, the British Prime Minister, if he sold them out by doing any deal with the Republicans or the South. One was bringing in hard drugs which he was selling to soldiers in the

British Army and the other was trying to purchase arms and munitions in the immediate aftermath of the Good Friday Agreement. In other words, he wasn't buying into the Peace Process."

"OK. That strengthens the case for some sort of British involvement in this, but it doesn't explain the link between those cases and ours. Why start up now? After all this time? And why in Dublin?"

"That's why we're paid the big bucks Boss. To find out."

"What else did she say that might help us?"

"She came back to the variation in the way the murders were carried out."

"A pattern?"

"Yes. Roger split the murders into what he labelled as Civilian and Conflict related. The Civilian murders were just plain gorier and crazier, to be blunt. The Conflict murders were more efficient and, I don't know, professional?"

"Like he was just following orders. Executions."

"Exactly."

"Can we be sure it's just one guy?"

"She said Roger was positive it was just one person."

"What were the threads connecting these murders. I mean, thirty-nine is one hell of a big number. Did she shed any light on the common elements?"

"Better than that, she has Roger's file."

"What? I assumed it had been taken by whoever went through Roger's study? That's great."

"Well it's a copy. She discovered it just before she moved to France. She cleared out a safety deposit box they had in London on her way to Nice and it was tucked away in the middle of the other documents. She'll give it to me tomorrow. She wants me to call over in the afternoon."

"So the trip to Ventimiglia and Ospeditiale was what? To check us out? Get to know us?"

"Well she knows me. It's you she wasn't sure of."

"And I passed?"

"Well she's giving us the file, so, yes."

"Maybe we'll get some more answers in that. Did she say what's in it?"

"Dunno. She reckons it's pretty up to date as he had visited the bank a couple of days before he died and I'm guessing it was to update the copy."

"I'm surprised whoever is behind his death didn't know about the safety deposit box."

"It was registered in her maiden name. In effect it's her box and he just had access."

"Smart."

"Roger was no fool, just unlucky to discover what he did and too honourable to leave it alone."

"Back to Dublin. Why now and why after all of this time?"

"At this point, I don't know Boss. Could it have something to do with the University? Or those kids we interviewed? The killer could have mistaken the victim for the girl we interviewed, Beth. But what happened to the Plenderleith's was just right back to what I saw in the Shankill."

"OK. So what would he want with Beth? If we follow Roger's line of reasoning. He may have had a professional interest in her, whereas the Plenderleith's fit more into the Civilian mode?"

"Prendergast checked her and her pal Dane out and nothing in their background or history jumps out except that the guy Dane was the victim of some paedophiles when he was a kid in foster care. It was a pretty nasty case."

"Could he be our perpetrator?"

"Why would he kill someone who was just wearing the same outfit? Besides, he has an alibi for the time of the murder, he was toting Beth across campus and sobering her up back in his flat. She verified that and Garda Sweeney found some security guards who spotted him."

"He's good, isn't he?"

"Sweeney?"

"Yes"

"I think he's got potential."

"So if it wasn't Dane and it was someone else and nothing stands out in their history then it must be something related to their present," Tiberius was thinking aloud. "or their future."

"As in?"

"This software they've built. Maybe it's valuable."

"Enough to kill for?"

"I'm from California, Doyle. The home of Silicon Valley? A piece of software can be worth millions, billions even. Believe it."

"That's motive."

"Yep and we don't know yet what it does. There may be something in its functionality which adds value or significance other than just financial gain to whoever's interested it and... Damn!" Tiberius cursed. Doyle looked up from his plate quizzically.

"I just remembered I contacted my sister to talk to her about it. She's pretty hot on technology. Made a ton of bucks in tech a few years back."

"Oh, OK. Why not ring her now?"

"Doing it." Not finding any reception for his mobile phone, Tiberius got up and headed outside to the cobbled street. The phone rang for several minutes but wasn't answered. He rang it again but inserted a digit which he knew would put him through to Rayne's voicemail and he left a message asking her to ring him back.

CHAPTER ELEVEN

Tiberius and Doyle had returned to their borrowed apartment after their meal. Rayne had not contacted Tiberius yet which shouldn't have surprised him. She had a lot more in common with their bohemian and wildly erratic mother than Rayne might like, Tiberius thought. Doyle's phone rang, disturbing him from his awkward, cramped efforts to type into his laptop.

"Hi Gillian?" Doyle looked at Tiberius quizzically.

"No, it's not too late at all." He said and then listened to whatever she was saying. After a few minutes he replied to her saying "I think Roger was probably right but it's your decision at the end of the day." He stopped and waited. "OK well, we can call out tomorrow at whatever time suits you. Yeah? Fine. See you then." Doyle ended the call and grinned at Tiberius.

"Well?" asked Tiberius.

"She says she re-read Roger's file and has a good idea of who the guy is. If we call out tomorrow, she'll tell us who she thinks he is and why."

"Why not tell us before now?"

"A couple of reasons. I think she wanted to be more comfortable with us, which may be the reason for that shopping trip to Italy. Secondly as she just said on the phone, Roger warned her that if she ever spoke about it to anyone, she would put herself into immediate danger."

"From whom?"

"I reckon some individual or group within the British Secret Service."

"You sure about that?"

Doyle stopped, looking warily at Tiberius, who continued carefully. "Well I sometimes think it's easier for you guys in Ireland to blame the British for everything that happened relating to the problems in Northern Ireland. I'm not trying to insult you or anything but they're very convenient fall guys and I don't want us to miss anything vital because our attention is fixed on the wrong people. OK?"

Doyle stared at his screen for a long moment and Tiberius was concerned that he had offended the man. He was always conscious of being an outsider and not having a full understanding of the intricacies which formed a part of the confusing tapestry that defined modern Ireland.

Then Doyle sighed and ran his hands through his hair and said quietly. "I take your point and I get where you are coming from, Tiber. But my comments are based on a combination of my own previous research shortly after Roger died, Roger's own conclusions and Gillian's comments to date. Also you have to put their perspective into context. They're Protestant and Unionist. Staunch supporters of the British presence in Ireland and would under normal circumstances die to defend the Union between Northern Ireland and Britain. So pointing the finger at any element of the British Establishment is something which would have come very hard to them. Believe me, they would have preferred if the bad guys here sprang from the Nationalist side or the South."

"OK. Good. Now we have more clarity yes?"

Doyle smiled, realising now what Tiberius had been doing. It was a tactic he had used on subordinates himself in the past. Prodding them to make them re-evaluate their approach to a case and their assumptions about it.

The following morning the two of them headed out. They walked east along the sea front and up the long slope to where the promenade curved around and then dropped into the harbour. They stopped for a moment looking back west to enjoy the view along the coastline towards Cannes. As they turned to descend the hill to the harbour Doyle suggested a slight deviation to their plans.

"We're about an hour and a half early so why don't we stroll out along that breakwater below to the Lighthouse?"

"Fine with me."

They walked into the port and turned back towards the sea, heading out along the quayside past the yachts and super yachts lining it. "Bit like a caravan park on the water when you think about it," commented Doyle with a grin.

"The herd instinct always wins," replied Tiberius laconically.

As they ambled out along the narrow causeway, Tiberius stopped about fifty metres from the square stone tower topped by a red pillbox affair to house the light, which Doyle had informed him was no longer in situ.

"Where's Gillian's place from here? Can we see it?"

Doyle stopped beside him and looked eastwards.

"Do you see the building on its own with the diving boards and different level balconies?"

"Yes."

"That's La Reserve. When I win the lottery I'm going to stay there and eat myself silly for a solid week. They've got at least one Michelin Star, maybe two!"

Tiberius smiled at Doyle's enthusiastic description.

"So just about one hundred yards or metres, if you prefer, along the road to the right is Gillian's place. It's the whi..............."

A massive burst of flame exploded from the top right corner of the building they were looking at. A split second later they heard the roar of the explosion across the water.

"Damn," muttered Tiberius. "That's"

"Gillian's place," finished Doyle.

"Come on." Tiberius pivoted and began sprinting along the breakwater.

Doyle cursed and ran after him.

As they approached the port Tiberius glanced to his right

and vaulted a barrier. He ran up the street beside them where he had spotted an approaching taxi. He jumped in and after a few moments, Doyle fell into the back seat, wheezing and coughing. "Oh God! I think I'm going to puke up me lung!" he gasped.

They were silent as the taxi sped around the harbour and headed up towards Boulevard Franck Pilatte, the sounds of approaching sirens getting steadily louder.

The taxi slowed just fifty metres short of the apartment block. Tiberius threw some Euro notes at the driver and leapt out. Doyle was beside him as they rushed through the crowds moving towards the scene of the explosion. Two gendarmes stopped them just short of the building.

"We are police officers," Tiberius told him in his faultless French, both of them displaying their warrant cards. "We were on our way to an appointment in that building."

"Bon, then you will be 'appy to assist us with our enquiries." the Gendarme said back in accented but equally good English.

"Sure thing, but do you have any idea if there were any fatalities so far?"

The Gendarme gave the question a little thought as though weighing up whether or not to be of any assistance to this tall American. After a moment he said, "just one. We think it was the inhabitant of the apartment which was the location of the explosion."

"I suppose it's too early to know what caused it?"

"Yes, however, at a guess, it looks like a gas leak, but you must wait for my colleagues to discuss it further. So," he lifted the tape strung across the road. "Can you both please wait over by the wall?"

There being nothing more to be done, Doyle and Tiberius walked over and sat on the low wall with their back to the sea and stared above the fire engines to where a fireman stood at the top of a ladder spraying a powerful jet of water over the balcony and into the fiercely burning apartment.

"They got here quickly," commented Tiberius after a while.

"Hmm?"

"The fire engines and police. They arrived on the scene pretty fast."

"They are on high alert around here due to the possibility of terrorist activity," replied Doyle dully.

They were silent watching the devastation.

After a while, a long while, Doyle said, "this was no accident. Gas explosion my arse!"

"Let's see what they say."

"I know. I know. I'm just saying it." He fell silent and then asked, "how much do we tell them? Or let me rephrase that, how much can we shagging tell them?"

"On the one hand we are duty bound to tell them everything. On the other hand our investigation has just gotten kinda messy involving as it now does the police force of another country. So I'm kind of thinking that one through right now."

"Well let me know when you come to a conclusion," replied Doyle sarcastically.

Tiberius just swivelled his head to look at Doyle in his quiet way. After a few moments, Doyle muttered "sorry. I just really liked her, y'know? She was a real lady and when things were difficult for me at different points in the past she was always very kind to me."

"I get that, but we need to be of one mind on this. Not taking our emotion out on each other right now. Yeah?"

"Yeah. Gotcha."

After another hour, they were approached by a tatty looking individual dressed in jeans, sneakers, a grubby grey teeshirt and black stained hoodie.

"You Doyle?" he asked Tiberius brusquely in English.

"No, I'm Frost."

"Ah l'Americain. What are you doing with the Police Irlandais?"

"Excuse me pal," Doyle had stood up and moved in front of

Tiberius, "but who are you?" He asked belligerently.

The Frenchman looked at Doyle coldly for a minute and then began rummaging in the pockets of his hoodie. He brought out a wallet which he flipped open. "I am Detective Inspecteur Maurice N'Dour and I have the misfortune to be in charge of this disaster. So M'sieu Doyle what are you doing here and why?" The French Policeman deliberately omitted Doyle's title.

Doyle glared back at him, until Tiberius intervened saying in French, "I apologise, Inspector N'Dour but my colleague is old friends with the lady who owned the apartment which blew up and he is upset. We will of course do everything we can to assist you. If you need to check us out further, we met with Sergeant Pelous yesterday at Sûreté headquarters to inform them that we were in town to speak with the lady in question."

The French police officer said in a more pleasant tone. "I see. Thank you for your explanation Inspecteur Frost, we will contact Sergeant Pelous." He turned to Doyle and said in a sympathetic tone, "I regret, Sergeant Doyle, there appears to be one body at the scene which we think, and it is of course too early for a definite identification, but we think it's a female. I am sorry."

"Thank you. The lady we were to meet who was the owner of the apartment was called Gillian MacAllister." Doyle told him.

"OK. Good. We'll get her records and that should speed up the process of identifying her."

"Ahh, Inspector. Are Forensics up there now?" Asked Tiberius

"Yes."

"So, how long before Forensics have finished, do you think?"

"You want to see?" Asked N'Dour in a surprised tone.

"If that would be acceptable to you. We may have something to contribute."

"I will consider it" answered the Frenchman. "Please wait

here." N'Dour turned and walked away.

"That can't be an easy station," commented Doyle as they watched him walk away.

"Sorry?"

"He's African. Possibly or probably Muslim and this is a difficult time in relations between France and its own Muslim community and Muslims in general. Poor guy probably gets it from both sides, from his own people and his colleagues."

"He strikes me as a tough, savvy guy" replied Tiberius

"Ditto."

They sat on the low wall and waited again. After another hour or so a young French policeman approached and offered them a couple of bottles of water. When they thanked him, he said it came from N'Dour and he would get back to them as soon as he could, but they were free to leave if they wished. They looked at each other briefly and Tiberius replied that they appreciated the Inspector's courtesy but they were happy to wait.

The sun continued to beat down on them as they waited but they stayed where they were. Every now and again a French officer would glance over at them, but no one approached.

Sometime later, after Doyle's ears had turned bright red from the Sun, the young Gendarme came back and asked them to follow him. He led them past the cordon of police vehicles, ambulances and Fire Engines which completely blocked the road. They entered the wrought iron white gates which led to the main entrance of the smoke blackened, streaked building. Amazingly the gates were still perfectly white and dripping as though one of the water jets had cleaned them at the end.

N'Dour waited just inside the marble entrance hall with gloves, booties and blue jumpsuits for them.

"Gentlemen, I don't need to remind you not to touch or disturb anything." N'Dour paused and then added "but I would be grateful for any insight you can give." As soon as they were suited and booted, he turned and led them up the stairs.

The room was black. A charred, smoking, steaming ruin with an underfoot carpet of water, sludge, broken glass and debris. Everything was blackened and turned to charcoal or scorched black. All of the soft furnishings in the room had vanished. Fuel for the inferno which had consumed Gillian MacAllister's home. But she remained.

A vaguely human shape sat in what remained of a steel framed chair in the middle of the room. Doyle glanced at Tiberius, who studiously ignored him, moving slowly around the room, his attention fixed on the remains in the middle.

"From the stature and initial estimates of the pelvic girdle, at this point, we think it's an adult female." N'Dour said in a low dispassionate voice. "What baffles me is why she would just sit there? Was she suicidal? Or perhaps surprised by the explosion? But if that was the case surely she would have smelt the fumes of so great a volume of gas. Perhaps she was overcome by the fumes, but then she would have slumped in her chair and this body is sitting completely erect. We think she may have been tied up as the marks on the back of the skull suggest that her head may have been tied to something, like a piece of wood. In which case she may have been tied up prior to death and therefore unable to escape." He paused. "What do you think?"

Tiberius walked silently out of the room and halted at the stone parapet of the balcony, staring out to sea.

"You may be right." Doyle spoke after a few minutes. Tiberius turned to look at him and nodded.

Doyle continued, "it demonstrates similarities to a case we are dealing with in Dublin." N'Dour stared at him intently.

"In the Dublin murder the victims were tied up facing each other and tortured for several hours prior to death. The autopsy may find patterns of blade marks on some of the corpse's bones. Also the floor around the chair should be checked for bloodstains. It's unlikely anything organic like blood survived the blast but you might get lucky," Doyle said in a deadened voice.

"I think we should get out of here while I get the Forensics guys back in." N'Dour said "and then I'm going to buy you guys a drink while you tell me all about it."

Tiberius had continued looking out to sea, watching but not seeing a medium sized cabin cruiser style boat in the bay pull up its anchor and move off. Nor did he notice the person standing in the stern looking back at the apartment through binoculars.

"Let's go DI Frost. We have things to discuss" came N'Dour's voice from inside the room. Tiberius turned and they went downstairs again. They shed the dirtied forensic outfits and walked out into the bright sunshine. N'Dour led them along the road to a bright red American muscle car.

Once they got in and the engine roared into life. N'Dour drove along the road towards Cap Ferrat. He said in an embarrassed tone, "I apologise for the ludicrous transport, but I was about to initiate an undercover operation near here when the call came in about the explosion."

He headed off the main road and drove out along a road which snaked its way past the stunning villas and mansions which made up the ultra-rich enclave of Cap Ferrat. He pulled up by a small beach and they sat on the veranda of a small café bar overlooking the sea.

N'Dour ordered three large beers and once he had taken a long drink from his glass, wiped his mouth and settled back in his chair. He regarded the Irishman and the American in front of him and finally said "Well?"

Tiberius said, "this could take a while and before we start you've got to agree that some of it has got to be off the record."

"Unofficial background data, as it were" chipped in Doyle.

"I can't promise that gentlemen. Look why don't you just tell me whatever you think is relevant to my case. Anything which might help me solve it and let me be the judge of what

I need to place into the case files. How does that sound?"

After a short pause, Tiberius said, "OK." He turned to Doyle. "You deal with the North and I'll take Maurice through the Dublin case."

"OK Boss."

Tiberius turned back to N'Dour. "The first thing I need to explain is that we think have a good idea why Gillian Mac-Allister, assuming that the body back in the apartment is Gillian MacAllister, was murdered. It was no accident." He paused and then said, "it's because she was going to give us the name of the perpetrator of a double murder we are investigating back in Dublin. My view is she was killed to prevent her from doing that, which also means that somehow the person or persons who were involved in her death knew that we were in Nice to talk to her. They may even have been in a position to monitor our conversations with her and therefore able to take action to prevent her from giving us any further information. If we are correct then she was also tortured prior to her death to discover what she may have told us up to that point in time."

He sat back and then Doyle took up the tale. Half an hour later, having been interrupted several times by N'Dour, on different points and seeking certain clarifications and explanations, Doyle finished. Tiberius then took up the story again and filled in as much as he felt able to about their investigation in Dublin.

"Merde," said N'Dour sitting back in his chair, "this is seriously above my paygrade on one hand and on the other.............."he tailed off, thinking hard.

"Above your paygrade? How" asked Tiberius.

"Only in that it may involve elements of the Intelligence Services of the UK and Ireland."

"Ireland?" Doyle queried.

"Bien sur. I would not be surprised if the UK and the Irish Intelligence people had some form of collaboration to keep this going for so long." N'Dour paused, watching the people on the beach. "I think this guy may be an assassin and he is or was working for one or both of the intelligence services. Most likely, the British. Based on what you have told me, he tortured Gillian MacAllister prior to the explosion, either for his own pleasure or to discover if she told you anything dangerous to him or his masters or both. The poor woman."

"So what's he doing in Dublin?" Asked Tiberius, impressed with N'Dour's incisive comments.

"OK. First, he's smart, very smart. He has to be to have survived so long, no? I would imagine also he would not kill in such an obvious and trackable manner if he wasn't confident that his past misdemeanours were all fully covered up. Yet he or some other colleagues of his followed you here and killed Madame MacAllister to stop her from enlightening you any further, which also means that they know what you are doing. You have a leak inside your investigation or among those to whom you report, mon ami. This is what triggered them to follow you to Nice and take such drastic action. Hence my comment about the Irish intelligence service possibly being involved."

Doyle said to Tiberius, "it makes sense."

"Yes but everything relating to the investigation is being sent to at least three different people in our command chain and there is no real requirement for confidentiality beyond the norm." said Tiberius. "Also we don't know where the information is going from there."

"Exactement" N'Dour added emphatically, "or who is sharing it with whom."

"They better pray we don't find them!" Doyle said grimly.

"Well. Thank you for your courtesy in sharing your information with me, as one professional to another," said N'Dour standing up. I will drop you back to your hotel or wherever you are staying and then return to my investigation. I will bear in mind what you have told me and interpret my findings accordingly. I trust you will complete your investigation before I complete mine so I can then add all of this data to our findings without compromising yours. OK?"

Tiberius stood up and shook N'Dour's hand. "Thank you Maurice. I'm grateful."

CHAPTER TWELVE

Doyle and Tiberius disembarked from their Ryanair flight and walked across the wet and raining tarmacadam to the Terminal building at Dublin airport. They skipped the passport queues, showing their police ID at Passport Control and as they only had carry-on bags arrived at the taxi rank quickly. Fortunately, there were two taxis waiting and having noticed how tired and drawn he looked, Tiberius made Doyle take the first taxi. As Doyle's car pulled off, Tiberius turned to get into the second taxi when a woman asked him, "do you mind asking him if he can radio for another cab?" He turned to discover the mother of Doyle's rugby playing protégé.

"Why don't you take this one?" he offered smiling.

"No. No. I couldn't. You were getting in."

"Well I'm not gonna take it and leave you standing here in the rain, uh?" He paused. "I'm sorry I don't know your name"

"It's Ashling. Look let's just share the cab and get out of this rain?"

"Deal. I'll put our bags in the trunk." Tiberius held the door open for her and asked the taxi driver to pop the trunk.

"Ya wamme to do wha?" asked the Driver in a strong Dublin accent.

"Open the boot so he can put our bags in." interjected Ashling.

"No problem love."

The boot opened and Tiberius put both bags in, closed it and got into the taxi at the other side.

"Awri!" said the driver wearily. "Thanks be to Gawd, youz

decided to share coz I thought I'd be here all night waitin'. Where to?"

"I'm in Dalkey." Said Ashling.

"I'm at Port View Apartments, Ringsend." Said Tiberius.

"Perfeck. Feckin Perfeck," said the Driver. "I'll go tru de tunnel an' drop you first, and den head for Dalkey. Awri?"

"Great thanks," Ashling smiled. "I know those apartments you're in. My father in law was involved in that development."

"A buddy of mine bought one when he was over here setting up a US finance house and he lets me have it cheaply. It's got great views."

"Just right for a single guy eh? Or do you share?"

"No. Uh. Just me."

"What floor are you on?"

"The top floor, hence, the view."

"De penthuuus? Lucky bastarrrd?" the taxi driver interjected.

"So were you travelling on business or pleasure?" she asked.

"Business, I'm afraid. What about you?"

"I was visiting my best friend who lives in Italy. A sort of bi-annual pilgrimage where I tell her all of my woes and she sort of advises or rather lectures me on my shortcomings and makes me be nicer to my sister."

"Doesn't sound much like pleasure to me."

"She has the right intentions, just the wrong way of expressing herself sometimes. She's high octane and lives life to the full, but she cares."

"I have a sister too. I tend to provide that function for her rather than the other way around."

"Lucky her."

The cab suddenly lurched as the taxi was merging into the motorway traffic from the slip road they were travelling along.

"Bollix!" shouted the driver as he swerved back onto the hard shoulder. "Dat fella should be shot!"

Ashling had been thrown forward and across Tiberius who had grabbed her. Their faces were momentarily inches apart, her eyes wide staring with surprise. After a millisecond too long, Tiberius released her and she sat back.

"Are youz awri?" asked the driver anxiously.

"I'm fine," Ashling said.

"Yeah. Just take it easy buddy. We're in no rush," said Tiberius

"Not my fault pal. It was that nutbag in the Merc who cut me up."

Tiberius ignored him and glanced at her again. She was looking out the window as the taxi entered the tunnel which would take them to the Dockland area of the city.

They were silent as the car sped under the city and then emerged into the softening evening light.

"The rain has stopped," she said in a conversational tone.

The taxi made its way over the Liffey river along the East Link Bridge and then turned into the Ringsend area, pulling up outside Tiberius's apartment building.

"Can I get you coffee or something?" Tiberius found himself asking her, his hand on the door handle.

"Thank you but better not." She replied smiling at him. "I have an au pair who's probably screaming for release from looking after Cian right about now."

"Yeah. Of course. Sorry, I..."

"It's just not convenient right now. However, perhaps I can take a rain check on it? OK?"

"Sure. Anytime."

He handed some money to the taxi driver as he got out and retrieved his bag. The taxi sped off as soon as he closed the boot. Tiberius watched the car drive to the corner and then, just as it turned, she looked out the rear window and smiled back at him.

*   *   *

Six hours later Tiberius stood in his boxers at his open window, troubled, watching the rain fall in heavy sheets over Dublin bay. Way out to sea he could see the lights of a boat slowly emerging from out of the dark sea as it headed towards the port. There was little wind and the dense rain obscured and softened every edge and blurred the lights from the port and lighthouse at the tip of Howth promontory right out at the far side of the wide, flat bay. Truth be told, Tiberius liked the rain. He found it soothing. When he first arrived in Ireland, it had been in late October and turned into one of the wettest winters on record. The difference from the arid perma-sunshine of California was like a blow to the senses. He couldn't believe how long it lasted. It explained the frenetic activity along the seafront and in the parks dotted around the city once the weather became dry or that treasured rarity, sunny.

He had awakened, distressed and sweaty, from a very restless sleep or rather from a recurrent nightmare. As before he was standing at the door listening to her laughter and staring with a sickened dread twisting his stomach and making his knees weak, at the trail of blood going up the stairs. Then his hands would begin to hurt and he would look at them to see more blood, blueish in hue, flowing slowly from his fingers. The weakness would spread from his legs up through his body to his head. Then his vision would go black and he would feel himself falling. He always woke with a start just as he hit the blood soaked floor.

He went to the kitchen and poured himself a glass of water. As he stood drinking it, he heard a soft bing. It was from his mobile in the bedroom. Picking it up he saw a text from Doyle.

Sorry it's so late but my mobile didn't work in France - just turned it on to see text from Gillian's phone

She sent just one word – blaxo. Doesn't make sense? If you're awake ring me.

Tiberius dialled him.

"Hope I didn't wake you," Doyle's voice sounded tired.

"Nope. Couldn't sleep. You?"

"Working on my thesis when I remembered to turn on my phone. When it had powered up all of my messages came in and this was among them."

"Can you tell what time it was sent?"

"She sent it a few hours before the explosion, about six am."

"We need to email N'Dour to see if we can narrow down the time and location. Take a screen capture and attach the image to the email."

"I'll get onto it."

"Any thoughts as to meaning?"

"Not sure Boss. I googled the word and it's not proper English. It's like a name."

"Could be a mistake."

"Sorry?"

"She may have intended typing another word on her phone. Some or all of it may be typo's," he paused, "especially if she was under stress." Tiberius's comment was followed by a long silence. Both men thinking of what Gillian had endured at the hands of her killer or killers.

"Let's see what N'Dour thinks, Doyle?" Tiberius added briskly. "He may be able to shed some light on it."

* * *

N'Dour was walking slowly towards the front door of Nice Sûreté headquarters. His head was pounding. He really didn't want to be doing this but he knew he had to go in. Hangover be damned.

Dinner last night had been intended as a thank you for their neighbours. Marc and Didier were a gay couple who lived upstairs and had helped out when Chantal and he had to spend a week in Paris urgently. About six weeks ago, her mother had been taken to hospital with a heart attack. While they were

128

on their way, she had a second attack and by the time they arrived at the hospital she was in a coma. Maurice rang their neighbours and asked them to feed the cat as they couldn't be sure how long they would be in Paris. Marc and Didi had brought starters and dessert and two wonderful bottles of Bordeaux and Maurice had cooked the main course. Chantal wasn't up to much and had been very quiet. After they had eaten the first course, and he brought the crockery into the kitchen, Marc came in and told him that Didi and Chantal were on the balcony crying.

Maurice and his friend sat in the sitting room talking quietly and drinking the marvellous wine. In low tones they chatted about the mad bastard of a vigneron who had sold it to them, the previous summer when they had visited his vineyard on their motoring holiday. When Chantal and Didi came in and realised the two bottles were gone and their partners were more than a little drunk. Chantal smiled. It was a sad smile. She came over to him to sit on his lap, putting her arms around him and kissed him gently.

"You're a disgrace to the noble police force of France"

"Ah yes," he agreed drunkenly. "But I'm your disgrace. All yours."

They then broke out the other two bottles from that trip which everyone felt were slightly heavier and fuller bodied and complemented his cassoulet main course just perfectly.

After Marc and Didi staggered out and up the stairs of their apartment building. Maurice turned to find his beautiful wife fast asleep on the couch snoring gently. So he picked her up and put her to bed. Then he returned to the sitting room and in a rare act of drunken self-indulgence finished off the last bottle.

Several hours later as he made his way through the front door of the headquarters, N'Dour noticed a well-dressed elderly lady arguing in a loud voice with Bastareaud, the Sergeant who inhabited the front desk. Bastareaud walked with a limp as a result of receiving two bullets during a bank raid which he inadvertently strayed into some years ago. From what N'Dour understood, Bastareaud had kept his nerve, shot both raiders and called for backup and ambulances before passing out. He was promoted, decorated and moved to a variety of desk jobs until an exasperated Chief of Police realised his abrasive personality and general air of grumpiness was perfectly suited to the customer service role of running the front desk. A classic French solution. It worked. Sort of. The number of time-wasting complaints they had to deal with dropped through the floor but on more than one occasion they had lost out on genuine leads. Despite complaints from all of the detectives in the station, the powers that be persevered with Bastareaud and he was now a fixture, part of the entrance hall furniture.

N'Dour could see Bastareaud was trying to send the woman away and was making his way past the arguing pair when he thought she looked vaguely familiar. He spoke to her saying "may I be of assistance?"

She turned and said in an annoyed manner "Yes. I hope so. This horrible man doesn't believe me. You see."

N'Dour moved off and she followed him still talking. He was steering her gently to the front door when she said "I saw him. I saw him you see. God forgive me but I let him in. It's a terrible thing."

"Saw who Madame?"

"The gendarme, who called to the door."

"Where do you live Madame?

"Number Thirty One, Boulevard Franck Pilatte. I'm Gillian's neighbour!"

N'Dour halted their progress and brought her back past the bemused Sergeant and upstairs to an interview room.

She calmed down quite quickly once she saw she was being taken seriously. She explained that a police officer called to her apartment building at two or three a.m. as she had made a complaint about someone standing outside her window, three days previously.

It turned out that no police officer had been despatched to investigate because the elderly lady had made several identical complaints in the previous six months, all of which were fictitious. They were all the more unlikely as she lived on the third floor of the building and the only way to reach the window in question was to climb up the front of the building which was very well lit.

The police officer had told her over the intercom he had been requested to check the inside and outside of the building as an extra measure. She had been suffering from insomnia, so was awake when she heard a knock on the door of her apartment at about four am but was too frightened to open it. She said she thought that she heard a man's voice asking to come in to check the apartment but she couldn't see his face through her door and she was just too frightened so she hid in her bedroom. What saved her was quite simply that she had forgotten she had let him in. She couldn't remember any of this when she was being questioned immediately after the events. It was only early this morning that she had returned to the police station in an agitated state.

"I forget things you see. It began recently. I overheard my daughter speaking with the doctor on the phone last week. He told her I have dementia. I'm going to lose my mind." She began sobbing. N'Dour was momentarily flustered but the female officer he had called into the room when he began speaking with Madame Lagarde, got up and went around the table to give her a comforting hug. As his colleague calmed the woman, N'Dour thought Madame would be of little use to them if this ever came to court. Any good lawyer would simply trot out her medical records and tear her testimony to shreds.

No. Her use to them was as a sign-post to help them get closer to their quarry. He asked for her daughter's number, stepped out into the corridor and rang it. She told him her mother's dementia was in the very early stages and she could go for months between attacks. She felt since the recent events she was much improved. It was as though the dramatic explosion had shocked her back into a state of sanity. Something which she had discussed with Madame Lagarde's doctor who said it was very rare but not unheard of, although normally such an event would have the opposite effect.

As he looked back in the door at Madame Lagarde, N'Dour thought about how clearly and lucidly she had presented the information to them just now. It was all chronologically sequential which is always a pointer to how confused a witness is. He opened the door and asked Madame if she would mind looking through photos to try and identify the man she said she saw on the video intercom at the entrance to the building. If that proved unsuccessful they would get an artist to put together a sketch of the man. Madame agreed and his colleague said she would take care of it.

N'Dour went back to his office and picked up the phone to Tiberius who at that moment, was walking through the UCD Campus towards the office he had commandeered for his team. N'Dour related Madame Lagarde's information to him and added that he felt she was composed and mentally alert at present and that after speaking with her daughter and giving it some further thought he had decided to regard it as a firm lead. He also told Tiberius that the telephone company had reverted to them with the information that the text from Gillian's phone was sent at seven minutes past six on the morning of the explosion.

"What do you reckon Maurice?" asked Tiberius.

"I think he gained entry to the building at two, maybe three a.m.. Madame Lagarde let him in. Then, some time after entering the building, he got into Gillian's apartment. He tied her up and began interrogating and torturing the poor woman at that point. No one would have heard anything as the construction of the walls and floor are reinforced concrete. Forensics found what looks like a melted mobile phone under the chair she was sitting on so she may have had it on her person when she was tied up or whatever and managed to send that text to your colleague. From her records, it was the last number she contacted so it would have been easier for her to text or call it."

"She wouldn't have called it."

"Why?"

"She couldn't run the risk of her attacker hearing Doyle's voice answering it."

"She would have thought of that? Under all of the undoubted stress she was under?"

"Gillian struck me as a very cool, intelligent, self-possessed woman. On balance, I'd say it was possible."

"What do you think the word *blaxo* means mon ami?"

"We're not sure. It may mean nothing. Could be gibberish typed while she was in a great deal of pain and frightened. I'm meeting with my team in an hour and we'll see what we can come up with."

"I would offer the same but as her native language was English, I think we may be of little use."

"Yep. Let's see what we can figure out. I'll keep you in the loop Maurice."

"Same here Tiberius. Just one thing."

"Go on."

"Don't call me Maurice. Everyone calls me N'Dour. Bien?"

"Same as Doyle. No problem. Talk later."

Tiberius walked in the door of the office to find Prendergast, Doyle and Sweeney waiting for him. It turned out to be a pretty unsatisfactory meeting as not much new information had come to light. At the end, Doyle explained about the text and the circumstances of it and Tiberius filled everyone in on Madame Lagarde's information and N'Dour's conclusions.

"So what the hell does *blaxo* mean?" asked Prendergast.

"That's what we need to work out," replied Tiberius, noting with irritation that Sweeney seemed more interested in playing with his smartphone than contributing to the general discussion.

"Was she right handed or left handed?" Asked Sweeney, his head still buried in his phone.

"Ahhh. I'm not sure. Right handed, I would guess, on the balance of probabilities. Doyle?" Tiberius replied.

"No boss. She was left handed, definitely."

"OK. A ciotóg" said Sweeney in the same distracted way. He flicked his phone from his right hand to his left in a flash, showing amazing dexterity and coordination.

"Sweeney. What the fu…" Doyle began, but Tiberius waved him to silence, looking intently at Sweeney.

"Did she have a smartphone or a blackberry?" continued Sweeney still not looking up and switching his phone behind his back.

"A Samsung smartphone." Tiberius replied.

"Prendergast," continued Tiberius. "have the final forensics from the Glebe House come back?"

"No sir. Shannon has priority so God knows when we'll get them."

"I know someone over there. Do you want me to ring them to see what can be done Boss?" offered Doyle.

"Yes please." Tiberius was still staring at Sweeney.

Sweeney stopped slouching and sat up. He looked up at Tiberius and said, "I don't think it's *blaxo*."

"No?" queried Prendergast.

"I'm fairly certain it's *black*," replied Sweeney.

"On what basis?" asked Tiberius.

"If you're tied up and texting on a smart phone, one handed, your hand is quite likely to slip when texting. In fact it is more than probable that you will make errors. Remember, she couldn't see the phone. If she was in pain, then the likelihood increases. If we assume that she was concentrating hard on the first two or three letters and that they are accurate, bearing in mind that her left hand was her dominant hand and she would have had stronger muscle control over it. She would have been using the standard qwerty keyboard of her Samsung so if she did slip then based on the patterns of movement controlled by the muscles of her left hand, the neighbouring keys her thumb is most likely to fall on are the 'x' and 'o' keys. If you reverse the pattern and move in the opposite direction to the most likely neighbouring keys on the keypad which are 'c' and 'k'."

"Jaysus, Sweeney. You're a bloomin' genius." Said Doyle with genuine affection.

"Makes sense," added Tiberius. He looked at Prendergast quizzically. "What do you think?"

"Is it the only combination which becomes a real word or name?" She asked Sweeney.

"Yes. I've been trying various combinations. It's the only one."

"So is it a name or a colour or both, or a codename or what?" asked Prendergast.

"I'm fairly sure it's a name" answered Doyle. "A few hours earlier she told me she was going to give us the name of the person she thought had committed the murder in Dublin and several more prior to that, mostly in Northern Ireland."

Sweeney interjected, "several more?"

"Thirty nine," said Tiberius quietly.

"Oh my God!" Said Prendergast.

"Plus the two in the Glebe House, makes forty-one. Forty two if we include the girl in the pit," added Sweeney pedantically.

"However, some of the Northern Ireland cases might be classified as under the guise of military action" said Tiberius.

"We aren't sure at this point how many would count as directed assassinations and how many would be regarded as straightforward murder" Doyle added in a sarcastic tone.

"One sick bugger" muttered Prendergast under her breath.

*   *   *

Tiberius and Doyle walked from the office back to their car.

"So ahh, what did Sweeney call it? A key-togue is the name for a left handed person in Ireland? Is that Gaelic?" Asked Tiberius.

"Yes. It actually means an awkward person. It is spelt C, I, O, T, O fada, G."

"Fada?"

"It's a slanting mark over the O to remind you to draw it out. Sounds like the ending in the word brogue?"

"Gotcha."

"In many countries across Europe, they used to force kids to use their right hand for everything. Everything on the right was good and on the left was bad. For example, the word in Italian for left is 'sinistra', hence the word sinister?"

"You're a fountain of knowledge," Tiberius smiled at Doyle as they walked along. Doyle was quiet.

After a while Tiberius said "all right. Out with it."

"Sorry?"

"What's eating you?"

Doyle sighed and said, "In order to properly investigate this Black lead."

"It is that" Tiberius interjected.

"What?"

"A very dark lead. We better be prepared for where it takes us."

"True Boss, but in order to properly investigate it, we need to kick this upstairs in order to requisition the sort of access and support we need."

"Go on."

"Well. Firstly, every available resource is focussed on the Shannon Attacks so they're not going to want to give us any more than we've got. In fact, it's pretty amazing you've got as many as four in the team as it is."

"Well, we are investigating two separate murders, with three victims. Under normal circumstances in Ireland that would be a big deal." Tiberius reminded him.

"Accepted. Also, how popular is this idea that we've got a serial killer running around Dublin going to be with the upper echelons of our glorious force? In the light of what happened in Shannon, it's going to be the last thing they'll want to hear. Lastly, how concrete is the evidence on which we are basing all of this? Sweeney's interpretation of a dodgy text and an elderly pensioner's reminiscences which can't be checked any further because she's dead and we suspect, without a shred of evidence to back it up that it's our guy who happened to make a side trip to France just to take her out."

"I'm not so sure this guy is a serial killer. I'm considering that he's some kind of assassin, overly sadistic and probably a psychopath. Sooner or later the behaviour of serial killers spiral out of control. This guy is most definitely in control of himself." Tiberius drawled then sighed, "we need more, before we can go upstairs."

"Yes Boss, but it's a catch-22 situation. We need to go upstairs to get clearance and access to the relevant files and possibly to access British Police files in order to put together the information to back up this theory. But we need to prove the theory *before* we go upstairs, in order to persuade them to grant us that access!" Doyle sounded exasperated.

Tiberius grinned, slapped Doyle on the back and said, "you're forgetting that it's probably British or Irish Secret Service files we really need to access and I can tell you buddy, we ain't gonna get that. But then that's why we're cops. If it was an easy job anyone could do it."

"Wish it was that simple," grumbled Doyle as he got into the car.

CHAPTER THIRTEEN

A taxi pulled up outside the British Embassy on Dublin's Merrion Road. It was an unattractive modern building, quite out of keeping with the neighbouring collection of Edwardian and Georgian mansions which comprised the bulk of Dublin's embassy district. It had been built in haste and contravened all planning guidelines, rammed through by an embarrassed Irish government after the previous embassy had been attacked and burnt in rioting after Bloody Sunday. A particularly low point in modern British – Irish relations.

After a double check. First by an Irish policewoman outside the gate and then by British security personnel manning the gate, the taxi was allowed through to the courtyard to drop its two passengers and then left immediately. A tall young woman was waiting outside the entrance. She shook hands with them and invited them to follow her. To their surprise she did not go back into the building but headed around to the right and along the side of the building, walking across the grass. They could see an elegant, white haired man seated at a table, smoking a cigarette facing towards the sun. He got up as they approached and extended a hand in welcome.

"John, how are you?" He smiled at the massive Irishman in the dark suit and had his hand engulfed in a firm handshake.

"I'm well, Jocelyn." He gestured to the almost as tall, younger man who accompanied him. "this is Gavin. I'm sort of training him in. Are you happy for him to stay, or?"

"Perhaps on this occasion, you might decide how much you want to brief him once we've had our little chat. I trust I've not offended you, Gavin?"

"Not at all. I understand. I'll take a stroll around your grounds. Call me when you need me sir," the young man replied diplomatically.

As he walked away, Jocelyn said smiling, "That's a rare one. Most young buggers in London would be taking such a request as a slight on their reputation."

"Don't you believe it. He'll damn me with questions the minute we get into the car. He's just not stupid enough to do it in front of you." The Irishman gingerly settled his six-foot seven-inch frame onto a chair opposite Jocelyn. "So?"

"I've been well John and how are you?" teased Jocelyn.

"Come on Joss. I'm too old and tired for messing. What's up?"

Jocelyn dropped the smile like a mask falling and said "Black"

The Irishman stared at him and then asked, "what about him?"

"We think he's in Dublin."

"You think or you know."

"Um, fairly sure."

The big man was quiet, remembering and thinking. Then his face changed and he said, "the murders in UCD. Him?"

"Possibly. Well, the couple who were killed look like his handiwork."

"Is he employed?"

"No. No, we're keeping to our agreement on that. No, he appears to be here on his own account. We're not sure why."

"Jesus. This is the last thing we need on top of the Shannon attacks."

"Indeed."

"If you're right and he's caught then he's going down. You realise that."

"Which could be embarrassing for both of our governments."

"True. True. But three people are dead and two of them

quite horrifically. The only reason they're not splashed all over the media is because they're totally focussed on Shannon. However, they will eventually turn their attention to it, especially if he does it again and if no one's caught."

"Point taken, so what do you recommend, John?"

"He's not the sort who's going to respond well to a prison psychologist. Now is he?"

"Ever the master of the understatement, John. In the good old days, I'd make a phone call and have him put down."

"He is still your dog, Joss...."

Jocelyn looked steadily at his Irish counterpart, not a hint of emotion present on his face. Always a patient man, John sat looking back, with a slight smile.

"Obviously, we can't do anything in your jurisdiction John. No matter how needed it might be."

"Now Joss, we both know it wouldn't be the first time that happened."

"Different times, John. Different times." Jocelyn was uncomfortable at the turn the discussion had taken. Jocelyn's relationship with him had always been a very positive, cordial one marked by an unusually high level of co-operation between the two men. Both of them in similar roles at the top of their countries intelligence services. They had both made a point of informally keeping the other in the loop thus cementing their low key liaison. As a result they had discreetly cleared up a lot of messes for their respective countries and the flow of information between them had proven invaluable on several occasions over the past few decades.

Now he wondered how much John knew about certain operations which had taken place within the jurisdiction of the Republic of Ireland which he had not been able to inform him about.

"Perhaps we ought to evaluate this situation more carefully and talk again?" suggested Jocelyn.

"Fine with me. You know how to find me. Safe journey

back."

"Indeed. All the best John."

They both stood. The Irish spy shook hands with the English spy. John walked back towards the building, picking up his younger protégé and disappeared around the side.

Jocelyn sat back down and analysed the conversation they had just had. It was obvious that John wasn't going to do anything about the problem, beyond monitor it, allow the police to investigate the murder and then let events take their natural course. In fact, it sounded like he was tacitly encouraging Jocelyn to deal with Black in a more direct manner. An extreme manner. Yet, Jocelyn felt, it would be foolhardy to attempt to take any action to curtail or remove Black's freedom of movement while in the Republic of Ireland at this point. Although nothing would have given him more pleasure than to simply execute the bastard.

Realistically, it was unlikely the Irish police would manage to track down Black and arrest him. If they did then they would have managed to achieve something no other police force in the world could. In such an event, Jocelyn was certain Black would have absolutely no loyalty to his employers and indeed enjoy causing as much embarrassment to Her Majesty's Government as possible. It was a dead cert that the nasty little bastard would try to cause as much damage as possible to Jocelyn personally and Barty would probably be pretty damaged too. Maybe more so. *The situation might indeed get out of control,* Jocelyn mused. *So, although that scenario might be somewhat remote, nevertheless, preparations needed to be made.*

In a way, that was Jocelyn's greatest value to his government, his ability to analyse situations and create solutions for dealing with all possible contingencies. A final solution to Mr Black was something Jocelyn would relish if he was being honest. Barty would be a tad put out, but then one did have to break few eggs in order to make a decent omelette.

CHAPTER FOURTEEN

The massive spotlights roamed the stage and then a single bright white beam flicked to the side to pick out a slender man standing there in black jeans and a green t-shirt holding a microphone. "Hi everyone," said the man, striding confidently across the stage at the Web Summit event being held in the main exhibition space of the Royal Dublin Society, a collection of the largest indoor and outdoor arenas in Ireland.

The Web Summit is a three day event during which over twenty five thousand of the top tech people in the world gather in one place to do business. Hundreds of millions of euro change hands in deals, investments, mergers and acquisitions between some of the wealthiest people and companies on the planet.

The crowd roared. There were upwards of two thousand people crammed into the auditorium. It was the largest of about sixteen to twenty similar spaces of all different sizes, all focussed on specific different themes, such as Financial Technology or Fintech, IOT or Internet of Things, Marketing, Artificial Intelligence. In addition, each area was host to clusters of tiny booths which were home to start-up companies. The noise in these locations was deafening. It was thousands of human voices all talking at once. The staff working the booths were frantically trying to spread the word about their unique idea or approach to solving some problem or other in the hope of attracting an investor, of which there were many, prowling around, evaluating the different companies and ideas on show. It was a deal mak-

RUN FROM THE DEVIL

ing frenzy. A form of business lottery in which millions were being bet on *the next big thing*.

"I'm Chet Bryant and I'm so excited to facilitate this talk. Really! I want to just thrill you. I want to make you salivate." He paused and then sat on a chair, positioned to the left at a slight remove from of a group of four other chairs in the middle of the stage.

"But I don't have to." He added. "Because coming out to join me right now is Howard Markovsky of Google!" The crowd roared again as a small bald guy wearing a dark suit with an open necked white shirt made his way to the vacant chairs.

"Dana Pritchard of Wikipedia!" Another roar. This time a woman wearing a similar dark suit with an open necked white shirt.

"Patrick Collison of Stripe!" The loudest roar yet for a slender, ginger haired youth covered in freckles, wearing shorts and a dark t-shirt

"And my favourite entrepreneur turned investor?" He paused for effect "Rayne Frost!" A final roar which changed to applause as the last of the four members of the panel arrived out on stage and seated themselves.

"So now we're going to pick their brains. And what a collection. Four of the finest minds in Tech today. We're going to get their bets for the future. What do you guys see coming down the tracks. What excites you the most? Who excites you the most? Share with us your insights into what you reckon will be the next big thing. Howard, talk to us."

Tiberius stood near the door watching Rayne with pride. *This is such a massive validation of her talent and success,* he thought.

The Google guy chattered excitedly about driverless cars and open source Artificial Intelligence software they were working on. Most of it going over Tiberius's head. So he popped out to the Café area next door to the auditorium and bought a coffee, arriving back in time to hear the woman from Wikipedia finish talking about the role of Machine

Learning in Financial Software and transactions.

"So Patrick would you agree with Dana about where AI's greatest contribution will be? Fintech?" Chet asked.

"Nope," said the young man in a broad accent which marked him as coming from the city of Limerick. "It's a limited viewpoint. I think we're just scratching the surface. The applications of AI will be multitudinous. There will be very few areas which will not make use of or benefit from AI in the next few years. Transport of all sorts, the Internet of Things, from the most mundane and ordinary to life transforming sectors like medicine, space travel. You name it. I reckon we are only traversing ground zero of AI's development cycle and our imaginations can't really take us to the places where AI will bring us at this early stage." He sat back and folded his arms.

"I agree with Patrick," Rayne interjected.

"Rayne," chirped the facilitator delighted. "Share with us your perspective."

"Well Chet," Rayne responded smoothly. "I will. I'm going to take a chance now and share with everyone what I regard as the next big thing. And what you've got to understand is, I just met these guys a few days ago. Two young Irish students who are attending the University just up the road here have come up with the single most exciting piece of software I've ever seen. It's ground-breaking and the most disruptive development. It's going to change our world."

The other three panellists had swivelled their chairs and were no longer looking out at the audience but at Rayne. Chet looked like he was going to burst with excitement and shrieked "Rayne, come on. You have to bring us all in on this."

"Why not?" Rayne grinned. "I feel its impact will be global, truly far-reaching and its potential value I would confidently estimate as being in multiple billions right now. This software can accurately predict people's behaviour in advance. And when I say accurately, I mean it's been benchmarked at 100% accuracy. It works."

"Wow." Patrick, the red headed young man, who was arguably one of the finest coders in the world, was genuinely impressed, which delighted Rayne. "More detail." He demanded. "Prove it."

"Okay," said Rayne. "Using unique sophisticated machine learning algorithms, the software is able to predict patterns of behaviour by aggregating and analysing data relating to specific individuals or groups, which doesn't sound too new, but the thing is no one has ever been able to make it work. These two kids have done it.

At this early stage, proof of concept has focussed on the likelihood of an individual, or members of a group of any sort, committing a crime or crimes at some point in time in the future with the second part of the software focused on behaviour modification recommendations. In other words, it can determine what individuals or groups might commit crimes and can suggest alternative paths, thereby dramatically reducing the possibility of them offending in the future. The two inventors of this unique software feel that this platform could have a huge effect on the future and cost of law and order. Less police needed, less judges, lawyers, prisons, prison officers. You get the picture."

"But that's not all. Is it? I mean, it sounds like the basic platform should have more applications than just in the law and order arena?" interjected Patrick again.

This is going so well, felt Rayne. *Thank God Patrick is on this panel. He's just teeing up the ball for me.*

"That's right Patrick." Rayne continued.

"I'm not so sure about this." Dana from Wikipedia interrupted Rayne. "I mean, if it's true and it does work, it feels a bit like Big Brother to me. Y'know whoever owns this software will have massive power as it will give them the ability not only to effectively prevent crime but also to identify and accurately profile all sorts of people and all sorts of behaviour. For example, to determine how the stock market might react to different types of events or a governments actions, to predict legislation? Wars? When and what are the tipping points which could cause them. The possibilities are endless for a software program that can accurately predict people's behaviour and the wealth and power which will accrue to the possessor of such software would be unimaginable, which is actually quite frightening to me."

The facilitator leaned in his chair and said "Rayne? Would you care to speak to Dana's point?"

Rayne had been annoyed at the interruption but suddenly thought to herself it was OK. Dana and she had never gotten on and Dana was using the opportunity to hit out at Rayne in this public manner, but Rayne realised that all Dana had done was to just drive the price of the software through the roof by listing large groups of individuals and governments who would pay anything to be able to utilise the app.

"You may be right, Dana. I think you have very perceptively seen that the permutations and combinations of applications of this unique software are far greater than the inventors had originally envisaged." She sat back, very pleased with how things had gone.

Before Dana or any of the other panellists could reply, Chet, who had been sitting listening to instructions in his earpiece, stood up and invited the audience to applaud the panel for their contributions. He thanked them and moved on to announce the next event due on the stage in five minutes.

*   *   *

Rayne walked off the stage and moved fast through the crowd to a roped off VIP area. She ignored the people calling out her name and trying to speak with her. Once in the VIP area she pulled out her phone and turned it off. She then continued through another door, making her way along a laneway to a luxury SUV with blacked out windows waiting for her. She got in and the driver moved off through the delegates milling around. He drove out the gate and turned right along a Dual carriageway, heading South past UCD campus. After a twenty-minute drive he pulled up outside the front door of the Ritz Carlton hotel, situated on the side of a beautiful valley, deep in the forested Wicklow Hills. It was another world, yet minutes from Dublin and perfect for the next step in Rayne's strategy.

Rayne took the lift to the penthouse suite where she found Dane and Beth sitting on a couch crouched over a computer.

Beth looked up as Rayne came in and sprang up. "Wow! That was amazing. You were amazing," she bubbled happily.

Rayne was puzzled. "How do you know how it went?" she asked.

"Dane snuck in last night before the Summit opened when they were rushing around like lunatics trying to get it ready for today. He put a webcam with a microphone and a Wi-Fi connection on one of the pillars at the back of the hall. We were able to watch the whole thing, Rayne. You were great. You handled them all so well!" Beth high fived Rayne who came around to sit on the couch beside Dane and watched the somewhat grainy picture of the crowded auditorium.

"What was all that about the Big Brother type applications of the app?" asked Dane in a worried tone.

"Oh that was nothing." Rayne answered casually. She had expected this reaction from one or both of them and had worked out her response in the car. "Dana and I go way back to when we started out as interns in a failed startup. She has a serious chip on her shoulder and is always taking pot-shots at me. I apologise to you both if my personal issue with this woman has impacted on our enterprise here."

"That's no problem, Rayne," burbled Beth. "We don't have a problem with this Dana whatshername, do we Dane?"

"I guess not, but I'm a bit concerned about what she said. I mean what if someone buys in and wants to use it for something illegal or immoral? Or they're just bad to the bone?"

"I know where you're coming from Dane." Rayne said in what seemed like a considering manner, as though this had all only just occurred to her. "The first problem we have is, we've just told the world about the app. So as of right now, there are dozens of programmers and software development teams in companies all over the planet looking at this area and beginning or ramping up or refocussing their efforts on this area, and if they get to market before us then there's no telling what could happen." She was pleased the other two appeared buying this line of thought.

"I think," she continued in the same calm tone, "that what we have to do is make sure that whoever does come on board with us, signs up to strict legal guidelines which perhaps you might come up with Dane?" She smiled at him, tossing what she hoped was a responsibility he would not wish to shoulder back at him.

"Uh." Dane muttered, "not sure legalese is my area. I might screw that up. What do you think Beth?"

"Rayne's on the same wavelength as us on this Dane. So, if you don't mind, I reckon Rayne's probably the best person to deal with it." Beth smiled at Rayne.

"OK. Well I'll do my best. Are you happy with that Dane? Glad you raised it by the way."

"Sure. Sure. Makes sense." Dane was still staring at the screen watching the crowds inside the Web Summit.

Rayne stood up from the sofa and took her phone out of her bag. "I need to check these messages," she said and walked out onto the balcony. She stopped at the railing and gazed out over the lush Wicklow hills and valleys, gripped by a triumphant sense of joy. She hadn't felt this good in a long time. *And I played that perfectly,* she told herself. *Once I've sold this for as much as I can get from whoever wants it the most, I'll let Mr Bleeding Heart in there worry about enforcing an unenforceable covenant governing its application. I just need to be sure I'm paid up front or as close to up front as possible. I could make more out of this piece of software then I have out of everything I've done in my entire career.*

*　　　　*　　　　*

Back at the Web Summit, Tiberius walked slowly out the front doors and into a cloudburst which was sending everyone scurrying for shelter. He crossed the road and went into a little pizza place called Base, which, in addition to making wonderful pizza also specialised in pretty good coffee. He took his cup outside and sat on a wooden bench under the canopy, looking out at the teeming rain.

Tiberius had been stunned by the revelation that Rayne was closely involved with Beth and Dane's software. He had made the connection between the software Rayne had announced and what Dane had explained to him. He was still trying to tease out the different permutations and combinations.

Why hadn't Rayne told him she was involved with them? Granted I haven't had the opportunity to discuss the case with her in detail. Now he thought about it, he had only mentioned that it related to the areas of Big Data and AI.

OK. OK. He needed to call her and meet to clarify her involvement in this.

Another thought occurred to him which filled him with dismay. Rayne's involvement might just mean he would have to resign from the case due to his family relationship with an interested party. He knew his bosses in Harcourt Street were aware of his past problems and very public meltdown in the States.

Tiberius realised that while he was enjoying getting to grips with the challenges of the two cases, building and growing his team had become a real buzz. That plus the added bonus of his growing friendship with Doyle were not things he wanted to give up. He hadn't understood until now how isolated and lonely he had become once he emerged from his depression some months after his arrival in Ireland.

His experiences in L.A. had taken a long time to come to terms with and he was sure he still wasn't over what had happened. The nightmares proved that. It had devastated him.

He took out his phone and dialled Rayne's number. It went to voicemail again. This time he left a message which was stronger in tone. "Rayne, Tiber here again. Look we really need to talk. I think one of the cases I'm investigating may be related to this software you announced at the Web Summit earlier today. I need to speak with you as soon as you get this message. Face to face. Call me."

Then he rang Doyle who answered immediately. "I hear your sister made a big announcement at the Web Summit today, Boss." Tiberius cursed silently.

"Yeah. Wish I'd seen it coming."

"Well, I can verify how you've been trying to contact her about the case to get her input. Kind of lucky you didn't discuss it with her now?"

"True. I should have realised that someone like Rayne would be all over a development like this."

"Not your fault. Just coincidence."

"What are you up to tonight after work?"

"Home. Decant some sardines from their tin and garnish them with toast, why?" Doyle's humorous description of his non-existent culinary skills made Tiberius grin.

"Forget the sardines. I'll cook. I've something to discuss with you. OK?"

"Sure. Great. Anything but sardines."

CHAPTER FIFTEEN

Tiberius turned the heat on under a pot and uncorked a bottle of Italian Red wine, which he sloshed into a glass decanter.

"So it's Italian night?" asked Doyle. "Are you just reheating last night's grub then?" He asked with a grin.

"No," Tiberius ignored the sarcasm. "If you precook the sauce and gently reheat it before serving, it tastes much better. An Italian cop who was seconded to us in the States showed me how to cook pasta the way they do it in his hometown of Bergamo in Northern Italy. You boil it until it's nearly cooked and then drain off the water. Throw a little of the water from the pasta into the sauce and plate up the pasta. Then you just reheat the sauce, he did it in a microwave, and serve."

"You should be a TV Chef! Still, beats sardines on toast."

"Hope so."

The two of them sat on high stools at the island in the middle of the modern, somewhat sparsely furnished kitchen and tucked in.

After a while Doyle leaned back and rubbing his stomach said "Oh God, I'd come back to this restaurant again. You're some cook for one cook!" He eyed Tiberius warily and asked "What brought you to Ireland? I asked but all I got was that it was some sort of an exchange programme. Another person told me you were here as a private citizen and some high-ups brought you in?"

Tiberius was silent for a few moments and Doyle hastily added "hope you don't mind me asking."

"No. Not at all. In fact, that's why I wanted to talk to you tonight. This thing with my sister might create difficulties with the case and we need to discuss it. Unfortunately, you can't really have an accurate perspective unless I share with you some of my," he paused and took a drink of wine, "my career history, let's say."

"Before you ask, anything you say to me stays with me. I won't discuss it with anyone without your permission," said Doyle.

"I figured that." Tiberius paused again, thinking, then continued. "Look this is difficult for me. I've spent a lot of time trying to deal with this crap and I'm still not comfortable with it. Any way I cut it, it's relevant to what we're doing so I figure I've no choice in the matter but the only choice I do have is who I talk to about it. And I figure you are the most appropriate person. Also I trust you. So." Tiberius took a deep breath and began.

"The last case I worked in the States was a multiple homicide. The first was a young woman who was killed with an unusual knife. It's a knife used in Japanese cooking, called a fugu hiki. The subsequent homicides were all perpetrated with the same knife.

I was in charge of the case and we were making progress. Once we realised what kind of knife it was, we were able to track down the suppliers and manufacturers in the States and in Japan. It's quite a rare knife because it's only used for one purpose - to prepare sashimi from the fugu fish or pufferfish. The reason it's so unusual is because the fish contains lethal amounts of poison called tetrodotoxin. The poison is located in its organs. Basically the liver, the ovaries, and the eyes. The skin is OK, non-poisonous.

The method of death was an initial cut by the knife which was laden with the poison. The poison is what's called a sodium channel blocker so it paralyzes the muscles while the victim stays fully conscious but begins losing their ability to breathe and ultimately dies from asphyxiation. However, in these cases, as soon as the poison took effect, paralysing the victim, the murderer would take out their liver and ovaries and fillet them in front of the victim, displaying them on a plate at a nearby table."

"That's pretty extreme. Very unusual," Doyle was fascinated.

"Yeah. Well, I contacted a Japanese TV Chef by the name of Aika Sato. She had a food show on one of the West Coast Networks and I recalled she had written an article in the L.A. Times about Fugu and its preparation. Also she had prepared and eaten Fugu live on her show. So I figured she might prove a useful source. Bearing in mind you are only allowed to prepare Fugu if you have done three years of training and passed serious tests to get a licence."

"OK," encouraged Doyle, lifting his now empty glass with a smile. Tiberius refilled it, topped up his own and continued.

"The reason for all of this training and testing is because Fugu poison is over one thousand times stronger than cyanide, and there is no known antidote. So if the chef gets it wrong you die. Simple as that."

"That's a bit of a step up from eating a very hot vindaloo to impress your mates."

"Uh yeah, I guess so."

"Sorry Boss, I've got a smart mouth. Always making cracks. Go on please."

"OK. She proved helpful. Very helpful. As a result, we made significant progress with the cases. She identified the method used to prepare the victims liver. Confirmed that it had to be someone qualified. So we contacted the police in Japan and were able to get the details of all registered Fugu chefs and then started checking them out." Tiberius paused again and glanced out the window as painful memories flooded back. He had never been so low as the months after the case. He felt utterly bereft of self-confidence, self-respect. He had been devastated.

"In addition to its being a high profile case and very challenging," he continued, "I was having a problem with my partner on the case. It was our first time working together and after a while I began to realise she wanted a different kind of relationship with me. She wanted to be more intimate. Obviously, I said no, because the case came first, but I also said that once it was over we could go out for dinner, maybe and talk about things. My previous relationship had terminated abruptly a short time before. Freya was very intelligent. A great analytical brain and ferociously focussed, followed up every single lead, no matter how small and unimportant. A great partner but not very emotionally intelligent unfortunately."

"Sorry Boss. You lost me. I thought you said she was intelligent."

"She was academically and analytically intelligent. Her case work skills were superb, just not emotionally intelligent." He looked at Doyle and realised he needed to clarify further.

"She was immature and not very good at dealing with emotions. Hers or others?"

"Gotcha."

"Anyway. That seemed to resolve the issue and we continued with the case. We felt we were making progress, especially with Aika's help. I was able to report to my bosses that we were getting places, which took a lot of the heat off. Then, one morning, out of the blue, everything went down the toilet." Tiberius paused and this time Doyle refilled his glass.

"Thanks," he said absentmindedly. "This is difficult because it was so odd. Or maybe not so odd, but certainly embarrassing. I'll leave you to decide. At around eight, one Friday morning, Freya and I met with Aika on the street in front of her building. When we contacted her the night before she said she had to go to a meeting at nine but she would meet us as she left the building. We just wanted to show her a knife which we had located near one of the crime scenes.

It looked similar to a fugu hiki knife but we weren't sure. For some reason, the cellphone network we would have normally used to send her a picture of it was down all day Thursday and Friday morning. Actually, it was interesting to see how people reacted, well overreacted to being without their cellphones briefly."

"Why didn't you just email a pic of the knife?"

"She didn't use a computer. Did everything on her phone. Very Japanese apparently. Certainly very West Coast. Anyway, we showed up and showed her the knife. She said it wasn't anything she could recognise and certainly wasn't a fugu hiki knife. At that moment, the phone network came back up and Freya's rang. She moved off to take the call.

Aika and I were kind of left standing there. I didn't have any more questions and there was a kind of awkward silence. She wore this pale grey short dress which just looked sprayed on. She looked stunning. It was kind of the first time I noticed her in that way. I stepped back and offered to call her a cab, but she said no. She was smiling all the time. Next thing Freya rushed up and said that her dad had been taken to hospital and she needed to get there ASAP. She had driven us over so I told her to just head off and I'd get a cab back to office. So she did, and I was left staring at Aika in her killer dress, looking back at me.

She offered me a coffee and I don't know why but I said yes. When we got into the lift there already were a couple of elderly ladies in there with Zimmer frames talking at each other loudly. I made for the corner and Aika stood in front of me. Then the Janitor came in with a bag of tools and a short ladder and Aika was pushed back against me. One of the women looked over at us. She smiled and said, 'young love!' We got out of the lift at the top floor and went to her penthouse apartment. We hardly got through the door. She never made her meeting and I didn't leave until Sunday evening."

"Wow. You must have great stamina boss!" Doyle said with a big grin.

"Ha. Ha." Tiberius said drily. "Fortunately, no one realised what had happened and I went into work as usual on Monday morning, but I knew I'd crossed a line. What had happened was a complete no no. Totally unprofessional.

So I went back to her apartment that evening to sort it out and explain that it couldn't continue while we were both involved with the case but once again I left the following morning. I had no self-control when it came to her. She was my cocaine." Tiberius got up and went into the utility, emerging a few moments later with another bottle of wine.

"A two bottle story is it?"

"And then some," Tiberius replied quietly.

"For several weeks we continued the relationship. It was a total lapse of judgement on my part. I mentioned my fiancé? She died in a skiing accident the previous year and I hadn't been with anyone or been interested in any one prior to meeting Aika. And to be honest I had never experienced anything so intense in my life before that." Tiberius paused and looking away added in a guilty tone, "even with my fiancé."

He seemed lost in thought for a moment and then visibly gathering himself together continued, "during the time I was involved with Aika, there were three more deaths. All with the same M.O.. We were sure it wasn't a copycat because we had managed to put in place and maintain a complete news blackout on the case.

"OK?"

"Freya figured it out in the end."

"About the relationship?"

"No. She cracked the case. Figured out who the killer was."

"Great."

"Yes and No."

"No?"

"The killer was Aika."

"What?" Doyle looked stunned.

"She used me as an alibi for her final three murders before Freya caught her. I can't claim to have had a lot to do with it."

More silence. Tiberius staring into space.

"How did she catch her?"

"Simple really. I always had treated her as a source, almost as a consultant. Freya treated her as a potential suspect and investigated her. Basic Investigation 101. Everyone's a suspect until proven otherwise. She found that Aika had been filming episodes of her show close to the scene of each murder just prior or just after each event. She decided not to tell me until she could confirm her suspicions, on the basis that I may have been compromised and that she couldn't trust me. Which, to be fair to her, was correct, on all counts.

She started covert surveillance of Aika and they caught her in the act. I hadn't been well for some time and was in the hospital getting tests done. They found traces of a tranquilliser in my bloodstream.

When Freya and my superior officer Fred McMurray...."

"As in the actor?" interjected Doyle, then "sorry Boss."

"It's OK. Yes, same name but very different looking. Very different temperament also. Anyway, that night when they came through the door of the hospital room I was in, they looked very serious. I thought they had been informed of the results of my blood tests, so I asked them about it. They looked puzzled and McMurray asked what I was talking about. I told him that the hospital tests showed high amounts of a tranquilliser in my body. I said that it appeared that someone had been doping me for some reason. Which didn't make sense. I told them I was trying to figure who might have done it when they arrived.

They looked at each other and Freya said that my girlfriend had just been arrested in the act of trying to kill her next victim. She tried to keep the anger from her voice but she couldn't. My boss said that Aika had given me as her alibi for the other murders and said that she had been with me at the time and I could confirm it. However, it now appeared she had drugged me to make me sleep and slipped out. She had read the media report of my fiancé's death and determined that I would be vulnerable, easy to manipulate. And the bitch was right."

Doyle leaned forward and said in a reassuring tone, "psychopaths have no empathy, but they are unnaturally good at finding a weakness and exploiting it. So what happened next? I assume it all hit the fan?"

"Never a truer word, Doyle. It was an absolute disaster. The trial was a circus. I was suspended indefinitely because with all of the media attention they couldn't fire me and technically I hadn't committed a fireable offence. If I had contested a dismissal it would have cost them millions. To make matters worse, her lawyer tried to use me to reduce her sentence as much as possible, but she's serving several counts of consecutive life sentences in a max security penitentiary in California. She'll never get out. Thank God."

"So why did you come to Ireland."

"I was still officially attached to the L.A. Police force and I assumed I would never be allowed through the front door again, or the back door for that matter. However, after a while, Fred, my old boss, asked me to advise on a case which they were having problems with. When my advice proved useful, they began using me more and more. Unfortunately for them, by the time they came to me and proposed full reinstatement, I had decided to come here. I'm a quarter Irish, on my Dad's side and I had never had the opportunity to visit. So, I kinda took early retirement, which left my C.V. a bit neater, y'know? About a year after I arrived here, Fred came to Ireland for an Interpol meeting and told his Irish counterpart, a guy called Smith about me?"

"I know him." Said Doyle grimly. "Only too well. A political shite, if ever there was one."

"Well, he must have spoken to someone else because I had just returned from a trip to Dun Aenghus on the Aran Islands when I was approached to assist the Irish police on a temporary basis. Amazing place, by the way."

"Dun Aenghus? Yeah, pretty stunning," Doyle replied with

the casual indifference to the wonders of Ireland of the native Irish, "you obviously said yes?"

"To be honest I was bored. Well, kinda down really and at a loose end, so yeah. I did. It was that or go back to University and head in a completely different direction. Next thing I knew, I was fast-tracked into your Homicide Division."

"The good old NCBI, the National Bureau of Criminal Investigation, of which I used to be a member myself," said Doyle.

"Right. Well, initially I operated as a consultant and then it became more permanent, something which didn't endear me to many of my new colleagues."

"You got that right. There's plenty still waiting to see you trip up."

"Yeah. Which brings us up to today and my new problem. I think I may have to take myself off the case."

"Because of your sister?" Doyle sounded a bit incredulous.

"Yep."

"I'm not convinced it is an issue. Her involvement with our two nerds is a matter of public knowledge at this point in time. I suggest you report it to the Chief Super and let him decide what to do about it. That way you're in the clear. You just continue to work the case with the rest of the team while the Brass decide what to do. Bearing in mind they're short-handed because of Shannon right now, I reckon they'll let you continue on but on a tighter leash and maybe an increased level of reporting.

"Sounds like a plan," Tiberius replied. "They already know about what happened on the West Coast."

"Exactly. Look don't just give in, Boss. We're building a good team here. You, me, Prendergast and Sweeney. We click. We have complementary strengths and abilities. I think we have the makings of a great investigative unit and if we can crack these two murders then we have a chance of being left together as a team. Something I'd like to see happen."

"You've clearly given this a great deal of thought."

"Well, when I'm not slaving on my thesis, I tend to get my head around work matters."

The rain had stopped and Tiberius stood and slid back the Glass doors to the balcony.

"Coffee?"

"Yes. Thanks. And a glass of water please."

"Sure thing."

Doyle moved outside to a low rattan lounger under the canopy. When Tiberius returned, Doyle asked him, "did your sister call back yet?"

"Yeah. She said she came to Ireland to do a deal with Beth and Dane about their software. She is going to become a shareholder in their business and will be involved in fund-raising or selling the software to whoever, hence the very public announcement at the Web Summit today. Rayne knows how to sell stuff. That's for sure." Tiberius put a tray with coffee and water on the low table in front of Doyle and sat back on another lounger. "Guess how much it's worth?" Tiberius said in a casual tone, looking out at the bay.

"I wouldn't be the world's greatest techie, but based on what they claim it can do? I'm thinking, several million, which is a good enough reason for murder."

"Rayne said that right now it's worth somewhere north of five hundred million dollars."

"Well now that certainly changes things! It has got to be a driver in at least one of the crimes." Doyle was excited.

"Yes, but which one?"

"So, you think they're unrelated?"

"Not sure" answered Tiberius. The coincidence factor in time and location is too great to be ignored. That suggests there's more than likely a link between them but I've also been considering the possibility that although associated with each other they may have been committed for differ-ent reasons and possibly by different people."

"So one could be the latest instalment in this Northern Psy-cho's odyssey and the other an attempt to get at Beth and maybe Dane by an unrelated party."

"It's looking like that." Tiberius agreed and then went on sounding frustrated, "but why kill them? That's not going to secure you the software? If that was your primary motive."

"Well maybe it just went wrong? What if the murderer was just trying to get information? They realised they had given too much away or that they had been speaking with the wrong person. Maybe she could identify them so she had to be silenced?"

"And the other murders?"

Doyle rubbed his chin thoughtfully, "as you say it may be unrelated, but that's unlikely. Unless it is Northern Psycho's way of getting his jollies while he's sojourning in our fair city? It does replicates elements of his M.O.."

"I guess we need to sleep on it and keep digging." Tiberius stretched his long frame and slouched in his chair looking out at the night sky.

"And with that, I'll say goodnight," said Doyle rising, he drank his glass of water and turned to Tiberius, "I'll let myself out Boss. See you Monday unless you want to talk some more about everything. I'll be training little rugby monsters tomorrow morning again."

"Got it. See ya, Doyle." Tiberius remained slouched in the chair, lost in thought.

CHAPTER SIXTEEN

Shaylene dialled Rayne's number as she stood looking out at the Irish Sea.

"Hi Ms Frost?"

"Hi, who is this?"

"I'm calling on behalf of Deng Holman Lee? I'm his personal assistant."

"What can I do for you?"

"Mr Lee would like to meet you."

"I'm kind of busy at present, as I'm sure he already knows."

Deng took the phone from Shaylene. "Rayne, you know why I'm calling and why I want to meet," he said quietly.

"Oh hi Deng. How are you doing?" Rayne said brightly into the phone.

"I am well. Are we meeting? Or not?"

"Sure how does tomorrow at ten am suit? In the Intercontinental Hotel in Ballsbridge?"

"Too public. I have taken a house South of there. It's more private. I will see you there."

"Well now I..."

"Ms Frost, Shaylene Foster here again. Can I give you the details of where Mr Lee wishes to meet you?"

"I was about to tell your employer these arrangements don't suit me. Sorry."

"Mr Lee does not wish his presence in Dublin to become public knowledge. This is the best way of achieving it. It's a matter of personal security."

Rayne sighed. "OK. I'll see him at eleven am. Email me the address. Goodbye."

Shaylene turned to Deng and asked, "is eleven am tomorrow OK?"

He was standing watching the waves through the massive glass windows of the ultra-modern house she had rented for him.

"Yes."

Thank God for that thought Shaylene.

"Here?"

"Yes Mr Lee."

"Leave me."

Shaylene walked quickly to the door and closed it behind her. She stopped outside the door and sighed heavily. She didn't know why but she found him to be the most stressful person she had ever worked for, and she had worked for some right doozies. Folk who were totally out of control and difficult. Newly rich billionaires who were the only people who could pay her sort of fees. But this guy with his quiet, controlled, ferocious focus was pretty much the scariest human being she had ever encountered. If he had shown the slightest interest in her, even sexually, she could have coped. She knew how to deal with horny clients. But he was utterly immune to her, treating her as no better than a type of service robot. Even his personal bodyguard Riga Wong, ignored her unless absolutely necessary. She figured out early on that the best she could do was to try to anticipate Deng's requirements and then offer him a selection of options and let him decide. It seemed to keep him satisfied.

Deng stared at the cold white capped waves of the Irish Sea, remembering.

Nan Do Island is the most northerly island off the coast of North Korea. Unknown to the outside world it has been used as an ultra-discreet training location by the Chinese Army for over fifty years in return for Chinese support to the North Korean dictator. It is deserted except for a lighthouse on the southern tip and some sheds on the north west. It was February and the sea water was one degree above freezing.

They had all sprinted into the water, naked. The last one to the waterline was shot in the head by The Sniper. They swam through the icy waters to a raft with twenty poles on it. On top of each pole was a photograph of the Great Chairman Mao. Deng was the second to the raft. He shinned up the smooth pole grabbed the photo and put it into a small plastic bag he had stolen from the kitchen and then back down. He could see the boy who had been first to the raft, lower himself into the water and begin swimming back, other boys who had swam slower and were just reaching the raft, attacked him trying to get the photo. Deng got into the water at the other side, heading out towards the open sea, then curving around, giving the raft now heaving with boys a wide berth, and headed back to shore.

When he got to land, he was so cold he couldn't feel any of his extremities. He half hobbled; half limped up the stony beach to the soldier sitting at a desk on a concrete platform by the road. "Well, Gwailo?" the soldier sneered at him, referring to the fact that he was only half Chinese by calling him a foreigner. Trembling, Deng delicately extricated the photo with numb fingers and placed it on the desk in front of the soldier, who leaning forward, examined it, and jerked his head, motioning Deng towards the truck parked above on the roadway behind him. Deng slowly and painfully climbed up the bare, sloping face of the cliff, and then moved towards the truck. The base of the truck was at his chest and initially he just couldn't climb in. Weakened as he was, he kept trying until finally he managed to swing one leg up and roll over and onto the floor. He lay there panting. Then he got up and carefully paced around the darkened interior of the truck in his bare feet. He covered it inch by inch until he found a spot where the heat from the engine had risen, warming the floor. He sank down on the slightly warmer metal, crossed his legs and began the mental exercises he knew they were expecting from him.

After another few minutes he heard another shot. He knew

they probably rotated the snipers but he didn't care. To him it was always just The Sniper, who ruthlessly punished the weaker and less efficient children. Deng calculated. Twenty four boys and girls had lined up on the beach and with just two shots which meant that at least two were dead, not counting anyone who had drowned or been killed fighting for the photos. He nurtured one grain of hatred deep within him, which kept him going. When he was done with this life of torture and pain, he was going to come back and kill The Sniper or as many of them as he could locate. However, a quick end for The Sniper was not part of the plan. There would be no bullet in the head.

A few moments later the first of the others arrived at the back of the truck. Deng did not assist any of them in their painful attempts to climb in. There was no point. Tomorrow the nine year old might have to kill the person he helped today............. or be killed.

Deng turned away from the view of the grey, frothing Irish Sea through the windows and checked the time on his watch. After a few minutes he pulled a phone from his pocket and turned it on. It wasn't a normal mobile phone. It was a wireless IP phone which connected via Wi-Fi to a secure server in his office building in California. The phone had a built in encryption facility which scrambled whatever he spoke and then transmitted it to the destination phone which was also encrypted. That phone unscrambled the data and replayed it as sound to the other party. The only issue was that although it happened in real time, the instantaneous conversation occurred with each party hearing a default voice instead of the other party's real voice. Deng didn't care. It worked and was secure. It was all that mattered.

"Yes?" came the answer in a robotic sounding male voice with a neutral mid-Atlantic accent after a few moments.

"Did you get it?"

"No."

"Why?"

"He wipes his local machines when he's finished using them. Every time he leaves. Even for a short time. According to the Police files I accessed, he informed them that he has set up a secure virtual workspace where everything is kept. You would be better placed to locate it than I. It's not within my skillset."

"Yes." Deng paused, thinking. "It is unlikely we will either locate or be able to access this digital location."

"If you cannot do it with your resources then I certainly cannot."

"Continue to monitor both targets and be prepared to act swiftly. Have you located a secure facility at which to question them?"

"I suggest removing them from this country and interrogating them elsewhere."

"Do you have somewhere selected?"

"Yes."

"Are you able to transport one or both to the location undetected?"

"I'm working on it."

"Very well. I will inform you if I require you to do so."

"OK. I take it you don't wish to know where?"

"No. I have transferred the first payment of one thousand, one hundred bitcoin to the account you specified, which will be worth above the ten million we agreed. At today's rate, you will receive an excess figure of ninety-two thousand dollars. I do not require repayment of this amount."

After a few moments, the other voice said "I noted the transfer. I will continue to monitor the targets and prepare the location and the mode of transport."

Deng ended the call. Thirty kilometres away, parked beside a reservoir at the back of Weston Airport, Mr Black turned off his phone, smiled happily and turned on his car to head back into Dublin. Weston Airport is a tiny private airport which catered for wealthy travellers and corporate and private executive jets.

A few hours later, Mr Black was watching Beth and Dane. He was troubled.

To the best of his recollection, no one had ever done anything for him without requiring something in response. And usually the payment involved something he did not want to do or endure.

He considered the twin facts that not only was Beth the first person who had ever done something for him without expecting repayment but that she had also saved his life. What was even more annoying was that he was supposed to have been standing behind her, shadowing her. The movement of the crowd and her sudden halt had reversed their positions so he had decided to cross the road, get clear of the crowd and pick her up at the other side. He had been considering this when he stepped off the footpath and she grabbed him back. It was an unacceptable error in his tradecraft, in his method, which he had developed over several years and which had saved his life more than once. It was something which had never happened before. A total conundrum. What to do?

The obvious strategic option was to take both, transport them to his little hidey hole and interrogate them, playing one off against the other. If necessary torturing one in order to get the other to give him the information his client needed. Looking at the two of them, he felt they had a very close bond and that pressurizing one by hurting the other was the way to go. Unfortunately, on the basis that the male had all of the access codes and location of the data his client needed, the obvious candidate to use for leverage was the female, Beth. However, and he had real problems understanding this, he felt this bizarre desire not to damage her? He felt pressure building up in his skull as he watched her and tried to reason out the correct way to proceed. He was on very unfamiliar ground as he had never not wanted to hurt someone because bluntly he had never cared about causing pain.

Blood sports, which involved causing pain while painting a rich tapestry with the bodies of his playmates sometimes gave him pleasure. Granted, not a great deal of pleasure, but so little gave him pleasure that he treasured this occasional source. To Mr Black, humans were just animals, bags of meat and bones, including himself.

This was definitely a first. He was unaccustomed to the usually serene landscape inside his head being disturbed in any way.

The ideal scenario was where his client simply acquired the software by purchasing it and that would pan out over the next few days apparently. In which case, he would keep his fifty percent fee and receive a further thirty five percent as compensation, netting him approximately fourteen million dollars. Which was still a serious payday for doing very little and having a fun time in Dublin! Also he could still use the place in Dungeness for some blood sports with different candidates at some point.

Still, he had to work out how he was going to proceed if his client decided that the price for the software was too high and he wanted him to acquire it instead. He had been surprised when he overheard Dane and Beth discussing the value of it outside the tapas restaurant. He had even given some thought to acquiring the software for himself, but he realised he wouldn't last long enough to make money from it. The various interested parties in this little drama were just too powerful and too ruthless.

According to his contact, Dempsey, Sir Bartholomew had agreed to provide him with military transport to remove the targets from Dublin and transport them to Ashford Airport, a tiny airstrip outside the village of Lydd in the middle of Romney Marsh on the south Kent coast. A Landrover would be waiting to transport them to the location he had chosen for interrogation. It was a disused building which had been refurbished by the British Army. He had since upgraded it with some further improvements of his own.

It was located in a remote isolated area between the firing range at Jury's Gap and Dungeness Nuclear Power station. Dungeness was perfect. Very few people ever visit this barren spit of land, which was composed of a sea of endless shingle, on a sparsely populated part of the south Kent coast. It was called the Desert of England. A broad, echoing flatness with the famous nuclear power station on one side, the shingle dipping into the sea on the other, backed by one of the largest marshes in Europe.

Dear Sir Bartholomew was going to be very disappointed when he didn't deliver the software to Her Majesty's Government, but Mr Black was sure he could persuade him to be understanding once he revealed to him the naughty things he knew about him and would release into the public domain if anything untoward should happen to Sir B's favourite operative of choice! Oh, yes, he definitely had that chappie by the short and curlies! It was a pity he couldn't have some fun with tubby Sir B, but Mr Black also knew that doing so would arouse the ire of the only person in the world who actually inspired concern in him, especially as he had killed all of the others. Having said that, Sir B was not as clever as he thought he was and Mr Black reckoned there would be few in the British Intelligence establishment who would mourn his passing as long as they believed he had passed naturally.

Mr Black refocussed his attention on Dane and Beth sitting inside the window of a café in the middle of the University Campus. He noticed Dane jump up and run out of the café. He accosted a mature large breasted woman, dressed in garish flowing colours. He enveloped her in his arms, hugging her fiercely. Beth joined them and hugged her too. They went back into the café and sat at the window. Mr Black noticed how Dane seemed more animated than usual. He fussed over the woman, arriving back with more coffees and pastries. After some time and a lot of animated chat, the three left the café. After lots of fond farewells, Dane and Beth headed in he woman in the other.

...eful about this development, Mr Black
...t on a bus at the gates to the University
...town, getting off at a Quay beside the
...ity centre. From there she walked up a
...urned left past the main gates of the Guinness Brewery. She turned right and then left. After passing by some unattractive council apartment blocks, she walked along a terrace of small cosy looking redbrick houses, called Gray Street and disappeared into one. There was nowhere on the road for him to wait so Mr Black walked past the house, taking a note of the number and continued to an odd little cast iron religious shrine in the middle of the street. He walked around it pretending to look at it while he scoped out the area. He noticed a small white card in the window of a house opposite the one into which the woman had gone. He went over and was pleased to find it said, "Room to Lett."

Not too hot on the old spelling are we? Mr Black thought. He knocked. The door was opened by a skinny young woman with short crew cut hair, in a black vest and sagging black jeans, whose upper arms and neck were covered in tattoo's. "Yeah?" she snarled aggressively.

"I've come about the room to let? Is it still available?" Mr Black smiled nicely, while wondering what sort of sound her neck would make when he broke it.

"I'm looking for a woman."

"I'm going to be working locally so I don't need it for too long. Just a week or so but I'd be happy to pay a full month's rent in advance." He turned the full wattage of his smile and charm up.

She was nervous but said "it's six hundred a month an' I don't do food. You've to cook your own. You working in one of those techie companies then? There's millions of them around here."

"Tell you what," Mr Black really wanted to kill her at this stage, "as it's sooo convenient to my work. I'll give you seven

170

hundred. Is that OK? I won't need to use the kitchen. I eat at work, and I won't be around too much as we work all hours, programming you know." He rolled his eyes to heaven as though exasperated with the irregular nature of his work.

"Yeah. Yeah. OK." She said, uninterested. "Come in and I'll show it to you. Got the money on you?"

"No. I'll return in half an hour and pay you. You can give me the key then OK?"

"Yeah, whatever." She turned and walked up the stairs which began just three feet from inside the door. The tiny room was on the first floor looking directly over to the house he was interested in. He could see three or four children inside. Two more came barrelling out the front door with a soccer ball at their feet and disappeared down the road.

"They look like a lively lot. The family across the road," he said.

She looked over his shoulder and sniffed "s'not a family. Mary's a whatchamacallit? A foster mum. She has loads of kids there all the time. Some of them can be bloody annoying."

"She fosters kids?" he mused aloud. "OK."

He turned back to his potential landlady and said cheerily, "right ho! I'll be back in a jiffy with some money for you. OK? My name's James by the way."

"I'm Lindsey. So yeah, you need to hurry cos' it's in demand, this room. It could go real fast yeah?"

He looked at the faded wallpaper, the lumpy bed squashed in with a tatty wardrobe which probably wouldn't open fully, the threadbare carpet underfoot and smiled at her, "you're so right. But it's perfect for me." He headed out the door and down the stairs.

"Just one thing," she called as he reached the front door. "I'm gay, so I'm not interested alright? Just so you know. No funny business."

"Oh, no problem. Please don't worry yourself about it" and

he went out the door.

Mr Black whistled as he retraced his steps back towards the front gates of the Guinness Brewery, opposite which he had noticed an ATM machine. He took out some money and shortly afterwards knocked on the door of the house in Gray Street and paid Lindsey, receiving a key in return and left.

*　　　*　　　*

The black SUV Rayne was travelling in pulled up outside the front door of the modern house Deng was using. Two other SUV's pulled up also and six athletic looking men in dark suits got out. Two of them accompanied her to the front door which opened as she approached it. Shaylene stood in the doorway smiling. Rayne was unused to looking other women in the eye as she was taller than most, so she found Shaylene's height a bit disconcerting.

"Ms Frost? Mr Holman Lee is waiting in the living room. If you'll follow me?"

Rayne walked behind her lithe frame along a corridor with polished concrete walls, dotted with subtly lit pieces of sculpture. She opened a grey bare wooden door and stepped aside to usher Rayne through.

"Uh your bodyguards have to stay outside, I'm afraid." Shaylene said apologetically.

"Sure," smiled Rayne, "once they've checked out the room OK?"

She walked past Shaylene and towards the waiting figure of Deng Holman Lee who was standing at the glass wall, somewhat overshadowed by the striking view of the Irish Sea behind him.

"Deng, how are you?" Rayne walked towards him with her hand outstretched. He looked at it and her and then shook hands, but with obvious reluctance.

"Please sit," he said ignoring her polite enquiry and sitting in one of a pair of low leather easy chairs facing each other.

Rayne knew how famously rude and brusque Deng was. Unfazed, she sat in the seat he indicated, crossed her legs and waited. She recognised a tall, powerfully built Chinese man standing against the wall. He stood, quietly watching her bodyguards move around,

Deng stared at her while her bodyguards prowled around the room. The older one said to her "We'll wait outside Ms Frost. Call us when you're ready to leave or whatever?"

"Thank you, Dave, I will."

"Expecting a problem?" Deng asked her, his cold expression unchanging. "Did you think I would harm you?"

"Nope, Deng old pal. But I've got control of the hottest property in tech today, which we both know is worth a great deal so I'm just being careful wherever I go." She paused, "or rather, everywhere I go."

"Wise of you."

"Thank you. My guys left. What about yours?" Rayne nodded towards the other occupant of the room standing behind Deng.

"Riga. Leave us." Deng didn't look around. The man detached himself from the wall and slipped out through another door.

"Riga? Not a Chinese name," Rayne commented.

"Most Westerners can't pronounce our names so many Chinese pick new names for their dealings with foreigners." Deng replied. "In his case, he saw the word on a map. He wasn't aware it is the capital of Latvia, nor does he care."

"So the name he uses outside of China is Riga....?" She trailed off.

"Riga Wong."

"OK." She leant back in the seat. "So how much are you offering?"

He didn't quite smile. Rather, his mask cracked slightly. She knew Deng appreciated people who didn't waste his time. If he hadn't been such a scary, ruthless s.o.b., she would have liked to work more with him. Rayne reckoned that she got him.

"One hundred million for twenty percent."

"Nope"

"My offer values the company at five hundred million. However, my understanding is that total control is not on the table. Or is that incorrect?"

"Well, it's not quite accurate but, shall we say, open to interpretation?"

"Whose interpretation?"

"Mine"

"So what do you want?"

"Two hundred and fifty million for twenty percent. Obviously, subject to proper due diligence."

"I would need my people to see how it all works."

"Deng, there is no way I'm going to allow your people, especially that little creep Kent, to reverse engineer this software. We are willing to conduct supervised tests using it under controlled conditions to prove it works."

"What if I don't trust you? I know you're financially stretched at present; this could just be a scam to get money."

Rayne was initially a little concerned to discover that he was aware of her financial problems, but then relaxed remembering who she was dealing with. This guy was famous for his preparation and information. He had people everywhere.

In fact, she thought, *I would have been surprised if he hadn't known about my financial issues.*

She leaned forward and looking straight at him said "Deng, I do my research too, and with everything I know about you and where you come from. Your background in China? Do you honestly think I'm stupid enough to try and rip you off? I'm not suicidal you know."

Deng said nothing, staring at her. After some moments, he said quietly. "I will pay four hundred million for fifty one percent of the business, and I want pre-emption rights over the remaining equity. I won't have any competitors buying in at a later point in time."

Rayne knew Deng well enough to realise this was not a negotiating tactic. This genuinely was his final offer. She had sat on the other side of the table to him in the past. She was thrilled. He had come in one hundred and fifty million above the nearest bidder.

She stood up and held out her hand to him. "I'll talk with my partners about your offer and get back to you Deng, OK?"

"Not OK." He ignored her hand. "Will you recommend my offer to them or not?"

Rayne paused and then asked, "why should I favour your offer over other people's?"

"I will also buy your shares in the crappy mobile payments company you invested in for the price you paid. Forty-one million dollars, I believe?"

Rayne thought fast. *OK, it was a bit hokey to accept a commission in return for recommending his bid, but on the plus side his offer is the highest so I'm not really doing anyone a disservice here.*

Deng waited patiently.

After a long moment, Rayne said, "OK. You've got a deal. Contact Robe…"

"Robert Craig of Drexel Langham Partners. I know. It will be done and the funds transferred to Drexel Langham's client account as soon as contracts are signed."

"Nope. Once we proceed to contract negotiations, it means I've done my bit and put in the recommendation. At that point you buy my mobile phone shares. As you might expect I already have skin in the game so I will be doing everything I can to get the contracts signed ASAP."

Deng stared at her. Finally he said, "I will pay you twenty million once we have exchanged contracts and a further twenty one million once contracts are signed by both parties."

"That's fair," said Rayne brightly and got up to leave.

As she walked towards the door Deng said "Rayne?"

She stopped and turned to him, waiting.

"You have until I leave in one week to get them to the table."

"No problem," Rayne said breezily and opened the door to find her security team waiting outside.

Sitting in the back of the SUV on her way back to brief Beth and Dane, Rayne was ecstatic. She had only been hoping to get her money back, having agreed with them that her commission would be ten percent of the shares which would have netted her fifty million. Based on the deal she had just done with Deng; her shares were worth eighty million. She would get back the forty one million she had paid for her shares in the damn mobile payments company. More importantly she could use the twenty million down payment to pay off her CFD's, which meant she was in the clear financially. Her net worth would go from virtually zero to one hundred and twenty one million and who knew what the CFD funded shares would do in the future. *Hallelujah!*

CHAPTER SEVENTEEN

It was Saturday morning and Tiberius was walking along the back pitches of Blackrock Rugby Club again. He headed towards the group of parents on the side-line cheering on the pint sized rugby players. He scanned the group as he headed toward them but couldn't see Ashling anywhere. Doyle was on the side-line, calling out to his players who were playing against a team wearing jerseys with large black and white hoops. The ball came out over the side-line and straight above Tiberius. He reached up and caught it, firing it one handed, like a quarterback, back to the Referee. He turned to find Doyle grinning at him.

"Yer not in the Superbowl now. Boss!"

"Old habits," Tiberius grinned.

"We'll finish in about twenty minutes and I'll be free then OK?"

"Sure. How's your team doing?"

"We're hammering them." Doyle answered with relish. "Young Cian Clarke Brady ran in three tries already. Great little player."

"Yeah. He's a pistol, that kid."

"Pity Mrs C-B left early, isn't it?" Doyle remarked staring fixedly at the match unfolding.

"Yeah. Pity." Tiberius ignored Doyle's unsubtle jibe and turned to leave "I'll meet you back at the clubhouse when you're done. OK?"

"See you there, Boss."

Tiberius ambled back across the pitches towards the clubhouse and surrounding carpark. As he approached, he could see a woman sitting on the bonnet of a large black Mercedes speaking animatedly into a phone. Once he got closer he could see it was Ashling. She ended the conversation by calling the person she was speaking with a total bastard! She stuffed her hands and the phone into the pocket of her jacket and stormed towards him, head down. Muttering.

She headed straight for him and he wasn't sure what to do. When she got close, she lifted her head so he smiled at her and said "Hi."

She stopped, confused and he noticed she was crying.

"Hey. I don't wanna intrude, but are you OK, Ashling?"

"No. I'm bloody not! My bloody husband wants a divorce. The bastard has been banging our neighbour."

"Uh. Um. I'm sorry. Does little Cian know about any of this?"

"Oh God. Poor Cian. He'll be devastated. What am I going to do?" Her face crumpled and she began sobbing. Tiberius took her shoulder and steered her over to a quiet corner of the car park.

He plonked her up on a low wall where she sat facing away from the busy clubhouse area. She took out a tissue and blew her nose.

"Sorry. I don't know what to say. I discovered what they were up to last night at a party in another neighbour's house. I never even suspected. Now he says he's moving out and wants a divorce. He wants me to take Cian into town after this for a few hours so he can get his stuff moved out before we return. Robert says it'll be less traumatic for Cian. For God's sake!"

"I don't think there's an easy way to soften this news for Cian, to be honest. Been there"

"He just wants it to be less traumatic for him. The coward." She stopped and looked at Tiberius as though just realising he was there. "What do you mean 'been there?'"

"My folks divorced when I was nine. My sisters were seven and five at the time."

"Oh God. I'm so sorry. It must have been very hard on you." She sniffed wiping her nose.

"It was made more difficult because my Mom was a high-profile artist and my Dad was quite wealthy so it all kinda happened in a very public way." He looked past her shoulder and noticed Doyle walking towards them. Tiberius looked at Doyle and shook his head slightly. Doyle picked up on the message and turning pointed at the clubhouse, indicating he'd meet Tiberius in there. Tiberius nodded.

"Y'know it might not be a bad thing if his dad has physically moved out before you and Cian get back home, even though he may be suiting himself primarily. It will give you time to work out what to say to Cian. How to handle it?" He looked at her, thinking that even with streaming eyes and a runny nose she still looked amazing.

"You may have a point, but, oooooh, ohh!" she wailed again. Sobbing into her crumpled tissues. After some moments of unbridled distress, she gulped and visibly pulled herself to-gether. She took a deep breath and looked past his shoul-der in an unfocussed way and said, half to herself, "at least I know now why he didn't want to have sex with me. Bastard was getting it elsewhere."

"Guy must be nuts," Tiberius thought and then she looked up at him quickly, surprised.

Tiberius groaned and looked skywards. "I said that out loud didn't I?" he asked through gritted teeth. He looked at her to find her staring back but with a slight crinkle to her mouth.

"Thanks. I think." She was almost smiling now. "For the backhanded complimentary non-compliment."

Tiberius was deeply embarrassed. "I'm so sorry. I don't want you to think I'm hitting on you, y'know when you're vulnerable and at a low point."

"I don't think you're hitting on me. And I do think your perspective on the value of not having Cian watch his dad physically move out of home is accurate. So don't worry. I just have to figure out what to do with him for the rest of the day."

"Unfortunately, I have to work with Doyle for a bit. But if you want the keys to my apartment you can take him there. If you need somewhere quiet?"

"Thanks, but no. I'll go to my sister's and have a chat with her."

"Of course. Yes. Family is best at a time like this." Tiberius stopped himself in mid flow, thinking, *I'm babbling and putting myself into a place where I'm not wanted. The last thing she needs now is a horny Yank coming up with dumb suggestions.*

"Look," Ashling said, still smiling. "I do appreciate the offer and if I wasn't sure Aoife was around, I'd take you up on it. But I think I need to talk to her. She never liked Robert. Or his dad, for that matter. She's the strongest person I know. She's been through a lot and still going through a lot."

Ashling hopped down from the wall, she had been sitting on and gave her eyes a final wipe. Placing her hand on his arm, she squeezed it gently and said "Thanks, Tiberius." Then she turned and walked towards the clubhouse.

Tiberius stared after her, trying not to look at her ass and failing dismally. A pint-sized kid exploded from the clubhouse and sprinted towards her, yelling "Mum! Mum! I scored three tries! Three. Mr Doyle says it's a record for a first match. A record Mum! I'm going to play for Ireland someday. Just like Brian O'Driscoll. Mr Doyle says he was quite small for a rugby player too and he's the greatest!" The little boy was cut off as his mother bent down and swept him into her arms, hugging him fiercely as she walked along. Doyle emerged from the clubhouse and waved at Ashling and Cian as he made his way over to Tiberius.

"What's going on Boss?" he asked.

"She caught her husband screwing around. He just rang her and said he wants a divorce. She was a bit shook up."

"Jesus!" said Doyle. "That Brady is a total wanker. Why in

the name of the good Lord would you ever screw around on a woman who looked like her! And she's nice. I mean a genuinely nice girl. What a prick!"

"My thoughts exactly."

Tiberius and Doyle headed back towards the clubhouse and agreed to meet at a coffee shop on the sea front in Dun Laoghaire called The Promenade Café, where they could sit outside and talk.

CHAPTER EIGHTEEN

Mr Black stood at his window watching the house across the road. The woman had come in and out several times during the morning and the kids were constantly coming and going. He had heard Lindsey get up and go to the loo a few minutes earlier and then he could hear her bed springs as she got back into bed. He reckoned she spent a lot of time there, watching TV and doing a lot of nothing.

A soft buzzing sound came through the wall and he heard a sigh.

Hang on a second now! He grinned to himself. *What's going on here Constable?*

The buzzing continued and the sighs increased in frequency until he could hear a deep groan from the other side of the wall. Then the sounds stopped and he resumed looking out the window, but this time with a slight erection.

I wonder do I have time to go in and have some fun with her? he considered. *Better not. It would be a pain in the ass to have to clean up this bloody place and remove any traces of my visit.* He moved a table to the window and sat on it. *Still,* he mused. *A fire would effectively achieve that. And, as long as I was careful with whatever knife I use, then no one would ever know. Mightn't even use a knife.* He was enjoying this train of thought. *She's such a scrawny little thing. I could just tie her hands and strangle her slowly while I fucked her............mmmmmmmmmm.*

The thought of her frantic futile struggles, coupled with her obvious distaste for men, excited him. Then he discarded it abruptly and forced himself back to his mission. He refocussed on the woman across the road who was standing in the doorway talking to a teenage boy. *Come to think of it, she has a nice hefty body. A bit like dear Jessica, though somewhat more careworn and less elegantly dressed, methinks. I definitely would enjoy using her to encourage her little protégé Dane to spill the beans. Just got to figure out how to get her out of here and discreetly transported. She needs to be out of circulation for long enough to achieve my objectives.* Mr Black smiled as he looked fondly across the street at the unsuspecting woman. He rubbed his crotch as he looked at her and decided he had seen enough.

Two hours later, Mr Black walked along a busy, down at heel shopping street near his temporary home and stopped outside a surprisingly trendy café called Legit Coffee. He ordered and received a nice latte and was enjoying sipping it when he noticed two women standing uncertainly inside the doorway of the shop. One nudged the other and said "gowaun! Dey won't bitecha." The nudgee walked up to the counter and ordered "tew capichinoez pal, an tew scones" in a broad Dublin accent. She turned back to her friend, the nudger, and giggled. Mr Black was mildly amused by the pair who behaved like schoolgirls when neither were ever going to see their thirties or even their forties again. He moved sideways along the large table where he had been sitting and gestured to the empty spaces, saying with a smile, "Ladies?"

"Tank yuuz." Said one of them and they both sat at one end to wait for their coffees.

"Been in here before?" enquired Mr Black, smiling, knowing full well this pair were totally out of place among the uber cool collection of art students, techies and assorted hipsters who were currently inhabiting the café.

"Jaysus. No. It's a bit classy for us. But her son Mikey says dat de coffee's nice, and we're meetin Mary, a friend of ours."

Mr Black moved along the bench further, saying "I'll just give you a bit more room then, for your friend."

"You're dead nice. Tanks mistah."

The coffees and two huge fruit scones with butter and raspberry jam arrived and the girls busied themselves plastering the scones with too much butter and jam and glugging down the coffee. Had they realised the monster they shared the table with they would have ran for their lives and never stopped running. Mr Black returned to his newspaper.

"Hi girrrls." A new voice intruded and he looked up as one of the pair slid along the bench towards him. To his delight, the newcomer was his target, who he had decided was probably Dane's foster mother.

"Hi Mary. Jawanna coffee? What sort?"

"Same as youz girrrls."

The woman on the outside swivelled around and called out to the trendily dressed camp man behind the counter, "anudder capichino pal? Over here, yeah?" Without waiting for a reply she turned back to her friend.

"So tellus Mary. What's de story pet?"

"Ah look. The doctor wants me to go into the hospital and get a mole on me back removed."

"Sore ting Mary. Very sore, Pet. I had a wart removed on me tit two years ago and it was agony."

"Ah no Terese. He said it won't be painful, just uncomfortable for a few days."

"They said that to me an all, Mary. It was excruciating, so it was."

"Problem is Terese, I can't get the lazy bastards in the health services to get someone to come in and mind the kids while I'm in hospital. An' after the last time, I want to be sure they don't send me another pervert."

"Jaysus Mary. I forgot about dat bastard. He was a right paedo wasn't he?"

"Yeah. So what can I do? The kids need watching and feeding, but I promised meself I'd get dis done. An' now it's all arrayanged"

"Don't yuuz worry pet. We'll mind 'em. An I'll talk to one or two udders in the street. We'll do it in pairs. An Noreen here and me'll sleep there during the nite times OK? When-ave you gotta go in for de ol' slice'n'dice pet?"

"Thursday. I've to be in Beaumont Hospital at nine in de mornin. I'll take a taxi. "

"No bodder pet. We'll sort it by den. You'll need to leave de house at about eight if you're to get to Beaumont by nine, love?"

"Yeah, I'll walk to Thomas Street, probly get one dere."

"Yeah."

Mr Black stared at his paper, smiling and thinking this must be his lucky day. *I must have done something very, very good in a previous life for God to favour me so. Now all I have to do is fig-ure out how to extract young Mister Wilson and we're good to go.*

CHAPTER NINETEEN

Tiberius stretched his legs under the table, feeling the pleasant ache which came from having ran earlier in the day. He had enjoyed jogging through Dublin's Georgian streets, half empty, as they were, at six thirty am on a Saturday morning.

Doyle sat and passed over a black coffee to him.

"So, putting the delectable, and soon to be sensibly divorced, Mrs C-B to one side for the moment. Have any striking breakthroughs occurred to you overnight Boss?" asked Doyle.

"I reckon we're on the right track. We need to find out what this guy Black looks like and issue a photo, sketch or whatever to the rest of the force. We need to find him. I reckon he's like a killing machine and there's no stop button. I also think he's mixed up with this other killing in some way, maybe through the two kids and their software? Maybe he's after it."

"Well we already know he has operated in a professional capacity for the British. Well Roger was convinced he had and that's good enough for me, frankly."

"Yes, I….." Tiberius's phone rang and he answered it.

"Hi. No, you're not disturbing me Sweeney. Go on. Is that so? So you were right. Well that narrows things down. Thanks for the call. I'll tell Doyle. No. He's with me right now. Talk to you on Monday. Well done."

Doyle looked at him and raised an eyebrow. "And?"

"That was Sweeney. His hunch was 100% on the money. Jo Anne Sutherland had foreign female DNA on her lips and just below one earlobe. She had been kissing a woman."

"So, our murderer, may have been a woman."

"Yes. Quite likely. And the pathologist reckons the internal bruising in her vagina was caused by a hard object, unlikely to have been a man's penis."

"Smart boy, our Sweeney."

"Yep."

"So, are we looking for a woman for both murders or just the girl's?"

Tiberius didn't answer so Doyle continued, "y'know, it's looking more and more like we do have two different perpetrators. A woman did the first and a man, probably this guy Black, did the second." Doyle paused. Tiberius was still silent, encouraging him to continue with this line of reasoning.

"Boss, if the software is as valuable as you say and we're fairly convinced both murders are somehow connected to it then we have may have two different parties after the software, who are capable of murder?"

"Right."

"Let me rephrase that, we may have two different parties that we know about who are after the software. There may be others, so shouldn't we be thinking about providing some sort of protection to young Dane and Beth? Or keeping an eye on them at least?"

"We are unlikely to get approval from Harcourt Street for that. Not enough resources."

"True. True. So what do we do then? We can't protect them ourselves and run an efficient investigation?"

"Let me ring Rayne. She may have put some protection or security in place. If not, then we'll have to figure something out and step in."

"OK. In the meantime, I'll look up this geezer, Black, on our systems to see if we can locate a photo or even a description of him. If that doesn't work I might talk to an old pal of mine who works in Intelligence and see if he can help. He has lots of contacts with the UK Services going way back to the Troubles so perhaps he can locate the information we need?"

"Great, Doyle."

*   *   *

Rayne had just sat down to eat with Beth and Dane when her phone rang. She glanced at the screen and realised it was Tiberius again. She stood and excused herself, answering the call as she walked away from the table.

"Hi Babes!"

"Hi Rayne. Got a second?"

"Sure. Fire away."

"I need to ask you if Beth and Dane have any security in place?"

"Sorry Babes?"

"I know. This is kind of out of left field but we're investigating two murders, one of which may be a case of mistaken identity." As Tiberius spoke, Rayne suddenly felt cold, a queasy feeling spreading in her stomach.

"Mistaken identity?" She managed to ask.

"Yeah. We're not sure but we think the girl who was killed on the UCD Campus may have been mistaken for Beth. In addition, we cannot rule out the possibility that there isn't a link to the second murders. I don't want to alarm you but I know you're in the middle of things with them so I just wanted to check whether or not they have security in place. For what it's worth, I have no concerns about your safety. This could just be an inaccurate assumption we've arrived at, but I'd rather be safe than sorry."

"Ahh. No. Tiberius. I mean. I have but you know me. I'm ultra-careful when I travel at all times, so......," Rayne realised she was babbling a bit and stopped herself.

"Of course. I understand that Raynie. If they don't already have security then I need to put something in place for them. Just for a short while. Can you talk to them for me? I would like to arrange a meeting to discuss this."

"Uh sure. Sure thing. I'll talk with them. Listen, I could always add them to my security guys' watchlist, if that'll solve it? They're important to me too."

"That's what I was hoping you'd say Rayne. That's a perfect solution, because right now our resources are seriously stretched as a result of the Shannon attacks."

"I can imagine. OK Sweetie, just leave it to me."

"Bye Rayne. Thanks."

"Bye." She ended the call and put the phone into her pocket. Thinking furiously.

Mistaken Identity. If only Tiberius knew how close he was.

Rayne's mind went back to the awful moment when recognition came into the girl's eyes.

"Hey, you look familiar. Didn't I link to you on Linkedin.com? You're that internet entrepreneur Ray something yeah? I'm Jo Anne. Jo Anne Sutherland!" she said drunkenly. "Wow! Wait until my friends hear who I scored. Ohhh wow!" Panicked, Rayne had suggested they go somewhere more private and have a little fun. "I've some great coke if you want to try some?" she had whispered huskily to the girl. "Ohhh yeah. Great. Us poor students can't afford expensive stuff like Coke. Well not too often. Lead on!."

Rayne and Jo Anne half walked, half staggered away from the venue and along the path into the wooded area. Satisfied they hadn't been noticed; Rayne diverted them through the bushes just stopping in time to avoid banging into the barrier surrounding the massive hole in the ground. In the darkened copse of trees Rayne couldn't see the bottom but thought it couldn't be better. In fact, the deeper the better. The girl bumped into her from behind, giggling and hiccupping. Rayne grabbed the silly bitch and kissed her deeply. Then she swivelled and slipping behind her, cupped Jo Anne's breasts. She nuzzled Jo Anne's neck, licking and sucking on the skin just below her earlobes. Rayne slid one hand down the front of the girl's belly and slid it through the opening at the front of the fancy dress suit and into her panties. Jo Anne began to pant as she became more excited. Rayne unzipped Jo Anne's suit and eased it off her shoulders and down over her hips leaving it pooled around her knees. Rubbing her breasts again with one hand Rayne took out a small vibrator and slid it gently into the girl's vagina from behind. The girl held onto the barrier in front of her as she writhed and gyrated.

Jo Anne jerked once, twice three times and exhaled heavily. "Jesus, that was great! Didn't even need the drugs," she laughed leaning over the barrier. After a few moments, Rayne took out a small black object from her own pocket. It looked like and performed the functions of a portable memory flash drive, but if you pressed both buttons on either side in a particular sequence a small but viciously sharp blade popped out.

The back of Rayne's hand brushed the girl's lips in the dark and suddenly whipped back across her throat. The pain was sudden and intense. Jo Anne tried to scream but she felt like she was drowning. After a few minutes she was still, slumped over the barrier. Rayne knelt down with one hand on the girl's back and put her other under the crotch of the suit, pulling it up. Then she explosively shoved and lifted the dying girl's body up and over the barrier. She heard a crunching sound as Jo Anne landed on bushes or brushwood in the dark below.

She checked herself with the spotlight on her phone and was pleased to detect no blood spots or smears. Rayne looked into the black maw of the pit but couldn't see the body. She didn't want to risk turning the spotlight into the hole in case someone saw it and anyway it wouldn't reach very far. Rayne turned and left the woods.

*   *   *

Deng's phone rang as he was lying on a massage table. His

back was dotted with acupuncture needles. He recognised the ring tone and said to his therapist, an elderly man from Beijing, "I need to be alone to take this call."

The old man tut tutted and removed some of the needles.

"Leave," said Deng. He picked up the phone and still lying on his belly, propped himself up on his elbows. His bodyguard followed the old man to the door and looked at him questioningly. Deng nodded and Riga left the room also. He waited until he heard the door close and then spoke into the phone.

"Yes?"

"I am ready to extricate one target and am confident I will have the leverage which will enable me to get the information you require."

"Only one of them?"

"Yes."

"Why."

"We only need the male. He has the information we require. I do not need the female any longer. I have discovered someone who is more important to him, who can be acquired easily. However, the current window of opportunity is narrowing. I will need your instructions by early Thursday at the latest, preferably Wednesday evening. Otherwise we will have to begin again."

"One moment," said Deng. He looked out at the sea. It was smooth and calm this morning and the sun was shining. He considered the pros and cons of the different strategic options open to him.

If Rayne persuaded the two to sell to him then it would establish his top cost for acquiring the software at four hundred million. He would control it and it was a risk free route.

If he had his unknown employee, now waiting patiently, acquire the software, it would cost him approximately twenty million, but this was an illegal option and it might just be traceable back to him. It was unlikely but one never knows. It would also deny him any future benefits from the work of

Dane Wilson as he would undoubtedly have to be disposed of after interrogation. Yet he would save three hundred and eighty million, which was a sizeable sum. Was there a third route?

"I have two questions," Deng said.

"Yes," came back the answer.

"Can you get the information without damaging the male in any way? And can you get the information so we do not have to dispose of him afterwards as I may have a further need for him?"

"The answer to both questions is yes. That is partly why I have selected this different route, utilising a different female for leverage."

"Make the arrangements. Call me on Thursday morning for my final instructions."

"By that point I will have acquired the leverage."

"I don't care about the leverage. Just be in a position to execute if I require it."

"Yes."

The phone went dead.

Deng put it down and pressed a buzzer to summon the elderly therapist to finish the acupuncture session.

CHAPTER TWENTY

Aoife stroked her sister's head gently. They had gotten little Cian to bed and Aoife had given her husband his meds, ignoring his feeble pleas for a "wee drink." They sat in the kitchen and opened an excellent bottle of Gran Reserva Rioja wine. Ashling had moved through a bewildering array of emotional responses to the situation, encompassing rejection, anger, self-doubt, self-pity and then just tears and more tears. She had eventually sobbed herself dry and was now lying on the couch, head resting in her sister's lap staring dully at the wood burning in the glass fronted stove in the living room where they had moved, accompanied by a second bottle of Rioja.

They had always been close. When Aoife's husband James developed Multiple Sclerosis, it was a double tragedy for a sculptor who had been beginning to make a serious international reputation. Ashling was always there for Aoife and helped her as much as she could.

James and Aoife had met at a party thrown in honour of Ashling and Aoife's mother Ingrid Campbell, one of Irelands most celebrated living sculptors. Ingrid was a member of the RHA, the Royal Hibernian Society and the Royal Irish Academy. Kellett, a Canadian, was corralled in a corner by a fat, red-faced, very tipsy author, when Aoife rescued him. "I think the President was looking for you Charles," she said quietly into the author's ear. He twirled around and scampered towards the diminutive figure of the Irish President, who having earlier presented a ceremonial golden necklace called a Torc to Ingrid was now saying goodbye to her at the door.

"Oh God. Thank you so much for saving me," he said in a Canadian accent.

"Not God, just Aoife," she grinned.

"Beautiful name. I shouldn't ask but, how do you spell it?"

Dear God what a stupid question! He thought. *She's going to think I'm a complete Jerk.*

"A-O-I-F-E," she said patiently, "pronounced EE-FA. Apparently, it means Beauty in English and refers to a mythical warrior princess who went to war against her sister, was defeated by Cuchulainn but eventually became his lover before his untimely death. But I'd never go to war against my sister, Ashling's my best friend."

He looked at her intently.

"So that's A-S-H-L-I-N-G," she continued spelling it out, "pronounced ASH-LING. It means Dream or Vision and believe me if you saw her you wouldn't be bothering talking to me. She really is stunning."

I'm babbling, she thought. *His eyes are hazel and kind of flecked. He's gorgeous.*

"No. I'm quite happy with the way things are right now," he said smiling.

"So what brings you to this august gathering of Irish greatest living artists? Our version of the Academie Francaise?"

"I'm a sculptor, and I came to Ireland to work with a particular kind of wood which can only be found in bogs. My sister's husband is Irish and he owns large tracts of bog in the midlands of Ireland. So, I'm here to see what I can do. Are you an artist?"

"No. I haven't one ounce of artistic talent, I'm afraid. My sister and I are great disappointments to our mother as neither of us are in the slightest bit creative. I'm a police officer."

"OK," he sounded a bit hesitant

Here we go, Aoife thought. *This is where he makes a run for it.*

"Fancy a drink?" He smiled.

"I'll just get my coat." Pleasantly surprised, she turned and walked away.

Outside it was raining heavily and he slipped on the sloping walkway from the restaurant to the street. She grabbed his arm and steadied him.

"You OK?" she queried, concerned.

"Fine. Just clumsy. I'm lucky you were here eh?"

They went to a well-known Dublin pub around the corner and managed to find a little cubby hole where they had several drinks and ended up in her apartment that evening.

Eight months later, they got engaged. Then one day the world stopped turning and came to a crashing halt. James brought her to Sandymount Strand and sat her down on one of the wooden seats looking out to sea, telling her he had something serious to talk to her about.

He didn't beat about the bush, just said bluntly he had been diagnosed with Multiple Sclerosis and that it was a particularly aggressive form of it. She looked at the heartbreak in his eyes and cried for him. James said he had intended to tell her for the past week or so but couldn't find the courage and that he would understand if she wanted to end things.

"Don't be so bloody stupid," she snapped at him, angry now. "You don't have a very high opinion of me do you?"

"Look Aoife, this is only going one way. Eventually I'll lose the ability to use my hands. I'll no longer be able to sculpt and shape the wood. Aside from dealing with the physical deterioration, it's going to be very difficult for me to handle. After that it's all downhill. I'll need constant care and medical attention. I'm luckier than a lot of MS patients because I inherited a lot of money from my parents and it'll pay for everything."

"Oh, so you're saying you don't need me." She couldn't help herself; bitterness stole into her voice.

"No! No! God no! Aoife, I love you. This is so hard for me. It's because I love you so much that I don't want to condemn you to years of dealing with this. It's going to be horrible."

"James, I love you too. So, bollocks to this disease. Let's get married and have as much fun as we can for as long as the MS allows you. You work as much as you can so you can feel you took your chances and I'll support you."

It was all very romantic, until James' Multiple Sclerosis worsened to the point where he could not work anymore. Gradually, as he dropped the chisels more and more and the disease ate away at his motor functions, he became frustrated and bitter.

They had been unable have children so the house was quiet when she was out at work. James began drinking heavily which contributed to the more rapid than normal deterioration in his condition.

Over the past year Ashling and her parents had worried about the effect this was having on Aoife. She had become increasingly sharp tongued and short-tempered with everyone. It was clear that dealing with James' deteriorating health and state of mind was having a growing effect on Aoife. Unfortunately, there was little anyone could do. James was right and she had been wrong. The reality was horrible and she was trapped in it. Prior to calling to the house that afternoon, Ashling hadn't spoken with Aoife for about three weeks after a very unpleasant family dinner where Aoife had been vitriolic with her mother for suggesting that perhaps James now required more full time medical care and shouldn't she consider moving him to a facility which specialised in the treatment of MS.

When she had arrived at the door Aoife's face had been hard and unsmiling until she realised Ashling had been crying and suddenly it was as though no estrangement had occurred between the two siblings. Aoife kept her fury at Ashling's errant husband under control, just focussing on Ashling and Cian and what could be done to alleviate the effects of his actions on his innocent family.

In an odd way, it diverted her from brooding and agonising over her own misfortunes and the constant tragedy of James' situation. Bizarrely, helping Ashling and focussing on her was having a positive impact on her emotionally.

Hours later she brought Ashling up to the guest bedroom, where Cian was already asleep in a small single bed built into the Bay window of the room. She folded the covers back and tucked them around Ashling who looked like a little child herself.

"We'll work things out better in the morning Ash," she whispered and then kissed her sister on the forehead.

"Thanks Eef, I don't know what I'd do without you," Ashling replied sleepily.

Aoife closed the door and walked along the hallway to her own bedroom. They had brought in a special bed and installed it into an adjoining room when James deteriorated to the point where he needed nursing care during the night. Sometimes she lay awake and listened to him crying. Initially she had gone into him and laid beside him but more and more he had pushed her away as anger and bitterness at his unjust fate, ate away at him.

One night, the thought had insinuated itself into her mind that she was trapped in this awful reality due to her own stupidity. She had the opportunity to walk away on that beach and she hadn't taken it. She felt guilty even thinking like that and had gone into James' room and climbed on to the bed beside him and put her arm gently around him. He woke up and realising she was in bed with him angrily told her to leave him alone. There wasn't enough room and did she want him to fall out? Devastated by this latest rejection she fled back to her own room and sobbed herself into a broken and shallow sleep. After that she became much angrier and harder on herself and everyone she encountered. It was so easy to just lash out. The only exception was little Cian. Every time he smiled up at her, her heart melted a little. Just a tiny crack in the wall she had built around herself, which disappeared with Cian when he left.

Tonight, she noticed as she looked in on James that his breathing was very shallow. He was asleep but seemed a little restless. She was very tired, both physically and emotionally and just a bit drunk too so she decided not to telephone the nurse who was on call tonight but to discuss it with her replacement who would arrive tomorrow morning at eight thirty. She closed the door on him and continued on to her own room.

Tired as she was, she couldn't sleep. She lay there going through everything Ashling had told her. Then, a little guiltily, she realised she hadn't thought about James and their problems for some hours. Guilty, because she knew that even though Ashling was going through an awful experience, it had at least the unintended benefit of helping her to concentrate on something other than her own problems.

*   *   *

"UncaJameswonwakeup!" Cian exclaimed from the foot of Aoife's bed. Aoife was groggy and not feeling one hundred percent, courtesy of the volume of wine consumed the night before, so it took a minute for her to realise what the little boy was saying.

Then it hit her. She jumped out of bed and dashed past Cian out the door and into James' room. He was still. Lying there, unmoving. Not breathing. She moved towards the bed like she was swimming through water. The rational part of her told her there was no point in trying to do .anything because he was clearly dead for some time. He had passed away during the night.

She moaned harshly and dropped to her knees at the side of the bed, lowering her head to the surface, her arms outstretched across his legs. She felt blasted. Wasted. A hollow shell struck by lightning and now emptied of all emotion, all feeling, all humanity. She did not hear Ashling come into the room behind her but felt her arms around her and she turned into her sister's embrace as her poor battered heart broke.

Cian stood at the door watching, bewildered but silent. He

was confused. He walked over to Ashling and Aoife and carefully kissed his aunt on the forehead. "Is he gone to Holy God, Aunty? Is he gone to heaven?" His voice quavered, on the verge of tears himself. The sight of the little boy's distress gave Aoife pause and she disengaged from Ashling and reached out to him and gently hugged him. "Yes pet. He's gone now, and he has no more pain, so that's a good thing, isn't it?"

"Yes Aunty," he said through his tears.

*   *   *

Doyle stood at the back of a queue of people stretching out of the Funeral Home, across the yard, through the entrance gates and thirty or forty feet along the street. He felt a heavy hand on his shoulder and turned to look up at the smiling face of the giant who had shouldered his way in to stand beside him.

"Well Doyle. How's the man?" asked John Burke.

"Ah John. I'm good. I'm good. And you?"

"Never better, with the exception of the back giving me a bit of gyp now and again. You were looking for me the other day?"

"Ah yes, I wanted to ask you about something but maybe later, yeah? Once we've a bit more, ah, comfort?" Doyle smiled.

"Excellent stuff, Doyler." John replied. The two friends had created a private language of phrases and key words when they were working together in Northern Ireland during the Troubles which had served them well in disguising their conversations from others. But any phrase with the word 'comfort' in it was a simple invitation to go for a drink in whatever bar was to hand.

The two friends began talking about rugby, having both played on the same rugby team as young men and were both still passionate about the sport. The time passed and they

found themselves at the entrance to the funeral home. They
filed in and passed along a line of grieving relatives, expressing their sympathies with the time honoured expression
"sorry for your troubles." Then Doyle was stunned to find
himself shaking hands with Ashling Clarke Brady. "Hi Ashling. I'm so sorry. I didn't know you were related?"

"James was married to my sister Aoife." She replied quietly.

"Right. I'm so sorry for your troubles. My deepest sympathies." Doyle said and moved on to stand in front of Aoife.

"If there's anything I can do to help, you only have to pick
up the phone," he said quietly to her. "Anything at all. At any
time. Please don't hesitate." He looked frankly at Aoife and
smiled.

"Thanks Doyle. I appreciate that." She was distant but held
his hand firmly and gave him a brief return smile.

Outside the funeral home, Doyle caught up with his friend
John and they walked down the street to a small pub where
they ensconced themselves in a quiet corner and ordered
two pints of Guinness. Doyle noticed John's casual gaze
around the pub and when he turned back to his friend, John
smiled broadly and said simply, "force of habit."

"Some things never change."

"No," he paused. "Been doing it too long, I suppose. Getting
sloppy too if a dopey sod like you noticed."

"So, how many in here and what's the story on them?" Doyle
grinned, starting a game they used to play in their down
time when they were both working in Northern Ireland.

John stretched and said, "well the couple at the bar have a
serious issue. From the way she's talking at him rather than
with him, I reckon he lost his job. She's the main breadwin-
ner but now they can't afford the mortgage. They've got at
least one kid, possibly more. The old guy at the end of the
bar is just topping up the alcohol content in his blood. If
they cremate him when cirrhosis of the liver finally kills
him, it'll cause a natural disaster and will probably acceler-
ate global warming. Irrevocably." He paused to take a deep

long swig of his pint. Put it on the table and continued. "The Barman is married to the woman who carried a tray of sandwiches into the lounge bar but based on the looks he was giving the young lad playing the poker machine over there, he's gay. As for the young lad, he's unemployed. He has never worked in a full time job, scraped through his school exams, barely passed or perhaps barely failed and therefore has little chance of making much money. I'd say he's probably a good touch to buy some gear from, though. He smokes grass or hash and sells a little to supplement his unemployment benefit."

"You're some cynic, d'you know that?"

"True. True. Life and hanging around with the likes of you has done it to me."

The frightening thing though, thought Doyle to himself, *is that John most likely nailed all of them. He's rarely wrong. I've certainly never proven him wrong.*

"So are you going to tell me what has you bothering an old man like myself in the twilight of my career, Doyle?"

"It's related to an investigation I'm working on at the moment."

"An investigation? I'm glad they finally saw sense and let you back at what you're best at. Although I have to say I was cheering when I heard you beat the daylights out of that nasty little creep Slevin."

"In hindsight, it was a dumb thing to do John. I should have done something else. I shot myself in the foot. Anyway. at the moment, we're dealing with two separate investigations and we think that one, a double homicide, was committed by a character who may have been active in the North, during the Troubles."

Doyle noticed that John had his pint to his mouth but was not drinking. Eventually he asked, "got a name?" and continued to drink.

"Well we're not one hundred percent sure about it but we think his name might be Black. Ring any bells?"

"I'd need to think about it. Can I get back to you?"

"Sure John." Doyle was watching his friend closely. After a moment, he decided to poke the fire a little and added "we think he may have committed a murder in the South of France while we were there also. Although that's a wee bit of a long shot, admittedly."

"Oh?"

"We think he may have tortured and murdered the wife of Roger MacAllister. You remember Gillian, don't you?" Now he was throwing some petrol on the fire.

"Yes. I remember her. She was a nice lady, tough but decent. So was Roger for that matter."

"She had a hard death."

"Did she?"

"He's evil, John." Doyle pushed.

"I'll look into it. OK?"

"Thanks. Anything which might help with this investigation would be great."

"Sure." John sat back regarding his empty glass and leaned over towards Doyle, staring at him coldly and said quietly "It's your round, you stingy sod."

Doyle laughed and got up. As he stood at the bar with his back to his friend he could see from the positioning of various mirrors in the pub the massive man in the corner regarding him intently.

CHAPTER
TWENTY ONE

Mr Black lounged in the doorway of a darkened shop, watching. The row of taxis inched forward like a big lazy crocodile, swallowing up drunken, noisy revellers at the front and sweeping them off into the night. Although it was a Wednesday night, Camden street was buzzing. Hopping. People flowed up and down the street and in and out of the bars, restaurants and clubs lining it. He ignored it all, staring intently at the taxis. One in particular had caught his attention. It was quite smart, black and had darkened windows. It was large, could carry seven or eight people and importantly had wide doors for disabled access.

It looked just right.

He waited until it was just one from the front of the queue and crossing the road quickly, stopped behind three young girls negotiating with the taxi at the front. He turned and looked straight at the driver of the black vehicle and raised his eyebrows questioning. The driver beckoned him forward and he got into the back.

Three hours later the taxi drove out of the car park of a remote woodland part of Wicklow mountains south of Dublin. Mr Black whistled as he drove.

Moving those rocks was hard work but a little robust exercise never did a body any harm did it?

Several years ago he had been part of a covert unit which tailed two IRA hitmen to this forest. The two republicans had gone deep into the woods to a tiny glade with a small depression in the middle and a jumble of mossy rocks at one end. They had surprised the pair as they finished levering up a large slab and took them out. The others in the team slipped the two bodies into bags and humped them back to the van they had brought around to the car park area. Mr Black and the commanding officer pulled open the door set into the ground which had been uncovered. It wasn't really an underground room more of a storage area but it had contained boxes of guns, ammunition and some explosives. The munitions were humped out next and Mr Black and the commander covered back over the door and heaved the slab back into position and dressed it with some more rocks. As they walked back to the car park and their ride back North, Mr Black made a mental note of the location and possibilities of the, now empty, hidden facility.

He had re-visited it a year ago, racing from Belfast to Wicklow on a powerful motorbike and noticed that the rocks had been disturbed. Doubtless the IRA mens' colleagues had come to check up on them and to see what had happened to their guns. He was pleased to see that it was still empty. Clearly, the IRA had decided to stop using it.

Well it served him well tonight and now it had a new occupant. He smiled remembering the little drama he had created with the unsuspecting taxi driver.

First, he had agreed to the exorbitant price the cabbie had demanded to take him the twenty five kilometres out to Enniskerry, a picturesque village nestled in the foothills of the Dublin Mountains. Then he gave the impression that he was upset about the driver's request for more money "cos he wouldn't get a fare back into Dublin, now would he, pal?"

As they approached the entrance to one of the many forest car parks he pretended he was going to throw up and the driver jerked to a halt telling him loudly to "gerrout of my car if'n ye're gonna puke pal!" He got out and staggered along the wooded laneway and then bent over with his hands on his knees. After a few minutes, possibly concerned that

204

his fare might try legging it, the driver got out and walked towards him. He put his hand on Mr Black's back and was asking if he was OK, when the sick man's arm straightened and sprayed the drivers face quickly with a small black aerosol can. The driver jerked back and gurgled. He raised his hands and fell to his knees looking up at Mr Black in surprise. He fell forward onto his face. Mr Black quickly dragged the unconscious man to the open rear door and dumped him inside. He jumped into the driver's seat and headed to his final destination. Once he got there and carried the man from the taxi to the hidden store in the woods beyond. He worked out that he was slightly behind schedule and regrettably had no time to play with the driver so a swiftly punched blade through the eye socket into the brain dealt with that issue.

As he drove back to Dublin, Mr Black decided he would park near the target's house in the next hour. He would monitor the house from his rented room and when she left the house, he would go out and just drive around the corner to create the happy coincidence which should encourage her to use his taxi.

He had a wheelchair in the boot and blankets to cover her with if necessary. However, he had already prepared two 'body boxes'. The 'body box' was a little device of his own invention. He had originally noticed the sturdy wooden crates, which normally contained engine axles, in the yard of a British Army outpost on the border and realised that they were strongly constructed, the perfect size for most bodies and that the black lettering describing the contents along the bottom would hide several small airholes for the sedated or expired occupants. *I'm such a creative little fella!* he smiled to himself as he drove along.

*   *   *

Mary opened the front door and stepped out into the quiet of an early morning. She hoisted the small overnight bag onto her shoulders and turned right heading up the slight hill. She was nervous and hadn't slept much the previous night worrying. Being the kind of person she was, her concern was not for herself but for the foster kids asleep in the house behind her. Thank God, Terese had shown up last night and was asleep on the couch with the alarm set, ready to give the kids their brekky and send them off to school. *I'm no great shakes of a cook but at least they all get some proper food in the morning to set them up for the day,* she thought to herself as she walked along.

Mary heard a car engine come up behind her and glanced to her left as a large taxi cruised slowly past. *First bit of luck today,* she said to herself. "Hey!" she called out and raised her hand, but the taxi was at the corner turning right into Meath Place, obviously heading for the busier streets. "No!" She moaned and bustled to the corner after the taxi. She turned and was delighted to find the taxi stopped in the street with the passenger window wound down. She leaned in and asked, "will you take me to Beaumont Hospital?" Surprisingly, the handsome driver got out and walked around to her. He politely opened the door for her and she got into the back, thinking that this was a great start to the day. He picked up her bag and placed it on the seat beside her reaching for the seat belt to strap it in securely. He smiled at her and said "you need to put your seatbelt on too? Can't have you getting hurt, now can we?"

She smiled at the very good looking younger man and then twisted away to fumble for the seatbelt which was behind her bum. "Got it," she said turning back to find his hand holding a can inches from her face, she felt a spray of something on her face. She became nauseous, like she was going to faint. Then it all went dark.

Mr Black was on one knee as he took the seatbelt from her limp hand and secured it. He did a visual check of his surroundings and could see there was no one on the street. He turned back to her and tilted her head back to rest on the back of the seat. He grabbed her large breasts and gave them a hard squeeze. Not a budge from the unconscious woman. Excellent. Indulging himself further, he opened her legs pushing her skirt up and slid his hand along her thigh. She had a nice firm, fleshy crotch. *This is going to be fun,* he thought, *she's in better shape than I expected. She should last longer than that annoying old woman in Nice.* He re-adjusted her clothing, got out and closed her door. Then he got into the front, turned off the for hire sign and drove away.

Shortly afterwards, Mr Black parked in the deserted carpark of the Stillorgan Shopping Centre. It was the oldest shopping centre in Ireland, had only one storey and free parking but most importantly, powerful free wi-fi. He took out the IP phone and dialled his employer.

"Yes" answered the digital voice.

"I have secured the leverage we discussed. I'm ready to extract the other party now if you wish me to?" he asked.

There was a long pause. Mr Black waited patiently. One thing he had learned early on was never to pressurize a client and besides, he didn't mind whether he took and interrogated Dane or not. He was going to have fun with wee busty Mary in the back seat no matter what. So it really was a win-win situation, he smiled.

"Take him." The answer came back. Then the phone disconnected.

Mr Black was pleased. He drove out of the car park and headed back towards the city centre along the Dual Carriageway until he came to the University grounds. He turned left at the corner of the Campus and then took a right through imposing pillars into the driveway of the Nova UCD centre where Dane had his office. Mr Black knew Dane liked to work very early in the morning but that he would head back over towards the main campus for his breakfast before the other Nova staff had arrived.

He drove the taxi along the drive passing the Nova buildings on his right and stopping just where the road split in two. The left hand fork was blocked by a metal gate which was unlocked and Mr Black opened it and drove through, turning the taxi around to face back the way he had come but hidden by a hedge from the other spur of the road and the block in which Dane had his office. Mr Black got out and walked around the corner and along the side of the dark windows of the silent Nova building, until he came to an office with the lights on. It had a glass door which led directly out to the road, allowing the user to access it at any time of the day or night, which suited Dane perfectly. Mr Black was pleased to see Dane was in the office hunched over a laptop, with the windows open and the door ajar.

As he walked back to the taxi, he noted the time and realised Dane would be heading for his breakfast shortly. He lifted the dead weight of Mary out of the passenger seat and carrying her in a fireman's lift, walked around the corner to the edge of the building. He placed her against the wall with her legs out in front of her on the roadway and her head lolling to one side. He tilted her slightly so when Dane touched her she would slump to the left, prompting Dane to turn towards her, with his back to Mr Black as he approached. He then checked that her face would be clearly visible to Dane once he came in sight of her. He heard the alarm go off in Dane's office and retreated around the corner of the building where he would not be seen by Dane as he approached the body. He heard the door close and then Dane's boots on the tarmac getting closer.

He could hear Dane mutter "What the?" The sound of the boots ran closer. Then "Mary! What are you doing here? Are you OK?" Mr Black rounded the corner to find Dane knelt over Mary's body with his back to him. He quickly stooped over Dane, and his hand swept around to spray directly into Dane's face. Mr Black stepped back, as Dane attempted to rise, got on one knee and then toppled over sideways.

That is such wonderful stuff. Just a whiff and they're gone for hours and it acts so fast. I must find out where dear Sir Barty gets hold of it? Mr Black mused happily as he returned to the taxi. He reversed back towards where the two bodies were lying in the roadway. He jumped out and lifted each into the back seats where he put on their seatbelts and positioned them as though they were asleep, with her head on Dane's shoulder and his head lying back on the seat rest. He had decided to make it look like they were drunk or stoned after a night out on the town just in case he was stopped by the police. *He's a big boy*, he thought so he leant in and sprayed Dane's face again.

There was no problem getting through Dublin at that early hour of the morning and his route was very straightforward. He headed out to the M50 motorway which circled the city until he came to the turn off for Galway and the M4 motorway to the west of Ireland. Quite soon he was on the N4 Dual Carriageway heading for Weston Airport.

He drove past the airport and turned through a gateway into an industrial area where he stopped the taxi behind a large shed. He got out and lifted two large wooden boxes which had been placed by the wall under a tarpaulin and slid them into the passenger compartment. He got in and closed the door behind him, confident no one could see through the tinted glass windows. He opened one box and put the unconscious woman into it with her bag at her feet. He then secured her with straps which had been installed in the box for that purpose. He checked her pockets and found her mobile phone. He took out the sim card and the battery, putting them into one pocket and the phone into the other. Then he closed the box. He did the same with Dane and added the phones and sim cards to his pockets. He heaved Dane's box on top of hers, pushing them both up against the edge of the closed door.

Mr Black hopped out and took off the taxi sign, placing it on the rear seat. Then he got back in the front, put on a full face mask of a British film actor and checked his watch. *Not long now.*

After about twenty minutes, he could see a small speck approaching in the Eastern sky. The plane landed and stopped surprisingly quickly. Then it taxied up towards the industrial area he was parked in. It had no markings, just a number on the back. He turned the engine on and watched as it moved towards where he was waiting. The plane stopped again and turned slightly as if to taxi across the runway to the area in front of the main terminal. The pilot raised his hand and Mr Black drove swiftly to the side of the plane. A door was already opened and three men in military fatigues with crewcuts hopped out. They ran the twenty or so feet to his cab, opened the side door and took out the two boxes as though they were weightless. They ran back to the plane in single file, with the man in the middle holding each box, with just one hand in front and one behind. Mr Black was impressed by this display of strength, co-ordination and balance. The trio reached the plane door and slid the two boxes inside. They jumped back in and closed the door. The plane immediately moved off towards the Terminal.

The entire process took just under twenty five seconds. Once the passenger door had closed Mr Black took off the mask, stuffed it in his pocket and was already reversing back towards the sheds from which he had briefly emerged.

He turned around and headed back out to the main road and went right. He turned again after three hundred metres and drove along a back road until he approached a bridge. Just before he got to the bridge he turned right off the road onto a rough grassy track running through some trees, along the side of a large reservoir. Three minutes later he spotted a tree with a red cord tied around the trunk and turned the taxi sharply left just before the tree, pointing the vehicle towards a small gap in the trees at the water's edge. Mr Black left the engine on with the automatic transmission in Neutral and turned the lights off. He got out and leaned a wooden pole against the side, checked that the front tyres were pointing straight ahead and then tied the steering wheel to a lever under the driver's seat. He unwrapped the red cord from the tree and put it in his pocket. Next, he opened all the windows in the car. Then he took a heavy stone which he had placed at the foot of the tree when he scouted the location some days previously and quickly put it on top of the accelerator pedal. The engine roared and the loud sound made him nervous. He took the pole, reached in and tapped the gear lever to pop it into Drive. The taxi leapt forwards and tore through the undergrowth, up a slight incline and soared some three or four metres to splash into the dark waters of the reservoir. The loud sound of the engine was muted almost immediately by the inrushing waters and the taxi sank out of sight. Mr Black turned and walked away, taking off the gloves he had worn since getting into the taxi the night before.

He walked along the bank of the reservoir until he came to a chain link fence at the boundary of the airport. Mr Black lifted away a section of fence which he had cut earlier and climbed through. He replaced the section of fence behind him and continued along the edge of the reservoir which had now turned into a river until he came to the edge of the apron where a group of small planes were parked at the side of the Terminal building. The jet he needed was parked closest to him and the side door was open. He walked towards it and got in, pulling the door closed behind him. The boxes were on the floor at the rear of the plane behind three rows of two seats and strapped in. There was no one else in the cabin. He walked to the closed cockpit door and knocked three times, paused and then knocked once. He walked back into the cabin and sat, noting with satisfaction the engine starting. There was a small jerk and the jet moved forward.

CHAPTER
TWENTY TWO

Beth walked into the café and headed to their usual breakfast spot beside the window. She dumped her rucksack and coat and bought a large plate of fried food and a large coffee. She began eating, pleased that she had actually arrived before Dane for once. He was a morning person and she, most definitely, was not! She wanted to talk to him this morning with no one around and this was the reason for her dragging her unwilling body from the cocoon of her duvet at such an unearthly hour.

Yesterday they had been playing around with a new piece of technology they had purchased called a Tile, which she wanted Dane to return to her, but where was he? Since she had installed an alarm app on one of the computers in his office he was always here at this time for breakfast. Fifteen minutes later Beth finished eating and walked over to Dane's office in Nova. When she got there she could see the lights were still on but the door was locked and his laptop bag was on his desk.

Beth figured he may have gone back to his apartment so she turned around and walked over there. As she walked, she rang Dane's phone. It went straight to voicemail so she left a message asking him to contact her. Dane had given her a key so she was able to enter the building and his apartment. As usual it was spotless and ultra-tidy. The diametric opposite of her dump. Unfortunately, it was also empty. Outside the apartment building, Beth thought for a moment and then rang Mary Gill, Dane's foster mum, just in case she might have some idea where he was but it went immediately to voicemail too, so she left a message asking her to call her as she was trying to find Dane.

She walked to the main road and caught a bus into town, getting off in Donnybrook. She headed down along Anglesea Road and turned right into Simmonscourt Road where the Intercontinental Hotel was located. She and Dane were supposed to be meeting Rayne there, so Beth figured she may as well show up in case Dane had made his own way and was already at the hotel, but when she got there he wasn't in the lobby, where they had met in the past. So she headed up to Rayne's suite on the top floor. Rayne answered to her knock with a bright smile. "Hi Beth. Good to see you. Isn't Dane with you?"

"No," said Beth. "I thought he might be here. I can't locate him. It's not that big a deal but he's normally so reliable. A creature of habit..." she stopped. Rayne was looking at her fixedly, with a concerned expression on her face.

"Beth, look. One of the reasons I wanted to talk with you guys this morning was to discuss security."

"Security? What sort?"

"Personal security, Beth. I have my own people who look after me and I was going to include you guys within the umbrella of their surveillance. Just to be on the safe side."

Beth stared at Rayne and then asked in a determined tone "why?"

Rayne took a moment and then said, "because my brother asked me to make sure you guys were safe. He's a cop, works with the Irish police, the Guardians or Gardee or whatever they're called. You've met him, his name is Tiberius. Tiberius Frost."

"Tiberius Frost? DI Frost? This is weird. I mean, yes, I've met him. He's investigating that girl's murder. He talked to Dane and me. Do you think this is related to that murder? Is that why he asked you? Is Dane in trouble?" Suddenly Beth was upset, becoming frantic about her best friend and unsettled by the news of the link between Rayne and Tiberius.

"No Beth. I don't think they're related," answered Rayne quickly. "Tiberius asked me to up our security because we're in possession of a very valuable asset. Your software. It's worth a great deal of money which puts a different complexion on everything." Rayne got up, pacing back and forth, thinking hard.

"OK," she said after a few moments. "Let's not overreact. There might be a perfectly legitimate reason for his being late. So, what we do is wait until noon. No, let's make it just after lunch, say about two thirty. If we can't track him down by then, we'll call Tiber. He'll know what to do. He's great at this kind of stuff. OK?"

Not knowing what else to do, Beth agreed miserably. The hours dragged by. After a brief discussion about the bid process, Rayne went into an adjoining room saying she had to make some calls and get some work done, while Beth sat on the couch, with her laptop open, and her phone, alternating between them. Checking emails and constantly scanning them both in case Dane got in contact.

By one thirty, Beth was ready to scream, when Rayne re-entered and suggested ordering up some lunch. Beth wasn't hungry but managed to eat some sandwiches and drink a coffee. By two pm she had had enough and said to Rayne there was no point in waiting any longer. They needed to alert Tiberius and get his input.

Rayne agreed and rang Tiberius. His phone wasn't answering so she left a voicemail asking him to contact her. Just to be sure she sent a text also.

"Now what do we do? Should we contact the police anyway?" Beth asked.

"Nope. Let's just give Tiberius a chance to get back to me. If he's not back to me by, say three or three fifteen pm then we'll ring the police in Donnybrook station. I think that's the closest place to here. OK?"

CHAPTER TWENTY THREE

Tiberius stood at the back of the church having arrived too late to get a seat that Thursday morning. It was a very large church and packed with people. Doyle had told him earlier that Ashling's sister was Aoife Kellett and that her husband had died, so he felt he ought to show up in solidarity with his colleague, but if he was honest, the involvement of Ashling was the primary driver in his decision. His initial encounter with Aoife was such a negative one that he was stunned the two women were related in any way, but Doyle's information about James' illness and the pressure that would have placed on DS Kellett gave him pause to reassess his view of her.

The religious service was lengthy and, to Tiberius, largely unintelligible. However, it was mitigated if somewhat lengthened further by a soprano possessed of a stunningly powerful voice singing some beautiful hymns and songs throughout. The music soared through the vaulted spaces of the massive church and lifted the otherwise turgid and sombre proceedings to a special place. Even a died in the wool atheist like Tiberius felt moved by the beauty and serenity as she sung the Latin version of the hymn Ave Maria at the end. He could see people around him were moved to tears.

Gotta hand it to the Irish Catholic church, he thought to himself wryly, *they sure know how to put on a good show.*

At the end of the service people shuffled forward to the front of the church to commiserate with the bereaved family, which seemed to consist of just Ashling, Aoife and her parents and the little kid Cian. Tiberius decided against joining the massive queue and headed outside. Quite a few of the attendees were waiting outside also and Tiberius moved through them to the side of the large open space at the front of the church. He turned on his phone and checked his messages. Rayne had rang a few times and Doyle had sent him some texts. He rang Doyle first and was pleased to hear Doyle had managed to speak with his contact about their suspect and that he hoped to hear something shortly.

There was a movement in the crowd around the door and they moved back as the coffin was carried out on the shoulders of six men in identical black suits. They were followed by Aoife and Ashling and their parents. Once the coffin was placed in the hearse, the crowd moved towards the family and they were the centre of more hugs and handshaking and expressions of sympathy.

He was surprised to see some people with cameras outside the boundary of the church grounds on the public pathway. Doyle hadn't said that Aoife's husband was famous or maybe it was some other member of the family. Tiberius remembered going to a remembrance service for a school buddy who had been killed in an avalanche in Aspen and how those attending were plagued by aggressive paparazzi who were following up on a rumour that Britany Spears was going to attend. It turned out the organisers of the service had misspelt the name of his buddy's daughter Brittony, who had married a guy called Sears. These guys were more respectful though.

He began to move forward towards the family but by the time he got to within fifteen feet of them, they turned and got into the limo waiting for them. Tiberius was uncertain what to do as he didn't know whether or not it would be appropriate for him to go to the graveyard. He was uncomfortable. He felt out of his depth.

A tiny old lady was looking at him quizzically and said in an amused tone, "you look like a fish out of water, young man!"

"You got that right Ma'am," answered Tiberius with a grin. "I've never been to an Irish funeral before."

"And you don't know what to do next," she cackled. She was laughing at him but with a merry light in her eyes which suggested deep reservoirs of humour. "So let me analyse your situation?" She said, "you were heading for the two O'Malley girls? Which one?"

"Ah, I know them both Ma'am." Tiberius felt like a schoolboy being quizzed by a headmistress. She stared at him waiting.

"In a professional capacity," Tiberius added lamely.

"Well you certainly don't understand the real function of an Irish funeral, young man." She said sniffily.

After a moment, Tiberius, now thoroughly intimidated by this diminutive sparrow of a woman, asked her, "Umm, perhaps you could advise me as to whether or not it would be appropriate for me to go along to the graveyard and sympathise with the ladies there?"

She beamed up at him. "Yes indeed. Well done young man. There are approximately five opportunities to sympathise with the bereaved at every funeral not including Wakes, of course. I'll tell you what," she grabbed his wrist with a ferocious grip, "you drive me to the graveyard and back and I'll combine directions and illuminating your poor American mind with valuable cultural information. Is that a fair deal?"

"Sounds good to me Ma'am."

She turned and Tiberius found himself heading for his car, with his new-found companion's hand resting on his forearm, much like an old fashioned beau and his girl. Once they were settled in his car and following the funeral cortege, she piped up "So you never asked me my name. You're a very trusting sort for a policeman."

"How did you know I was a cop?" Tiberius was amused and surprised by her shrewdness.

"The files on the back seat have the Garda Logo on them.

And Aoife is some sort of policewoman as I recall," she said dismissively.

"My name is Tiberius Frost and you were going to tell me yours?" Tiberius was trying to head her off before she started interrogating him about his cases or the files on the seat behind. He figured there was nothing this feisty old lady wouldn't say or do!

"What a wonderful name! Named for a roman emperor. You had interesting parents, Tiberius. My name is Anne-Marie Bulloch. The name wouldn't mean much to you but my father was quite well known in his time. They even named a harbour after him. I, by way of contrast, am a humble psychologist."

"Ahh, so you've been analysing me?"

"Not at all. You Americans are as open as a book. Which is rather refreshing, I might add."

"So, what's the deal on Irish funerals?"

"Ahh, well done. Good memory, Tiberius! Well they provide a far more important service than just burying the recently deceased. They enable Irish people to meet, connect and, most importantly, reconnect. Also, the one excuse every Irish employer will accept is when someone says they have to go to a funeral. They are social events and gatherings. Usually the only sad people are the deceased's nearest and dearest, or those cut out of the will." She cackled again.

"As to the etiquette, well, one can approach the bereaved and sympathise with them at various times. Just prior to the saying of prayers in the Funeral Home or at the private dwelling of the bereaved where the corpse is laid out in the coffin for all to view. Just after the saying of prayers at the Funeral Home. Just before the Funeral Mass and just after the Funeral Mass, both of which opportunities you fluffed, by the way. And finally, at the graveside, just after the prayers are said and the body has been placed in the grave and buried. Although it is more customary to place a cover over the grave now and fill it in later. In times gone by, the male members of the bereaved's family and their closest friends would have filled in the grave by hand. Gone are the days! So you will have your opportunity to speak to your friends once all is complete, yes?"

"That's very helpful. Thank you, Anne-Marie."

They had arrived at the graveyard and parked. Tiberius escorted Anne-Marie along the grassy pathways between the graves as they followed the other mourners to a spot in the far corner of the graveyard. At Anne-Marie's insistence they walked right up to stand at the side of the grave opposite the funeral party. Tiberius looked up from the grave to find Ashling looking at him with surprise on her face, which slowly gave way to a soft small smile. He nodded to her and their attention was grabbed by a burst of loud and discordant feedback from the priest's portable P.A. system. Everyone grimaced and Anne-Marie said loudly "Lord knows why these fools need all this technology nowadays. Modern priests no longer have the lung capacity to project their voices properly. Milksops, every one!"

Tiberius stifled a grin, noticing others doing the same.

The harassed looking young priest began reading the prayers with the people around the graveyard automatically responding to the prayers in a rhythmic manner. Then they stopped and the four gravediggers lowered the coffin slowly into the grave. After a few moments, the priest began again and then was silent as Aoife stepped forward and dropped a single soft reddish-pink rose into the grave.

"How appropriate," murmured Anne-Marie quietly beside him. He looked at her. "It's a Canadian Wild Rose," she whispered. "James was from Calgary in Alberta. It's the national flower of Alberta. Lovely thought."

A few moments later the priest nodded at the grave diggers who came forward and placed a large cover with a green artificial grass top, over the grave. Then the Funeral Home attendants began placing floral tributes on top.

Slowly people moved towards Aoife and Ashling and began

shaking hands and embracing them. Tiberius felt a poke in the side from Anne-Marie. "Now young man. You can take me over to speak with the family." At this point in time Tiberius had decided he was just going to do whatever she ordered. He figured it was the simplest solution. So they joined the short queue and patiently shuffled their way forward. Then they were in front of Aoife. Anne-Marie gave her a hug and whispered something in her ear which Tiberius didn't catch. He put out his hand to her and said "I'm really sorry. I should have been here yesterday too but I didn't know. Doyle rang me and I'm just very sorry."

"Thanks." She seemed distant. "It was good of you to come."

Numb, he reckoned. He hadn't been looking forward to the encounter, if he was honest, knowing how sharp-tongued she could be. He wasn't sure she would even accept his presence, but he hadn't properly understood just how upset she was. Though, she didn't seem to be hugely distraught. Just cool, distant, collected. Under control. *One strong woman,* he thought.

The person behind moved close to him and he moved forward to find Anne-Marie kissing Ashling on both cheeks and pinching her hip. "You need to put on weight Missy." She admonished the younger woman. "Too much of this exercise nonsense and gymnasiums and that! Now you've gotten rid of that cretin Brady, you need to find a nicer man! Are you listening to me Ashling?"

Ashling leant forward with a big smile and gave the old lady another hug. "You're incorrigible Anne-Marie. So naughty!" She looked at Tiberius and he put out his hand again. They shook quite formally and he said, "I'm really sorry about your brother-in-law passing."

"Thanks Tiberius. We're having some tea and sandwiches back at my parent's place if you want to bring your girlfriend." She winked at Anne-Marie, who retorted archly. "That won't be possible as he has to take me home. I'm quite tired now."

"Ah. OK, sure." Tiberius just agreed and moved forward with Anne-Marie. Ashling smiled sympathetically at him and said, "see you another time." Then "I hope?"

"Definitely. You've got my number so just call whenever it suits."

"OK."

Anne-Marie whisked them along the line of chief mourners and marched Tiberius briskly out of the graveyard and back to his car.

"Actually, I wasn't serious about getting back to my home. I just don't get on with Ingrid any more. She's their mother. We went to school together. She's a good sort but a bit of an idiot." She informed Tiberius, once they were back in the car. "We could go for afternoon tea in the Shelbourne Hotel, if you like. My treat?"

"I've never had afternoon tea," he replied, a little warily.

"Well, once again it falls to me to elevate your colonial cultural awareness and introduce you to the concept of afternoon tea in one of the nicer hotels of Europe. Although it is more lunchtime than time for tea but I'm sure they'll accommodate me."

"OK Anne-Marie. Whatever you say."

"What a good boy you are, Master Frost!" she purred triumphantly.

Forty minutes later they were ensconced in the very elegant surroundings of the Lord Mayor's Lounge, part of the two hundred year old Shelbourne Hotel overlooking the leafy expanse of St. Stephen's Green. Much to Tiberius's amusement the staff fluttered around Anne-Marie as though she was royalty.

When he asked about it, she remarked casually that the hotel manager was her nephew. "I have lots of nephews and nieces, dotted all over the place, usually in quite useful roles."

The food was very nice. Very simple and tasty. A selection of sandwiches, dainty pastries and cakes on a three plate display unit, each on top of the other. Tiberius hadn't realised how hungry he was and when Anne-Marie informed him she wasn't and that he would have to make up the difference, it was all the invitation he needed.

Anne-Marie had been telling him all about the history of the hotel and some of the famous people who had stayed there, when she stopped suddenly and asked him "how long have you been enamoured of Ashling?"

Tiberius choked and spluttered. He drank some tea and eyed her warily.

"Sorry, what do you mean Anne-Marie?" he asked, stalling for time.

"Oh I think you know well what the word 'enamoured' means. It's from the French word 'amour', to love!" She flashed back at him.

"Well. I've only met her a few times."

Anne-Marie gave him what could be described as an old fashioned look.

"She's very nice but going through a tough time at the moment so I reckon the last thing she needs right now is more confusion in her life." Tiberius continued.

"Good man. That's exactly what I told her. So I've contacted some mutual friends and arranged for her and Aoife and little Cian to go to the French Alps for a few weeks skiing." She watched Tiberius alertly as she spoke.

"That's a great idea. They all probably need a break." Tiberius was surprised to feel a bit put out Ashling wouldn't be around for some time.

"Your enthusiasm for my suggestion is somewhat less than convincing." Anne-Marie teased.

"No. I think you're on the money. It's just what they all need. Do they ski?"

"Ahh yes indeed. In fact, I would have to say Ashling and Aoife both ski like goddesses! Minimum effort married to maximum style and all totally natural. Which is why the best way to teach people to ski is when they're ridiculously young. Do you?"

"Ski?"

"Yes. What else did you think I meant." Anne-Marie was enjoying herself hugely now at Tiberius's expense.

"Sure. I ski. Lots of Colorado trips when I was a kid."

"The Rockies, eh? Challenging off-piste I'm led to believe. Never skied there myself. I primarily skied in Europe and Argentina, before I got too old and withered. So, Ashling." She returned to her topic, like a dog with a bone.

"Yes?" Tiberius reverted to his normal monosyllabic style, under this verbal bombardment from Anne-Marie.

"Will you be looking her up on her return, peut-etre?" She asked

"Who knows" he replied.

"Well don't be too laid back pardner," she stressed the last word. "Once word gets out she's single again, Ashling won't be lacking in suitors, my dear."

"Ah. OK. Anne-Marie."

"Just trying to be helpful," she smiled.

"I get it."

"Try some of these little cupcakes, dear. I can't touch them. My cardiologist would have a fit, but you should be able to polish them off quite easily." Satisfied her point was clearly made and understood, she moved on to chat about other things. The time flew and when they were leaving she refused point blank to allow Tiberius to pay, saying "your money's no good here Tiberius. They won't take it. Trust me."

They left and he drove her south to a beautiful old Georgian house looking out over the bay. It had been her family home but she explained she had arranged to have it subdivided into eight large apartments, to provide her with an income and a home with no stairs for her to fall up or down "as I totter towards my final curtain."

"I shan't invite you in today Master Frost as I'm quite tired, but perhaps you might come and visit an old woman sometime in the future?"

"I'd be delighted." Tiberius replied sincerely, thinking he hadn't had such an interesting or pleasant time in quite a while.

"Then it's a date." She reached up and pulling his head down to her level, pecked him on the cheek and turned to go into her home.

As he drove away, Tiberius thought to himself that he had just met one of life's great characters. One of those unique souls whose lust for life and amazing energy impacted positively on everyone she encountered.

He checked his watch. It was three pm and when he stopped at the next set of traffic lights he checked his phone to see several missed calls from Rayne.

He called her and she answered immediately.

"Hi Rayne, sorry I missed your calls I was at a funeral. Did you speak with Beth and Dane?"

"There's a problem Tiberius. We can't find Dane."

"I take it that's unusual for him? Where's Beth?"

"With me."

"Where are you? Are you secure?"

"We're in my suite at the Intercontinental and my security guys are in place."

"I'm on my way."

CHAPTER TWENTY FOUR

Tiberius met Doyle inside the front door of the Intercontinental Hotel and they grabbed the first lift to the top floor. Two large gentlemen in dark suits and sporting earpieces were waiting outside the lift. "Mr Frost?" The taller, more muscular one asked.

"That's me," Tiberius answered.

"This way please." They led them down the hallway to a door at the end where a third clone in a suit was standing. He opened the door and Doyle entered ahead of Tiberius. The head of the team placed his hand on Tiberius's arm and said quietly. "My name's Gant. We've two in the hallway at all times. One on the door. One on each of the balconies to the suite and two in the suite next door. OK?"

"Thanks," said Tiberius, impressed with the other man's discreet, efficient approach and went through.

Beth rose from the couch she had been sitting on and approached Tiberius quickly. "Dane's missing."

"How long?" He asked.

"Since sometime this morning," Beth replied.

"That's less than twenty-four hours," interjected Doyle. "Usually we don't regard someone as missing for at least that period of time."

"You don't understand." Beth replied hotly. "Dane's a creature of habit. Of absolute habit. Especially when he's coding. And he's coding at the moment. He's improving the security of the platform, so he would never vary his routine. Not even slightly. It means that for the next week I would know exactly where he'll be and what he'll be doing at different times of the day. He's a bit OCD like that."

"Dane is OCD?" asked Doyle.

"Dane had a tough childhood and his teenage years were no joke either. If it wasn't for Mary, his foster mother, God knows what would have happened. She changed everything. Took care of him. Protected him. The whole nine yards. She's amazing. Anyway. He's very, very predictable. It's one of the benefits of his Obsessive Compulsive Disorder. Seriously, I know where I can find him at any point in time. Any variation in his routine is out of character and a big deal. Dane being missing for several hours has never happened before."

"I'm sorry Beth, but I have to make the point that Dane does sound like he may have mental stability issues and as such this may be just a function of one of them." Doyle replied to her rapid fire monologue.

"No. No. No. This is so out of character. You just don't understand."

"Am I right you've both recently been informed by Rayne as to the value of this software you've created with Dane?" asked Tiberius.

"Yes. So?"

"I guess Tiberius is concerned that such a life changing event brings with it, its own stresses," added Doyle, trying to slow things down, to bring some perspective.

Rayne spoke up for the first time. "I think Beth has a point. What's inside Dane's head is potentially worth billions. Having said that, I've spent some time with the guy recently and I don't think he's wacko. Nor do I feel that he's had some sort of breakdown, and I've had some experience with mentally unstable people." She stared at Tiberius in an unspoken reference to their mother whose mental problems had blighted their youth.

"OK. What do we know at this point?" Tiberius asked. "When was he last seen? Where was he last seen, and has he missed any appointments?"

"Last night, we all had dinner together and my driver dropped Dane and Beth off to their apartments on the University Campus. I've checked with him and he saw Dane go into his apartment building in his rear-view mirror as he was turning the car." Rayne answered.

"The last thing I said to him was that I'd meet him for breakfast this morning in our usual spot, and he agreed." Beth followed up.

"There was nothing odd or unusual about his tone?" asked Doyle. "Did he seem under any form of pressure or was there any extra emotion present in his voice that you can recall?"

"No. Everything was very normal. Very ordinary." Beth replied in a flat voice which radiated disapproval of Doyle's line of questioning.

"So, at this point he's missing for the past seven and a half hours." Tiberius said automatically, thinking hard. He turned to Beth. "You mentioned his foster mother. Mary, was it?"

"Yes. And before you ask, I rang her number a couple of times but she hasn't called back."

"Oh?" Doyle sounded interested.

"She's a foster mum. She has tons of kids in her tiny little house in the middle of The Liberties." Said Beth. "It's a part of Dublin central," she added in answer to the unspoken question on Tiberius's face."

"OK. So you just called her cellphone?" continued Doyle.

"Yeah."

"Does she have a landline into her house?"

"I think so."

"Do you have it?"

"I'll check." Beth crouched over her phone.

Tiberius looked over her head at Doyle, who said "I'm on it. I'll check with Social Welfare."

"Maybe try the Garda Vetting section first. She would have had to be checked out before they allowed her to take on fostering kids."

"Good thinking, Boss."

Tiberius turned to Rayne and said quietly. "Well?"

"Well what Tiberius?" she sounded annoyed.

"Do you reckon he could have lost the plot or are you concerned about his security?"

"The latter. Definitely the latter. He's a cool cucumber, highly intelligent and I think he's quite together, Bro."

"OK, thanks Raynie."

"I have her home number," said Beth.

"Call it out." Answered Tiberius.

"Oh One Eight Eight Three Oh Five Seven One."

Tiberius punched it into his phone.

"Hello?" a woman's voice answered.

"Hi is Mary there please?"

"Who want's ta know?"

"Sorry, I'm Detective Chief Inspector Frost of the Garda. I'm trying to locate Mary to discuss one of her ex-foster children with her."

"She's gone to the hospital."

"What happened?"

"She has ta gerra yoke removed from her back by the doc."

"Which hospital?"

"Hang on pal." He could hear the woman shouting in the background "Noreen! Wha hospital's Maree getting dat thingy removed from her back?" He couldn't hear the reply but a moment later the woman was back on and said "Beaumont hospital, an if yuuz are talkin to her, will ya teller dat Noreen an me's got it all under controwel, OK? Everything's hunky-dory wid de kids."

"Will do. Thank you." Tiberius put down the phone. "Doyle, Beaumont Hospital." He called out. "I reckon an elective procedure for some kind of skin surgery?"

"OK. I'll check."

Tiberius turned to Beth. "We'll track down this lady and hopefully she'll shed some light on Dane's whereabouts. Is it possible he might have gone to the hospital with her?"

"Yesss," Beth sounded unsure for the first time. "If Mary asked him to, he'd do anything for her."

She was silent for a few moments and then piped up "but he would have contacted me somehow, and he would never have left his office with the servers on and his laptop wasn't in the safe he keeps there."

"Sorry Beth, can you explain the significance of that? What does it mean in terms of his likely movements?" asked Tiberius.

"Well, he would have put the laptop in the safe if he was going to return and do more work, ditto with leaving the servers running. There are failsafe's built into the servers and they will power down if he doesn't return within a certain timeframe, but that is a pain in the ass because if they haven't been manually powered down by Dane then it takes ages to get them operational again as the system assumes a breach. If he left the laptop there it means he was definitely going to return after we had had breakfast together, but the fact that it's still there and that the servers hadn't powered down means he never made it back."

"That's very useful Beth." Tiberius said encouragingly. "It narrows down Dane's movements even more."

"Boss?" Doyle called Tiberius over.

"Yes."

"She never showed up for her hospital appointment." Doyle said quietly and looked at Tiberius with concern on his face.

"OK. We need to escalate this."

"I'm on it." Doyle headed for the door.

Tiberius turned back to Beth and Rayne. "We can't locate Mary either. She didn't show up for an appointment she had in a Dublin Hospital to have some elective surgical procedure. The impression I have is that it isn't an easy or a simple task for her to take time out as she had to arrange for two other ladies to mind her foster children in her place. So, it's unlikely she would have just skipped the appointment or done something else."

Beth looked stricken. "Ohhh no!" She moaned. "This gets worse by the minute."

Rayne put her arm around the upset girl. "Beth," she said "Tiber is really good with this kind of stuff, honey. If anyone can find them it's him."

"Oh God. I hope so." She looked up at Tiberius with tears in her eyes.

Tiberius's phone rang and he went into the bedroom to answer it.

"Frost here."

"Boss, it's Prendergast. Doyle rang and instructed us. We've put out missing persons alerts and Sweeney is working the computers. He's located pictures for both of them already. Fortunately, he had just installed a computer system here in the Campus Office so we are using that instead of heading into Donnybrook. Saves time."

"Good work"

"Yeah, well that's the only good news, I'm afraid."

"It's early days yet."

"No. I mean we've a problem with resources."

"Go on."

"They reckon some suspect related to the Shannon attacks might be still in the country and is trying to get out so they've got priority. Our little request is going to go to the bottom of the pile."

"Do what you can. Just ensure every point of exit is informed and get the photo's out ASAP."

"Sure thing, Boss."

*   *   *

Later that evening, Beth and Rayne were sitting in a little bistro a few hundred yards from the Intercontinental Hotel called "The French Paradox."

"It's really authentic and casual, so perfect for us," Rayne had explained as, yet again, she overrode Beth's protests that she wasn't hungry.

They were sitting at a table in the very back of the narrow restaurant. The table nearest to them was occupied by two of Rayne's less obvious security team members with another two parked outside in an SUV.

"There must be something we can do." Beth sounded frustrated.

"I doubt it Beth." Rayne answered. "Unless you've got a magic wand we have to go through the official channels, but at least we've got Tiberius on the inside and he'll keep us updated." Beth subsided and continued eating in a distracted way.

When they were finished eating and had just been served coffee, Beth said "look, this may sound a bit scatty but I can't help feeling there's something we're missing here. Or maybe something I'm missing. I just can't figure it out. I know it sounds a bit arrogant but I'm sure there's something I'm not seeing which would provide us with some answers."

"Can't help you there Beth. Maybe you should sleep on it? Might come to you in the morning?"

"That's the problem. I don't want to sleep on it. I feel time is essential here. I think Dane may not have the luxury of time."

"Beth, if you don't mind my saying so I think you're being a bit melodramatic, which, believe me, this situation we're in doesn't need right now."

"Rayne. I know I'm right." Beth sounded more forceful as they argued, more sure of herself.

One of the skills Rayne prided herself on was what Tiberius called her 'bullshit detector'. She could tell when someone was talking BS and when they were genuine. She realised Beth was convinced she knew something that might help them.

"I'm serious Beth. When you're stressed like now, it's very difficult to figure things out, to find solutions. In fact, at times like these, the harder you search, the more elusive the solution becomes. Why don't you stay in the suite tonight? There's three bedrooms and my guys will be on duty all night. You'll feel more secure and I won't be worrying about you."

"OK. Why not?"

They got up and Rayne paid the bill. Thirty minutes later Beth was lying on the large double bed in her room staring up at the ceiling, wide awake. She got up and went into the private bathroom adjoining her bedroom and washed her face. As she dried herself, she looked around and decided that the bathroom was larger than her studio apartment on campus. She went back and lay on the bed again, but sleep refused to come so she turned on her laptop. She started going through emails which she and Dane had exchanged recently to see if she could find any clues. When that proved fruitless, she logged on to the secure messaging system she and Dane used and began trawling through recent online chats between the two of them. She couldn't shake the feeling that she was missing something important. Something which could help Dane. But what? Until she figured it out sleep would continue to elude her. A noisy wind had sprung up outside which was the forerunner of a storm coming in from the West.

Rayne was also awake. However, she was trying to work out whether or not to tell Deng about Dane's disappearance as she sat in front of her mirror brushing her long hair. *Come to think of it,* she thought to herself. *I wouldn't put it past that sneaky little creep to have kidnapped Dane and be sweating the information out of him. Saving himself millions. No. Hundreds of millions.* The concept was compelling. She thought about it from different angles while she mechanically swept the brush through her hair in long slow strokes. The more she considered it, the more likely it seemed.

As a possible scenario which would explain the disappearance of Dane, it presented her with two problems. Firstly, should she share this with Tiberius or not? Secondly, how could she use it to ensure Deng didn't cut her out of the pie? If she shared the idea with Tiberius and he was able to locate Dane, would he do so in time? In this case, 'in time' meant before Deng or his employees were able to secure sufficient information from Dane so they wouldn't need to complete the deal she had negotiated. If Tiberius didn't locate him in time then Deng didn't need her and her lifeline was gone.

Then it struck her she might still be able to sell the software to another buyer, albeit for a lesser amount, as long as no one knew that Deng already had the Intellectual Property.

Well Deng certainly wasn't going to be broadcasting what he had done, she reasoned. *So maybe do nothing and let matters take their course. A text to the next highest bidder alerting him to the level of Deng's offer might just spur him to increase his bid. At a valuation of two hundred and fifty million, I will still make enough to resolve all of my problems but hey, the more bidders the merrier!*

The other alternative would be to contact Deng directly and tell him that she knew what he had done and try and extricate some money in return for her silence. That, however, was a very risky move. Rayne was under no illusions as to what Deng might be capable of. She had researched him in the past when he was bidding to acquire a previous business she had been involved in and her contacts had come back to her with a warning not to get involved with him in any way. One guy in particular had said that people who got mixed up with Deng either ended up doing whatever he told them to or having very unpleasant experiences, with the emphasis on unpleasant.

Still, if I'm not greedy, perhaps just twenty million? Is that a fair price for allowing Deng to get his hands on a billion-dollar property? Or rather not getting in his way while he did so? Rayne decided to take her own advice and sleep on it.

CHAPTER
TWENTY FIVE

Ashling looked around for Cian. She couldn't see him anywhere. Suddenly worried, she jumped to her feet. She relaxed when she saw him in Aoife's arms. Aoife had come
from a meeting in police headquarters at Harcourt Street
which meant she couldn't travel to the airport with them.
Cian had obviously spotted his aunt and ran to greet her.
This trip to the French Alps for skiing was only partly Ashling's idea. Now she thought about it, it was probably ninety
five percent Anne-Marie's idea seeing as she had pretty much
organised the whole thing. Although it was only the day
after the funeral, she felt it would be good for Aoife to get
away and as Robert hadn't properly moved out of the family
home yet, it would take her and Cian away while that was
going on also.

The night poor James had passed away and before they all
went to bed, Aoife had recommended a lawyer she knew
to advise Ashling on what to do next. The lawyer had responded to Aoife's text by ringing Ashling the following
day. When Ashling told her about James' passing, she briskly
apologised for interrupting matters but turned out to be
pretty tenacious and quickly persuaded Ashling to take the
initiative and begin divorce proceedings. She also told Ashling that it would be a sensible idea to take a break and that
she would monitor Robert's departure and protect her interests while she was away. Fortunately, Aoife knew this lawyer
detested Robert and his father, going back several years. So

Ashling was content they would be less likely to try on any of the sneaky tricks, she knew Robert's father was famous for.

She stood up and hugged Aoife. "Hi Eef, how are you?" She whispered in her sister's ear.

"Grand," came the terse answer. Then Aoife sat and said "well to be honest, I don't really know how I am. I suppose guilty is the dominant feeling?"

"Guilty? What have you to feel guilty about? You were so loyal, and supportive to him. And even when you discovered about the MS you still stuck by him when a lot of other girls would have ran for cover!" said Ashling indignantly.

"No. It's just that ...." Aoife tailed off. "It's just. God this is so hard!"

"No rush. Let it lie for now, yes?"

"No. I want to say it to someone. I feel guilty because I'm ... just ... so ... terribly ... relieved ... he's ... gone." Aoife was staring at Cian who was excitedly looking at all of the planes moving around on the apron just outside the window of the departures area they were sitting in.

"Oh." Ashling was uncomfortable. Unsure what to say.

"I know. What a bitch?" Aoife smiled ruefully.

"No. No. Why are you relieved? Because he was suffering so much?"

"Honestly? Him and me. We were both in hell if I'm totally honest about it."

"Well you shouldn't feel guilty." Said Ashling stoutly. "You paid your dues Eef! You more than paid your dues."

"Yeah. I don't know, Ash. Maybe once some time passes and I get a better perspective, I'll begin remembering why we were together and some of the good times. It's just that everything was drowned in the godawful suffering he went through. That illness killed more than James. It killed our marriage, our love for each other," she sighed heavily.

Aoife noticed Cian climbing up on the metal barrier protecting the glass wall of the Departures Lounge, as he tried to get a better view of the planes and hive of activity below on the tarmac. She smiled and said "anyway, let's get this little guy on board before he gets so excited he jumps through that window and hijacks something just to get going."

Ashling grinned, taking it as a positive sign that Aoife had made an, albeit weak, attempt at humour as they watched Cian bouncing on his feet and hanging onto the barrier, staring out at the planes.

"Did your meeting go OK?" she asked Aoife

"Yes. I've gotten compassionate leave, although I know they're not happy about it."

"Not happy?" said Ashling. "The bastards!"

"Look Ash, the Shannon situation is very complex and a huge drain on resources. I don't think that we as an investigating body have ever been as stretched. Even during the Troubles." Aoife looked up as the flight was called and Cian headed back towards them. "Actually, they reckon one of the suspects may be still on the loose somewhere in Ireland and it's all hands on deck trying to locate him. They're not happy with me taking time out now. Normally they'd be very understanding but...." She trailed off as Cian arrived and clamped her in another ferocious hug. Ashling gave Cian his headphones and he put them on, grabbing his Mum's hand tightly while they queued up to present their travel documents at the Departure Gate.

Shortly after that, as they headed down the steps and across the tarmac to the plane, Aoife turned to Ashling and said, "I discovered Tiernan Doyle pulled some strings to help me get the leave."

"You sound surprised."

"Oh Ash, I've been a complete bitch to that man any time our paths crossed. So, yes, I'm surprised he would lift a finger to help me."

"You never know who the good ones are until you need someone's help. Did you say Doyle? Is that the guy who works with Tiberius Frost?"

"Yes. How do you know Tiberius Frost? He came to the funeral, didn't he? Can't remember properly. So many faces."

"Tiernan Doyle is Cian's Rugby coach in Blackrock and Tiberius Frost meets with him after training on Saturday mornings."

"Doyle? Wow, never would have thought that."

"He's very good and very fair with the kids."

They stood in the obligatory Ryanair queue for the plane, at the bottom of the steps.

"Another point in his favour is that he told Robert to get lost when he tried to muscle in on the coaching and wouldn't take no for an answer. Robert was livid. Wanted to take Cian out of the club," added Ashling as they shuffled along.

"Another argument?"

"No Cian dealt with this one. He threw the mother of all tantrums and Robert backed down. But, of course, he never came to another practice or game."

"God! He's the child not Cian. So has Robert ever seen Cian play in a match?"

"No."

"You might be better off."

"He's his father Eef!"

"No. I mean if he thought Cian was any good, he'd be all over it like a rash. Messing things up even more."

"Yeah. Maybe. Anyway, it's a moot point now isn't it. That lawyer has initiated divorce proceedings for me."

"She's pretty ferocious, isn't she?" Aoife smiled.

"My God. I'm glad she's on my side and not Roberts."

"No chance. She went to University and then studied Law in the same class as Robert, and of course, when he discovered she was gay, he made her life as miserable as he could."

"Eef. You're dreadful. Still," Ashling added, "if she nails him to the wall, it can only be to my advantage. As long as everything is done discreetly. I don't want any publicity. It would upset Mum."

"Did you make that clear to her?"

"Yes."

"That's fine then."

They had reached the doorway of the airplane.

They had booked three seats in a row and they put Cian in the middle playing a game on a computer tablet. After an hour or so, Aoife was gazing out the window. As she looked out of the window of the plane, she thought of how each small town gradually appeared and disappeared like tiny golden spider webs, dotted here and there against the darkening French countryside below. She felt strangely secure and comfortable flying high above them.

Shortly afterwards they arrived at Nice airport and were met in arrivals by Ashling's friends who were hosting them in their cosy house in the picturesque hamlet of St. Etienne de Tinee, high in the mountain range which runs between Southern France and Italy.

Later that night, Ashling was sitting by the window of her bedroom on the third floor of her friends' house looking at the dark and empty village street below. Snowflakes swirled through the beam of light from her window. She loved snow. They didn't get much in Ireland due to the temperate climate of the island. Fortunately for Ashling her parents used to bring her to St. Anton in the Austrian Tyrol every winter. She learned to ski there and began a lifelong passion, spending as much time as possible in the wintry mountains of Europe. She was pleased to see the snow as they arrived, knowing it would create excellent skiing conditions. Now they were settled in, she finally felt a measure of calm and an objective distance from her problems. She felt cosy and safe in the warm bedroom with Cian sleeping soundly in the bed behind her. She could hear her friends chatting with Aoife in the kitchen on the floor above.

Her mind went back to the funeral and how she had suddenly seen Tiberius standing at the far side of the grave. They had shared a moment then. Definitely a moment. God!

What was she thinking? At her brother-in-law's funeral, flirting with a guy she hardly knew.

Still he was pretty good looking, in a lean, dark kind of way. And you could drown in those eyes. He came across as compassionate and kind and pretty sincere. Everything about him pointed to his being a straight-up, genuine, kind of person. Which would be a relief after Robert, who was so habitually deceitful that his right hand didn't know what his left hand was up to!

OK Kiddo. You need to stop now, she told herself. *This is all a bit Mills & Boon-ish. The last thing I need right now is to get involved with someone else.*

What was really surprising though, was how he knew Anne-Marie? She was such a character and always up to something despite her advanced years. She wouldn't be surprised if Anne-Marie had bullied Tiberius into escorting her to the funeral. And God alone knew what she forced him into afterwards. Tiberius was such a nice guy that he would be like putty in the hands of Anne-Marie, one of her Grandmother's most formidable friends. Actually strike that, Ingrid's most formidable friend. She was the only one of Ingrid's friends who would take her to task for some of the outrageous things she came out with and had actually called her "a blithering idiot" at a dinner party once.

She had always known that Anne-Marie, whose nickname amongst those who knew her best was 'Ammo', didn't like Robert. The first time they had met, at a party in Ingrid's house, Ammo had quietly looked at Robert, who was holding forth about some new legislation or other and declined Aoife's invitation to introduce her, saying "no introduction necessary dear girl. I've seen enough!" And that was that. Robert was persona non grata whenever Anne-Marie was around. The way she was hanging off Tiberius's arm, Ashling reckoned Anne-Marie had a considerably higher opinion of him, which, in retrospect was not an easy thing to achieve.

When a previous Irish Taoiseach offered her a lift from

Achill Island where she had been holidaying back to Dublin in one of his son's helicopters. She informed him she only travelled with people she could trust. When the leader of the Irish government had protested that his son's pilot was very competent, she replied coldly she wasn't talking about the pilot, but about the company. She compounded the insult by then sweetly inquiring did he intend walking back to Dublin, in which case she'd reconsider the offer?

CHAPTER TWENTY SIX

The pilot's voice came through a speaker above Mr Black's head. "Strong winds at Lydd Airport. Going to make landing tricky."

Mr Black cursed softly, undoing the buckle on his seatbelt in preparation to go to the cockpit and insist that they land, when the pilot added "we're going to do our best to land but it will be bumpy. Please ensure your seatbelt is securely fastened." Mr Black sighed and sat back, closing the buckle on his seatbelt.

The plane had initially diverted to RAF Portreath Airbase on the south western tip of Cornwall to try and go around this growing storm but it had changed direction, so they ended up heading straight along the coast for Lydd Airport.

The plane began dropping height and the impact of the turbulent atmosphere was immediately felt in the cabin as the plane seesawed around the sky. It ceased briefly and calmed down. For a few moments, he could see the lights of some town far below begin to get brighter and take on a little definition through the rain outside his window as the plane lost height. However the plane resumed being buffeted by the elements as it continued to approach the airport.

The turbulence increased as the plane got closer and closer. Mr Black was gripping onto the seat to keep steady. He twisted in the seat to check the two boxes were still securely strapped into position. They hadn't budged. As he turned back the plane bumped heavily, with the wings tilting wildly up and down. Mr Black could hear the screech of the rubber on the landing wheels. Somehow the pilot got the nose down without dragging a wing along the ground and then corrected sharply as the plane was pointing diagonally across the runway. Mr Black knew a bit about flying having taken lessons in the past and was impressed at the pilot's skill. He understood how tricky the landing had been.

The plane continued along the runway heading north east, seemingly taking time to slow down. Mr Black jumped out of his seat and went to the two boxes. He put his ear to a small hole in the wooden cover of one box and listened intently. He could hear what sounded like steady breathing and was satisfied. However, when he went to the second box with Dane inside, he heard what sounded like a groan. He took out his aerosol from his jacket and fitted a small straw to the nozzle which he then fed into the hole and depressed the button on the spray sending some more of what he called "Sir Barty's Magic Mist" into the box for the occupant to ingest.

He waited a short while and then put his ear to the hole. Normal service had resumed and the occupant was breathing heavily. It was important that both occupants were unconscious for the next part of the journey. He went to the door, put on the mask he had used in Dublin and waited. After a few more seconds, he could hear the plane's engines slowing down as the plane turned about. He had the door open before the plane had stopped. Four men dressed in black combat gear were waiting outside on the tarmac. Mr Black retreated immediately and went to the rear of the cabin, entering the galley and closing the door behind him. He could hear them jump on board and walk to the boxes, lift them and carry them to the door. After a moment he heard the door of the plane slam closed and he could see the men place the boxes in the back of what looked like a long wheelbase military Landrover with blacked out windows and drive away towards a large u-shaped building over to the side of the runway.

Mr Black took off the mask and walked back to his seat. The engines increased their noise and the plane taxied back towards the Terminal building. The pilot turned right just before the Terminal and taxied to the end of tarmacadam apron past eight or nine other small planes. Mr Black went back into the galley and waited. About ten minutes after the plane stopped and the engines were turned off, he could hear the door to the cockpit open and then the side door. Then it slammed shut. Still he waited patiently in the darkened galley for another half hour.

Mr Black took out a black balaclava and put it on. Then he walked slowly around the interior of the plane carefully scanning the view through all of the windows in all directions. The pilots had left the door to the cockpit open and he stood just inside the corridor in the open doorway checking there was no one around. Finally satisfied, he opened the exit door and climbed out, closing the door gently behind him. He walked around the rear of the plane heading for the field which bordered the area where the planes were parked. The rain and howling wind were perfect camouflage as he made his way across the grass heading towards the runway and turned left about one hundred yards before it. He slipped behind a couple of sheds where he found a track which he followed taking him parallel to the runaway and back to where they had unloaded the boxes.

He walked for about three hundred yards along the track until the u-shaped building loomed up ahead in the darkness. He slipped around the end of one wing to find the Landrover parked in the lee of the building. He checked the two boxes in the back and got into the driver's seat. There was a chain and an open padlock sitting on the front passenger's seat. He turned on the engine and with just the sidelights on, he drove over rough ground towards an open gate. Mr Black drove through the gate and stopped. He got out, closed the gate behind him and secured it with the chain and padlock.

Then he jumped in and drove away.

Ten minutes later he was driving along the eastern edge of the tiny village of Lydd and heading south. Leaving the village behind Mr Black drove along a variety of small concrete roads until he had passed into the vast firing range known as the Lydd Ranges which ran from south of the village all the way to the coast. He left the road and turned onto a rough track taking him deeper into the bleak and remote landscape. The wind had finally blown the rainclouds away and a bright full moon shone. Every time he visited, Mr Black felt that it was like travelling through a pebbled wasteland. Its remoteness was one of the reasons why it was one of the British Army's oldest Firing Ranges. Miles and miles of smooth small stones rounded and shaped by the sea which had heaped them along the coast and then smeared across the landscape by the constant wind, moving and shifting them against each other like an unsatisfied sculptor, unhappy with their shapes as it ground them down, day after day. None of this mattered to Mr Black. He just knew he wouldn't be disturbed and that Sir Barty's influence guaranteed it.

About fifteen minutes later he came to the sea's edge and a small wire compound containing an ugly, battered looking building looking out over the stony beach. He got out, unlocked the gate and drove through, locking it again. He turned the Landrover around and backed up to the side of the entrance to the building. He opened the back door and then knelt at the wall and opened a small door that was about three feet square. Mr Black then slid out one of the boxes in the back of the Landrover so that the front edge was resting on the concrete step of the doorway. With a grunt he lifted the back of the box and slid it into the black hole. He could hear it sliding down a ramp and then come to a halt without too much of a bang. He reached into the back of the Landrover and took out a cushion and a staple gun which he used to fix the cushion to the front edge of the box. He slid the box to the side and then out and shoved it into the hole and down the ramp. He listened and heard a muffled thump as one box banged into the other below. The cushion seemed to have done its job and softened the impact of one box hitting the other and not damaging it or the occupants. *Not that it's too big a deal*, he smiled. He closed the hatch and locked it. Then he drove the jeep into a shed on the right of the gate. He got out and closed the doors. He was whistling merrily as he walked back to the main building, where he unlocked the main door and went inside.

CHAPTER TWENTY SEVEN

Beth was eating a croissant which was perfectly cooked and still warm but from which she derived no enjoyment. She was sipping on a coffee when Rayne came into the kitchen area of the suite.

"Good morning," said Rayne brightly.

"Morning," Beth's head stayed bent over her food. Rayne looked at her with mild annoyance, thinking that she really didn't need to have to deal with this crap first thing in the morning. *Still*, she thought, *to be fair, Beth is just trying to process a situation which would be outside of the bounds of normality for most folks.*

Actually, Beth was doing nothing of the sort. She was carefully going over her movements of the last few days to see if she could come up with the answer to whatever it was that was bugging her. She was more and more convinced that if she could solve this, it would help lead them to Dane.

The bell rang and they could hear one of Rayne's security team open the door. They heard Tiberius's voice talking to the man and then he came into the room.

"Great." His eyes lit up. "Croissants. I haven't had breakfast yet."

"Any news?" Rayne poured him coffee and he sat back opposite them taking a huge bite out of his pastry and following it with a mouthful of coffee. Beth didn't even say hello. Once he had swallowed both he said "Very little. There has been no sighting of either of them at any airports, ports or elsewhere. And we've little to go on. However, a jogger said that she saw a dark taxi, possibly blue or dark grey, driving into the Nova facility very early yesterday morning and she thought it was odd because she knew the buildings didn't open for another few hours. So we're trying to trace that at present. At least the storm last night went past us and hit the south coast of England otherwise it would have made things much more difficult."

"It was bad enough," said Rayne. "It kept me awake for a while."

"I think it didn't do too much damage," answered Tiberius, "just some trees down and tiles missing off roofs. That sort of thing."

He reached for a second croissant. "Good aren't they?" said Rayne.

"Yeah."

Beth looked up suddenly, a light in her eyes. "Sorry, what did you say?"

They both looked at her.

"What do you mean?" asked Rayne.

"Tiberius, what did you just say about roofs"

"Just that some folks might have lost tiles and stuff. Why?"

Beth sat back triumphantly. "I've got it."

"What?" asked Tiberius

"I know how to find Dane."

"Go on," prompted Tiberius.

"We were playing around with a new toy the day before he disappeared. It's a tracking device!"

"You're joking me!"

"No. We chipped in some money together and bought this tracking system. It's called, wait for it," she paused then announced dramatically, "a Tile!"

"I've heard of them," added Rayne.

"How does it work?"

"Basically it is a small little tile shaped device which you stick onto whatever you want to keep track of. Hence the brand name, but where it really helps us is because it has created what could be the world's largest lost and found community. You buy a Tile and then download their app to your phone. Now, every app updates the location of each Tile device it detects and with more than eight million Tiles sold, it's a massive network which we should be able to leverage as long as Dane had it on him when he disappeared. It's only a matter of time before he pops up on the network.

We had been planning a trip to the West of Ireland and decided to register for a car sharing service called GoCar. But we would only have a single key card to access the car so Dane decided that with my history of losing things we should attach a tile to it. He installed the Tile app on both of our phones and the key card with the tile attached should be in his pocket. Now here's the sexy bit." Beth exclaimed as she took out her phone.

"All I have to do is open the app and select 'Notify When Found.' The really cool thing is that once any other member of the tile community comes close enough, Dane's tile location will pop up on a map on my phone automatically.

"What's the range?" asked Tiberius.

"It uses Bluetooth technology to connect to phones, tablets and other devices so about one hundred feet max."

"We need to monitor your phone constantly. Can you come into the Campus office we're operating out of?"

"Sure, I'll get my coat," Beth jumped up and ran to the bedroom.

"Do you want to take security with you?" Rayne asked Tiberius.

"No. I can take it from here and Sweeney's parked out front. She'll be in our care at all times."

"Fine."

"You don't seem too happy about this?" Tiberius detected a quietness about his sister and assumed that she was concerned about Beth moving from the security of her team of elite bodyguards to the local police.

"I am. I am, but unfortunately this situation has put a multi-million dollar deal in jeopardy."

Tiberius looked at her, surprised by what appeared like a lack of concern about the welfare of the young man.

She caught the look and said quickly, "I mean. It seems like you have a good chance now to find him, Tiber and there's nothing I can do to help with that, so I need to focus on what I can contribute. I'm trying to think beyond when you get Dane back. I still have to deliver to him and Beth on this deal, as I promised, yeah? Otherwise this will all have been for nothing."

"Right." Tiberius was unconvinced, but Beth's return, bouncing into the room, interrupted his line of thought and they left.

*   *   *

Mr Black was not amused. Clearly the extra spray of chemicals he had applied after landing had knocked out Dane again as intended but nothing, it seemed, was going to wake him up until the effects wore off. Mr Black was unsure as to how long it would take. He was casting his mind back and trawling through the previous occasions he had used the spray. *How long did the bloody stuff take to wear off usually and what kind of impact did more than one application have? Would the silly man ever wake up? Come to think of it he'd given him three times as much as the woman.*

He had been out cold for four hours since Mr Black sprayed him on arriving at Lydd airport. If he rang Sir Barty there would be questions. Too many questions right now. He didn't have a way of contacting the person who supplied the spray as Sir Barty had just shown up with a box of them for him to use on the basis that they would be conducting quite a few extractions and interrogations over a sustained period of time. He had a feeling Dane was going to be out cold for a number of hours.

He had taken both of them out of the boxes and fitted them with thick plastic bracelets around their wrists, neck, thighs, upper arms and ankles. Each bracelet was attached to a high strength wire, one centimetre thick. The wires snaked across the polished concrete floor to long connected slits running in different directions across the walls and ceiling. The floor, walls and ceiling of the interrogation unit were painted white, which maximised the effect of the hidden lighting.

He tested the cables on the woman who was lying on her back on the ground, using a small touch sensitive computer tablet, which displayed a 3D image of a human with the wires attached. As he dragged his finger away from her right hand, the cable attached to the bracelet retracted until it was taut. He did the same to her left hand and was pleased to see her body move into a cruciform shape with her arms stretched out. He attached a second series of wires to each bracelet and played with the tablet moving her unconscious body into a variety of positions suspended off the ground until he was happy everything was working OK. It was a very sophisticated restraint system and very effective. Finally, he left her lying on her back with her arms and legs apart. When she awoke she would have a very limited range of movement.

He attached a second set of cables to Dane's bracelets and did the same with him, going through the same set of tests and ultimately leaving him lying in the same position. Each body, lying on its back, with their feet just ten feet from each other.

Mr Black was frustrated that he couldn't commence and for a moment considered trying to wake her up to at least initiate some fun with her but decided against it. Or perhaps he would just use her while she was unconscious? He knelt beside her running the palm of his hand over her breasts, squeezing and kneading them, then along her belly and caressed her inner thigh and between her legs again squeezing and kneading her vagina.

No. He stopped and got up. The end game was too import-ant here and far too valuable to him. Using her unconscious body would not get him any closer to his goal, even if he would experience the pleasure of watching her wake up to realise he was violating her. It was one of his favourite ex-periences. Looking into a person's eyes as they woke up and came to the horrible comprehension of what was happening to them. No. No. He needed her in good condition to exert maximum pressure on Dane. He needed Dane to see him break her down, turn her into a whimpering wreck, pref-erably begging Dane to give him everything he required, if only to end her torment. Secondly, it would be useful if they both woke up and fed each other's fear while waiting for something to happen. There was a value in building a sense of dread, using the time spent waiting to ramp up the ten-sion prior to a session.

If the man would just bloody wake up!

CHAPTER TWENTY EIGHT

Rayne was still wrestling with her dilemma. She stared out the window of her SUV at the sea. She had gotten her driver and security team to drive her to this car park on the sea front where she could sit in the front passenger's seat and stare out at the bay. She made her team and driver get out and leave her alone with her thoughts.

Should she initiate and escalate negotiations with another buyer immediately in the hope that Tiberius recovers Dane in one piece and the tech is still available for sale? Or should she contact Deng and attempt to get as much money as possible from him in return for her silence? It kind of boiled down to whatever shape Dane was going to be in when Tiberius found him. If he was dead or screwed up, as a result of his experiences, then the tech might be dead with him. If he was relatively mentally and emotionally intact, and the tech was therefore still available to them, then the safest option was to initiate negotiations with another buyer. Trying to shake down Deng was a massive risk. No matter how good her Security team were, she would always be looking over her shoulder.

Still if Dane was going to be useless to her then she had to shake down Deng. Certainly, she should behave as though everything was normal in her dealings with Deng. Can't let him think she suspected him. There would be less danger in putting another buyer into the pot. In the unlikely event Deng was not involved in Dane's disappearance he would be annoyed by the development but not surprised she was keeping another horse in the race just in case things didn't work out with him. Having said that, unless negotiations commenced promptly she would lose her twenty million bucks down payment.

She looked far out into the bay and could see a bevy of small yachts racing each other way out in the distance. They looked small enough. Two man dinghies, most likely. Her mind went back to a warm sunny day in California, her sister Godiva and herself, pushing off their little boat from the low wooden wharf and scrambling aboard. They usually sailed with Tiberius, he was so good at it, quietly competent, but that day he had had football practice so they were alone.

Hours later, when Rayne was finally rescued, she was sitting on the upturned boat cradling her dead sister in her arms. It brought Tiberius and Rayne closer together and they comforted each other in their grief. It also meant that from then on Rayne could do no wrong in Tiberius's eyes.

Their dead sister hated the name her mother had inflicted upon her and her siblings called her "Goddy", unless they were arguing in which case it was "God" or "Diva." She was absolutely stunning. Slim, swanlike with pale skin, which was unusual for California, and resulted in Tiberius calling her "Vampirella." She had piercing blue eyes and the face of an angel. Their father had refused on several occasions to allow her to model, which resulted in massive rows with their mother, who could see a glittering career for her youngest daughter which would, of course, illuminate her own artistic endeavours. Their mother was a performance artist who was guilty of the unusual names of her children. Goddy was sweet natured and adored Tiberius, but fought constantly with Rayne, her strong-willed older sister over just about everything.

Their mother changed her own name from Sylvia to "Marsala" after the brandy, "because drinking it is a wonderful, earthy experience, just like me!" Her behaviour embarrassed the kids when they were younger. She organised art events and often took part, performing nude in live performances and on one infamous occasion having sex with another woman and a man.

By contrast, their father Whitaker was a reserved man who had inherited great wealth and spent most of his life as an academic, researching and writing about 18th Century American Poetry. By the time Godiva died, the children were living with their father and a small army of staff, north of Los Angeles on the coast. He got custody once their mother somewhat lost the plot at the final custody hearing. At one point asking the judge what was wrong with her children and their friends seeing her breasts and then whipping off her top to display them in order to prove it. She also scored an absolute zero with her liberal attitude to children being exposed to drugs.

Marsala had been horrified when Tiberius joined the police after university and resolved never to speak with him again. Her resolve lasted until the following Christmas when she rang to give out to him for not contacting her all year.

Thinking back to when she was rescued clinging to the boat with Goddy's dead body, things had gone very wrong with her plan but though it all came right in the end. The little bitch was dead. Bizarrely, afterwards she felt an odd desire to confide in Tiberius. She came close on more than one occasion but did nothing. Sometimes you protected yourself by sitting on your hands and keeping schtum. He'd never have forgiven her.

Yeah. OK. She would do nothing for the moment. Now was not the time to lose her nerve. She drummed her fingers on the dashboard. *Let's just see how things play out. If Deng calls to get a progress update, I'll tell him they were having difficulty getting the two founders to agree. If he pushes, I'll say we reckoned Dane had gone off on a bit of a bender, to celebrate the offer from Deng and that we can't locate him? Not great but it should placate him in the short term. I'll push the lawyers to move forward*

ASAP, so I get my twenty mill at least.

Of course, if Deng doesn't ring, which would be unusual, then it would go towards proving that he already knows where Dane is and what's happening to him.

Decision made.

Do nothing.

Just wait.

*   *   *

The door banged open and Doyle gingerly edged his way through it, holding two trays of takeaway coffee, one stacked on top of the other and a paper bag dangling below. He was stabilising the top row of coffees with his chin.

He set the bag on the tabletop and then carefully placed the coffees next to it. "Right," he called out. "Who's the latte?"

"Me" said Sweeney without looking up from the computer screen he was working at.

"The rest are cappuccino's and ye can grab them yourselves! Pastries in the paper bag are for those who are not looking after their waistline and are not currently members of Slimming World. Like me!" He reached in and extricated a massive croissant dusted with icing sugar and studded with flaked almonds. He sat in a corner, stretched his legs out and took a hearty bite of the pastry. "So nothing popped up on the ol' Tile App yet?" he addressed Beth.

"No," she said disconsolately.

"Have a coffee and a croissant, love. It might take some time before we get any progress on any front."

"Sorry, DI Frost?" Sweeney spoke up from what was the darkest corner of the room.

Tiberius turned with his coffee in his hand, "yep?"

"Regarding the report from that early morning jogger about noticing a taxi going into the Nova UCD facility yesterday morning? One of the staff at Nova UCD is in training for the Dublin City Marathon and noticed a taxi parked close to the missing person's office yesterday morning while they were also out running."

"Is that unusual? It's a big building. Lots of offices."

"Not this early in the morning. Also, it wasn't parked out front where they normally do. It was further into the grounds, just around the corner from Mr Wilson's office. This staff member's usually the only person around, apart from Dane, who he knows by sight."

"OK. Anything else?"

"He said that when he looked out his office window fifteen minutes later the taxi was gone."

"Description?"

"Large Black vehicle, tinted windows, probably an eight man taxi, he reckoned."

"Same type of vehicle the other jogger described. Did it have a taxi plate on the roof?"

"Yes, but he didn't notice the number. If that's what you're after."

"Sweeney?" Doyle interjected. "Any taxi's missing or stolen in the past week or two?"

"Just checking that Sir." Sweeney was always very correct and formal with his senior colleagues and as everyone on the team was senior to him, he ended up being that way with them all. Doyle smiled and glanced over at Tiberius to whom he had remarked earlier that he reckoned Sweeney was still nervous and afraid that if he was overly familiar with them, he might screw up this career opportunity.

They lapsed into silence. Tiberius was focussed on his laptop, Doyle on his Croissant and Beth on her phone, constantly refreshing the Tile app in case Dane's device popped up on the grid.

"A taxi and its driver went missing a couple of nights ago, Sir. They picked up a fare in Camden Street in town and drove the passenger out to Wicklow. The driver hasn't been back in contact since then and the taxi hasn't been seen," said Sweeney.

"Prendergast get the details of the vehicle and driver and circulate them immediately. Well done Sweeney!" Tiberius got up and nodded imperceptibly at Doyle as he did so. He left the room and Doyle followed him out shortly after. Tiberius was downstairs in the foyer of the building. Doyle sat in a chair beside him. "Well Boss?"

"It's an ideal vehicle to transport a body."

"Or two."

"Precisely."

"Get Prendergast to do a house to house in the area immediately around the missing woman's house."

"OK. The area is called The Liberties. It's an old closely knit part of the city. So, while they don't like us..."

"The Police?"

"They'll be willing to do whatever they can to help us locate Mary Gill. Prendergast should focus on the taxi?"

"Yep. It's a long shot but..."

Doyle turned and went back inside to brief Prendergast. Tiberius called after him, "keep Sweeney focussed on that cab too."

*   *   *

"Wakey. Wakey!" Mr Black crouched over Dane's unconscious body and slapped his face a few times.

Annoyed, he abruptly stood up and administered a fast, sharp kick to Dane's thigh.

"Damn! Wake! Up! Now! You!" Each word was punctuated by another kick to different parts of Dane's dormant body.

He stopped and stood over the body, his breathing slightly elevated. The silence in the room punctuated only by his own breathing and then.

"Oooooooh!" A long low groan came from behind him. A gentle smile stole slowly across Mr Black's face as his eyes swivelled and his head and then his body turned to follow them. Mary was sluggishly moving on the ground behind him.

He walked over to her, picking up his control tablet from the ground. He stood a few feet away examining her condition intently. She stopped moving and returned to her unconscious state. However, Mr Black knew she was edging closer to waking up. This was the moment he savoured the most in these type of situations.

He walked to the side of the room and picked up a scissors from a deep shelf bolted to the wall. Returning to Mary, he used the control tablet to gently pull her legs apart. He knelt between her legs and carefully cut a hole in her dark tights. Then he rolled down the top of her tights and cut her panties at both sides, carefully rolling the dark tights back up over her belly. He pulled her panties through the hole he had made in her tights, exposing her vagina and anus. Humming quietly, he moved to her side and cut her woollen jersey along both sides and both arms until he was able to lift off the front part of her jersey. He left the other part underneath her as it would fall to the ground when her body was lifted into the air by the pulley system. Her blouse was shiny, wine coloured and too tight to contain her bulging heavy breasts, as evidenced by the apertures between the straining buttons, which exposed her bra and the skin of her belly underneath. He sat for a moment staring at her upper body and then finally came to a decision. He put down the scissors and deftly but slowly unbuttoned the blouse, enjoying the sight of her abundant flesh being exposed. He snipped the bra straps and pulled it off.

She groaned again and he noticed slight goose bumps on her breasts. He picked up the tablet behind him and adjusted something. He could hear the air conditioning and heating system kicking in. It was a very responsive and powerful system which he knew could raise the temperature in the room to a level so hot you could literally cook the occupants, or to the other extreme where frostbite was a very real possibility. The system was, like this underground room, totally insulated for sound. The temperature in the room increased slightly.

He returned the scissors to the table and walked back to her. Mr Black was dressed in a matt black, skin-tight suit from head to toe with attached boots. The facial area was usually covered by a full face mask, which he had left in a bag beside his little escape route on the roof.

The skinsuit as it was called was designed for use by Special Forces Units on night-time missions. Mr Black had begun wearing it when he had someone at the facility. He wanted to get used to wearing it in a variety of conditions but he was also pleased to discover it was easily cleaned. Just stepping under a shower would wash away any blood or other mess. He had modified it, enlarging the crotch unit allow the wearer to urinate and defecate through separate small openings which could then be closed and resealed to maintain a watertight seal. The alterations also meant that when he reached down to the front of his trousers he could expose his full scrotum. *For when I'm having fun,* he grinned to himself. *And now it's time for a little blood sport.* From a hidden pocket at the hip he took out a packet, tore it open and pulled out a condom. He gently rolled back the foreskin on his now stiffening penis and then carefully rolled the condom up along it. As was always the way, it only went halfway up. Mr Black had an unusually long and thick appendage. It bounced along in front of him as he moved over to a shelf by the wall and picked up a tub of clear gel. He applied a generous amount to his organ, covering it with the lubricant. Satisfied, he walked back to Mary, holding his cock with his gel covered hand as he walked. He knelt between Mary's legs and slowly rubbed the lubricant into her groin, making sure to insert his fingers inside her vagina and to coat her internally with the lube. She moaned, writhing but she was trapped still, below the surface of wakefulness, protected from the horror awaiting her. Nevertheless, her reaction delighted Mr Black and his cock stiffened even further.

Nearly ready now. He thought. *She reminds me of someone.* The thought struck him. *But who?* He stood back and observed the mature, heavy, brutally exposed body of the woman on the ground. It bothered him, that he couldn't place her. He thought hard. His mind's eye flickering through the pages of all the women and men he had used over the years, those he had killed, those he had tortured, mutilated, sexually abused but he could not place her, couldn't link her. He thought back, to what he considered his "glory days." That fallow period known internationally as "The Troubles" where the one million or so inhabitants of Northern Ireland served as his happy hunting ground, but no one came to mind. So, he thought back further to his late teens. Nothing. Eventually it came to him. He was nine or ten, or maybe eleven? She was lying on their bed. His father had tied her ankles and wrists to the bed posts. Her tights were shredded at the crotch and her panties likewise. Her big solid breasts lolling to either side of her chest, bruised and discoloured, semen leaking from her gaping, reddened vagina. She stared at him with mounting horror and then up at his father who was standing behind him, his giant hand fixed firmly on his shoulder.

His mother.

CHAPTER TWENTY NINE

"Oh! My! God! Everything aches! I don't think there's a part of my body which isn't in pain. This was not a good idea Ash! Not a good idea. I thought I was fit? Well I wasn't. Dear God, I think even my fanny aches!"

"Eef. Don't be disgusting." Admonished her sister, shocked at Aoife's crudity. "Cian might hear you."

"Sorry Ash," said her sister shamefacedly, "but I'm really sore. Do we have to go back up again this morning? I genuinely don't think I can stand up properly, let alone ski down a bloody mountain. I need some time to recuperate."

"I thought all of you police officers were supposed to be fit?"

"I was, but over the past few months, what with James's condition deteriorating, I prioritised getting home early over working out in the gym. I'm probably the heaviest weight I've ever been, and the least fit."

"OK. Well, how about I take Cian up to the Nursery Slopes to his ski class. You stay here and chill and then when I get back, we'll just take the morning off?"

"Deal."

After Cian and Ashling left, Aoife got up slowly and painfully from the kitchen table and headed over to a low comfortable armchair beside the window with a brightly coloured soft cashmere rug thrown over it and put her stockinged feet up on the low table in front of her, legs crossed. She sipped from a mug of coffee and looked out the window and along the valley. She could see up the valley sides as far as the snowline. It looked like melted ice cream on top of each peak.

She burrowed into the chair, pulling the rug around her. She felt like a wounded animal, curling up, looking for comfort, warmth, respite.

She did miss James. How could she not? She had loved him and he her. That damned disease had damaged both of them emotionally, leaving their relationship scarred and battered. Maybe after some time she would be able to see past the most recent period with James to happier times and put their love into a clearer and more balanced perspective. She hoped so.

She was so pleased they had come out here. This break was just what they all needed. And to think it wouldn't have happened without Tiernan Doyle. She had been convinced he disliked her. God knows she had given him enough reason to.

Some years earlier, Doyle had been a rising star in the police force. So, she had been shocked to hear he had been demoted because he had assaulted another police officer, one Detective Sergeant Marcus Slevin. Instead of being kicked out of the force and prosecuted, he was reassigned to Sligo Station in the North West of Ireland where he had spent a year and a half before being moved to Donnybrook, working occasionally under her, for the previous year. She didn't know any more about it and taking what she understood to be the case, an assault on a fellow officer, on face value, gave him quite a hard time.

However, a few days ago, she met a friend she had trained with and who now worked in a senior position in Garda Headquarters. Her friend had told her Doyle had intervened on her behalf to get her the compassionate leave. Puzzled, Aoife asked why Doyle would have done this? Her friend's view was that he was a good guy and regarded very highly by a lot of people in Harcourt Street. Aoife also questioned her about the assault Doyle had been involved in. What had actually happened?

Apparently, Doyle was angry because the police officer in question was being allowed to retire with full benefits. Doyle had led an investigation that proved he had been heavily involved with a paedophile ring. The rumour went that this was happening because that officer, D.S. Slevin, had confidential information which would be very embarrassing for the Irish and the British police forces if it was released to the public.

Apparently, Slevin made the mistake of visiting Doyle in Garda Headquarters in Harcourt Street to taunt Doyle who promptly punched him in the face breaking his nose, to the cheers of his colleagues. Unfortunately, Doyle then completely lost control, kicking Slevin several times breaking ribs and smashing his jaw, teeth and cheekbones. The cheers died and several people jumped up to pull him away. Slevin spent several months in hospital and had to have facial reconstruction surgery and a burst testicle removed.

According to her friend in Harcourt Street, this time the information held by Slevin cut a different way and actually protected Doyle from charges of Assault and Battery and dismissal from the Police Force. However, the incident was sufficiently serious for his superiors to demote him and effectively derailed his career.

Well I got him totally wrong, She thought. "I'll have to apologise to him when we get back," she muttered.

"Apologise to who?" Ashling's voice sounded from the doorway to the kitchen.

"Jesus. You gave me a start!" Aoife exclaimed.

"You can call me Jesus, Sis. A somewhat belated beatification," said Ashling cheerfully. Flopping into the armchair at the other side of the coffee table. "Or should that be deification? Not sure."

"I was speaking to myself."

"Yes. First sign of madness they say."

"No. Answering yourself is the first sign of madness."

"Well as long as you enjoyed the conversation. So?" Ashling

grinned at her.

"So?"

"What unfortunate has joined that massive list of yours?"

"What list?"

"That list of people you have to apologise to!"

"Piss off!"

"Ohhh. Add me to the list please!"

Aoife sighed heavily and looked out the window. A silence descended on the pair and Ashling wondered if she hadn't gone a bit too far with the teasing. She was trying to lift Aoife's spirits. However, she now thought she had picked the wrong approach this morning.

"Doyle." Aoife muttered out of the side of her mouth.

"Hmm. I always liked him and he was very kind to Cian and very tough with Robert so he scores highly on all fronts with me."

"And he's become best buddies with that Yank you fancy!"

"I don't fancy him Eef. But I've got to say he was very nice to me the morning I found out about Robert. Really kind and considerate. Why don't you like him?"

"I don't dislike him, actually. He was parachuted in above me to run an investigation into a murder and I was very pissed off about it. Although, Harcourt Street have been known to do that sometimes. Also, I didn't realise they were going to use me on the Shannon Attack. Oh, and James was declining fast at that stage. And. And. And." Aoife paused. Then she continued, "add a little P.M.T. into the mix and you have the bitch from hell! He never had a chance with me. Not that it fazed him in the slightest. He just walked in. A cool, Californian gunslinger. He charmed my team out from under my feet, put me in my place and took over. In a matter of minutes. It was unreal."

Knowing Aoife's notorious temper and recent temperament over the past few years, Ashling sensed that this was progress. Of a sort. Although she had borne the brunt of Aoife's bad moods, particularly recently, Ashling was devoted to her. She knew Aoife loved her very much and was very loyal to her.

I'd hate to work with her though, she thought wryly. *Or for her. I can see how Tiberius would have been seen by Aoife's colleagues as a saviour.*

"So why do you think Doyle, helped you out?" Ashling gently prodded her sister.

"Don't know really. I was just thinking I've never given him any reason to."

"You mean you were horrible to him."

"Jesus Ash. Give me a break will you?"

"Sorry Eef, but you can be pretty .... Well. Strong with people, y'know?"

"I'll admit it."

They lapsed into a more companionable silence, which Aoife broke by saying "maybe he's just a nice guy?"

"Maybe."

"Let's go for a walk, Ash? Get on our snow boots and stroll around the village for a wee while?"

"Sure thing."

*   *   *

"DI Frost?" Sweeney called out.

"Yep?"

"I've been monitoring all reports relating to all vehicles in the past forty eight hours and a call went into Kildare District Headquarters from a Canoe Club in Leixlip. One of the members was there early working on a boat and he says he heard a loud splash from across the reservoir."

"So?"

"Well two things brought it to my attention sir. Firstly, I've been out there and although it's really quiet, especially at that hour of the morning, whatever caused the splash must have been large, in order for the sound to carry several hundred metres across the water to the Boat Club premises and secondly, the caller says that the splash was preceded by the sound of an engine racing. Says it might have been a car engine, but he's not sure. And there's no road at that side of the reservoir."

Tiberius turned to Doyle. "Let's go."

"What about me?" asked Beth.

Doyle looked at Tiberius quizzically.

"I'd like you stay here with Garda Sweeney. It would be safer."

"But.."

Doyle interjected. "You need Wi-Fi for that app yeah?"

"Not really, it just improves the performance and I…"

Doyle cut across her again, "where we're going there's no Wi-Fi and I reckon it's vital to give Dane the best chance to come in contact with us, don't you?"

Beth subsided, "I guess you're right," she muttered glumly. Doyle turned and walked out. Tiberius was putting on his coat and walked out past her, paused and put his hand on her shoulder, looking into her eyes.

"This is the toughest bit," he said quietly. "The waiting. Not everybody can hack it. But I know you can do it. For Dane."

She smiled up at him and answered "you're right. Of course. I'll call you if his Tile activates on the network."

Tiberius had a thought. "Sweeney?" He called over to the police officer hunched over his laptop. Sweeney immediately straightened up and turned to face him. "Yes sir?"

"Can you and Beth see if you can replicate the Tile app and account on your laptop? It might make sense to be monitoring for Dane using more than one device? What do you reckon?"

"Absolutely Sir. I should have thought of it earlier." Sweeney sounded abashed. "Leixlip caller's name is Potts sir. Nathaniel Potts."

"OK thanks." Tiberius looked at her again, "So, Beth can you assist Garda Sweeney?"

"Sure."

"OK, thanks. See you both shortly and call us if you get any-thing on that App." Tiberius followed Doyle out.

As they were in the car on the way to Leixlip Reservoir, Doyle said "smart move Boss. It'll keep her occupied."

"And focussed. I'm concerned we might miss that Tile pop-ping up somewhere."

"Yeah." Doyle kept his eyes on the traffic merging onto the M50 motorway.

About thirty minutes later they turned off the M4 Motor-way onto a side road. They drove along by the side of Weston Airport, which Tiberius stared intently at as they went past. A mile and half down the road, Doyle turned right and after crossing over a bridge, turned right again and into the grounds of the Canoe Club.

As soon as he parked, Doyle cursed and began fumbling in his pockets for his mobile phone. "Sorry Boss, I forgot to ask Sweeney for the name of the caller."

"Sweeney told me before I left. His name's Nathaniel Potts."

"Jaysus. Great name. Belongs in Salem though!"

"Is it an unusual Irish name?"

"Well it wouldn't be common, y'know?"

They got out and walked around the clubhouse to the water. Nathaniel Potts turned out to be a living breathing advertisement for Abercrombie & Fitch. He was a tall, rangy man in his early twenties, good looking, freckle faced and barelegged in boat shoes.

"Hi. I'm Nat." he said cheerfully after they introduced themselves and showed him their ID.

"Hi," said Tiberius.

"So, like wow, you guys got here quick? I didn't expect any-thing really. It was just something weird, cos it was at, like, the crack of dawn, man."

"Can you take us through what you saw?" asked Doyle.

"I'll show you," and Nat turned and strode away from the clubhouse along by the water's edge. He stopped at the little jetty furthest away.

"So I was, like, working on Tiffany's boat? Cos' I promised her at the party last weekend, yeah? I have a lot of stuff to get done today so I figured I'd make an early start on it. I carried it over here cos' it's a messy job and we don't really use this jetty too often." The young man stopped at the end of the jetty and pointed across the reservoir to a wooded section at the far side.

"I heard the car engine first, but like, it didn't penetrate, you know, I was concentrating on what I was doing, but the splash was loud and it got me looking up. I could see like, a disturbance in the water over there." He pointed to a spot on the opposite bank about two hundred and fifty metres away. "And that was it. I couldn't see anybody and didn't think any more about it until I like, had some brekkie and it just bugged me a little so that's when I called the cops over in Leixlip."

"Thanks for your help." Tiberius shook hands with him and turned. Doyle was ahead of him.

Nat stared after the two policemen, wondering at the abruptness of their departure, but then he spied Tiffany arriving around the corner of the Clubhouse and hared over to her, like an eager, albeit horny, puppy.

Doyle and Tiberius got in the car and drove out of the Canoe Club, turned left and headed back across the bridge. They drove slowly along the fence until they came to a gate. They parked and Tiberius checked the gate. The padlock was useless as the chain had been cut and the gate opened easily. He walked through and glanced back to see Doyle crouching over the chain.

Doyle walked after him and as they crossed the grass they could see parallel tyre marks in the soft ground. They followed the trail of the tyres until they could see where it turned towards the water. The tyre marks changed here and a deep groove had been dug into the ground with mud flung off to both sides. They moved carefully around both sides of the tracks and noticed broken branches in the bushes and a hole in the undergrowth through which they could see the water clearly.

"Went in here then."

"Yep. Water looks too deep and dark to see it. Got a torch?"

"Yes Boss, waterproof too."

"Get it."

Doyle looked at him questioningly.

"We don't have time to waste here, Doyle. We can call divers in after we've finished but we've got to know if anything like a vehicle is down there."

"OK," Doyle left and Tiberius looked at the trees beside him, checking them. He found a sturdy looking one over-hanging the water and climbed up into it. He lay along a branch looking down into the dark water, but he could see nothing.

Doyle returned and called out "Boss?"

"Up here"

"Ah OK. Everything all right?"

"Yeah. Just stick that torch in the water pointing down at a thirty three or forty five degree angle and in the direction the car might have travelled into the water. From the tracks, it looks like it might have gone in pretty straight."

Doyle looked at the edge of the reservoir, sighed, took off his socks and shoes and rolled up his shirt sleeves followed by his trousers. Carefully he stepped into the water, turned on the torch and after allowing a few moments for any mud to subside, held the torch under the water which was up to his elbow. Tiberius stared intently.

"Well? Anything?" asked Doyle

"Nope." Tiberius sounded frustrated.

"How about I sweep the torch from left to right and you watch the beam in case anything breaks it? I'll try it at a shal-low angle first and then at a deeper one."

"Sure, go ahead."

Tiberius watched as the powerful beam from the torch moved along under the water, but nothing showed up

The beam swept back and still nothing showed up.

"Try a deeper angle." Tiberius called down to Doyle.

"OK."

Tiberius could barely see the beam now. Still he followed it fixedly. Then the beam abruptly shortened. He watched it closely as Doyle swept the beam back in the opposite direction and the beam shortened again in the same place.

"There's something there."

"Great, can I get out now? The water's freezing."

"Sure, thanks."

"How big is it?"

"Can tell how long but, say, six to eight feet wide?"

"I'll call in the divers."

"Do that. I'm gonna walk in this direction OK? To see if a person can access the airport directly from here?"

"Good thinking. I'll call them and then I have an appointment with the towel in my boot. See you back at the car."

Tiberius walked along by the side of the reservoir keeping the tree lined water's edge to his left. After four or five minutes the wooded belt widened blocking his path. He walked through the trees and about thirty or forty metres later came out to the edge of a runway. He tracked along by the side of the chain link fence until he came to a section that had been cut. He put on a glove and lifted one side back like a curtain.

Simple as that, he thought. *Very organised.*

Doyle was sitting in the car with his stockinged feet up on the dashboard, intent on his phone. As Tiberius reached the car a squad car came over the bridge behind him and pulled up. Doyle opened his door and put on his shoes. He walked up to the uniformed police officer who got out of the car, spoke with him and then brought him through the gate and walked along to where they figured the taxi had entered the water.

Tiberius was still leaning on the roof of their car when he returned.

"OK Boss. They'll deal with it from here. Back to UCD or Weston Airport first?"

"Weston."

"Right."

They drove to the turn and went left heading back along by the side of the small airport until they came to the entrance. They parked up outside the main entrance of the small yellow terminal building, which had the words Weston Airport and incongruously "BAR" above the front doors. "They take flying seriously round here," Doyle quipped as he put a police sign on the dashboard. "Actually," he continued on in a more conversational tone, "Weston Airport is the only airport in Ireland with odd distinction of having a runway which has a county boundary running across the middle of it, so one half is in County Kildare and the other in County Dublin. Just another piece of random information no one needs," he said.

When they went in, they saw a grey haired man adjusting a display of large purple and pink flowers on a very ornate marble table which wouldn't have looked out of place in a palace but was stuck in the middle of an otherwise functional reception area of the Terminal building.

"We're looking for the boss." Doyle said to his back.

"That'll be Conneely. He's in Ballinasloe, sorry," the man answered without turning around.

"Then we need to speak with someone else in authority." Doyle's voice hardened.

The man turned around with a hostile look on his face. "Why?"

"Police business." Doyle rapped back, now thoroughly annoyed.

"What do you want to know?"

"Who are you?" Doyle moved to stand very close to the man.

"I'm Joe Slater."

"What do you do around here?"

"Just about everything really."

Tiberius intervened, holding up his ID and said, "we want to access your records of all flights in and out of here for the past week please."

"Well I'm not sure abou…"

Doyle moved close to the man and put his face up against his and said quietly "Now."

The man couldn't move away as his back was to the ornate table behind him.

"OK. OK. No problem. Let's go through to the Airport operations office." The man's hostile tone had changed. He slid out to the side and they followed him through a door behind the table, emerging into a larger area with security scanning equipment and desks. He brought them into an office and rang someone, asking them to bring paper records of all flights for the past seven days. Whoever was at the other end of the phone was obviously not cooperating until he snarled into the phone "Lucy, just bloody do it alright! The police are here looking for them. Yes! Now!"

After a few minutes, a flustered looking young woman came in and handed him a file and abruptly left without a word.

Slater slid the file across the table to them. Tiberius opened it and began poring through the flight records. Doyle sat with his hands crossed, staring silently at Slater.

"What's this entry here?" Tiberius rotated the file on the desk and pushed it towards Slater, his index finger pointing at a line of data.

"There's no flight number? It just says R.A.F.?" he added.

"We have been requested to operate an arrangement with the British Government to allow them to use our airport."

"Who requested you to do that?"

"The Irish Government."

"We figured that much. What was the name or department of the individuals who requested this arrangement?" Doyle asked in a sarcastic tone of voice.

"We don't know what department but they gave the management a document which both parties signed and then they took it away."

"Names!" Doyle sounded annoyed.

"Look I wasn't present. Conneely's company only bought the airport a year or so ago. This is an inherited situation."

"OK. So how do we find the people who were present?" Doyle persisted while Tiberius continued poring over the documents.

"I don't know. You'd have to ask Conneely or some of his management team. Here's their number. He passed a business card across the table towards Tiberius who ignored it as he continued to study the list of flights. Doyle picked it up and put it into his pocket, "are you certain you don't know any names?" he continued in the same tone, staring at Slater with a stony face.

"From what I understand the guy who signed the documents on behalf of the Government was called John Burke."

Doyle sat up suddenly. "Burke?"

"Yeah."

"Are you sure?"

"Well that's what my predecessor told me. Said he was a hard guy to forget. He was a giant."

Doyle sat back. Tiberius glanced sideways at him. He then unclipped the sheet of paper he was studying from the file and stood up.

"Hey you can't take that!" Slater protested. "We need those records for the Aviation authority!"

"I'm not. Don't worry." Tiberius moved to the window and pressed the sheet to the sunlit glass."

"Why was this entry erased?" He asked over his shoulder at Slater.

"Sorry?" Slater got up and walked around to stand behind Tiberius, peering at the sheet. "Damn it," said Slater "need my bloody glasses." He returned to the desk and fumbled around looking for them. "Hang on. They're in my pocket. If

I had brains I'd be dangerous!" He laughed nervously at his own joke. No one joined in.

He went back over to Tiberius and after looking at the entry Tiberius was pointing to for a moment, he said "right. I see what you mean. It's been tipp-ex'd out. Looks like a plane landed yesterday at about eight thirty in the morning and took off again almost immediately, without anyone boarding or disembarking."

"Yep," said Tiberius. "One of those raf planes."

"That's R. A. F. mate. Not raf, Royal Air Force," Slater seemed pleased to correct Tiberius.

"Why was this entry deleted?" Tiberius asked as he sat.

"Dunno." Slater answered picking up the phone, "Lucy, need you in here again."

After a few minutes, the young woman returned.

"What is it now?" She sounded annoyed.

Tiberius showed her the sheet of paper and asked, "why was this entry erased?"

"Dunno."

"Try harder." Tiberius stared at her grimly.

"They are called secure entries. Sometimes we get a phone call requesting us to delete them. We call a pre-agreed number to get authorisation and then we do it. My marker ran out so I used Tipp-ex. Did I do it wrong?"

"No." Tiberius said as he took out his phone and took a photo of the page. Tiberius stood up and said "I expect this document to be preserved intact as it may form part of the evidence of a criminal investigation. OK?"

"Yeah. Sure. Whatever you say." Slater stammered.

"Where did it travel to?" asked Doyle in the same dead tone of voice.

"After it left here?"

"Yes."

"We don't have their onward flight plan logged. We are never given it, but once or twice I've met the pilots and they usually go to an airport in Southern England, somewhere on the Kent coast. Sorry but I don't know any more and that's just from some comments guys made."

They drove away from the airport in silence. Tiberius staring out the window, deep in thought. Eventually Doyle said quietly, "John Burke is one of my oldest friends."

"And?"

"If he's involved then the Irish Government Intelligence Services are all over this."

"This complicates matters."

"And how!" Sighed Doyle, "want me to ring him?"

"No. Not yet."

"OK."

CHAPTER THIRTY

Gary Tolhurst was pissed off. He had arrived at his usual spot on Dungeness Beach for an hour or two of fishing and every good spot for about one hundred yards was bloody taken by some Angling Club wankers from Southampton! And Gary hated Southampton to begin with so this made him even more annoyed. He had spent most Saturday afternoons of his youth fighting against the bastards whenever his beloved Brighton played them. Gary was seriously devoted to Brighton & Hove Albion. Best football club in the world as far as he was concerned. Although he did like kicking the daylights out of Crystal Palace fans more. Still Southampton ran them a close second on his hate list.

So, Gary took his gear and trudged down the shale beach away from the towering Power Station and the annoying cuckoos from Southampton sitting in his favourite spots and towards the long bare beach which ran along the edge of the Army ranges. He could see a low, ugly, concrete building up ahead surrounded by barbed wire. He'd never really noticed it before because the best fishing was towards the Power Station where the warmer water encouraged the fish. *You just didn't come down this way, unless you have to,* he thought bitterly.

He stopped about a hundred yards or so from the building and set down his gear, but when he took out his folding stool and opened it, he noticed the shale underfoot was a bit too steep and loose for comfort, so he moved closer towards the building, just a bit closer. He was ninety seven metres from the building to be exact.

His phone pinged. *That'll be bloody Gloria. Wanting to know what I'm up to or wanting to scream at me. Just cos' she's bored and wants someone to talk to. Well she can piss off an' all!* He ignored his phone and continued setting up his gear and preparing for the first cast of his rod into the choppy grey sea. Gloria had shown up when word got out Gary had won three million quid in the lottery. They had known of each other and seen each other around in the small town outside Brighton, in which Gary lived, but she had never shown the slightest interest in him previously.

Gary had a sense of satisfaction from the fact that when he had won the money he did the right thing. He bought out his Mum and Dad's house from the council and the same with his brother John. The accountants which the lottery people had introduced him to had persuaded him to put the cash he wanted to give them into a trust fund. Gary still didn't quite understand what that was, but he got that it would stop them blowing it all quickly. No one had known about Gary's win locally until his brother John went into the local pub, got pissed and told everyone about his great brother. What a dickhead! Gary was so angry that he considered taking the dosh back from the muppet but the accountants told him he couldn't and that dismantling the trust would cost a lot, so Gary had to satisfy himself with going round to John's house and punching him in the snot when he opened the door with a big thick hangover!

Gary could remember standing over John who was spouting blood from his smashed nose and roaring down at him that he was a no-account waster dickhead with a stupid big mouth and he would kill him if he told anyone else about Gary's win, and he'd take back his money and toss John and his family out on the road! That properly scared John and his missus, who had come running out from the kitchen when she heard the shouting. She was kneeling beside John trying to stop his nose bleeding and looked up at Gary and begged him to calm down and not to do anything more. Gary always liked John's missus Shelly, so he just contented himself by saying in a loud voice, "Just make sure he keeps his dopey mouth shut about my business in future, right Shelly?"

No, the real problems started after that. Suddenly Gloria was in their local and making eyes at Gary late in the evenings when everyone had a few pints in and things were heating up. Of course, Gary was the centre of attention now, wasn't he? Thanks to his dickhead brother. Every wanker in the place hanging around him, hoping to get a free pint. Fortunately, the first person to try and touch him for a few quid had been Nigel Pratt who Gary had always hated, ever since school. He had approached Gary outside the pub and when Gary had told him no and piss off, Nigel made one fatal error. As Gary turned away to go into the pub Nigel got a bit stroppy and tried to embarrass Gary by making a loud comment to his back about how he had always been a stingy sod in school too.

Gary had enjoyed battering him up and down the high street of their little village. After that, word went around and no one else tried sponging off him. Gary still got annoyed about the comment and glowered at Pratt any time he saw him on the street. The nerve of the bastard, Gary had always bought his round and continued to do just that.

No, he could go right back to the exact second when things went down the loo. When he put his prick into Gloria's fanny up against a wall in the laneway at the back of the pub, pissed as a coot on a Friday night about three and a half years ago.

Once she had him by the balls, she never let go. She was a big sexy woman and a great ride, in fairness to her. She was also as ruthless and as calculating a bitch as ever walked the face of the planet. She screwed her way into his bed and into his life and into his bank account. Hardly a week had gone by before she was telling people round the village she was his girlfriend and a few weeks later she was pushing him to make things more permanent. Then she moved onto talking about him moving out of his Mum's house and wouldn't it be nice if they had a place of their own where they could have a bit more privacy. Ooooh and the things they could get up to then! All his sexy fantasies would be easy to do then, wouldn't they?

She was so bloody clever. She saw me coming, didn't she? Gary thought bitterly as he set up his fishing gear. His phone binged again. It was a different sound to the normal text message sound so he plopped himself down on his seat and took it out of his pocket to look at the screen. *It was that stupid app she had installed on his phone called Tiled or summat. What the hell!* She was always messing with his phone and he had a suspicion she was trying to keep tabs on him. To see what he was up to. Well, that had been the way until she had given him the heave-ho out of the nice place they had built just outside the town. He could still see the kids crying as he walked down the drive with his bags.

It had been planned like a military operation. Her Dad and two brothers had been there with cricket bats in their hands when she told him it was over and he was to stay away from her and the kids cos' she couldn't handle his violent nature anymore. From the look on her Dad's face, Gary reckoned she had convinced him that this was the truth. Lying bitch then got a lawyer to go after the rest of Gary's money.

Gary's sister Dolores reckoned she had planned the whole thing from the start. Fortunately, the accountants came up trumps and got him a lawyer who was like a Rottweiler in a skirt. She even scared him. After he left her office, he felt things were back in control for the first time. Gloria wasn't going to get it all her own way for a change. Her careful plan was about to be taken apart, if his lawyer was as good as she seemed to be. Still he couldn't get over how much Gloria had wormed her way in and gotten control over almost every-thing in his life. Even this phone, he looked at it. The icon for the Tile app had a little yellow dot flashing. He tapped it and it opened up a map showing where he was and how there was another tile close by. Down about where that ugly building was, just off the shoreline.

To hell with that, thought Gary and he opened up the menu to see how to delete the App. He'd had enough of Gloria trying to run his life. But he couldn't figure out how to delete it so he shoved it back in his pocket and cast his line into the dirty grey waves of the English Channel and sat down again, looking glumly out at the sea.

*   *   *

Beth's eyes widened as the Tile App pinged and a bright yellow dot popped up on her phone. Half a second later Sweeney straightened up in his chair as the computer made a similar pinging noise.

"It's found him!" she said excitedly.

"Yes, but where?" Murmured Sweeney. Totally focussed, he clicked on the map onscreen and zoomed out.

"Southern Coast of England! Just west of Dungeness Nuclear Power Station." He opened up a second window on his computer with Google Maps and located the same spot. "Hey, that's weird," he said.

"What is?" Asked Beth hanging over his shoulder to see the computer screen.

"He's in an area owned by the British Army. Some sort of firing range or training place called Lydd Ranges. Very isolated. How did he end up there?"

Beth stabbed the screen just north of the dot. "That's an airport. Could have used that."

"Yes. Yes." Sweeney muttered. "Hang on, I want to narrow down the area." He arranged both windows side by side on his screen and zoomed back in on both. When he was satisfied he had the right location he circled two locations close to it. On a hunch, Sweeney opened another window and entered a search for coastguard/military lookout towers in a fifteen mile radius of Dungeness Nuclear Power Station.

"Galloway Lookout Tower." He sat back. "That's where he is

right now. Or where the tile is."

He grabbed his phone and dialled it quickly.

"Sir, it's Sweeney. We found him." Sweeney paused and said "Galloway Lookout Tower in Dungeness on the South Coast of England. It belongs to the British Military, Sir."

He paused again listening and then said in a surprised tone "Yes sir. You're right it's in Kent. How did…? Oh right. OK Sir."

Sweeney put the phone down.

"Well," asked Beth. "What's happening?"

"The fact that it's a UK Military Base is an issue we hadn't expected," explained Sweeney quietly. "The Boss is contacting his superiors and I heard Doyle in the background saying he'll ring some guy in Intelligence. So…" He tailed off.

"So?" Beth pressed him.

"Now we wait for them to figure out how to do this, I guess." Sweeney finished lamely staring at her. "Uhm, can I get you a cup of tea?"

"Tea! Tea? How can you think of tea right now? We've got to get moving! We've got to get on a plane and go to England and rescue Dane. Never mind bloody tea!" Beth shouted.

"Hang on," said Sweeney quietly. "We can't go off half-cocked. DI Frost and Sergeant Doyle are the people best placed to rescue him or to arrange his rescue, if that is what's needed."

"Of course, it's what's needed!" Beth shouted. "God knows what's happening to him!"

"Look Beth. All we know for certain at this point is that he's missing since yesterday morning. We don't know what actually happened or why. There are a million reasons why people go missing each year and they're not always sinister or suspicious. Quite often they are due to very mundane and ordinary circumstances. He could have had some sort of breakdown and just decided to go away for a few days to get his head together. I'm not saying it's the reason." He quickly added as Beth snorted and shook her head.

"But it's vital we go about this the right way to ensure we get him back safe and sound. I have the utmost faith in Sergeant Doyle and Inspector Frost." Sweeney felt out of his depth trying to reassure the emotional girl.

"I know but it's so frustrating and I know Dane, better than any of you. He didn't need time out or time away or whatever. He was so happy and pumped at the prospect of turning our idea into a huge success. Believe me, he wasn't going anywhere, unless it was against his will!" Beth slumped against the desk behind her and started crying. The tears ran down her face and she moaned, "oh God. Poor Dane. This is all my fault. I persuaded him to try and help make my idea happen. I wish I'd never gotten him into this."

Sweeney was at a total loss. He just didn't know what to do. If he went over and hugged her she might think he was being too intrusive and creepy and if he did nothing she'd think he was just a cold bastard. Finally, he got up and walked over to Beth. He placed his hand gently on her shoulder and said softly "I can't imagine how difficult this must be for you. I'm really sorry. You must be..." He was cut short when Beth hugged him fiercely and sobbed. Sweeney slowly put his arms around her and held her. After a few moments she stopped and released him. He moved back immediately and looking at her sad face said "let me get you that tea. OK?"

She smiled at him through her tears and nodded.

Sweeney stopped at the door and turned back to her "Actually, if anything should give you confidence in the team handling this, it's that Inspector Frost already knew Dane was in Kent. Somehow they independently narrowed down his location to there."

*   *   *

Tiberius was driving fast along the M50 motorway with the lights flashing and the siren wailing. He and Doyle had been silent since the call from Sweeney. Doyle knew the next steps were vital and he didn't want to interrupt Tiberius's thought process at this crucial point in the investigation.

Finally Tiberius said, as he stared grimly at the road ahead, "ring him."

Doyle answered, "OK Boss," as he reached for his phone and dialled John Burke's number.

A moment later Tiberius could hear Doyle say "John? Doyle here.

"Hi Doyler. How's the man?"

He paused and then said "I'm good thanks. Listen John, We've an uncomfortable situation here."

"Oh."

"Yeah we think our boy may have kidnapped two people and taken them out of the jurisdiction."

"Do you know where?"

"An isolated building on a British Army Firing Range on the Kent Coast."

John was silent for a few moments. Finally he asked, "anywhere near the Nuclear Power Station at Dungeness?"

"Jesus! John!" Doyle was surprised.

"I'm in Blackrock. Let's meet," John cut across his old friend.

Doyle thought fast. "How about the incident room we're using on UCD Campus?"

"As long as there's some place private to talk."

"Sure. I can arrange that. We'll be there in fifteen or twenty minutes."

"See you there." John ended the conversation. Doyle looked across at Tiberius and said "I think he knows exactly what's going on. Exactly!"

"Sounds like. What did he say that was important?"

"He already knew the location where Dane is probably being held."

"Good."

"Good?"

"Yep. We'll all get to the same page faster. Does he have pull or connections on both sides of the Irish Sea?"

"Absolutely."

"Good." Tiberius took an exit off the motorway and keeping the siren and lights going, scythed through the suburbs of South County Dublin, only turning them off when he entered the grounds of University College Dublin minutes later.

* * *

Tiberius and Doyle jumped out of the car and strode out of the car park towards their Campus Office. As they rounded the corner and approached the building they could see John Burke's massive figure standing just inside the doorway. He was speaking on his mobile and watching them through the glass as they walked towards him. John put his phone in his pocket and came outside. He intercepted them before they entered.

"Doyle." He nodded at his life-long friend.

"John." Doyle replied tersely. "This is my boss Tiberius Frost."

Tiberius shook hands with Burke, experiencing for the first time the humbling feeling of having your hand engulfed by something the size of a shovel.

"On second thoughts, can I suggest we get takeaway coffees and find somewhere quiet outdoors to have this wee chat?" said John. Although it sounded like more of a condition than a suggestion.

"Sure." Tiberius replied. "I'll get 'em, while you two get reacquainted. What's your poison John?"

"Americano, black, no sugar."

"You got it." Tiberius turned abruptly and headed for a café nearby.

As soon as he got out of earshot Doyle turned to John and said, "anything you want to say to me before he gets back?"

"Not really Doyler. Just promise me you won't go ape on me. You know better than most that there's going to be some stuff I can't talk about. But I guarantee you I'll do what I can."

Doyle stood silently, looking towards the massive pond in the distance. He didn't answer for a long time, while his friend stood stoically beside him. Finally as Tiberius approached carrying three coffees, he said quietly "you're going to need to do a wee bit more than that, kid."

Tiberius handed them the coffees and they headed around the back of the building away from the pond and walked towards the playing fields, which were empty at this time of the day. John looked all around them as they headed out into the middle of the pitches and, satisfied there was no one nearby, stopped and said "OK. What can I do to help?"

"We need to….." Tiberius began but Doyle cut across him.

"Who is this guy? What is his background? What does he have to do with the British Military? Is the kidnapping of this kid and his foster mother a British operation mounted in Ireland? How do we get them back before this demented bollocks starts to cut them up?" Doyle said in a rush.

Burke sighed, drank some coffee and looked from Tiberius to Doyle with a slight smile on his face. After a lengthy pause, he said "his surname is Black. He is a seriously damaged bit of goods and he's the most dangerous human being I've ever encountered. Quite frankly, he scares me."

Doyle stared at his friend. Tiberius considered how bad this guy could be if he was able to frighten this giant in front of him, whom Doyle had said was a seriously hard man.

"He killed a lot of people during the Troubles in Northern Ireland" continued John. "He has worked for our friends across the water on occasion. I reckon that he worked for them during the latter half of the Troubles, both on this island and in other countries, including the Middle East, the Balkans and the United States. If he transported the two missing people to Dungeness then it was for the purposes of interrogation and possibly with the support or at least tacit agreement of at least some elements of the intelligence community in the U.K.. Because that's what the facility at

Dungeness is used for."

"How do you know what it's used for?" asked Tiberius quietly.

"Let's just say we have developed a close, working relationship with our brethren in the U.K. Intelligence community over the past twenty or thirty years."

"Are you telling me we've sent people over to this Dungeness place to be interrogated? Tortured even?" asked Doyle in a belligerent tone.

"No, I'm not telling you that." John looked at him with a stony, emotionless gaze.

"OK." Tiberius interjected firmly. "How do we get 'em back? John?" He looked at the big man with a frank stare.

"Have you found out why he's kidnapped them? That may help me here?"

"The young guy is a tech genius and he's created this software which can predict people's behaviour with close to total accuracy. It's worth potentially billions."

Doyle shifted on his feet and added, as though it had only just struck him, "this software might also give a massive tactical and strategic advantage to any country in possession of it."

Burke said "OK. I'll make a phone call and get back to you."

John went to walk away but was arrested by Tiberius's quiet question, "When?"

"I'm going to walk over there," John nodded at the treeline just south of them, "and call someone to see what can be achieved."

"Time is of the essence here. This psycho could be at them right now" Doyle ground out the words. John just walked quickly away.

The pair stood watching John speaking into his mobile phone about fifty metres away. Finally Tiberius asked, "what do you reckon Doyle?"

"He'll do what he can, but it may not be much."

"Well if it's not enough then we need to ring our bosses immediately, catch a plane to the U.K. and get the local police involved."

"Sounds good to me. Uh oh. Here we go," Doyle noticed John's tall figure heading back towards them.

CHAPTER
THIRTY ONE

This has moved far faster than we could have hoped, thought Doyle as he fastened his safety belt and sunk back into the hard seat in the small jet taxiing along the runway at Weston Airport. *John must have a lot of clout to swing this. Possibly the powers that be at the British end owed him big time or they were happy for us to take this sicko out. Or maybe both.*

John had driven them to the airport immediately on re-joining them and delivered them to this nondescript plane which had been waiting for them. As John explained it was a stroke of luck that it had been in RAF Aldergrove airport in Northern Ireland and had diverted the hundred or so miles south to pick them up.

Tiberius ended his call and fastened his safety belt. "John says we'll be met at Ashford Airport by his contact. A guy called Jocelyn. He's in charge of the British end of things."

"OK."

"John says he's a good guy and very connected. There's going to be some special ops type guys there as well and they will accompany us to the place we've identified. We'll find out the rest when we get there."

"OK."

Tiberius grinned and leaned forward. "You alright buddy?"

Doyle sighed. "Usually I don't mind flying because you're in something which looks and feels like a great big bus. But this thing is tiny. Like a damn cigar tube with wings. If the weather is anyway dodgy, we'll be thrown all over the bloody sky in this. And the proper name is Lydd Airport, it's the marketing bods in the British Airport Authority call it London Ashford Airport," Doyle added with asperity.

Tiberius's grin slowly died away as he gave thought to what faced them. He didn't want to be bringing back either Beth's partner and best friend in a body bag or the woman who raised him, come to that. He was determined to do everything in his power to ensure that didn't happen, but he couldn't rid himself of the nagging feeling it might already be too late. Doyle, meanwhile, stared fixedly at the table and tried, but failed, not to jump at every sudden movement.

"Take it easy Doyle. We haven't even left the ground yet."

"I know. I know and it's completely irrational behaviour on my part but I just can't help it Boss."

Tiberius looked out the window remembering his conversation with Sweeney, Prendergast and Beth. He had asked Sweeney to put him on speaker so they could all hear him. He told them that their contact had arranged for them to go straight to the location where Dane, and hopefully Mary, were being held and that the British authorities were co-operating fully in their efforts to rescue them. He asked them to monitor the Tile app and to contact him immediately if the location changed.

*   *   *

It was dark and bucketing rain when they landed at Ashford Airport. The plane turned right and taxied right past the cluster of airport buildings to the end of an open tarmacadam apron. As it stopped, two men in dark military fatigues appeared near the plane. They got out and were greeted by the taller of the two. "Welcome to Lydd gents! Worst bloody airport in Britain." He shook hands with them and motioned them to follow him to a nearby Landrover. They were shown into the back seat and their welcoming party got into the front with the smaller of the pair in the driver's seat. He whipped the vehicle around and sped straight down the apron, turning right and slipping into a narrow gap between two tallish hangars and then along the approach road to the airport.

"Where to now?" asked Doyle.

"Won't be long" came back the equally brief reply.

Never one to make idle chatter Tiberius looked at Doyle, shrugged and settled back into his seat with his eyes closed.

Doyle could just about make out large areas of water or swamp through the deepening gloom on either side of the road. Eventually they came to the outskirts of a small town and stopped outside a gate of some sort of military base.

They were stopped and the driver's pass inspected, then waved through.

After a brief period, the Landrover drove into a large hangar like building and stopped. As they got out Doyle noticed soldiers closing the large doors behind them. Once the doors were closed more lights were turned on and they could see a scene of controlled busyness. Men were loading other vehicles with boxes and other men were entering into the vehicles and seating themselves.

"How do you do? I'm John's contact, Jocelyn. You must be Tiberius, correct?" a clipped upper class British accent came from behind them. Tiberius turned to find an elderly well-dressed man roughly the same height as himself had come up to them with his hand outstretched.

"Hi," said Tiberius shaking his hand.

"Excellent. Come and join me in the office back here and we'll grab a cuppa and go through what happens next. All right?" Jocelyn turned on his heel and strode swiftly away. Once again the tired pair of policemen followed.

Shortly afterward they found themselves sitting on some stools with cups of coffee at a high table with a large detailed map on it.

"Can you confirm precisely the location you believe this chap Dane to be at?" asked Jocelyn.

Tiberius leaned over the map, scanning it carefully and

finally placed his finger on a structure at edge of the sea and in the middle of an oddly marked area. "There." He said, "but what's all this stuff around it?"

"It's a mixture of Shale, swamp, sand and water, m'dear fella. Most miserable stretch of countryside in all of the British Isles, I dare say, and absolutely perfect for training our boys."

"And this building? What's it used for?" interjected Doyle.

"Not sure actually. Hang on. Carmichael?" Jocelyn called to the soldier who had greeted them at the airport and was now standing quietly by the wall.

"It's a lookout post sir." He answered in a low soft voice. "or at least it was. It was taken over by B Directorate several years ago. I'm unaware of what they wanted it for."

"Well, we're about to find out. We believe we have a potential hostage situation ongoing in that building. There are two Irish nationals who have been kidnapped and are probably being held against their will by a chap I suspect is a terrorist. I want your chaps to quietly surround it. Go in, neutralise the hostile and liberate these people. Got that?"

"Yes sir."

"Now," continued Jocelyn in a pleasant conversational tone of voice. "this is the awkward bit. All a bit hush hush. Once liberated, we will be returning these misfortunates to the plane currently refuelling at Lydd airport. And I don't want a bloody word of this to ever escape the lips of any one of your boys. If it does happen, I'll personally nail his goolies to the nearest fence post and that's just for starters. Do we understand each other Colonel?"

"Absolutely sir."

"Excellent."

Jocelyn took a mighty swig from his mug of tea. "Now, D.I. Frost can you shed any light on the, ahh, individual in question?"

"He's a psychopath. Killed at least four people that we're aware of in a variety of bad-ass ways. I believe he has absolutely no regard for human life and if he is armed he will take out as many of your guys as he possibly can, especially if he thinks he is cornered. And he will definitely take out the two hostages unless they're already dead."

"They're in his possession for around forty or so hours now, so who knows what he's done to them by this point in time," chipped in Doyle.

The Colonel nodded coldly, processing the information he was receiving.

Doyle looked at the soldier thinking that he was a bit of a scary individual himself. Tiberius meanwhile was looking at Jocelyn with the distinct impression that he had just wasted his breath, describing Black to someone who already knew him, or knew of him. This felt like it was all for show, this guy wanted them to be the ones to identify Black to the Colonel for some reason. Maybe he needed to be able to disavow Black to some extent?

"How soon can you move?" asked Tiberius.

"Carmichael?" Jocelyn prompted.

"Forty-five minutes from now, Sir," came the clipped quiet answer.

"Excellent. Now, we three will not be involved in this operation gentlemen. However, we will be in attendance and we will be able to enter once the building is secured. At that point DI Frost, you will take charge of the hostages or, God forbid, what's left of them and return to the Emerald Isle with them. Alright so far?"

"I'd like to go in with them sir?" Doyle asked.

"Sorry, not going to happen," Jocelyn answered before Tiberius could reply. "You'll disrupt the operation of the Colonel's team. You don't know any of these chaps. You haven't trained with them. You are unlikely to have handled similar weaponry, so you see it's just not a good idea. And then there's Catch 22."

"Catch 22?" asked Doyle belligerently.

"Indeed. You wouldn't be allowed to go in unarmed."

"And?"

"And you do not possess a firearms permit for the United Kingdom. Catch 22." Jocelyn smiled to soften the impact of his logic.

Tiberius put his hand on Doyle's forearm to forestall the argument he saw coming and said "It's their show Doyle, and I have absolute confidence in the Colonel and his guys. I'm happy just to tag along on this one."

Doyle stood, "where's the jacks?" he asked in a sour voice.

"Through that door at the end, Tiernan," answered Jocelyn.

Doyle did a double take, as he realised that the Englishman had used his Christian name, something very few people actually knew and even fewer uttered. He walked over to the door and left the room.

Once he left, Tiberius swivelled on his stool and faced Jocelyn and the tall soldier standing to his right.

"I don't think you guys really needed my intel on the ah 'hostile', as you called him?"

Both men just stood there quietly looking at him, giving nothing away. The silent moment between them grew.

"Y'know," Tiberius continued quietly, "it occurs to me that there are many interpretations of that word. Neutralise. Personally, I'm not too concerned about how extreme that neutralisation might be. How do you feel about that Colonel?"

The soldier looked at Jocelyn, who nodded. He looked back at Tiberius and said in his oddly soft voice, "my instructions are that the hostile subject is to be fully neutralised. If he escapes then he is to be hunted down by my team with a view to achieving the same outcome."

"Good, because based on what I've witnessed, I don't want to see this sonofabitch enjoying the hospitality of the Irish Prison Service until he gets old and fat. Where I come from we have a different perspective on law enforcement." The three men shared a moment of complete understanding and then Tiberius turned back to the map. "So how far is this lookout post from here?"

"Three point one miles by road. The road surface is poor quality. Some of our team are already on their way by boat and expected to make landfall in one hour in a synchronised approach from the sea. Another team left three hours ago and are making their way on foot from the West across Lydd Ranges. We will split our team here into two groups. One group will approach directly along the northern access route to the lookout and the other will drive to the beach fishing area at the end of Dengemarsh Road, which is East of the Lookout and they will approach along the beach. They will leave fifteen minutes before the other group as it will take them slightly longer to get into position." the Colonel answered.

"Good stuff, Carmichael. You have it all in hand as always. Perhaps we can let you go now, I'm sure you have plenty to do before we're ready to leave." said Jocelyn.

"Yessir." Carmichael saluted Jocelyn but remained standing, looking at the older man.

Joss said with a sigh, "you want me to address them?"

"I believe they need to know what we are up against sir. I have already briefed the groups who are en route, however it would be far better coming from you."

"Very well. Just send someone to get us when you're on the move. Yes?"

Carmichael turned and left the room.

Tiberius asked, "does anyone ever call you Joss?"

Jocelyn looked at him, surprised. He reappraised this quietly spoken American. After a moment he said "yes."

Doyle walked back through the door.

"Feeling better?" asked Joss, smiling.

"Yes thanks. That flight did nothing for my stomach."

"Indeed. I don't like flying in small aircraft myself. I always get airsick." Joss murmured in a sympathetic tone.

Tiberius watched admiringly as Joss easily manipulated Doyle out of his grumpy mood and into a more malleable one. He realised that the man was a master at getting people to do what he wanted. *Which was great when he's on your side,* Tiberius thought.

CHAPTER
THIRTY TWO

The rain pelted hard against the windscreen of the Landrover they were travelling in, defeating the best efforts of the windscreen wipers to clear it. The toughened suspension of the military grade vehicle bounced along the poor surface of the road. They weren't going too fast but it felt like it.

Doyle and Tiberius were crammed into a side facing bench type seat in the rear with a group of soldiers, having been waved off by Joss a few minutes earlier. He explained that he was "too old for this sort of fun nowadays" in response to Tiberius's query as to whether or not he was accompanying them.

Tiberius cast his mind back over Joss's briefing of the team of soldiers before they departed. It had been fascinating. Joss stood on the second from bottom step of the stairs leading from their room to the main area in the hangar, the soldiers all standing in a circle around him. Tiberius and Doyle had observed from inside the room above. They couldn't hear what was being said but the level of respect the soldiers had for Joss was in no doubt.

"Gentlemen," Joss had begun quietly. "We need you to do what you do better than anyone I've ever encountered. We have two innocent hostages incarcerated at the Galloway Lookout and I am asking you to bring them out safely. I am, however, taking a moment of your valuable time to tell you a little about the individual holding them. Colonel Carmichael and I are one hundred percent united in our agreement that he is one of the most dangerous foes you will ever face. I should know because I bloody well trained him."

The men shifted, surprised at that admission.

"Please do not underestimate him. Even if he is bound hand and foot he is still capable of inflicting damage and potentially escaping and or killing. Do not take any chances at any point in time during this operation. Do not trust anything he says. Be wary of everything he does. He is always thinking several steps ahead. Colonel?" Joss nodded at Carmichael who had been sitting on a crate to the left of the stairs.

"He is the hardest bastard I've ever met." Carmichael said clearly.

"Worse than Straker, Sir?" asked a cockney voice. The men laughed.

"Do you recall the tests at Breakheart Beacon?" Asked the Colonel.

"Jesus! Do we what Sir!" Again the men laughed.

"Who has the record, Sykes?"

"Straker, Sir. Fifteen hours." Came back the quick reply from the young man.

"Well this bastard we're after tonight did it in nine hours."

"Jesus Christ!" The group of soldiers were taken aback.

Carmichael grimly looked around the group.

Then Joss said, "he was sixteen years old at the time and fully loaded."

"C'mon Sir, that's not possible."

"That's who we're after tonight," said Carmichael. He paused to let his words sink in. "So, remember what I've said and don't mess it up."

"Sir?" came the cockney voice again.

"Yes Sykes."

"You saying he's one of our own?"

"No Sykes. He may have completed Breakheart Beacon, but he is most definitely not one of our own. Now move out."

The Landrover hit a particularly deep pothole and Doyle

was thrown against Tiberius for the umpteenth time. They were travelling South in a fast-moving convoy of military vehicles, all painted some dark indistinct matt colour, which Tiberius noticed seemed to absorb the glare from the floodlights back at the barracks.

A sergeant sitting across from them grinned at them. "You gents will have to remain with the vehicle until we've made the area secure, Sir. Colonel's orders."

"We know," answered Tiberius.

"We're to bring you in once we've finished. Is that OK Sir?"

"Fine."

"Sir?" He looked at Doyle, who nodded in return.

The vehicle began slowing and Tiberius noticed the driver had turned off the engine and the headlights and was coasting slowly along the road as they came to a gradual halt.

The sergeant noticed Tiberius's attention and smiling, said "no sense in letting him know we're arriving is there?"

"Smart," answered Tiberius.

The door at the rear opened and the soldiers all got out quietly, flipping down night vision goggles over the front of their helmets. The sergeant was last out, leaving Doyle and Tiberius in the vehicle with one soldier sitting in the driving seat.

The driver leaned back and whispered, "we have a hybrid infra-red/satellite display of the target location and our lads, if you'd like to watch Sir?"

Tiberius and Doyle clambered forward. Tiberius sat in the front passenger seat with Doyle hunched forward in the middle. They could see a dark satellite image of a building with fencing around it and four rows of brightly coloured blobs moving steadily towards it from different directions.

"How will they get in?" asked Tiberius.

"The one advantage of this target installation is we bloody well own it, Sir, so we've got all the keys and entry codes. They should be able to effect a relatively silent entry. Based on what the colonel told us back there, we're going to need it. Wish I was with them though."

"Instead of babysitting us, you mean?" said Doyle, still a little annoyed at not being involved.

"I've just had surgery on my knee so I'm lucky to be here at all. Another guy was supposed to drive but he came down with some bug this morning, puking and crapping himself. Poor sod."

Tiberius was staring at the screen intently. "Can you zoom out a little so I can get a better view of the surrounding terrain?" He asked.

"Sure thing. Though we only need to keep eyes on what's going on at the installation."

"Maybe so." Tiberius was still looking intently at the screen.

Suddenly there was a flash up ahead and the building was illuminated briefly. They all looked up and could see figures sprinting into the building entrance.

"Thought you said you had the keys?" Doyle smirked.

"Funny that innit? Wonder why they had to blow it?" the soldier said, half to himself.

Tiberius had resumed watching the screen.

"There!" he said pointing. "What's that dot moving away from the building. It just appeared out of nowhere well outside the perimeter."

"Damn!" The squaddie rapidly typed commands on the keyboard below the screen and moved the screen to centre on the blob, then zoomed in to show a crawling body, moving away from the installation, heading roughly North West across the shale desert. He thumbed his communications unit and spoke urgently "Strike One! Driver One here. Urgent you respond. Over."

A moment passed. Then another. Then a metallic voice came back. "Why are you breaking radio silence, Driver One?"

"Just spotted a body moving away from the installation, Sir. Heading West North West. About three hundred yards away."

"Well done." The voice.

"Thanks, Sir." The driver turned to Tiberius. "If you hadn't requested we zoom out and spotted that, the bugger would have gotten clean away. I'll just lock in on his heat signal and he won't be able to hide while he's travelling over the shale." He typed rapidly and crosshairs appeared over the heat blob. Then he zoomed out and they could see the blob moving North West of them. More blobs began to appear from the installation and pursue. Some that had been stationary on the beach moved westward along the beach and then north up the shale banks.

"Bugger's fast inne?" The driver said. "Still he won't outpace our lads, and they know the shale lands and the marsh like the back of their hands."

"What's that dark area up ahead of him?" asked Tiberius pointing at a large blob."

"Water."

"Will that mask his heat signature?"

"Yes, but we'll get him again once he comes up and out."

"Unless he stays down or finds a feeder stream that's running to or from the water?" suggested Tiberius. "Can you see one?"

"You're right," said the Driver. He thumbed his comms again. "Strike One?"

"Yes?" came back the voice. They could hear movement in the background.

"Target is making for a body of water, dead ahead. There's a feeder stream at the north-west corner."

"Understood. Out."

The driver leaned back, locking his hands behind his head and stretching. "He'll send some guys to curve northwards towards that stream and intercept from there."

"OK."

"Driver One? Strike Three here. Over."

"Sir?"

"Send in the observers with Vehicle Two now."

"Yessir." He turned to Tiberius and Doyle and said, "that's you. Hop into the LR beside us and they'll take you to the installation. Hope it was worth it."

Tiberius and Doyle hopped out of one Landrover and into the one parked next door which immediately drove along the road, through the wire gates and up to the front entrance of the building. As they got out, they could see that one door was hanging askew by a hinge and the other was on the ground. Two soldiers were talking in the doorway and one walked past them stony faced.

Colonel Carmichael stood in the doorway.

"Right. One of the hostages is in a pretty bad way, a woman. The man seems to be out cold, drugged we think, but alive and untouched. We think he was in the middle of things when he caught wind of our approach. Our tech guys reckon that he had added some extra non-standard security which picked up on our boys on the beach as they approached. He escaped through some sort of tunnel. We think. We haven't found it yet."

The Landrover that had ferried them to the installation turned on its headlights and a flash of light above caught Tiberius's attention.

"Maybe he used a zipline?"

"Sorry?" asked Carmichael. Tiberius moved backwards and took a small torch from his pocket, which he pointed up at the mast above the building.

"Damn." The colonel cursed. "Well spotted. He went out over our bloody heads." He went back inside along a hallway and opened a cupboard door. There was a ladder inside the cupboard and an open hatchway above it. "Clever bastard," he said.

"How bad?" asked Tiberius.

"Sorry?" The Colonel was looking up at the hatchway.

"How bad is the woman?"

"Our medic says he raped her and then started on her with a

knife. She's lost a lot of blood but Doc is one of the best there is, so if anyone can save her she will. We have a Medevac helicopter on the way."

"And the male?"

"He seems to be out cold. Drugged with something."

Can we view the scene?" Tiberius asked.

"Yes, but brace yourselves," Carmichael said over his shoulder as he led them into the middle of the building and down a stairway.

"We've seen crime scenes before," Doyle sounded annoyed.

Carmichael turned around. "He took her eyes out," he said quietly.

"Bastard." Doyle growled.

They walked along a short corridor with a row of small bare rooms along one side. The door of each was ajar and Doyle could see there was nothing inside each except a ring bolt set into the wall and another into the polished concrete floor.

Carmichael stopped before a door at the end of the corridor.

"What are those rooms used for? Cells?" Asked Doyle.

"Holding rooms, we reckon." Carmichael replied tersely.

He opened the door and they followed him through into a white basement room which was surprisingly large. The walls, the ceiling and the floor were white. Doyle reckoned it extended beyond the external walls of the facility which led him to wonder what was holding them up. Hidden floodlights lit everything up and created a glare, which threw the red drenched scene in the middle of the room into stark contrast. Three soldiers were crouched around a body, lying on the floor in the centre of the room in the middle of a large splash of blood. Two soldiers were off to one side, placing a second, inert body onto a stretcher on the floor.

There was virtually no sound in the room, so when Carmichael spoke again his voice startled them. "Coates, our medic, gave her a shot immediately so she could work on her and to put her out of her misery. She was very distressed when we got here. Coates reckoned he had only just started on her and that's why she's still alive and may just survive."

"But will she want to? After what she's been through?" asked Doyle, talking to himself more than to any of the others.

"Once she's stabilised and able to travel we'll send her back to Dublin. Coates reckons the male is just drugged up to the eyeballs and." He stopped, realising abruptly what he had said. "Oh. Sorry. I meant."

"We know Colonel. Go ahead." Tiberius said quietly as he looked around the room.

"Once he comes around, he should be able to transit back to Ireland with you chaps." Carmichael continued as though neither of them had spoken. Tiberius looked at him and reckoned that this was the man's way of coping with situations like this. All business and logistics. Leave the trauma for someone else to handle. Although he was unquestionably shook.

"Strike One?" Carmichael's comm's unit crackled.

"Yes."

"Strike Three here. We can't locate the target. We think he went into a body of water. Either he's drowned or he's a very good underwater swimmer. No sign of him. Instructions?"

Carmichael walked away from them and out the door. They could hear him walking up the stairs.

Tiberius was ignoring him, staring at the woman being tended to by the army medics. They finished applying dressings to different parts of her body including her eyes and had covered her. They moved her carefully onto a stretcher and strapped her in.

One of the medics, a woman, stood up slowly and turned around.

"Colonel said you might want to go back with them in the chopper?"

"If I thought we could assist in the search I would offer, but I don't, so yes please," answered Tiberius.

Doyle followed the men carrying the two stretchers towards the door. He realised Tiberius wasn't beside him and stopped. "Boss?" he called back to Tiberius, who was standing in the middle of the room looking around him. Tiberius ignored him.

Tiberius turned to look at Doyle. His eyes intense and angry. "Dammit, we should have gotten here sooner."

Doyle couldn't think of anything to say, any way to respond to Tiberius's anger with himself. Eventually he just said, "c'mon Tiber. Let's go."

"Yeah."

They left the room and walked up the stairs and out into the driving rain.

*   *   *

"Snapes!" Carmichael barked into his comm's unit as he went up the stairs two at a time. "Deploy the Drones."

"Weather's too bad Sir. We could lose 'em."

"I don't care. Deploy them. Find him and if you get a shot take it."

"Yessir!"

The rear doors of two Landrovers were opened and four large boxes taken from each. A dark figure pulled what looked like an awning out from the side of another vehicle and flipped down sides and a front cover, creating an instant if flimsy looking tent. Carmichael arrived outside to see the first of the copter drones lifting off. Designed in a joint venture between the British and US armed forces, they were an absolute godsend to units like Carmichael's. Easy to assemble and almost silent, their dark colouring made them invisible in low light and at night-time. They carried an ultralight, long barrelled plastic gun which fired twenty individual shots and had a lightweight plastic explosive embedded in their cowling. This meant that they could be used as a remote controlled bomb as well. They were also equipped

304

with ultra-violet, infra-red and thermal lenses for tracking. Best of all was the link between them. They operated like a hive mind. Each drone was aware at all times of the location and status of the others and acted accordingly. Images from each were transmitted to each other in real time therefore what one saw they all saw, instantaneously and this overall digital vista was collated together and transmitted back to their controller's display. Lastly they constantly beamed a sonar signal to the ground which created a 3D layout of the terrain within which they were operating.

Carmichael approached the Landrover with the extension and entered. A soldier was sitting at a keyboard, facing the side of the vehicle which had opened out to display a bank of computer screens with one large one in the middle. Windows were popping up, side by side along the top half of the central screen. Each displayed a murky video feed. When the ninth window opened, the windows all merged to become a single image covering the entire screen. Silvery crosshairs labelled North, South, East and West appeared in the bottom left corner of the screen.

"Thermal" said the operator pressing a button on his keyboard. The screen flashed and Carmichael could see a line of four bright green blobs in the top left-hand corner. The operator touched a joystick and the screen shifted towards the line of blobs. As the drones moved, detail began to be added to the image. A large flat matt area materialised along which two lines of blobs could be seen extended out on both sides. Four more blobs appeared intermittently within the area.

"Good." Carmichael relaxed slightly as he had been concerned to ensure that he had men in the water also, so their quarry couldn't double back that way.

"Can you increase the area being covered?" he asked the Operator.

"I'd have to go higher Sir. Not recommended in these type of weather conditions."

"Do it."

"Yessir."

"Can you improve the terrain data?"

"Yessir" The operator pressed keys and more detail and patterns became clear on the landscape being displayed.

Carmichael peered at the screen. "Move half a klick north west?"

"Yessir."

He could see a long black line snaking north from the body of water. A feeder stream. It seemed to run through a large fenced enclosure and beside three or four buildings. The operator moved a mouse and crosshairs appeared above one of the buildings. The buildings solidified and information scrolled down a neighbouring screen.

"It's a farm Sir. Owned by the."

"I can read Corporal." Carmichael snarled at him.

"They're an old Marsh family Sir. The Chitty's have owned that land since the sixteen hundreds," the operator volunteered, knowing that this local knowledge wouldn't be on the databases they had access to.

"Well if that's where he's gone, then the family line will come to an abrupt bloody end."

"Yessir." The operator focussed on his screens.

Carmichael was angry. Angry with himself and increasingly frustrated with the looming feeling that the target was going to get away. He was aware that the target knew the area equally well and that he was probably following a preplanned escape procedure. He turned away and took out a phone.

"Yes Colonel?" came Joss's cultured tones by way of answer.

"Permission to involve the local police and set up roadblocks Sir?" Carmichael asked.

"Permission denied," came the reply. There was a brief pause and then "you lost him?"

"Not yet, but he prepared for an eventuality like this."

"Hmmm. Unfortunate, and somewhat awkward."

"I want to send a unit to a farm owned by a family called

Chitty. I suspect he may have some transport stashed there, or access to some transport located there."

"Anybody home?" asked Joss.

"Probably."

"Better send a clean-up crew too, under the circumstances." Joss sighed.

"Will do."

Carmichael turned off the phone and turned to the operator. "Is the portable control unit operational yet?"

"Yessir."

"Good. Switch to it immediately and head for that farm. You need to maintain contact with the drones and they're at their outer limit. I want them searching the area around it."

The operator jumped up and walked to another Landrover which sped off.

*   *   *

Mr Black moved stealthily out of the water and crawled quickly across the mud towards the lee of the building. It was an ancient half-timbered haybarn. He crawled along the wall until he came to old stone steps leading to an ivy covered wooden door which was rotten at the bottom. He took the handle and lifted the door a few centimetres sharply and then pushed it in. He entered and closed it behind him. The passageway was pitch black but he knew it well and had cleared it of anything he could trip over, a year or so previously. He counted nine steps and reached out. His knuckles grazed a metal ladder and he ascended it, pushing up a trapdoor at the top. He felt around until he encountered a small wooden box. He took out a small torch and turned it on. The narrow beam briefly illuminated the ground floor of the barn which was crammed with machinery and equipment

He picked his way carefully along the rear wall to the corner and pulled at a dirty tarpaulin to reveal an all-black motorbike, with not a hint of chrome or light coloured metal anywhere. He had it custom made and placed it here several months ago when he began working on the possibility that he might need a fast and efficient means of exiting the area if the British Government ever decided that his value had dipped and wanted to be rid of him.

The elderly farmer who lived here with his wife and daughter had a problem selling anything and used the barn to store machinery, equipment and bits and pieces which he just refused to sell or dump. His hoarding habit had created the best place to hid the bike.

About a year ago, he had seduced and shagged the farmer's unattractive daughter. He wanted to scope out the place and also needed a reason to be on the land. If he was ever caught there he could always say he had wanted to meet her. He wasn't really looking forward to having sex with her as he found her spectacularly uninspiring but once he realised she liked it rough, he had buggered her brutally on her parent's bed when they were out. He finally understood her rather cruel nickname of "Shitty Chitty", but he had been surprised at her enthusiasm. He had to exert massive self-control to stop himself from fully indulging his appetites and barely managed to leave her lying half naked on top of the floral quilt with her bruised, large, spotty bottom stuck in the air. "Will I see you again?" she asked in a muffled voice, her head amongst the pillows. "Oh yes," he replied. "Definitely. I'll be around."

"Good," she said as she turned to face him, smiling happily, "cos' you're the best I've ever had. That cock's a monster! I've seen horses with smaller ones. Ain't no one round here with anthin bigger. An you're so good lookin too." She squirmed around on the bed to a sitting position, her large breasts bouncing wildly. "You're gorgeous. For a guy. Best lookin guy I've ever fucked!" She gushed.

It was worth all the effort involved in riding her, he thought. He had been able to check the place out fully and locate the best hiding space for his bike. Then he shook his head as though to banish the memory and pressed the starter. The machine immediately growled into life. It emitted a low purr as the engine idled sweetly. The sound dampened exhausts were functioning efficiently and the engine noise was drastically minimized. It also reduced the heat plume from the engine so it would be more difficult to pick up his thermal signature. He turned it off after just a few seconds and picking up a set of night vision goggles, walked along the side wall until he came to a door. He had replaced the lock on the inside but left the rusted external handle. His lock only allowed the door to open from the inside and he had also replaced and greased the hinges so it would open silently and only from the inside. To anyone trying it from outside it would look like an old battered door whose locks and hinges had rusted shut. He put on the goggles before slowly opening the door. Standing in the doorway, he scanned the area from right to left and back, knowing he was hidden against the dark interior of the Barn. Satisfied, he went back inside and peeled off his top. His movements were swift and economical. Practised. He took out a first aid kit from a pannier on the bike and applied a spray to a bullet hole beside his shoulder. He reached around and sprayed the exit wound. He attached a bandage front and back and then pulled out a heavy jacket, trousers and boots which he put on over his one-piece skinsuit. He made no sound while treating the wound and dressing. He wasn't impervious to pain, just used to it.

Mr Black slid out the slim mobile phone he had on him when he escaped from the lookout building and took out the sim card. A secateurs which he had left in the wooden box chopped up the sim nicely. He put the phone into a bag which he placed on top of a heavy wooden block and hit it a few times quickly with a heavy metal hammer. He took out another mobile phone from the wooden box, replaced the torch in the box and tucked the bag with the smashed phone into his pocket. Then, he wheeled the motorbike to the door. Before exiting he lifted a piece of fabric on the left of the doorway and pressed a button. He continued out. Holding the bike with one hand, he closed the door quietly behind him. Then he wheeled the bike along the back wall of a second outbuilding and along the side of a hedge which lined the driveway leading from the old farmhouse to the laneway that went to the public road.

No dogs barked during the entire time he was on the farm as he had killed the latest ones some months before. Over the past three years he had poisoned or drowned five dogs. The first was the original one the farmer had owned and the next two were his replacements. After he drowned the fourth and fifth candidates, the farmer didn't replace them. The key was to make it seem like it was just a run of bad luck which was where the daughter came in, she was easy to convince and she in her turn convinced her father it was just that, bad luck and perhaps they should leave off buying any more dogs for a while. After all it wasn't like they had any livestock any more was it?

He ran the bike along the grassy verge by the side of the gravel driveway, until he got to the road. He took out a black helmet from one of the panniers and put it on. There was a slight slope from the gates of the farm to another road so he ran alongside the bike for a few yards and hopped on, allowing it to roll silently down the slope and around the corner. The hedgerows on either side increased gradually in height and when they were over six or seven feet tall and interspersed with trees he thumbed the starter and steadily increased speed. He would leave the headlight and tail lights off for as long as possible, relying on memory to guide him along the twisting roadway as he headed northwards from the coast. As he drove along he scattered bits of the broken phone and the fragments of the chopped-up sim card into the ditch which ran along the side of the road. It had taken just five or six minutes from emerging from the water to driving away. He had constantly rehearsed his movements until he had reduced the time to the minimum. The Drones were overhead by the time he was rolling the bike towards the road but he had anticipated their infra-red capabilities and was on the bike as the soldiers entered the farmyard. He heard the noise of an explosion behind him and could see a flash of light in the rear view mirror. He smiled.

CHAPTER THIRTY THREE

Tiberius sat opposite Carmichael and Joss in a quiet corner of a canteen back at the Army barracks, the three of them hunched over large mugs of tea. In the other part of the large room several soldiers were tucking into food after their night time "exercise."

"Thank you for everything." Tiberius said quietly.

"No problem Mr Frost," said Joss. "Just wish we had nabbed the bugger as well as saving the two unfortunates he had taken. Thank God, he had rigged the explosives in the barn on a timer rather than a trip switch or we'd have lost more of our boys."

"And gotten to the lookout ten or twenty minutes earlier. We might have saved her some damn agony." Carmichael said gloomily.

"I'm just glad you got there," answered Tiberius looking directly at Carmichael.

"Indeed. Indeed." Added Joss.

"One of the boys reckons he might have nicked him, Sir," said Carmichael quietly

"Where did he hit him?" asked Tiberius.

"Possibly shoulder or chest area. Not really sure. Too dark."

"So…." Joss said after a few moments silence. "Just a wee bit of housekeeping, as it were." Tiberius looked up at him quizzically.

"I've been in contact with John back in Dublin and briefed him on what has transpired here tonight, he in his turn has contacted your colleagues and put the wheels in motion for your return. He paused. "Now the lady, ahh?"

"Mary Gill."

"Yes. Yes." Joss continued. "She has been airlifted to a hospital where she'll get the best of care available. You have my word on it and as soon as she has recovered sufficiently to travel, she will be repatriated. John is looking after matters at the Irish end of things. I understand the poor lady is a sort of foster mother and obviously the children in her care will need to be catered for, until things are clearer for her. I should add, unofficially of course, that because these events occurred on British Army property, albeit without their knowledge and one feels a great deal of sympathy for Mrs Gill, I will use my best endeavours to try and arrange some sort of stipend for her to ease her way in the future." Joss paused and looked at Tiberius expectantly.

When no reply was forthcoming, he continued. "As for Mr Wilson. We have been given to understand that the excessive dose of drugs he was given, in order to render him unconscious and possibly easier to transport, etcetera, will wear off shortly and our medics are monitoring him closely in order to assist him to regain consciousness. However, they have indicated they are uncertain as to how long that might take. We have a plane waiting at Lydd airfield to take you, Mr Doyle and Mr Wilson back to Ireland and I suggest we repatriate you gentlemen without waiting for him to awaken. The medics have assured me he will be able to undertake a flight even in his current condition without any repercussions. Any questions?"

"Do you think he was interrogated during his captivity?" Asked Tiberius.

"No. The medics reckon based on the levels of the drugs cocktail in his bloodstream that he's been pretty much out of it since he was initially taken. By the way, I am sorry we had to refuse Mr Doyle's request to accompany Mrs Gill to hospital but we really did need the room on the helicopter for medics and equipment. Also, I felt it would be preferable if both of you were there in case Mr Wilson awoke at any point."

Tiberius looked steadily at Joss and said "when can Dane or another of us visit her? Can you tell me where she is being taken?"

"Please don't worry dear boy. She is genuinely in the best of hands. I can't divulge the location of the hospital as it is a top level secure unit. However, I will be delighted to facilitate visits to her by one or other of her nearest and dearest, albeit under strict security conditions. The medics have recommended we try and arrange someone familiar to her be available when she regains consciousness once she recovers from surgery, which I understand is anticipated to occur sometime in the next forty-eight or so hours, as soon as they are satisfied her condition is sufficiently stable to allow her to undergo surgery."

"OK." Tiberius nodded.

"John will meet you at the Irish Airport you originally departed from and he will brief you as to arrangements at his side."

"Fine." Tiberius looked at Carmichael who has stopped staring at his mug of tea and straightened up. He looked as though he was about to say something when Joss placed his hand on Carmichael's forearm.

"We will get him," said Joss, looking levelly at Tiberius. "Bugger took out two of our boys from the roof with a bloody bow and arrow, if you please! Silent but deadly eh? I don't care how far he goes or where, but he is now persona non-grata with Her Majesty's government and we have a surprisingly long reach dear boy. Trust me when I say it's a case of when and not if."

"We need a P42 notice sir," said Carmichael staring at Tiberius.

"Oh, I think we can do better than that, Colonel. I've put it out on the bush telegraph that he is a terrorist and is in possession of knowledge considered to be dangerous to the wellbeing of the realm. He is to be terminated on sight. I've also informed the Americans of this order and of course John is already fully aware. We'll get him," Joss reiterated.

"Good," Tiberius said. He could see Doyle approaching them in the reflection of the windows behind Joss and Carmichael and he turned in his seat, pulling out the one beside him. "Well?" he asked.

"He hasn't come around yet. They gave him another shot to keep him calm for the journey in case he wakes up enroute. Some kind of Beta-blocker, I think." Doyle took a long mouthful of tea.

"OK. So, when can he leave?" Tiberius asked.

"Immediately, according to the doctors. I just came in to get you, and this," he lifted his mug appreciatively. "Good tea."

"I have always felt that the appreciation of a good strong mug of tea is another thing which bonds our two nations together, Tiernan," said Joss with a smile.

"True enough." Said Doyle.

Doyle drank his tea, holding the mug with both hands and staring into space. After a few moments he stirred and said, "what I don't understand is why?"

"I beg your pardon?" said Joss.

"Why torture the poor woman? In fact, why take her in the first place? He was just doubling the amount of hassle and increasing the likelihood of detection? We have been operating on the basis that he was after Dane Wilson, so why bother with her?"

"It's a classic interrogation technique. Helps to break down the target quicker," said Carmichael quietly with his back to them as he looked through the window at his men below.

"Joss?" Tiberius looked at the older man, questioning.

"Unfortunately, the Colonel is correct. She was probably taken in order to add pressure to young Mister Wilson during interrogation. Once he had regained consciousness then she would have been used to make him talk."

"Yeah, but he didn't wait did he?" Tiberius said quietly, "why?"

"Because he's an out-of-control psycho and something triggered him. He screwed up." Doyle said savagely.

"He was waiting for Dane to come around, but it was possibly taking too long?" suggested Tiberius

"Indeed, that is quite a possible scenario." Joss said.

"Will you keep us informed of progress apprehending this guy?" asked Tiberius.

"Insofar as operational security and the powers that be permit us, dear boy," said Joss.

"I suppose it'll have to do." Tiberius sounded unhappy.

"In other words, not at all," interjected Doyle in a sarcastic tone.

In order to deflect Doyle from having a go at Joss and Carmichael, Tiberius abruptly stood up and extended his hand to Joss, who also rose and shook it.

"Thanks again, Jocelyn."

"Call me Joss dear boy. Do keep in touch, especially if you feel we can be of further assistance." Joss said pleasantly and turned to shake Doyle's hand. Carmichael walked around behind Joss and stood by the side of the table. He shook Tiberius's hand and said quietly "I'm sorry I couldn't get him this time. But if I ever get another chance I guarantee you he won't walk away. I lost two good people and another injured by the boobytrap he set."

Half an hour later, they strapped themselves into their seats on a similar small jet with Dane's trolley lying on a few seats behind them and a medic in attendance. Doyle brought a smile to Tiberius's face as he grumbled about the pathetic size of this cigar case with wings but at least they were going home.

After a few minutes, Doyle said "I'm not looking forward to telling that lad what happened to his foster mum."

"Nope. It ain't gonna be fun."

"Maybe, it would be better coming from Beth? From what I can tell she's the closest person in the world to him?"

"Nope. It's gonna be our deal. Sorry."

"Yeah. You're right."

The plane moved forwards and headed for the runway. Tiberius smiled again as he felt Doyle tense beside him. Then he settled back and tried to get some sleep.

*   *   *

John Burke came into the office where Sweeney, Prendergast and Beth were waiting.

"I have just been informed they have rescued Dane Wilson and Mary Gill. They're both alive."

"Oh, thank God!" said Beth and immediately began sobbing. She turned into Sweeney, who had no option except to put his arms around her.

John raised his eyebrows and looked at Prendergast who just grinned.

"Would you like to accompany me to the airport to meet their plane? It's already on its way and scheduled to land in about fifty minutes or so." He asked.

"Please. That would be great." Beth abruptly moved away from Sweeney towards John. "Can they come too?" she asked him.

"Perhaps Garda Sweeney should accompany you?" John suggested in a serious tone belied by a twinkle in his eye.

"Thank you." She said.

Sweeney, now thoroughly discomfited, reached for his jacket, trying to ignore the subtle punch in the arm Prendergast gave him as he passed her by.

Ten minutes later, they were sitting in the back of an unmarked car heading for Weston Airport with John in the front passenger seat and a tall, silent, younger man driving.

"Are they both alright, Sir?" asked Sweeney.

"Well, from what we can make out, Dane Wilson was

drugged and, fortunately for him, unconscious during the entire ordeal."

"And Mary?" asked Beth.

"She sustained some injuries and is being treated for them in hospital in the UK. It was agreed with D.I. Frost that she should remain there for treatment. Her injuries are not life-threatening though. She is expected to pull through."

"How serious are her injuries, Sir?" asked Sweeney.

"I don't know yet."

Sweeney caught the tone of Burke's voice and decided not to ask any more questions.

"Will Dane be able to go home?" asked Beth.

"No. My understanding is that he still has a significant amount of drugs in his system, so we will need to monitor his condition for at least twenty-four or forty-eight hours."

"Can I stay with him?"

"Yes."

They lapsed into silence as the car travelled swiftly along the motorway.

"What hospital will he be in?" asked Beth. John looked at the driver.

"Leopardstown Park," the tall young man answered.

"I've never heard of it. Where is it?" Beth asked.

John twisted around to look back at her smiling. "It's an interesting little hospital. It was originally established for shell shocked Irish soldiers returning from the First World War. More recently it is being used for elderly residential care and for people recuperating from surgery. We have the use of a section of it which we use occasionally for people who need a little extra privacy and care."

"Oh, OK. Thanks"

The car turned into the entrance road to Weston Airport.

A short while later they were sitting in a waiting room waiting for the plane to land.

*　　　*　　　*

The equipment stacked around Mary's bed blinked with a number of red lights like an ugly technological Christmas decoration. A variety of low electronic noises were being emitted at different intervals. Under normal circumstances they would be turned off but in this high intensity medical unit everything was turned up, so as to alert the staff to any changes in the patient's condition even if they were not in the room, which didn't have a door, just a green plastic curtain.

Beep! Beep! Beep! Beep! Beep! Beep! A loud noise came from the monitoring equipment beside Mary's bed.

A nurse rushed into the cubicle, followed immediately by a doctor.

"She's losing blood pressure, Doctor," the nurse said urgently scanning the monitoring equipment beside the bed. "Dropping rapidly."

"Like a stone," the doctor replied in a puzzled tone, "she was stable when they brought her in. What changed? Did we do anything?"

"No. Well…"

"Well?"

"Doctor Mekhtar evaluated her on arrival. He came back half an hour ago and as she appeared stable he switched her from blood to saline plus vits and antibiotics. She had received a lot of blood."

"Put her back on the blood immediately." While they were rapidly discussing Mary's condition the doctor was examining her and checking the monitoring equipment. "Damn, we're losing her."

The beeping noise changed to a solid tone.

Other medical staff had entered behind them and one wheeled in a portable defibrillator, which was immediately put into use.

After some few minutes, the doctor who had entered the room initially with the nurse, went outside. She took out her phone and made a call.

"Yes?"

"Sir Jocelyn, this is Doctor Graham here at St. Swithins."

"Yes Doctor?"

"I'm afraid the female patient your people brought in has died."

"I understood she had been stabilised. That's a bit sudden."

"Yes. To be frank, we're somewhat surprised. She experienced a sudden, rapid deterioration." She paused, expecting a reply. When none came she continued. "The patient went into an irreversible decline and died in a matter of minutes. We'd like to perform an autopsy."

"Please do and inform me of the results. Thank you for informing me Doctor."

"You're welcome." She replied, but the line was already dead.

Another doctor joined her. A tall, lean man of middle eastern appearance. "Julia," he began.

"It's OK, James. It wasn't your fault. I'd have done everything the same. I've permission to have an autopsy performed. It had to be something else. Something we weren't aware of."

"Do you want me to contact the next of kin?"

"James!" She was annoyed with his lack of comprehension of the situation. "This is a restricted unit exclusively reserved for government use. If next of kin need to be informed it won't be our responsibility. Our only role here is to keep 'em alive." She paused, "and we bloody failed."

Joss was patiently listening to Tiberius's ring tone. Finally, he answered.

"Hi?"

"Tiberius, how are you? Get back to Erin's green isle alright?"

"Oh. Hi Joss. Yeah got back no problem. Thanks for the use of the plane? Everything OK?"

Joss thought, *that was fast. He's quite intuitive, this fellow.*

"Regrettably, my dear fellow, things are not OK. I'm afraid Mary Gill has passed away."

"Damn!"

"Yes indeed. I'm so sorry. The director of the Intensive Care unit she was in, rang me to inform me that she passed away very suddenly. Quite frankly dear boy, they're a bit baffled."

"Baffled." Tiberius's voice was expressionless.

"Yes. However, I suspect I know what happened."

"Go on."

"I think that before we got there, he pulled a little trick which he's used before. Just delays the victim's death by anything from a few hours to a day or so."

"Cunning. Ain't he? How'd he do it?"

"Yes, he is. He is indeed." Joss paused, thinking *and we taught him everything he bloody well knows. God forgive us.*

"Basically he made a few very tiny holes in a specific area of the victim's heart. Eventually they rupture. Pretty ghastly."

"You got that right." Tiberius sighed. "I'll tell the next of kin and inform the Irish Authorities. She's responsible for a pile of foster kids."

"Right, mmm." Joss murmured.

Tiberius stopped for a second. "OK Joss. Level with me. How do you want to play this? Bear in mind it's already messy."

"Thank you for your understanding Tiberius." Joss was grateful for Tiberius's perceptive response, he went on "I have already informed John Burke. He will have it officially put out that Ms Gill was injured in a car crash, in North Dublin in which the driver was also killed and as a result it was not possible to identify the bodies until now. Fortunately, I know a wee bit about Irish funerals and I have suggested that her injuries sustained in the car crash would necessitate keeping the coffin lid closed."

Or maybe that should be unfortunately, Josh thought to himself before continuing, "I would ask you to persuade Ms Frontemont and Mr Gill to agree to accept the official version of events. Obviously, your team's discretion is already covered under the Irish version of the Official Secrets Act."

"Yeah, but I'm not."

A long silence developed.

"I'm an American Joss. Not an Irish citizen."

"Indeed." Joss's tone was frosty.

"Don't worry Joss. I won't contradict John or you. We're all friends, here right? Working towards similar goals?"

"Yes Tiberius. You're quite right." Joss was relieved and then realising what was not being said added, "and we'll owe you. Correct?"

"Like I said, Joss. We're all on the same side, pretty much."

"Well I shan't detain you any further, Tiberius. Thank you."

"Sure. See you around Joss."

CHAPTER THIRTY FOUR

One of the nicest things about Saturday nights, thought Barty to himself, *is that it's Book Club night.*

Barty's wife, Gwen, was a voracious reader and was a member of a Book Club composed of similar book devourers. Five speedreading ladies who Barty despised. To him, a book was something to take time over, to be savoured. Like he was about to do.

He was fascinated by medieval Japanese literature and read everything he could about the period. He also had an extensive collection of Japanese films by directors like Kurosawa and Takashi, mostly in Black and White and virtually all subtitled.

Tonight, he was settling into his favourite corner of a large couch in a cosy library room at the back of his house. Although Gwen and her bevy of literary greyhounds were in the front lounge, the massive walls and heavy oak doors in addition to the carpeted floors throughout the entirety of his family's seventeenth century home meant he may as well be alone, which, if he was honest, was exactly as he liked it. He loved Gwen and enjoyed any time he spent with her, but he treasured moments like this, snuggled up in a warm cosy corner with a good book, a large, richly aroma'd coffee and a box of nice chocolate biscuits and no one to disturb him.

I'm a simple man really. He sighed. He slouched back on the couch, his book propped up on his truly massive belly and began to read. After a while, comfortable and warm, he began to feel sleepy and drifted off.

A sharp sting to his fleshy neck woke him with a jerk.

"Owww! Bloody hell! What was that?" He grumbled as he struggled up to a sitting position, catching the book adeptly before it slipped off and fell to the floor. He placed it on the heavy wooden coffee table in front of him and took a chocolate biscuit and popped it into his mouth, all the while vigorously rubbing the skin under his hairline.

"What sort of insect could have stung me?" He wondered, remembering they had a large hornet's nest removed from one of the chimneys of the Orangery which abutted the back of the house, last summer.

He felt a bit odd. Sluggish, and his hand felt funny as he rubbed his neck. Like he had pins and needles on his palm and fingers. The area around his neck felt the same. In fact, his arms were now growing numb.

"Oh God." Barty mumbled as he realised what had happened.

"Hello Sir B.," Whispered a low voice with a soft Belfast accent into his ear.

Barty slumped backwards on the couch as his muscles lost their strength. Immobile. He watched in horror as someone walked around the side of the couch and sat on the edge of the coffee table facing him. Mr Black smiled at Barty and asked, "may I?" as he reached for a chocolate biscuit. He bit the biscuit in half and chewed it slowly.

"Very nice, Sir B. Very nice indeed. Belgian chocolate I suspect?"

Barty stared at him unable to move a muscle. Unable even to speak by this point.

"Y'know, your security is pretty poor. I was quite surprised at how easy it was to get in here. A pink elephant in a tutu could have waltzed past those fools walking around outside in the rain and they wouldn't notice a thing. Not quite the Queen's finest, methinks! And I know you've got an awful lot of windows in this Manorial pile, but you really should have alarmed every entry point Barty. I mean, there's at least three rooms on the first floor without any proper security. Dear me." Mr Black shook his head sadly. "Such inefficiency. You've compromised the safety of everyone under your roof."

Barty could only stare at him thinking about his wife and her book club in absolute horror.

"Now I don't want you to worry yourself about those lovely ladies in the front of the house. They can't hear us. And I have no desire, to pay them a visit," he paused, "at present." He beamed at Barty, whose eyes widened and from whom a curious whining noise emanated. Mr Black regarded him curiously for a moment until he realised Barty couldn't properly articulate and that this was a close to a howl as he could get at that point in time.

"But of course, what happens to them will depend on you, my old friend and mentor, and how willing you are to co-operate and most especially, not revert to your usual modus operandi and lie to me?" Mr Black leaned forward placed his gloved hands on his captive's fleshy knees.

"You'll be able to talk in a wee while, Sir B and we'll have ourselves a nice chat." He paused staring meaningfully into Barty's terror-stricken eyes. "About all sorts of things, but mostly about Dungeness and why you fed me to the bloody wolves."

CHAPTER THIRTY FIVE

Tiberius stood just outside the open door of Dane's hospital room, watching Beth sitting beside the unconscious figure in the bed holding his hand. She had finally stopped crying and was just looking at him red-eyed and exhausted, but grimly determined to be there when he woke up. She hadn't left his side since they had arrived at the airport.

Tiberius turned away and walked back down the corridor. There was a small waiting area, currently occupied by John Burke and Doyle. He could see Sweeney's shadow outside the glass door at the end of the hall. He flopped into an armchair and stretched out his long legs for a moment, overwhelmed by a wave of tiredness. Then, he sat up straight and looked at the other two.

"Are you OK with me informing Dane about Mary Gill?" Tiberius asked.

"Fine with me." Doyle sounded relieved.

"Ditto" said John.

"I think I'll tell Beth first and ask her to be there when I break the news to him."

"Will she be able to handle that?" queried Doyle. "She seems a bit young and, I don't know, immature?"

"I think there are hidden depths to that young woman." John said thoughtfully. "If you can get her onside, she may be very useful in helping and supporting the lad through this."

"Yeah, that's what I reckoned." Tiberius was pleased at John's support.

"Fair enough." Doyle agreed.

The three of them fell silent.

"So, what are we going to do about this psycho?" asked Doyle after a while.

Tiberius looked up to see a trace of an indulgent smile cross John's face. "From what you've both told me and based on what they've told me, it sounds like there's a lot more than the Irish police force's finest after him at this point and for some time to come."

"Yeah if you believe that slippery English bloke." Doyle grumbled. "I'm not so sure I do." Tiberius looked at Doyle with annoyance, thinking it was amazing that Doyle had ever risen to the high rank he had previously held within the Irish police force because his frankness and total disregard for being even the slightest bit diplomatic would certainly have derailed his career anywhere else in the world. On the other hand, Tiberius considered, Doyle's intellect was impressive, and he certainly was able to analyse behavioural patterns, evidence and developments within a case and come up with plausible interpretations, he just wished the guy would be a bit more sensitive to the audience now and again. Even when he was right.

Unaware of Tiberius's scrutiny, Doyle continued in the same angry vein, "the Brits knew exactly where he was, and they knew him! There was an unambiguous level of familiarity with him in the way they approached the whole thing. Initially I thought it was total overkill, but then I realised that they knew exactly how dangerous he was. What if they decide they want him to work for them again? Then they'll just protect him while he does their dirty work and we can go hang for all they care. According to Gillian MacAllister, they've done it before. We'll never catch the bastard."

John was about to reply when Tiberius said in a thoughtful tone of voice, "Jocelyn said something that didn't make sense at the time but now I'm seeing it in a different context."

"Go on," John encouraged softly.

"Well, he said that the way Mary died was a trick he'd used before. In other words, Joss is aware of this guy's killing techniques. Like Doyle said, they know this guy really well."

John sat quietly looking at the other two.

Doyle twisted his neck back and forth as though trying to work out a crick or stiff muscles. "C'mon John. Level with us."

"I don't think there's any doubt in any of our minds that this guy was at some point in time working for the British. The impression I get from them is that he has been deactivated, as it were, from active service for some time." John picked his words carefully, speaking in his measured manner.

The other two stared at him.

"And under observation." John added.

"Not enough though." Doyle replied.

"Sorry?" asked Tiberius.

"They didn't observe him closely enough." Doyle answered. "He still managed to wreak mayhem on our patch and in bloody Nice." He paused for a moment and added "So what happens now?"

John stared at his old friend, his face a mask. A totally emotionless façade, but inside he knew what was coming and was thinking hard about how to avoid being roped in any further into what, he could see, was turning into yet another personal crusade for this overly ethical and noble-minded man, who, despite himself, he cared deeply about and half admired.

"I can't see how we can simply let this drop," said Tiberius. "This guy needs to be put away so he can't harm any more people."

"Granted," said John in a thoughtful tone, "but how far does your remit extend? I can't see your superiors funding some sort of international manhunt? Do you?" He stared hard at Doyle in a gaze which held a lot of unsaid warnings.

"Bastard," grumbled Doyle.

"Whaddya mean?" asked Tiberius unsure for a moment of his footing and aware of the lengthy relationship between these two Irishmen.

"He's right. Bearing in mind what's going on in Shannon and the massive strain it's putting on the Department budget, we're unlikely to get much more by way of resources, and let's face it, we don't exactly have a solid file ready for the Director of Public Prosecutor's office to use, or a culprit in custody," answered Doyle glumly.

"So, when your conduct of this case and your progress in apprehending anyone for the crimes that have been committed are being reviewed, you don't have a lot to show for the time, effort and cost which has been expended so far." John stated bluntly, seizing the opportunity to try and dampen Doyle's enthusiasm further.

After a few moments of uncomfortable silence Tiberius sat up and said, "I'm just not convinced this guy committed all of the murders."

The other two looked at him.

"I'm pretty sure he did the couple back at the cottage in the back of UCD, Gillian in Nice, and Mrs Gill in Dungeness but I don't think he killed the young woman in that big hole or whatever the hell it is."

"You don't?" John sounded surprised. Doyle continued staring at the floor. He had heard all of this before and felt that Tiberius's instincts were correct.

"Nope." Tiberius answered.

"I reckon it was unplanned, spur of the moment and what little evidence we have points to the murderer being a woman." He continued. "I think whoever did it mistook the victim for Beth. What I couldn't figure out was why they killed her. I mean, I couldn't see a reason until just now. If the killer was trying to get information out of the girl, thinking it was Beth, and realised they had the wrong person, all they had to do was walk away and no harm done. After all everyone was in costume. A lot of folks were wearing masks. So why kill her?" Tiberius paused. He had the bare bones of a theory and was still thinking it through.

"Unless...," he added.

"Unless she recognised the killer?" Doyle jumped in.

"Exactly," said Tiberius.

"So, either the killer was already known to the victim or......." Asked John.

"Or the killer is someone with some kind of public persona which meant that the victim recognised them?" Doyle said excitedly.

"Yup." Tiberius agreed.

"It's an interesting hypothesis," John said cautiously.

"Here's another interesting thought," Doyle pointed out. "What event was on at the same time or just after the murder? An event which would bring a lot of high profile people to Dublin?"

"The Web Summit," answered John with a growing sense of despair that this case wasn't going to be as neatly wrapped up as he had hoped.

"It's a bit of a long shot." Tiberius said warily. "I mean, it could just be coincidence. But it's quite possible that the killer was trying for Beth and just got the wrong person. Someone who recognised him or her."

"Do we know what the victim was studying?" Asked John.

"Good thought. As it happens, Marketing."

"Nothing to do with Tech and the Web Summit then." John smiled.

"She specialised in Social Media. Internet marketing," replied Doyle quickly. "So, she would have known of and been capable of recognising a lot of the high-profile people in Dublin for the Web Summit. Y'know, potential clients or future employers. I think the killer was just plain unlucky, and you're right Tiberius, that's why they had to kill her. She recognised them."

"As a hypothesis, it's got legs and it kinda fits the facts we've assembled to date."

John stood up. "Well I've got to head back to Shannon, so I wish you luck with it guys. If I hear anymore from Joss or the UK, I'll forward it to you. Keep me in the loop, Doyle." He paused and turned to Tiberius. "Is that OK with you?"

"Sure thing." Tiberius stood and extended his hand to the taller man and shook. "I appreciate everything you've done John."

"Think nothing of it. I owe this wee pixie here plenty." John grinned.

"No, we wouldn't have gotten that kid in there back without your help. Thanks man." Tiberius said in a definitive tone.

"Ah well. Pity we couldn't have saved them both," said John.

"Talk soon Burke." Doyle stayed seated; legs splayed out in front of him.

"Sure thing," John turned on his heel and left.

Tiberius sat back down and as he did so, his mobile phone buzzed in his pocket. He took it out and checked the text message which had just arrived. It was from Ashling.

"Back from skiing tomorrow. What do you know about Rugby?"

"Uh, Doyle?" Tiberius stared at his phone with a slight grin.

"Yes Boss?"

"You know a lot about rugby, right?"

"Rugby? Jesus, you have some brain Boss. You go from one thing to another with no time to pause. What do you want to know about Rugby?"

"Is there a big game coming up soon?"

"Yeah. Ireland are playing England in Lansdowne Road on Saturday. Whoever wins, wins the Championship. It's a big deal seeing as the World Cup is next year. Tickets are like gold dust. Did someone just offer a heathen like you, tickets?"

"Not sure, but it might work out like that."

"You must be connected Boss. That game has been sold out for months. You can't get tickets for love or money." Doyle stopped looking shrewdly over at Tiberius, who was working on a reply text. "It's a great day out though. If you do get to go, you'll love it. So, don't screw up whatever it is you're saying there."

"Hmm? Yeah." Tiberius was focussed on his reply. He tapped the screen of his phone and put it back in his pocket. "Let's meet tomorrow morning at the Campus office with the rest of the team and go through everything. I suggest that Sweeney escorts Beth home and we'll put a beat cop outside her apartment, OK? Rayne's security guys can take it from there. I'll meet Beth tomorrow and brief her about Mary Gill. I might have Sweeney present again as he seems to get on well with her. I think she's sweet on him, actually."

"Oh, a real lady killer is our Sweeney, but you'd be hard put to find a beat cop in Dublin, Boss." Doyle added straight-faced.

"Smart ass." Tiberius looked at him coldly.

"I'll organise for a member of the *Garda Siochana* to perform that function for you." Doyle emphasised the name just to tease Tiberius further.

"You do that." Tiberius remarked drily. "See you tomorrow. We've now got two killers to catch." Tiberius stood and headed out.

*   *   *

Ashling and Aoife walked up the airbridge from the plane to Dublin Airport terminal. Cian had sprinted ahead and was standing at the entrance to the building, waiting impatiently for them to catch up. They headed through the building, picked up their cases in the baggage area and walked through customs. As they entered the arrivals area Ashling scanned the crowd looking for a particular face.

"Don't worry Ash. I doubt Robert would be stupid enough to show up here. Especially after everything that's happened." Aoife had noticed her sister anxiously looking around.

"Yeah. Yeah. I guess you're right." Ashling answered. *Only that's not who I'm looking for,* she thought.

They moved through the crowd quickly, their bags on a trolley with Cian gleefully perched on top and hopped into a taxi which sped straight into town and deposited them at Aoife's house.

After about an hour their parents arrived laden with bottles of wine and precooked dinner in tinfoil containers. A real treat as Ingrid was not just a good cook. She was a stunning cook. They fed Cian and got him off to bed, which for once wasn't hard as he was exhausted, having been dragged off the ski slopes a few hours earlier in order to make their taxi to the airport.

Once they had finished their main course, a family council of war was convened by her mother. Ingrid was very angry with Robert and just barely managing to refrain from saying, "I told you so" to Ashling. So for once, she left the talking to her husband, a mild mannered and gentle man whose easy-going manner belied his shrewd brain and calm, analytical approach.

As they chatted, they all agreed that Ashling had the best solicitor available and she was most likely to give Robert & Co. a drubbing in court. Her mother informed them that while they were away, she had rung the lawyer and persuaded her to arrange for a locksmith to visit Ashling's home and change the locks. A second locksmith had visited their summer home on Achill Island on the West coast of Ireland. She fished a large envelope out of her hand bag and deposited it on the table announcing that it contained four sets of keys to both properties. The alarm company would change the alarm codes and contact information for both properties tomorrow.

Lastly, Ingrid wanted Ashling and Cian to move in with them for a few months while things were going on. The lawyer had assembled an impressive team and was able to fast track the initial divorce. Ashling and Robert had married in

London which had really annoyed Ingrid at the time. However, that was now going to work to Ashling's advantage as the divorce process in the UK took a lot less time to work through than an Irish divorce. Roughly between sixteen and twenty weeks as opposed to three or four years in Ireland.

Under normal circumstances Ashling would not have welcomed her mother's interference but on this occasion, she was delighted that her family were rallying around her. She felt a warm glow as she looked around the table. She leaned back in her chair and put her hands in her pockets. As she did so, she realised she had left her phone on the table in the hallway when they had arrived. She got up and went out to get it.

"Sorry, I know nothing about Rugby, but I used to play football back home? What have you got in mind?" He had sent straight back.

She thought for a moment and typed *"I've got tickets to a big game on Saturday. Want to come with Cian and I?"*

"Great." Came back his reply within a few seconds.

"I'll call you tomorrow to arrange things," she sent.

"Look forward to it."

"Ash?" Aoife had followed her out into the hall. "Everything OK?"

"Yep. Things are getting better, slowly but surely, Eef," she replied enigmatically.

Aoife looked at her quizzically.

"You can continue to stay here too, Ash," Aoife said quietly. "To be honest, I'd welcome the company."

"Are your sure Eef? I don't want to impose too much. and I know Cian can be a bit challenging. He has so much energy." Ashling smiled.

"No. Like I said. I'd be happy for you both to stay here for a while. The house is a bit quiet and probably too big for me on my own, especially right now." Aoife continued as they re-entered the kitchen.

"Of course, you could all move back home with us. The house is big enough you know!" Their mother interjected.

"Ingrid. I think the girls have come up with a good solution," their father said quietly.

"Well, I'm outvoted then. As usual!" Ingrid said petulantly.

Ashling smiled and swivelling on her chair gave her mother a big hug. "I love you Mum," she whispered into Ingrid's ear.

Mollified, Ingrid suggested they try some of the Lemon Meringue Pavlova she had baked for dessert and they duly tucked in.

CHAPTER
THIRTY FIVE

"Everything OK darling?" Gwen popped her head around the door of Barty's study.

"Yes. Yes. Everything's fine. Girls gone?"

"Yes. I'm going to bed. Don't be too late." She was ducking back out the door and then stopped and looked harder at him.

"You look very pale Bartholomew. Are you sure you're alright?"

"Yes. I'm fine. I'll follow you up shortly."

"And you're perspiring. I hope you're not coming down with something."

"I told you. I'm fine." Barty snapped.

Gwen took a step back, surprised.

"Well, if you're sure?" She said hesitantly.

"Yes. Apologies if I'm a tad grumpy. Been fielding calls from work unfortunately."

"You're so dedicated Bartholomew. If people in this wretched country only knew how hard you work on their behalf."

"Thank you dear. You go on up to bed." Barty looked away from her and stared at the ashes of the log fire. He barely noticed her leave the room. He was considering the full ramifications of what had just happened and what action he needed to take next.

He had given Black nearly bloody everything. From the names of the Irish and American police officers who had followed him to Dungeness, to how they had located him. He also told him that high level liaison between the Irish and UK intelligence agencies had facilitated the operation. He had managed to not mention Joss's involvement as he hadn't been asked a direct question about it. Thankfully, Black believed him when he said that he had not had any involvement in the attack on the Interrogation Facility.

Joss should probably be his next port of call, but he didn't want Joss to know he had deliberately reactivated the asset. Secondly Joss would want to know why Black didn't just kill him and what he had traded in exchange for his life. Lastly, and most importantly, he just never wanted Joss to know about this. Any of it.

Having said all of that, if I don't tell Joss, what will stop this bastard coming back here again and carrying out his threats against me, or, God forbid, Gwen?

Barty sat up in his chair. He took off the rug covering his lap and looked down at his sodden trousers. Thank God, Gwen hadn't noticed the acrid smell of his urine-soaked clothing. Mr Black had found it hilarious.

Oh God. Barty put his head in his hands and rubbed his face roughly. For the first time in a very, very long time he was unsure of his path ahead. He stood up unsteadily. *First things first. I need to clean off, change, wash the trousers somehow and clean the chair. Then we'll deal with the unknowable future.*

CHAPTER THIRTY SIX

The street was crowded. From one side to the other, thousands of Rugby fans sporting a mixture of green Irish jerseys and the white of the English team. People were chatting happily, making their way along the wide road to the Irish Rugby Stadium at Lansdowne Road. Cian was ecstatic! His first time watching the National side, ever. He told Tiberius that his dad had promised to bring him a lot of times, but he never did. Ashling looked over Cian's head at Tiberius and smiled sadly. Then she stopped Cian and knelt down to tie his trailing shoe lace, while people navigated around them. They resumed their progress towards the ground.

At the crossroads of Shelbourne Road and Lansdowne Road, the crowds became more dense. Ashling moved them gradually to the right-hand edge of the mass of people and joined a queue moving at a snail's pace towards a police barrier which filtered out the fans entering the stadium from the Lansdowne Road side. Concerned they might be buffeted by the boisterous people around them, Tiberius suggested to Cian that he might like to get up on his shoulders. "Cool," Cian answered enthusiastically. "Good idea," said Ashling. Pressed together by the surrounding crowd, Tiberius was acutely conscious of her body to his right. Finally, they got to the barrier, had their tickets scanned and went through it to the relatively empty road beyond.

"Want to come down?" Tiberius asked Cian.

"Nope" came back the answer.

"OK buddy." Tiberius grinned at Ashling. They walked along the street of substantial, elegant Edwardian redbrick houses which led to the headquarters of Irish rugby. Tiberius looked up at the plastic covered, curved stadium and remarked, "Doyle reckons this stadium is shaped like a bed pan. It does seem kinda lopsided"

"That's because the residents of a small square at the other end refused to allow them to build the stadium up to the full height." Ashling answered. "They had to lower the stand. Apparently from the air it does look like a bed pan. Only in Ireland!" She smiled and turned to walk through the entrance to the Corporate Section of the grounds.

Their seats were on the Executive Seating level at about the halfway line. "Good seats, huh?" Tiberius asked Cian.

"The best. We can see everything. Thanks Mum." The little lad turned around and gave his mother a tight hug.

"You know I'm not too up on Rugby, Cian. Will you help me with some of the rules when the match starts?" Tiberius asked him.

"No problem." Cian replied and added after a few moments "Buddy."

Ashling looked over Cian's head at Tiberius and smiled indulgently.

The two teams came out and everyone went berserk. Then they were silent while the English national anthem was played, and the Irish national anthem followed it. Tiberius was about to sit down when the band struck up another song which was sung with great gusto by the crowd.

"You got two national anthems?" He asked Ashling.

"I'll explain later." She grinned.

"Look Mum, the President!" Cian said excitedly. "That's the President of Ireland," he informed Tiberius.

A tiny white haired elderly man walked jauntily along, being introduced to the massive rugby players of each team. Although dwarfed by the huge men he was shaking hands with, he radiated a sense of serene calm and authority. He was certainly well loved by the crowd, having come out onto the pitch to be greeted by a massive roar of approval.

Tiberius couldn't help but notice the disparity in size between the diminutive president and one Irish player who towered over everyone at around seven foot tall. Cian looked up at him and said, "that's Devin Toner. He's the tallest rugby player in Europe."

"Make a good basketball player too," said Tiberius.

"No way. Basketball's for sissies. He plays rugby," answered Cian scornfully.

Strike one for me, thought Tiberius as he caught a faint smile on Ashling's face, who was staring fixedly ahead.

Cian squirmed around and said to Tiberius "we have two songs cos one's for the Protestants, y'know, the guys from Northern Ireland? My granddad said they won't sing our song, so we wrote one specially for them."

"That's pretty nice of you," Tiberius said.

"Well not me. I'm only a kid, but someone else did it."

"Right. Got it."

Down on the pitch the two teams lined up and the game kicked off. Doyle's lessons the day before on the rules of rugby proved very useful and Tiberius found that after a while he began to enjoy the game. Cian talked non-stop throughout except when a penalty kick was being taken. He whispered to Tiberius "we gotta show respect for the kicker. So, we all stay really quiet when he's kicking the ball. Do you do that in America?" Ashling threw her eyes up to heaven.

"We're not so good at that as you guys," answered Tiberius.

Halftime came, and they went inside to the bar to get a drink. Tiberius hoisted Cian up onto the table they were standing at and the boy divided his time between a bottle of water and a burger.

"So, what do you think?" Ashling asked Tiberius.

"I'm having fun. I got Doyle to explain the rules to me yesterday so I'm beginning to get the hang of it. What interests me is that no one gets up during the game to get drinks or food. That happens all the time in the States."

"Oh, it would be seen as bad form to do that during the

game. It would mark one out as not being a real fan of the sport." She smiled.

"Right. Different cultures, I guess."

"Do you like rugby?" asked Cian through a mouth full of burger, his face smeared with ketchup and mustard.

"You're a messy pup Cian," said his mother as she wiped his face clean, "and please don't talk with your mouth full."

"Sorry mum," answered the little boy.

"Yeah. I do. It's different to American Football but I reckon I could get to like it," said Tiberius.

"Well, you can come and watch me play tomorrow morning against Old Belvo, if you want" ordered Cian.

"Sure. I'd like that. Thanks for the invite," Tiberius enjoyed the little boy's enthusiastic, full-on approach then he stopped and turned to Ashling, "that's if you don't mind?"

"No. No problem, and he'd be delighted."

"OK. See you there." Tiberius glanced up at the nearest TV screen and said, "we'd better get back out there, the teams are coming out."

CHAPTER THIRTY SEVEN

The mountain wind howled around the small stone building. Mr Black had banked the fire previously and it radiated a low-level background warmth throughout the tiny space. He acquired the old one room cottage and surrounding land high up in Snowdonia several years ago from an elderly farmer who had since died. He subsequently purchased a sizeable acreage from the man's daughter in a second cash deal and allowed a neighbouring farmer to graze his sheep on it for free. It meant that he pretty much owned the whole valley and that only one other person had any reason to visit. The property was registered in the name of an infant who had died years ago on one of the Orkney Islands, whose details he had appropriated.

It was a tiny little bolthole he visited infrequently over the years. Only when he felt the need for some solitude, to re-centre himself, or just to heal, like now.

Mr Black sat, quiet, unmoving, his gaze unfocussed. It didn't look like meditation. He didn't sit cross-legged. He been taught to drop into it in any position, so the British Military psychiatrists and doctors who had examined him had mistakenly called it a fugue state. They didn't know about Oul Feng.

He could see the tall Chinese man now, cigarette dangling from the corner of his mouth, bobbling around as he talked in his rapid way. *"You no worry about this silly Buddhist Taoist, Zen crap, gotta sit cross-legged to meditate and shave you dumb head. OK? Boy? Listen now. You figure this one out and you able to control you mind. You able to control you emotions. Then you able to mess with everyone else's heads. That's when the real fun start. That's when you make real progress. You doin good with exercise and physically but remember there always gonna be some bastard bigger than you! So! If you more focussed, more able to control youself then you gonna beat him every time. When you come from a place of calm you see everything more clear. So learn this and learn it good, Boy. This gonna save you life sometime. Mebbe."*

He could remember the day his father had brought him into Oul Feng's restaurant. He had never seen a Chinese person before. He wasn't sure why his father had brought him there. All he knew was that his father was in a very unusual state of mind. He seemed to be in good form. Not exactly happy but definitely not angry or dour. The Chinese restauranteur's name was a bit of a misnomer as Oul Feng wasn't old. He was younger than his Dad, maybe thirties or early forties? But for some reason, everyone called him Oul Feng. Apparently, he had inherited the name. His father had been called Oul Feng too.

Oul Feng knew who his Dad was though. Everyone in the place stopped talking when they walked in, but then that happened everywhere in Belfast. Even in Londonderry, on the only occasion they were there and went into a pub. People noticed when his father went up to the bar.

He always thought people were respectful of his Dad. It wasn't until much later that he realised it was fear. No one wanted to attract his attention. To stand out and be noticed. His father didn't like anyone who wasn't Protestant and Ulster born and reared, so he was surprised when he stopped in front of a slender, tall Chinese man. George Black towered over him as he shook his hand. *Who was this man?*

Mr Feng seated him and his father in a booth at the very back of the restaurant, where his father could see everyone and all entrances, including the door to the kitchens and toilets.

A waiter handed Mr Feng menus. His father said, "same as the last time."

Mr Feng smiled and asked in strongly accented English "and the boy?"

"Same for him too."

"OK." Another waiter came up behind Mr Feng with a plate of what looked like massive thick white crisps.

Mr Feng placed them on the table saying "Prawn Crackers. Call me if you need anything else? Food on the way." His father did not reply, just sat quietly looking around the room.

He sat on his hands staring at the mound of crackers. He was hungry. He had never seen anything so odd looking before and was dying to try them, but he knew better than to ask for the food or to reach for it before he was given permission.

After five or six minutes his father reached out and took a cracker, popped it in his mouth and chewed it slowly. He looked down, rather than let his father see the desire for food on his face.

His father took another.

"Ye can have one," his father said after another while.

"Thank you, Sir," he answered politely and reached out to the plate. He took a cracker and bit into it. A small bite because he wanted to make it last, not knowing if he would be allowed to have another. It tasted amazing! Salty and light and fluffy. Kind of sticking to his tongue and then dissolving. He had never tasted anything like it in his short life.

"There'll be a man coming to see me here. When he gets here I'll give ye the nod and ye piss off out that door over there beside the kitchen. Wait outside till I get ye."

"Yes, Sir." He kept his head down.

"G'waun. Have another." His father said magnanimously.

He couldn't believe it. *What was going on? Was this a prelude to some awful new experience?* Still, only fools left crumbs on the table when they might be hungry tomorrow. He took another and again subjected it to a slow dismemberment.

The main door opened, and three men came in. One walked towards them and the other two went back outside. His father growled quietly, "out." When he made to take his coat with him his father said, "leave it." He looked up in surprise to see that look he knew so well and dreaded most, come into his father's eyes. His shoulders slumped in resignation and he got up quickly and walked to the door his father had pointed out earlier, not looking at the man who passed him on the way to his father's table. *Shouldn't have touched that second cracker,* he thought.

He went outside and stood in a laneway at the side of the restaurant. It was narrow and dark in the Belfast twilight and cold. Small mounds of dirty snow lay at the edges of the lane and the bins all hosted soft white hats. God knows how long he was going to have to stay out here. He moved into the middle of the lane and looked around. He noticed clouds of steam coming behind a large bin beside the doorway. He walked around and saw it was coming from a grill, set low into the wall.

He moved over to it and stood directly beside the plume of mist. He smelt it. Yeuch! It smelt of some very strong, pungent but sort of sweetish odour. He didn't know what it was. He had never smelt fried garlic before. So now he had a dilemma. If he stood in the warmth of the steam he would stink, and his father would notice, which would result in further and probably worse punishment. On the other hand, he didn't know how long he was going to be stuck out here and the temperature was below zero. His weak and treacherous body began shivering.

He looked further along the alley and noticed several large black plastic bags piled against the wall. He went over to investigate them and opened one. It was full of empty white boxes. He took the boxes out and piled them neatly against the wall. He sniffed the inside and outside of the bag. There was no detectable odour. He brought the bag over to the steam vent and placing it right beside the vent of warmed air got into it, pulling the back edge over his head, the front edge up to his chin and leaving a space for his face to look out. He hunkered down to wait. *I look like a wee papist nun,* he thought smiling to himself. *But if I look like a Taig bitch, at least I'm a warm Taig bitch!*

Time passed. He wasn't sure how long, but his legs began to cramp, and he had stood up a couple of times to stretch them.

Then he heard footsteps. More than one person, he reckoned. Stealthy footsteps. He wasn't sure why, but he pulled the top of the bag right down and covered himself completely. He breathed slowly and as quietly as he could. Something he had learned to do the hard way. To make sure his Dad didn't notice him.

He could hear footsteps moving towards his location. They passed him, moving along the alleyway. As they receded, he risked peeking out of the bag, just one eye. He could see two men's backs moving slowly away from him, each man staying at the edges of the laneway, moving in and out to avoid obstacles. When they got to the end. They stopped, and one said in a low voice he could barely hear. "Brat's not here."

"No. We must have missed him somehow. Let's check again."

"We checked and he's not here."

"We would have seen him if he'd come out of the lane, so he must be here."

"There's loads of doors and windows. He could be bloody anywhere."

"Whaddya mean?"

"I know we saw him sent out here, but he mightn't be in the lane. He could have come out yon door and gone in somewhere else. D'ye see?"

"Aye."

"Still no harm in checking again, eh?"

"Aye."

He carefully pulled the bag closed and listened. He could hear them moving back towards him, noisier this time. Like they were physically opening bins and kicking bags.

"Be a feather in our cap with the Central Command, if we were able to nab that bastard's kid. Serious leverage," one grunted.

"Aye," the other voice replied from somewhere much closer.

He began to worry they would find him. They were checking everything. At this point he was sure it was him they were looking for. His knees quaked, and his stomach roiled. Those prawn crackers didn't seem like such a good idea now.

He heard the footsteps approach his hiding place, snow and gravel crunching underfoot. They stopped. Someone was standing near him, breathing heavily.

A new sound. A door opening. Footsteps. And then a voice coming closer to him. "What you lookin' for boys? I hep you, mebbe?"

"Ah no, yer grand, Mr Feng. Joe here went for a piss and thinks he lost a fiver out of his pocket."

"Oh my God. Joe! You must have a bloody huge one! If it knock money out of you pocket? Ha! Ha! Ha!" Oul Feng chortled, one of the men laughed with him.

"I don't like losing money." The other man said dourly.

"No problem. No problem. Your boss my frien'. I sort you out. Here."

"Ah that's not necessary Mr Feng."

"No! No! I insis'. Sean's boys all good customers. I look after you guys. Take it! Take it!"

"Oh. OK so. Tanks Mr Feng."

"So, who watching Sean's car while you look for money, boys?" Mr Feng's voice sounded innocent.

"No problem Mr Feng. Y'don' think we'd come here shorthanded d'ye?"

"You smart boys. You come back for dinner soon OK?"

"Thanks Mr Feng. Be seeing youse."

"OK. I need a cigarette. You got a light?"

"No. Neither of us smoke Mr Feng. Those things'll kill youse."

"I tink you boys gotta worry about other stuff killing you. Cigarettes the least of your worries no?"

The two men laughed, and he could hear them continuing to move away.

Then silence. After a few moments, a match was struck, the gentle hiss of combustion and someone inhaling and exhaling strongly nearby.

Finally, Mr Feng said softly. "You stay in there kid. Until you father come get you. OK?"

He said nothing. After a few more minutes Mr Feng said quietly "good boy."

Then footsteps and the door opening and closing.

Hours later in the car on the way home, his father said, "Mr Feng told me what happened in the alley."

He sat quietly, waiting.

"You did well."

"Thank you, Sir."

His father drove on in silence. Eventually, they passed the first Loyalist Murals on the end of rows of houses and he said, "Mr Feng offered to train you."

He was surprised and confused.

"Train me?"

His father's voice sounded annoyed. "He reckons you would do well, with what he has to teach you. I'm not so sure."

He was annoyed with himself for the lapse. He would pay for the question causing a change in his father's mood.

However, instead of continuing home, his father turned the car right and eventually pulled up outside a redbrick house in the middle of a row of identical houses.

"C'maun." His father got out and he followed, recognising that they were outside the home of Jamie Wilson, an old friend of his fathers.

Mrs Wilson was standing outside the house next door talking with another woman.

"Ladies," his father saluted them in a serious tone, "is he home?"

"Aye, go on in George." Mrs Wilson said. His father pushed the door and walked into the house. He followed quietly, head down.

As he entered the house and was closing the door behind them, he heard Mrs Wilson mutter to the other woman "Puir chile."

"Aye," said the other woman in an equally quiet voice, "havin' that psycho as a father."

"No Moira and this might be a strange thing to say. I'm telling you now. I reckon my Jamie is a truly bad man. If I didn't know he loved me dearly, I'd be terrified of him." She paused as the other woman made a surprised sound. "But George Black is a totally different story. One hundred times worse. He'll never go to Hell because the Devil would be afeard to let him in. I shudder to imagine what that wee chile's life must be like."

"Not to mention Morag's," the other woman added referring to his mother.

He closed the door softly and stood with his back to it. His father had gone into the kitchen and he could hear him speaking. Another man's voice replied, and the kitchen door opened as the two men came out and went into what he knew was regarded as "the good room". It offered the most privacy in the house also.

As he passed by, the other man, Jamie Wilson ruffled his hair and said "What about ye, wee Master Black? Are you being a good boy for your Daddy?"

"Yes Sir," he replied in a monotone.

"Well g'waun into the kitchen and play with my kids. Have a wee bit of fun."

"No." Interrupted his father. "He'll wait there."

"Yes Sir." He replied in the same monotone.

Jamie shrugged his massive shoulders and closed the door to the room, leaving him standing in the darkened hallway. In truth, it was a relief not to have to spend time with the Wilson kids. They were all older and bigger than him and took great pleasure in tormenting him. Although the bullying had lessened after he broke a broom handle and went at the two brothers Ivor and James who were the closest in age to him. They had been kicking and punching him in the tiny backyard of the house during their last visit. When he had finished beating them with the stick, he noticed his father looking out the window at him.

His punishment that night was particularly severe, but as his father said, it was caused by his stupidity in leaving marks on them. Marks that had to be explained away. "Next time," grunted his father as he hit him with a leather tawse, "Hit them in the stomach so there's no marks. It's the best place."

"You." Bang! "Stupid." Bang! "Wee." Bang! "Cunt. Bang! Bang! Bang!"

One of the Wilson kids peeked out the kitchen door at him. He stiffened and moved slightly forward, whereupon the other boy banged the door shut.

He settled back and breathed slowly, calming himself, quieter. Listening to snatches of the muffled conversation he could hear in the room.

He moved closer to the door to listen.

"So that's what we'll do about it then." He could hear Jamie say.

"I'll deal with it." His father replied.

"You sure you don't want the boys in Larne to handle it George?"

"No. They're too soft."

"I still think that we should use Cushendal. It's a much quieter port."

"Listen Jamie, and this is the last time I'll say this. Quieter places will be exactly where the authorities will be checking. Larne's a much bigger port. Everyone working in Larne will be onside by the time I'm finished. It'll be safer in the long run."

"Like hiding in plain sight."

"When this civil rights malarkey blows up in the faces of those fools in Stormont there'll be civil war. We have to be ready to protect our own."

"And our business."

"About that. I'll be going to London next week to do a deal with those niggers. A good supply means that if everything goes according to plan, we'll drown those bastards down South in drugs and fund our own operations from their money."

"How did your meeting with Docherty go?"

"Exactly as planned." His father sounded satisfied.

"I never doubted ye, George."

"Except for one small issue."

"What issue?"

"His pals tried to take my son."

"Bastards! What happened?"

"I sent him to wait outside in that alley beside the restaurant. Docherty's men saw him go out and went around the side searching for him."

"That puts a different light on things."

"Aye. They'd have got him too only Oul Feng spotted what was going on and persuaded them to leave before they got to the boy."

"How come they didn't spot him?"

"Feng says he must have heard them coming and hid in a rubbish bag."

"Good Lord, George. That's one smart lad."

"He'll do." Said his father in a disinterested, non-committal tone.

"Seriously George. None of my brood would have had the smarts to do that. They'd be sitting in a cellar in the Ardoyne right now."

His father was silent.

After a few moments he said, "you realise what this means Jamie?"

"Aye, it's not good."

"No. If they are willing to try that on while I'm negotiating with Docherty then they're getting arrogant. Ready to do worse. A lot worse. We need to be prepared. We need to take the initiative."

"I'm with you George. Always have been."

"I know."

The boy stood silently outside the door, breathing so slowly and carefully. He was equally petrified and torn between missing a word and letting them know he was listening, but he was determined to hear as much as he could. He felt that what he was hearing would affect his life for years to come.

"Oul Feng wants to train the boy." He heard his father say.

"Like his father trained us?"

"Yes. What do you reckon?"

It was Jamie's turn to be quiet as he pondered the question.

At last he said, "If Oul Feng is as good as his father, and your lad is as smart as I think he is, I reckon it could benefit us."

"How?" His father queried in that dead voice which raised the hairs on the back of his neck.

"We'll need soldiers for what's coming. They'll need training. The training we got from Oul Feng's daddy has stood youse and me in good stead over the past few years. Your lad could become a handy lad."

"Not so sure I want him to be handy."

"George. Let me ask youse. Is he an obedient lad?"

"Totally."

"Do you reckon he'll stay that way?"

"Absolutely," his father answered. "Or I'll bloody kill him," he added in a soft voice after a second's pause.

"Well then. Train the wee lad. Train him hard. Turn him into one of ours. If he's anything like his Daddy, then we'll be a lot stronger and better able to deal with what's coming."

The front door began to open behind him and he shot up, jumping to the wall opposite the "good room" door.

"Oh, Good Lord!" exclaimed Mrs Wilson. "You scared me. What are ye doing standing there in the dark?"

The door to the "good room" opened and his father looked out. When he saw his son was standing against the far wall, he nodded and turned his head to look at Moira Wilson.

"He's fine there. We'll be leaving soon."

"Oh aye. George. Whatever you say." She said nervously and bustled quickly along the short corridor and into the bright and noisy kitchen beyond. His massive father stayed in the doorway looking down at him silently. Then he went back into the room.

One wet Saturday morning about two weeks later he cycled over to Oul Feng's restaurant to begin his training.

CHAPTER THIRTY EIGHT

Rayne woke up to her mobile ringing.

"Rayne? Did I wake you?" It was Beth.

"No problem, honey. Any news?" answered Rayne.

"Yes. I'm here in the hospital with Dane."

"What?" Rayne was shocked. "Is he OK?"

"Yes. Sorry. Look, they won't let me talk about it over the phone. So, can you come to meet me, and I'll fill you in on everything?"

"Sure. Where? What hospital?"

"Uhm. Hang on."

Rayne could hear a muffled conversation in the background.

"Oh OK." She heard Beth say to someone.

"Rayne? I'll meet you in the Coffee Shot Café. It's in the Plaza at the Beacon South Quarter."

"OK. What time?"

"In an hour? Is that too soon?"

"No honey. See you there."

Rayne swung out of bed and headed to the shower.

An hour later her black SUV's pulled up outside the Café. Her security staff got out first scanning the area.

Rayne hopped out and, noted with annoyance that the door to the rear of the café was locked with a sign saying that high winds has forced its closure and would patrons mind walking around to the front entrance.

A short while later, she and Beth were sitting in a corner on cushions, made from coffee bean sacks.

"You OK Beth?"

"I've been getting takeaways here since they brought Dane back. The coffee in the hospital is, well, just crap, really."

"Back from where? Can you fill me in?" Rayne asked urgently. "I'm really concerned about him," she added as an afterthought.

"Sure. But he's OK now." Beth said quietly.

Rayne noticed the rings under the younger woman's eyes and how pale she looked.

"I can't imagine how worried you must have been," she murmured.

"Oh Rayne. It was awful!" Beth gulped her coffee.

"So, where do things stand now?" Rayne prompted again.

"Well. He was kidnapped. That's a definite and either the police don't know who the guy or guys were, or they do know and they're not saying. Either way, they got away, whoever they were. His foster mother died yesterday in a hospital!" Beth stopped, her voice shaking.

"Take it easy Beth. Just take your time. How's Dane now?" Rayne wanted to get through what she regarded as the emotional crud and reach the nub of things.

"He's fine." She sniffled. "Well, he's still unconscious, but improving. They reckon he'll wake up in the next few hours. I need to be there when that happens, to talk to him."

"Do they think he'll make a full recovery?" Rayne couldn't contain herself............. she needed to know.

"Yes. They're optimistic he should be OK."

Rayne relaxed back in her seat and sipped her coffee. *Thank God for that. We're back on,* she thought.

"So, uhm, Beth. Do you have any idea of what actually happened to Dane? I mean, why was he kidnapped and what happened to him?"

"Not really, Rayne. All I know is he and his foster Mum were kidnapped, drugged, brought to some awful place in England, somewhere on the South Coast and then rescued. The only blessing is that the doctors and the police believe Dane was probably out for the count the whole time. Whatever they used to drug him with was very powerful"

"So, is it something to do with his foster parent? Or something else?"

"They are not saying, but I reckon your brother may have figured out who did it? Just some comments I overheard. Do you think he might tell you more?"

"No harm in trying."

"I think we need to find out more Rayne. How do we know it won't happen again? Especially if it's related to our work."

"You've got a point. I'll speak with Tiberius and see what I can find out. Promise."

*   *   *

Mr Black continued sitting still. A wood louse crawled across his bare leg, slipped down into the hair of his groin and fell further to the floor. He might have been carved from stone. Oul Deng reckoned he would have made a great monk if he wasn't such a stone cold psychopath.

He no longer felt the pain from his wounds. They were distant from him. The fire had gone out and the temperature in the little room dropped but he remained impervious. He just sat still, cocooned in silence.

*   *   *

Beth was thrilled. Dane had awoken and was taking food. It looked like things were moving in the right direction finally. Then that bloody American detective intervened. He had taken her for a walk around the grounds of the hospital. He said the doctors and consulting psychiatrists had advised him that Dane should now be able to handle the news about what had actually happened during the ordeal he had endured. She was very wary about dumping all of this on him, but Tiberius had been insistent.

It was crucial Dane was given the opportunity to process everything and also vital to his ongoing mental health. Therefore, she was, she felt, being pressurised into explaining what had happened to him and answering any questions he might have as it was felt she was the closest person to him that he would identify with and trust. Especially now Mary was dead. The psychiatrists felt that she rather than Tiberius should handle the discussion with Dane.

Tiberius clinched the argument when he pointed out that Dane would start asking questions now he had recovered. It was felt he would become more and more agitated if his concerns were not addressed. Therefore, it was far better that a sympathetic source, someone he trusted, gently explained what had happened. The doctor responsible for his primary care and a psychiatrist would be present in the room, just to lend her support if it was needed. Tiberius told her specifically not to question Dane about his ordeal but if he gave her any information about it, then he wanted her to relay it to him. "I need to know as much as possible so we can track down the perpetrators and also to protect Dane going forward. OK?" Beth nodded, unconvinced.

Every step bringing her closer to the secure unit Dane was in felt like a pound of weight was being added to her. She just felt weighed down, dragging increasingly heavy chains behind her slight frame.

Too soon, the door to his room appeared. She took a deep breath, all the way to her toes, she felt. Then she pushed the door and walked in. *The difference between Dane's handsome face and the white sheets is minimal,* she thought to herself as she looked at him. It had taken a lot out of him. Suddenly she considered, *what if they had gotten it wrong. What if he simply wasn't ready? What if this might damage him? Set him back? Jesus! It was too great a responsibility.* She sighed again and thought. *It was what it was.* She just had to do it and help him to deal with the reality of it all. She owed him that much. He would do it for her and, at the end of the day. He was her closest friend and he would do the same for her.

"Hi." He smiled the word. Hardly heard. Faintly whispered.

"Hey, Mofo!" She called him that when she wanted to rein in his huge brain, to focus him on something. His expression changed. The smile, gentle and fleeting, disappeared. The beautiful deep eyes looked at her with laser intent.

She had the bizarre thought that he looked like someone in that instant before a disaster, braced for impact. Almost as though he knew that the next brief spasm of time would bring him nothing but pain, like a punch-drunk boxer waiting for that flashing movement, which would knock him out and heralded the darkness and a relief from the punishment he was enduring. But Dane knew it was all ahead of him. His expression said it all.

"Mofo" was short for "Motherfucker". Dane and Beth had spent a warm, boisterous, sunny evening during a rare Indian summer in Mary's tiny back garden amidst the debris of a truly great barbecue, arguing about which of the rude words and phrases they had heard throughout the afternoon were sufficiently worthwhile and useful to the massively difficult challenge humans faced in communicating accurately with each other. After a lot of cheap Pinot Grigio and burnt sausages they had agreed that "Motherfucker" was such an obnoxious phrase that it had a value in stopping one short and alerting that person to a momentous communication. Something which was of great importance to one or both parties to the interaction.

However, they also agreed that abbreviating it to something like "Mofo" made it more palatable. And then they both cackled at the ludicrousness of the whole thing. How silly they were being. They laughed out loud because they realised they were really acting like two pretentious young graduates. But they just didn't give a toss.

When Dane initially cracked the complex mathematical algorithms which underpinned the technology and made Beth's vision a reality, he rang her at four am. She was, under-

standably grumpy and sleepy on the phone until he said
"Beth, Mofo, listen." She knew immediately that this was of
major importance.

So, this was the quickest and kindest way she knew of preparing him, as she sat on the edge of the bed and began to
speak in a low tone.

*   *   *

"Hi?"
Tiberius felt a pleasant feathering in his chest as he recog-
nised Ashling's voice on the phone early one Sunday morn-
ing just after he returned from a run.
"Hey," he answered.
Hope I didn't wake you?"
"No, I was out running."
"Oh"
Then
"Where do you run?"
"Out along the Bull Wall to the lighthouse and back."
"Feel like brunch?"
"Absolutely." Then he thought, *oh God that sounded so
desperate.* But she laughed into the phone and said, "Great.
Meet you at my Mum's place in Monkstown at eleven?"
"Sure." He paused, "where is it?"
"I'll text you the address. OK?"
"See you there." The phone went dead.
Shortly afterward, as he stood under the shower it occurred
to him that they had only spoken about twenty or thirty
words but that was all which was needed. The only other
person he had experienced that with was Alexa. He felt a
sudden pang of guilt, thinking of Alexandra who had been
his first love and who had been cruelly taken from him as
they had been setting out on their journey through life together. But then, he reflected, maybe he was being given a
second chance. "So just take it, Tiberius." He told himself an-

grily and got out of the shower.

He walked to the DART train station overlooking the Grand Canal Docks and took the train which ran along the coast southwards. He got off at the Salthill & Monkstown Station. He walked across the bridge over the line to the path running between the railway and Monkstown beach, then turned left and strolled along enjoying the morning sun on his face and the smell of the sea.

This is a pretty nice place to live, He thought to himself. Eventually he came to a round granite tower. He noticed several people. Some sitting around sunning themselves. Some in swimming gear heading into or out of the sea. He walked around the tower and passed along a terrace of low set beautiful Victorian villas with a narrow road between them and the sea. He looked right out over the bay as he walked.

"Hi Pardner!"

He turned from the diverting vista of the bay to see Cian bursting down the narrow road towards him, followed by Ashling with that amazing smile, which kind of shook him right down to his toes.

He realised as Cian neared him that the little boy wasn't going to stop so he grabbed him and lifted him, swinging him around and receiving a tight, quick hug before he set him back down and of course Cian immediately sprinted back to his Mum.

"Hi again," she said.

"Hey you" he answered. "You look great."

"Thanks. Things are going better, so I feel good too. How about you?"

"I'm good thanks."

She gave him an old-fashioned look which suggested that while she didn't believe him, she wasn't going to argue the point.

"C'mon." She turned and walked back towards what looked like a dead end. The road was a cul-de-sac and there was a large wooden gate set into the wall at the end. Ashling keyed a code into a pad on the right of the gate and it slid to one side. He followed her and Cian into the courtyard of an ultra-modern single story building with what looked like glass walls. He could see through the glass to his right and out beyond it to the sea. There were people sitting on what looked like a terrace beyond.

Cian yanked on a section of the glass wall and managed to slide it to the side and ran through to the terrace, yelling "Tiberius's here! My pal Tiberius is here!"

Ashling looked back over her shoulder at him, grinning and shrugged as if to say, "what am I going to do with him?"

"I don't think I've ever had such an enthusiastic introduction before," Tiberius said to her.

"Hope you live up to your billing," She said mischievously, paused and added "pardner."

An elderly couple got up as he stepped out onto the terrace and the man offered his hand to him saying " welcome to our home, Tiberius. I'm Ashling and Aoife's Dad. Call me Joe."

"Thank you for having me sir," answered Tiberius politely.

"Maam" he added, nodding at the taller striking looking woman with long flowing white hair who was looking at him quizzically behind her husband. She rounded him and offered Tiberius her hand. "No. No. You're very welcome. Anyway, I'm sure you're as keen to meet us as we are to meet you" and she laughed.

Ashling raised her eyebrows at him and said "OK Mum. Let's not try overwhelming our guests before they get to sit at the dinner table. Yes?"

Aoife came forward and shook Tiberius's hand giving him a warm smile. "Thanks for coming the other day. I appreciated it," she said.

"You're welcome. How are you doing?"

"Taking each day as it comes."

"That's the only way I reckon."

"OK everyone. Let's eat!" Ordered Ingrid. And everyone duly obliged.

About an hour or so later, Tiberius had to beg Ingrid to not offer him another slice of pie because he said "I have no will-power to control my appetite in the face of such amazing cooking, so I'll probably say yes and then burst. Sorry if that offends, Maam," he added hastily.

"Not at all. You know, and this is a very Irish thing to say but you remind me of someone."

Aoife snorted and said "Mum don't try on the Irish six degrees of separation thing with Tiberius please! There's only over three hundred million yanks in America."

"No. no." Ingrid said in a thoughtful tone of voice. "I never forget a face and Tiberius is looking increasingly familiar."

"Too much Chablis, Ing," her husband said amiably.

"My job, for lack of a better way of describing it, involves understanding faces and facial structure and I'm increasingly sure Tiberius reminds me of someone," she insisted.

Tiberius was looking at her quietly, wondering if she had done some research on him before dinner. So, he decided to float a line on the surface of this tributary which the conversation had meandered down.

"What do you know about the Art world on the West Coast of the States?" he asked Ingrid directly.

"Well, I've exhibited there a few times in the Getty Museum and some other places. And we had that wonderful holiday in the late eighties, didn't we?" She turned to look fondly at her husband. "Why?"

"Uh, my Mom was, sorry is, an artist."

"What was her name?" asked Ingrid, fascinated.

"She had a bit of a reputation on the West Coast for being a little out there." Tiberius temporized.

"Ohhh, do go on." Ingrid said fascinated.

"Well my surname is Frost? That's your first clue."

"Oh! My! God! Marsala Frost!" Ingrid said dramatically, clapping her hands together.

"Right first time." Tiberius said looking quietly at her.

"Who's Marsala Frost?" Ashling asked.

"She is one of the foremost Avant Garde Artists of the late 20th Century. Personally, I never understood her move into performance art, but she was one of the most skilled draughtspersons I ever encountered. Her early works in pen and ink and her charcoal drawings were right up there with some of the best in the world." Ingrid said a little bit sniffily.

"Yeah well try living with her," Tiberius said drily.

"Did I read that your parents divorced?" Ingrid pushed Tiberius.

"Yep."

"That must have been traumatic."

"Mum!" Ashling interjected. "I really don't think Tiberius came to lunch to be grilled about his parents!"

"Sorry darling but it's so rare one encounters one's peers. Or at least people closely connected to them, offspring even. You must tell me all about her. She's still working, of course?"

"Sorry to disappoint but we had very little to do with my Mom once my parents divorced, so I have no idea about her work or her whereabouts."

"Who wants Coffee and what sort?" interjected Joe diplomatically.

The girls asked for various coffees and Cian wanted a hot chocolate, which his mother objected to but was charmed out of her resistance by his grandfather. Ingrid requested a tisane and Tiberius asked to be shown the toilet, partly to put a little distance between himself and the imperious and inquisitive matriarch of the Clarke family.

Ashling got up to show him the way. Once they left the terrace and were walking along a corridor, out of earshot of the party, she turned and put her hand on Tiberius's arm.

"I'm so sorry about my Mum Tiberius. She can be insufferably nosy sometimes, and like all artists is not good at knowing when to stop. I hope she didn't upset you."

"No. That's OK. No problem." Tiberius paused. Then clearly deciding to trust Ashling, he added. "My folks divorced when we were very young, and we just never knew her. She apparently visited once or twice early on but broke the rules laid down by the divorce judge so that was the end of that. We had a really great childhood. My dad was a little quiet but a genuinely good guy who cared deeply about us."

He covered her hand with his and looked at her smiling. Time stopped for a fleeting moment of quiet in the hall.

A door banged behind them and Ashling turned again to open another door and say brightly "here's the loo." She moved away, restoring a physical space between them.

CHAPTER
THIRTY NINE

"How did it go?"

"Oh God. I never want to have to do anything like that again. I don't know. I just don't know. The fog outside didn't help, made the light even more gloomy."

"Yeah it's kinda weird the way it just rolled in from the Bay. Is it a regular occurrence in Dublin?" Tiberius tried to distract her.

"No. Not really." Beth was sitting opposite Tiberius in the hospital canteen drinking a coffee. She was miserable and felt like a wet rag. All washed out and emptied.

Sweeney entered and walked towards them.

"I think the Doctor has sedated him. He's sleeping now," he said as he sat down.

"Why?" Beth asked a little querulously.

"It's another part of the process I guess. Effectively getting him to sleep on it," replied Tiberius.

"Oh. They think that'll help?"

"Yep. How are you doing? That was a tough job you took on."

"OK. A bit tired now."

"Well Sweeney will take you home if you want to catch some sleep or whatever." Tiberius smiled gently.

"That'd be good." Beth replied. "Are you sure you don't mind?" She turned to Sweeney.

"It's no problem Beth," said Sweeney.

"You guys head off. I'll see you later." Tiberius nodded at

Sweeney.

Tiberius headed along the corridor to Dane's room and looked in through the glass observation panel in the door. The young man was asleep. He turned to go when he noticed someone outside the window, barely distinct in the solid grey mist. Whoever it was, they were looking in. He took his phone and rang Sweeney.

"Sir?"

"Have you left yet?"

"No sir. Just got into the car. It's gotten really foggy."

"OK. Tell Beth to come back inside, that you forgot something. When you're back outside the front I'll give you further instructions."

There was a pause. Then Sweeney said "OK sir. I'm outside now, standing outside the front door."

"Good. There's someone standing outside Dane's room, looking in. Make your way around the side of the building. Keep your phone on, use your earphones. I'll come from the other side and let's see if we can catch this guy. Seems male, wearing a dark hoodie, possibly black or navy. Don't approach him, just get him in your sight line and monitor him. Got that?"

"Yes sir."

Tiberius strode towards the back of the building where he knew there was an outside smoking area which he could access and then head around the side towards the suspicious figure. As he walked, he gave thanks for having people like Sweeney on the team, who quickly understood his superior's request, asked no unnecessary questions and just followed instructions with the minimum of fuss.

Tiberius softly popped the horizontal locking bar on the glass door to the smoking terrace and climbed over the low railing onto the grass. He turned right and moved along by the side of the building. At the corner he stopped and crouched down. Rather than stick his head around the corner, he turned on the camera on his phone and set it to selfie, then inched it out where he could see around the corner. He cursed as the fog was too dense to make anything out. He felt a slight breeze for a moment and tensed when he could finally make out a figure standing by the window about twenty five metres away.

Satisfied the person was angled away from him he risked poking his head out and watched. The figure seemed to be stretching up high, maybe placing something against the glass, but he couldn't' be sure. Tiberius moved further out from the corner. The person was quite tall and broad-shouldered and he felt it was a man.

Suddenly he heard the muffled sound of glass breaking. The figure whirled, turning away from Tiberius, to stare at the far corner, from where the sound had come.

Sweeney appeared around the corner and moving towards the figure, called out "Stay where you are. I am a police officer."

Tiberius cursed silently. What was Sweeney up to?

The figure suddenly darted left and sprinted away from the building. Tiberius figured the boundary wall was about thirty metres away. He and Sweeney ran after him. However, the intruder easily reached the wall before them, leaped up to grab the top and effortlessly disappeared over it. When the two policemen arrived at the wall just seconds after the intruder, Tiberius jumped and grabbed the top of the wall. Rather than jump, Sweeney bent down and grabbing Tiberius's foot, hoisted him up. When Tiberius was sitting on top, Sweeney asked, "which way did he go Sir?" Tiberius pointed to the right and Sweeney sprinted along the inside of the wall while Tiberius dropped over the other side and chased after the man.

Tiberius dropped into a car park full of cars, vans and trucks into which the intruder had disappeared. He could see the vehicles right beside him, but everything further than twenty metres appeared as vague blobs in the fog. After a few moments he could hear footsteps and Sweeney appeared running towards him.

"He pass you?" Tiberius asked.

"No sir."

"Right. We keep within each other's eye line at all times. No more than two or three cars apart and let's try and see if we can find this guy." With that they separated and walked slowly through the car park. Tiberius ducked down occasionally to see if he could see the intruder's feet under the vehicles but to no avail.

They slowly paced along the ranks of vehicles, constantly alert, but if the man was there, he was abnormally good at stealthy movement. Also, the dense fog muffled all sounds and they felt like they were totally insulated from the normal world.

Sweeney was sweating heavily. He was wearing his full uniform and it was a heavy cloth with a "stab vest" over it. Suddenly he felt horribly exposed. Vulnerable. It occurred to him this guy was probably armed and like the vast majority of the Irish police force, Sweeney and Tiberius were not.

As they advanced across the carpark the light seemed to decrease more, becoming even more grey and opaque, which did nothing to improve Sweeney's mood.

They came to the last line of parked vehicles and Sweeney checked to his right. He turned his head to signal Tiberius, when a large dark Lexux SUV which had been sitting in the middle of the lane at right angles to the cars swept silently towards him. It caught him in the thighs and threw him into the air. Sweeney felt the impact on his legs and then he was weightless for a few seconds which felt like forever, until he slapped onto the hard tarmacadam. Suddenly Tiberius's face was there, but fuzzy, out of focus.

"Sweeney! Sweeney! Can you hear me? Can you speak?"

He could hear his own voice answering but it sounded like it was miles away.

"Sorry sir. I didn't see a bit of glass on the ground. Stood on it. Alerted the bugger. Sorry sir. Sorry. I bloody hurt. Oh man.

Oh." Then he couldn't feel anything, and it went black.

*   *   *

Doyle walked down the corridor and stopped beside Tiberius.

"How is he?" Doyle asked.

"Touch and go."

"Sorry?"

"He was lucky it happened so close to a hospital, but he's pretty badly smashed up. The doc said their primary objective right now was to stabilise him. He may be bleeding internally."

"Jesus! Who was the guy?" Doyle's voice spilled over with anger.

"Don't know. I never saw his face."

"Was it that bastard Black?"

"Not sure. Sweeney might have gotten a look at him, but I'm not optimistic. The fog was very heavy. The kid stood on a piece of glass when we nearly had the guy cornered and alerted him. So, he took off but before he did, he must have looked straight at Sweeney. Unfortunately, he would have been thirty to forty feet from him. Physically he seemed smaller in stature than I would expect Black to be."

"What about when he was hit by the car? He would have been closest to him then?"

"Nope, the guy drove into him from behind."

"So, if he pulls through, we mightn't even get an ID?"

Tiberius didn't answer for a while, just turned to look through the window of the Intensive Care Unit, in which Sweeney was the only occupant.

Eventually, he turned away and said quietly, "If, being the appropriate word here."

"I was getting to like that kid. Very smart too. Still waters and all that."

"Same here."

Doyle turned to walk away and then stopped. He realised Tiberius needed to leave and either talk about what happened or to just occupy his mind. Doyle felt Tiberius was possibly feeling guilty for what happened to their young colleague. So, he suggested they return to their base of operations in the University's Police facility.

"I'll check with the Hospital admin to see if anyone on staff owns a dark Lexus SUV before we leave. It's their overflow carpark and is mostly used by staff as I recall." Doyle added.

Tiberius agreed and they left via the Administration office of the hospital where a staff member said she'd email him a list of registered carpark users and their cars.

Doyle drove slowly back to the office through the fog. Doyle asked, "do you think it might have been our suspect?"

"Not sure."

"Percentage?"

"Can't say at this point. He definitely escaped in England but the Major reckoned one of their guys winged him. So, I can't see how he could move as well as the guy we chased."

"What do you mean? How well did he move?"

"Once he was alerted to our presence, the guy swivelled, sprinted around thirty yards in seconds and jumped or maybe vaulted to the top of an eight or maybe ten foot high wall. I'm pretty fit and a runner but I couldn't catch him, and I needed a leg up from Sweeney to get over that wall."

"A serious individual."

"Yes, and I reckon he's had some training in stealth tactics, because once we went into the car park, he was just gone. Even with the fog helping him, guy's a ghost. And that's training. Tradecraft. He made it to his SUV or stole an SUV in really quick time. If he stole it, then he's smart."

"Smart? How does that compute?"

"Because he picked a hybrid vehicle and he was already driving it on the electric motor, silently, out of the car park when he hit Sweeney."

"Which is why he got Sweeney. You said he hit him from behind. The poor guy didn't hear it coming?"

"Yeah, most of the lanes in the car park were gravel. Sweeney would have heard the vehicle on that surface and might have gotten out of the way, but the perimeter lane was asphalt. Son of a bitch was virtually silent."

The two men said no more until they arrived back at the office.

As they walked through the door into the room, Prendergast jumped up with a concerned expression on her face. "How is he, Sir?" she asked Tiberius.

At that moment Tiberius's phone rang. He didn't recognise the number and thinking it might be the hospital, he reversed his tracks and went out into the hallway, closing the door behind him to take the call.

After a few minutes he came back in. Doyle and Prendergast looked up expectantly from a computer screen they were huddled over.

Tiberius's face gave nothing away, then he said, "can you credit it? Sweeney wanted to know if his phone was bust when he was hit? And he's looking for his laptop." Prendergast smiled in relief and said "Oh! He's on the mend so!" She grinned at Doyle and held up her hand to high five him.

Doyle ignored the hand and grumbled "I'm not into these bloody Americanisms!"

Tiberius reached over him and slapped her hand. "It's better than expected. The internal bleeding was light and they stopped it. Apparently no damage to internal organs. Busted leg, arm, three cracked ribs. They reckon that going immediately unconscious stopped him from moving around and I didn't move him, which helped. They did brain scans and he doesn't seem to have any damage to his head."

"He was lucky it's not worse."

"Yeah."

"Where's Beth?" asked Prendergast.

"Glued to the seat outside the door of the Intensive Care Unit. She, point blank, refused to leave with us," answered

Tiberius.

"Ah young Love!" Doyle murmured as he stared at the computer screen in front of him. He sat back and put his hands behind his head. "OK! There are three Lexus SUV's which have parking rights in the carpark. One is white, One is a kind of light gold colour and one a dark charcoal. The dark one belongs to a Surgeon called Michael Brooks. I'll call him." Doyle pulled out his mobile and dialled a number from the screen.

Tiberius was sitting on the edge of a desk beside the window, seemingly looking out at the dense wall of grey outside. He was deep in thought.

Doyle ended the call and immediately dialled another number. "Hi this is Sergeant Doyle of the Garda. Can I speak to your head of security? Thanks." He sat back, waiting. After a few moments, he spoke again "Hi. Yes, thanks. He'll be OK. Can you do me a quick favour? Send one of your guys over to the car park where my colleague was hit and check on the car space marked Seven E? Should be a dark Lexus SUV there? Great. Thanks. You have my number on screen yeah? OK. I'll wait for your call."

The office was quiet except for Prendergast and Doyle occasionally tapping on their keyboards.

After about ten minutes, Doyle's phone rang.

"Hullo? Yes thanks. OK. That's very helpful. Thanks for doing it so quickly."

Doyle put down the phone and said, "No SUV there and the owner said that the last time he saw it was when he parked it there this morning. I'll put out an alert for the vehicle, description and registration. Maybe we'll get lucky."

"Doubt it. Like I said. This guy is smart."

After a few moments, Tiberius asked "It was sunny early this morning. What time did the fog roll in at?"

"Not sure, Boss. Why?"

"Contact the security guys at the hospital again and see if they have CCTV in the carpark. If they do and we can review it, we might be able to see him scoping out his entry and es-cape routes. Might even catch him breaking into the SUV"

Doyle picked up his phone and dialled the hospital. Fifteen minutes later they were on their way back. When they ar-rived the Head of Security Tony Devlin was waiting for them inside the foyer. He led them to a room with a bank of five large screens. Tony sat them in front of the screen at the end of the desk.

"I've set up the video feed from the server on this screen for you." He said. "Just click on those controls at the bottom of the screen to move backwards or forwards. The slider on the right hand side of the screen controls the speed of replay and the one on the left hand zooms in. You just grab the screen with the mouse to move to the location you want. If you need me, I'll be in my office, just dial zero four two on that phone and I'll pop back. We can give you copies of the video feed, no problem. It's set to begin just after Dawn this morn-ing, around six twenty am." Tony left the room.

Doyle took the mouse and clicked on Play and the two of them settled in to watch.

Initially the camera was displaying a panoramic view of the entire car park with the time displayed on the top of the screen and as nothing was happening, they speeded it up. Until around seven thirty am when a car entered the car park. Doyle focussed on the entrance to the car park and they watched as a variety of vehicles entered the car park. Then Doyle hit pause and pointing at the screen asked, "That it?"

Tiberius straightened up, looking at the dark vehicle just visible in the top right hand corner of the screen, approach-ing the entrance to the car park. "just move it forward slowly," he asked.

The vehicle crawled glacially through the entrance and into full view. Doyle zoomed in and confirmed that the num-ber plate was the one they were looking for. "We're lucky, it's a good quality system," Doyle muttered. He zoomed back out and the vehicle continued on its way to park near the end of the parking lane, where it was reversed into a space and the driver got out. He retrieved a coat and bag from the back seat closed the door and walked away.

"OK, so just zoom in on the SUV and fast forward the video?" asked Tiberius.

"Gotcha."

The video sped along until about two hours later the fog began to arrive and to their frustration the SUV disappeared from view. Doyle zoomed back out and back in again, but it was no good they couldn't see a thing.

Doyle paused the screen and asked "Now what? This could be a total waste of time, Boss."

"Just thinking." Tiberius was silent. "Where's the camera situated?"

"As far away from the SUV as it could be, unfortunately."

"Yeah but where?"

"About five metres from the entrance on top of a pole."

"OK. So, he's got to drive past it to get out, yeah?"

"Brilliant. Let's see what we get." Doyle altered the focus of the video and they were focussed on a piece of dark tarmacadam just in front of the camera and the entrance.

"I think that here will be our best chance to see the SUV leaving and, just maybe, the driver."

"Yeah, looks good. We'll know soon enough once another vehicle leaves. If we can see in and make out the drivers features." Doyle speeded up the video feed again and they waited to until a medium sized white van flashed past. Doyle slowly rewound the feed until they could see the van reversing back through their field of vision. As soon as he had the front of the van centre screen Doyle zoomed in and they could clearly see the driver was a woman, driving one handed with what looked like a mobile phone held to her ear with her other hand.

"Naughty girl," said Doyle. "I could do her for that. Using her mobile phone while driving a vehicle."

"OK so just speed up and let's see if we can make out this guy," Tiberius sounded impatient.

Doyle promptly set the feed racing forward again, only slowing every time a vehicle passed by.

"Stop!" said Tiberius. "Reverse it slowly. Can you pan over to the right a little and zoom in a bit?"

"Sure," Doyle answered, concentrating intently on the screen.

"Stop!" Tiberius leaned forward. "See him? Just keep moving it backward slowly." They could see a dark hooded figure moving along the right of the screen until it disappeared into the mist.

"We don't know it's our man Boss."

"No, but he's walking towards the general area of the SUV and he's doing it thirty minutes before we encountered the intruder outside the window. The dark hoodie and dark trousers are consistent and if you look at the way he moves, he's an athlete. It might be a bit of a stretch but he's not a million miles away from the general appearance of our suspect. Anyway, let's move on."

Doyle clicked the mouse and the screen moved forward again. He stopped when the time on screen showed the approximate time Tiberius and Sweeney had encountered and began pursuing the intruder into the car park.

Both men were tense until suddenly an SUV materialised on screen and swept past. Doyle hit rewind and slowed the feed to a crawl.

Frustratingly, they couldn't make out the features of the driver.

"Call Devlin. Get him in here," ordered Tiberius.

Within minutes Devlin arrived.

"Is there anything we can do to make the features on this driver clearer?" asked Doyle.

Devlin asked, "can I take over your seat?"

Doyle got up and stood behind Devlin, looking over his shoulder.

"OK," Devlin said, more to himself than to the two police-men. "Firstly, are we going backwards or forwards?"

"What difference does that make?" asked Tiberius.

"I don't fully understand it myself but whatever way this system is programmed, the picture is clearer and crisper playing forward than reversing. It's a video compression thing, I think."

As he spoke Devlin reversed the screen feed until the SUV disappeared again into the mist then he ran it forward at normal speed until it began to appear. He stopped the feed and then set it to advance one frame at a time. Gradually the screen filled with the front of the SUV.

"Now, we're probably a wee bit too close so there's some pixilation here. Let's pull back a little." Tiberius and Doyle leaned forward eagerly as the image shifted but sat back in frustration when they couldn't make out the features of the driver more clearly.

"Hang on now," said Devlin, sounding like he was thinking out loud. He picked up the phone and dialled. "Marga? Can you come to the CCTV monitoring room please? Yes, right away. Thank you." He turned to Tiberius and said, "I reckon we might be able to sharpen the image a bit more. Well, Marga should be able to do it. She's from Northern Spain and worked for a video software company before she married an Irish bloke and came to live in Dublin. Bit of luck really, she's significantly improved our usage of this system already. We're getting a lot more from it. Although, we are talking about cars banging into each other mostly. Nothing like this. "

After five minutes, the door opened, and a tiny brunette came in. "Hola Tony?" she smiled. Tony stood and gestured to her to sit in his seat. "Can you sharpen this image for us Marga? These police officers want to try and identify the driver?"

"Si, I will have a loook," she said in heavily accented English. Her hands began to fly over the keyboard and mouse. Windows popped up and disappeared rapidly. After some time, Tiberius felt the image was definitely improving, sharpening. Then it disappeared and a grey window appeared covering the whole screen.

"Now, ees going to render. So, we wait. Eet will not be queek because my program is running at the same time" said Marga quietly.

Line by line the image scrolled slowly down the screen, until a face came clearly into view.

"Jaysus," Tiberius could hear Doyle behind him. "Didn't expect that now did we?"

CHAPTER FORTY

"Mum? It's Beth"

"Hi Lovey. How are you?" Her mother's voice sounded surprised. "Everything OK?"

"I'm fine. Fine. Everything OK with you and whatshisname?"

"It's Felicien, Darling." Her mother paused and then sounded mildly irritated. "Please be nice Beth."

Beth sighed then continued "Have you any plans to use the Spanish place?"

"No. You know I haven't been there since your father and I separated."

"OK. Well I'm going to use it for a few weeks. A friend of mine had an accident and needs somewhere to recuperate."

"I won't be using it and have no intention of using it for a very long time, if ever. I'm surprised you're even asking me about it."

"Just checking. I don't want any surprise visits from you and whoever your latest boyfriend is."

"Beth. That's not fair. If you're not going to be nice, I'm going to have to hang up."

"Don't worry Mum. I'll do it for both of us!"

Beth ended the call and resisted the temptation to fling her mobile against the wall outside the ICU. She was still so angry with her mother and father for splitting up. Even now, two years after the fact. She felt betrayed by them and was dealing with it in what she knew was a very immature way, taking out her hurt and pain on them every time they spoke. Especially her mother.

Still, at least, she knew now she'd have the house free for the foreseeable future. Time to move onto the next part of the plan she'd come up with while sitting outside the Intensive Care Unit. She had been so relieved when the doctor came out half an hour earlier and told her Garda Sweeney was going to be fine. However, the relief was swiftly followed by the thought that while Dane was sitting in the hospital bedroom, he was vulnerable and when he left, he could be tracked and attacked again, or worse. No. He needed to get out of the hospital and in a way which meant that no one would know where he was until the two of them were able to figure out what to do about this situation they had gotten themselves into.

She dialled another number.

"Hi Beth," her father's voice was faint. He was somewhere very windy and she could hardly hear him. She found herself automatically speaking louder. "Hi Poppa Bear. Where the hell are you – sounds like a wind tunnel?"

"Nearly at the top of Ben Nevis in the Grampians, Pet. I'm amazed you got me, didn't think there'd be any coverage up here."

"Dad, it's a satellite phone," she said in an amused tone. "I got it because I never know where you're going to be next!"

Beth's father had reacted to his wife's infidelity and the subsequent breakup of his marriage by turning his interest in hill walking into a project to trek through and over most of the mountain ranges in Europe with some buddies. Beth's concern for his safety had prompted the purchase of the satellite phone which had a special facility for calling in a helicopter rescue in case of an accident.

"Of course! Of course! Anyway, what's up Beth? Do you need anything?"

"Can I borrow one of your cars? I want to drive Dane to the flat in Avila and take some time out. He's been in hospital and I want to help him."

"You're so good! Of course. Ring Joe and he'll sort you out

OK? Is Dane alright?"

"He's fine, just some health issues he's getting over. Thanks for the car, Dad."

"No problem, but why don't you fly?"

"Just want to take some time out. There's no rush to get there."

"OK Beth. I've got to go. We're hoping to make the summit and start back down before the weather closes in. Love you!"

"Love you too, Poppa Bear. You be careful."

*   *   *

Tiberius looked over Doyle's shoulder at the fuzzy image on screen. It was an oriental face, maybe Chinese. Tiberius and Tony left the room and stood in the hallway discussing it. After some time, Doyle walked out to them.

"Sorry, but Marga reckons it's as good as it gets." Doyle.

"We're unlikely to ID the driver" Tiberius said quietly.

"Nope."

"I'm sorry we couldn't be of more assistance," interjected Tony.

"You've been great. Really appreciate it," Tiberius turned to Tony with a tired smile and shook his hand.

Tiberius and Doyle left the hospital with Doyle driving and they went to the Intercontinental Hotel in Ballsbridge. They sat in the plush lounge waiting for Rayne.

"Hi Babes." Rayne leant around the side of the wingback chair Tiberius was in and kissed him on the cheek. She shook hands with Doyle and sat opposite them.

"Thanks for meeting us. Rayne." Tiberius spoke in a formal tone, letting her know the way he wanted her to approach the discussion.

"No problem. What can I do?"

Doyle surprised Tiberius by pulling out a printout of the image of the driver of the SUV and offering it to Rayne, saying "Any chance you've ever come across this guy?"

Rayne looked at the picture and her eyes widened for a split second. Then she took the paper, sat back and studied it carefully. She handed it back to Doyle, saying "No sorry. Who is he?"

"Just someone we are interested in," replied Doyle quickly, tucking the paper into his pocket.

"Why did you think I might know him?" Rayne asked sounding a little annoyed.

Doyle shrugged and said, "we're going to be showing this pic to everyone involved in any way with the case."

"He looks Chinese," Rayne remarked, "but it's a crap photo. What's he done?"

"He was covertly monitoring Dane's hospital room from outside. He fled when we challenged him and ran down one of my team with an SUV." Tiberius answered.

"God! Show it to me again? I didn't really look at it properly first time." Rayne held her hand out to Doyle. She took the picture and looked at it more carefully.

After a moment or two, she handed it back and said, "Well if he isn't local, then another thought is that a lot of Chinese and Far Eastern attendees came into Dublin for the Web Summit. He might be attached to one of those groups?"

Tiberius stared at her intently. "So you don't know him?"

"Don't think so, no. However, it's possible if he was around the Summit I might have encountered him there?"

Tiberius's face was like stone, betraying no emotion. "OK Rayne. Thanks for that."

Tiberius and Doyle walked silently to their car. They got in and sat there for a moment or two, Doyle making no movement to turn on the engine.

Finally Doyle said quietly as he stared out the window, "she knows him."

"Yep."

"Sometimes I hate my job."

"Same," came back Tiberius's reply.

"What do you want to do Boss?"

Tiberius was thinking hard. Silence sat in the car between them like another passenger, growing more oppressive with each passing second. Finally, Tiberius reached across himself and taking hold of his seatbelt he fastened it. The loud click seemed to turn on a switch inside him and he said, "start watching her. Her Security team will be very good so we need to be very careful. Can't be you or me. She knows us and they will have made us also. Rayne has never met Prendergast, so use her. Did you say Sweeney is able to work off his laptop in the hospital?"

"Yes?"

"Once we've ID'd Rayne's security team we need to check each of them out. Sweeney should be able to determine if any of them are oriental." Tiberius paused again, looking out the window.

Doyle broke the fresh silence and asked the question they were both wrestling with: "If she knows him why wouldn't she say?"

Tiberius sighed heavily and tapping three fingers in succession said "A. He might work for her? B. He might work for someone she is associated with? C. Neither A nor B are correct, but she does know him somehow and she didn't say anything to us because she might want to use it as leverage in some way?" Tiberius sighed. "I know my sister. If she is in the middle of a deal of some sort then she will not allow anything to get in the way of it."

"She sounds like a tough cookie."

"She is."

"OK so Prendergast? As I recall she did a course on covert surveillance and has done a stint with CAB, the Criminal Assets Bureau. I know one of the guys on it and he said she was like a feckin' ghost!"

Tiberius just nodded. His mind racing through the possibilities which might fall from Rayne's potential involvement, even if totally coincidental. It might be the thing that did take him off the case.

"We have to alert our superiors to this potential development." Tiberius said quietly.

"Yeah," Doyle agreed. "It would be safer Boss. Better coming from you in your usual weekly update to Harcourt Street?"

"Yeah. No choice really."

Tiberius's phone range held the screen up to Doyle – it was Rayne.

"Rayne?"

"Tiber, I just realised. I never asked how your guy who was knocked down is doing?"

"Thanks for asking Rayne. He's going to be OK. Some broken bones and bruises."

"Well I'm glad he's OK. You take care too Babes. Don't do anything crazy."

"Thanks. Gotta go. Bye." Tiberius ended the conversation and looked at Doyle who shrugged, started the car and drove out of the Intercontinental Hotel Car park.

*　　　　*　　　　*

Rayne stood in the window of a bedroom belonging to one of her security team. looking at the car driving out. She had raced to the room as soon as Tiberius and Doyle left her. She hoped the position of the room would give her a good view into the car. She wanted to observe the body language of her brother and his colleague.

Damn, Rayne thought. *Got a problem with Tiber now! That's all I need.* Rayne knew her brother intimately and could tell he was trying to hide his emotions during the latter half of their brief meeting. Watching the car before, during and after her call to Tiberius confirmed it. He was not a happy bunny. She had not convinced them she didn't know the Oriental man in the photo.

She sat in the armchair beside the window and considered the position. *There might be a benefit in alerting Deng that the police had a photo of his guy Riga. He would owe me. On the other hand is there a greater benefit in simply giving Tiber the name? I'd be in the clear and he would stop looking at me in the context of this case, which is vital."*

Rayne absently drummed her fingers on the screen of her mobile beside her on the table in the window, thinking through alternatives. *I could do nothing. Take a chance Tiberius would not have spotted my stupid reaction when I recognised Riga."* She stopped drumming her fingers and sat up. *I could also do both? Alert Tiberius either directly or indirectly as to who Riga is and also let Deng know the police have identified his employee.*

If she simply told Tiberius she got a direct benefit. If she did it anonymously he might still be concerned about her, so better to confirm Riga's identity directly. However, she would call Deng before telling Tiberius to give him time to get Riga out of the country.

Satisfied, she took out a different phone and made a call to Deng's PA Shaylene.

"Hello Ms Frost." Said Shaylene's husky voice.

"Hi Shaylene. Are you with Deng?"

"Uhm." Shaylene temporised, "I can reach him quickly?"

"Good. I need to speak with him on a secure phone. I have some information for him he needs to hear."

"This phone is secure. Hold on," came back the woman's reply in a cool, calm tone. A few moments later she heard Deng's voice "Rayne?"

"Deng. I am going to do you a favour. You remember the man you didn't quite introduce to me at that lunch in Bel Air last year?" Rayne was referring to a private lunch they had had in a very discreet upmarket restaurant Deng owned in Los Angeles, during which Riga stood menacingly behind Deng throughout the meal.

"Yes." Deng understood immediately who she was referring to.

"He ought to take a vacation, do some travelling."

"Oh?"

"Like immediately?"

Deng was silent, then said, "we should meet, I suspect."

"Sure but heed my advice."

"Will do. Let's talk soon."

"OK." Rayne said, "bye."

Shaylene came back on the line. "Perhaps you might like to meet here at our current residence, Ms Frost? Say two pm tomorrow?"

"Tomorrow won't work. How about later today?"

Shaylene's end of the conversation went silent for a few moments then she said, "four thirty?"

"Fine. I'll be there."

Rayne left with her security team and boarded the SUVs parked in the underground car park of the hotel. They drove her to the nearby beach at Sandymount. She got out and walked onto the flat sandy beach. As she walked along, she took out her normal phone and rang Tiberius.

"Hi Babes!" she said brightly into the phone.

"Hi Rayne. What's up?" Tiberius sounded distant.

"I've been thinking about that photo you showed me. I don't want to sound racist but I find it difficult to discriminate between one Chinese guy and another. They genuinely look very similar to me, but that picture's been bugging me since I looked at it."

"Go on." Tiberius sounded more interested.

"Well. Like I said it's been bugging me. When I initially looked at it I thought he looked a bit familiar but y'know not enough to say I did recognise him. I kind of discarded it?"

"Rayne. Get to the point," Tiberius sounded irritated.

"OK. OK. Jeez Tiber! Who's helping who here?"

"Sorry but things are a bit fraught."

"OK. Well anyway I think he works for one of the heavy hitters who attended the Web Summit. Don't hold me to it because it was a crappy photo, but I'm fairly certain I saw him in the VIP lounge at the Web Summit. I'm just trying to work out which person he works for, because it was very hectic at the time, as you can imagine Babes."

"OK Rayne. Thanks. Contact me if you can remember who he works for."

"Will do."

"Bye."

"Bye."

Rayne put the phone in her pocket and headed back to the SUV. After an hour or so, she arrived at Deng's house. He was in the same room, in the identical position as he had been during their last meeting, except that Riga was no longer present.

"Deng," she strode forward and shook his hand.

"Rayne."

"I'll get straight to it. My contact has informed me that a police officer was knocked down and injured by an oriental man driving a stolen Lexus yesterday."

Deng continued looking at her steadily, showing no emotion.

Rayne continued. "The Irish police have a photograph of the individual. I managed to get sight of the photograph. It's Riga."

"That is inconvenient."

"So I am not going to speculate as to your motives for sending Riga to the hospital and why he would have felt he needed to avoid the police. However, I don't want anything to interfere with our deal and that is why I am helping you." Rayne leant against the glass with her arms folded. "Nothing is going to interfere with our deal on your side Deng, is it?"

"No. We will honour our commitments."

"But what happens if I do everything I have committed to for my part and something else interferes with the completion of this deal?"

"I will still honour my commitment to you."

"I hope so. I'm taking a risk assisting you in this manner."

"I understand. Have you discussed my offer with your partners?" Deng switched the focus of the conversation adroitly.

"I have tee'd them up. We need to get a few codicils in place relating to the legal and ethical usage of the platform to satisfy my partners concerns about such matters." She shook her head, smiling. Deng picked up on where she was going with this.

"We will have our lawyers insert some sections into the agreements which should satisfy them."

"Excellent, as long as they're not too restrictive."

"They will be very restrictive and will apply to every country in Europe and to the United States." Rayne looked at him quizzically and then the penny dropped.

"You're going to site the servers for the platform somewhere else aren't you?"

"That will not be your concern."

"OK."

Deng shook hands with Rayne and she left. On her way back into the city centre she called Beth's mobile number but it went straight to voicemail so she said, "hi Beth. Rayne here. Just wanted to update you and Dane. I have been speaking with several parties about the platform and have narrowed it down to three serious contenders. I'm using Dane's suggestion about the ethical and legal usage clauses in the agreement to weed out any investors whose integrity we might have concerns about.

One guy, Deng Holman Lee, said that he welcomed my comments and that he would have his lawyers get to work on a mutually acceptable wording. I liked that. He has a reputation back in L.A. as being tough but a straight shooter. Anyway, I'll keep you guys updated as I move forward with the process."

CHAPTER
FORTY ONE

Tiberius stood in front of his Boss's desk and an impressive desk it was too. When not discharging his responsibilities which included the eight Special Crime Operations Units that reported to him, Assistant Commissioner Kane collected antiques. So when he had been promoted to his current position, he had made only two changes to his office. He had taken every picture and chart off the walls and he had replaced the utilitarian desk with this massive Victorian leather and mahogany Partner Desk.

"So Tiberius. Time flies by and from my perusal of your reports. We have not even a prima facie case constructed? Bit disappointing."

Tiberius knew better than to say anything at this point, so he just stood there. Kane was a man under severe pressure. The Shannon attacks had stretched the Police resources to breaking point and this was the guy who had to make it all work.

"Well, sit down," harrumphed his superior.

"Thank you sir."

Kane flipped open the file on his desk and said, "your latest update has given us some cause for concern."

"Sir?"

"You know what I mean. Your bloody sister man!" He growled. "Stuck in the middle of your damn investigation. An investigation which, from all appearances, has stalled."

"Yes Sir."

"Unless she turns out to be squeaky clean, you're compromised. Can't continue really," continued Kane in a conversational tone.

"Sir, I" Tiberius began

"No. No." Kane cut across him. "Tiberius. You and I both know the situation. Unless she's cleared of involvement, it would undermine the case if you were to continue in your current role. No. The question now is, what do we do?" Kane mused, talking to himself more than to his subordinate. "Who should take over? There are very few officers at your level available. And that's before we consider their capability in handling a sensitive, awkward bugger of a case like this."

"If I can make a suggestion, Sir?" Tiberius leaned forward.

"Go on."

"DS Doyle has been working as my number two on the case and although it hasn't been very long, I've been impressed with his abilities and approach."

"You want Doyle to take over from you? And keep you in the loop too I suppose?"

"No sir. I just feel that it will take time for another officer to be brought up to speed. Time we can ill afford and, to be honest, I reckoned you were going to can me from the investigation so I did a little digging into his history and other than one blot on his copy book, he has all of the skills, experience and training to get this case over the line, Sir."

"One blot?" Kane leaned on his desk wearily. "Detective Inspector Doyle, as he was then, nearly killed a fellow officer in an assault which occurred not fifty metres from where I am sitting. He has self-control and anger management issues, to say the least of it."

"Granted, but he's an excellent cop. Old style, straight and one of the smartest guys I have ever met Sir." Tiberius defended Doyle stoutly. "Furthermore, he has changed sir, and the proof is that after being demoted to a rank and file officer he was promoted again to Sergeant, which I understand is unheard of." Tiberius leaned back and folded his arms. "Sir, my recommendation is Tiernan Doyle, for the simple reason that I believe he'll get the job done. It is one of the most difficult cases I've ever encountered in my career sir, but I would instinctively trust him to see it through."

Kane's head was bowed, looking at the file. He leafed through it. "You think this guy Black killed the victims? Does Doyle agree?"

"Actually Sir, we think the suspect Black killed the Plenderleiths in Dublin, Gillian MacAllister in Nice and more recently, Mary Gill in Dungeness. We have reason to believe that a different perpetrator, possibly female, killed Jo Anne Sutherland and that it may have been as a result of mistaken identity."

"With the exception of the Gill woman, all evidence you have is circumstantial, though"

"True."

"The British have issued a P42 notice, which is a bit annoying. It would be better if we had done that first."

"I'm wasn't aware we could have done it also, Sir. That's a problem?"

"It means they get first dibs when he's caught," said Kane absentmindedly. "Yes." He continued. "I've read the files and your reports. If it wasn't for the Shannon Attacks, Black and your failure to arrest him, would be all over the newspapers." Kane was silent for a while, then he said in a decisive tone, "we've enough on our plates right now so the Nice murder is not our priority. I assume you've been liaising with the French police?"

"Yes Sir."

"I liked Roger MacAllister. Never met her. OK. We'll let Doyle run it, but he'll be on a tight leash and I want you to piss off for a while. Take a holiday somewhere. Get some sun on your bones. Dismissed." Kane closed the file on his desk.

Tiberius left the office and went out to the street where

Doyle was waiting for him.

"Well? How did it go? Are you OK, Boss?" asked Doyle anxiously.

"Coffee." Tiberius said and strode down Harcourt Street, making Doyle hurry to keep up. Tiberius ignored Doyle's queries until they were settled in the window of a café on a little side street off Harcourt Street.

Tiberius took a long drink from his cup, looked at Doyle and said, "I'm off the case."

"Oh great! They really don't want to solve it do they? Bunch of muppets!" said Doyle viciously.

"Well that was the bad part." Said Tiberius with a smile.

"There's a good part?" asked Doyle despondently. "How could there even be a reasonable part let alone a good part to that bloody news."

"I recommended you to take over the investigation. And they said yes."

"You are joking!" Doyle was astonished. "They really are in trouble."

"Nope. Kane agreed with my assessment that you were the ideal candidate for the job. It was easier than I expected so I reckon he had already considered it. I didn't have to batter down the door, just gave it a little push."

Doyle started to smile and then looked miserable again. "Tiber, I hate that good news for me springs from bad news for you. Really."

"I know, but I regard this as the best outcome in a bad situation. Just remember they'll be watching you like a hawk. If you screw up in any way, they'll dance on your head buddy and you'll never get a chance like this again."

"I know. I know. They don't trust me an inch. What are you going to do?"

"I've been encouraged to take a break."

"A break. A bloody break. Jesus!"

"It sucks, but it is what it is. So in my last report. I clarified what you and I have concluded regarding the case. Black killed the Plenderleiths, Gillian MacAllister in Nice and Mary Gill in Dungeness. We reckon that an, as yet unidentified, maybe female assailant killed the Sutherland girl. I also explained that Black got away during the firefight in Dungeness and at this point in time, neither the British nor we have any information as to his whereabouts.

I suggest you re-focus your attempts on tracking down the identity and whereabouts of the other suspect on the basis that unless Black appears again somewhere, it's down to just firming up the evidence, timescales and preparing a file for Harcourt Street to determine if a file should be sent to the Public Prosecutors office. Not that they can do anything without someone to try in court. With regard to the Sutherland case, keep slogging away at it and something will break."

"That makes sense. Will you inform the team or do you want me to?"

"You do it. Better if it comes from you and it'll go some way towards cementing your role quickly."

"OK." Doyle finished his coffee and stood. He offered his hand to Tiberius who shook it.

"I'm sorry Boss."

"Just call me Tiber now, but I'm still gonna call you Doyle"

"Wouldn't have it any other way."

Tiberius sat back down as his friend left. When the waitress came over he ordered a sandwich with another coffee, thinking as he did so that he had nothing better to do and it was also better to work out what he was going to do next on a full stomach.

Twenty four hours later, Beth drove through a deserted office park. She took it slowly as she was still getting used to driving her Dad's left hand drive SUV on the Irish roads. Here and there, lights gleamed in office buildings that were empty at the weekends and she was glad of it because she had turned off the headlights once she entered the office park. She turned into the front of a building with a For Sale sign outside it and drove around the side to the rear. She parked beside a gate set into a fence comprised of green perpendicular metal stakes, each about ten feet high.

Beth got out with a large bolt cutters and with a lot of difficulty managed to cut the chain. She had to virtually swing out of the bolt cutters to get enough leverage to do the job. *I'd never make a burglar or a secret agent,* she thought. *I'm no Evelyn Salt.* She returned the tool to the boot of the Porsche Cayman and, trying to keep the noise of her activities to a minimum, pulled the gate just sufficiently ajar to slip through into the gardens beyond.

Keeping to the perimeter of the gardens she made her way to the building at the far side. Beth counted the windows she passed as she moved carefully along the wall. When she came to the one she wanted, she tried to raise it gently. No joy. It was fastened on the inside. However, she was prepared for this and pulled a long thin piece of metal from her jacket sleeve and inserting it into the middle of the window pressed it to one side. There was a quiet click and she put the piece of metal away before climbing into the darkened room.

She stopped by the side of the bed and whispered quietly "Dane? Dane. It's me. Beth?"

The figure in the bed said groggily "wha? Who?"

"Sssh," she whispered urgently. "It's me Beth. Keep your voice down."

Fully awake now, Dane levered himself up in the bed facing her. "Beth. What's going on?"

She knelt so that her face was close to his.

"Mofo, I think you should come with me. I've got a place we can go to. Take some time out. You can rest and we can figure out what to do next?"

"Where?"

"It's abroad. I've got it all planned. We just go and tell no one."

"Uh Beth. I'm not sure."

"Dane, if no one knows where we are and we just use cash, no cards or anything. We'll be safe."

"Off the grid?"

"Bit melodramatic but, yeah."

He sat quietly for a moment and Beth resisted the temptation to try and persuade him further. She knew him well enough when to shut up.

Finally, after what seemed to her like ages, but was probably less than a minute, Dane slowly sat upright and swivelled on the bed, gingerly putting his feet on the ground.

"OK," he said.

Beth took off her backpack and took out a pair of jeans, teeshirt, a hoodie and a pair of shoes, all black.

"Pretty sure of yourself," he grunted.

Beth ignored him and made her way back to the window, sticking her head out and looking around.

Dressed, Dane went to the wardrobe and pulled out two spare pillows and put them in the middle of the bed and then pulled the covers over them.

"Let's go," she beckoned him over and slipped out. Dane followed her slowly and tentatively through the window. Weakened by his ordeal she had to help him through and stayed by his side, guiding him, as they walked back along the side of the building and retraced her route across the hospital grounds.

It wasn't very far, but by the time Dane reached the SUV, he was exhausted, and Beth had to help him into the passenger seat. She returned to the gate and pulled it closed. She then replaced the chain and padlock with an identical one and locked the gate. She stuffed the heavy chain and padlock into her pocket and got into the Porsche. Then she drove back around the side of the empty office building and out onto the road outside. Once she approached the main road, she turned on the headlights and made straight for the nearby motorway. As she drove south along the motorway she glanced at Dane. He had adjusted the seat backwards and was already asleep.

Two hours later they arrived at Rosslare Ferry Port in the south east corner of Ireland. Beth drove past the main entrance along the perimeter road until she came to a large yard full of containers. Driving through the yard with the stacked containers looming on either side felt strange. At the end Beth turned right and in front of her was a man standing beside a concrete ramp. She stopped and although it was daytime, flashed her lights once and waited. She sighed with relief when, after a few moments, he responded in kind using a torch in his hand. She drove forward, up the ramp, and into the container on a lorry standing at the concrete loading platform.

She sat silently waiting. The man appeared behind her at the entrance to the container and then disappeared. A few moments later she heard a whine from the engine of an electric forklift which proceeded to place a pallet of crates behind them. After seven more trips she could hear the doors being shut and shortly afterwards, the container jolted as the truck moved off. Beth stayed upright, hands on the wheel until she felt the angle of movement change and distant metallic bangs and clangs and then what sounded like a distant horn. She didn't take her hands off the wheel until she felt a gentle swaying movement. She tilted back her seat, cracked the windows slightly and surprisingly fell asleep almost immediately.

Beth was awakened by a loud bang and a jolt and light flooded into the container. She sat up and looked around. She checked her phone to find that incredibly, she had slept for about twelve hours straight. Dane looked comatose beside her. She leaned towards him and was relieved when she could see his chest gently rising and falling.

After a short while Beth could hear the engine of another forklift and after about fifteen minutes the last of the pallets were removed. A man came to her door. She wound down the window. He was grizzled looking with a crewcut. He leant in with his arm on the window sill and said "When I bang the side of the container once and then twice, you reverse out, turn to your right and drive straight out of the warehouse. The exit to the main road is straight ahead too. Take a right once you get outside and make sure you remember to drive on the right hand side. Don't stop for anything or anyone. You'll only have a short window of opportunity. They all head to their canteen for whatever the hell these French eat at this mad hour. OK?"

She grabbed his arm before he could leave and kissed him on the cheek. "You're the best Joe!"

He scratched his head. "Dunno about that, or what you're up to. Just be careful missy!"

"Definitely the best," she called softly after his retreating form.

Ages seemed to pass until finally she heard the three bangs and reversed carefully out of the container into a massive warehouse. She turned right and drove straight across the warehouse and out through the huge doors. The gates were open, and she went through and turned right. Ahead was a sign for Nantes and the E3 motorway which she followed. Within twenty minutes they were moving smoothly south.

Beth stopped off at a services area, parked and went inside. As she walked back towards the Porsche balancing two coffees and a plastic bag with various pastries and water bottles she was delighted to see Dane sitting up looking around him. He got out as she approached so she plonked the bag on the bonnet and carefully set the cardboard tray with the two coffees beside it on the sloping surface. Dane regarded her warily as she reached in and handed him a small bottle of orange juice. He looked at the bottle and then at her. "We're in France? Jesus, Beth! It seems like minutes ago we were in Ireland. You certainly move fast."

"I planned it carefully. I was lucky too. Joe, the lorry driver owes me, big time."

"How come?"

"It's not important Dane. How are you feeling?"

"Tired, but it's great to be outdoors." He looked at her for a long moment, then reached out and placing his hand on her shoulder, added, "thanks."

"No problem. So now I can give you the rest of the story. It's six am and we've left Cherbourg. We're heading south. It'll take us a couple of hours until we reach a little seaside town called Les Sables d'Olonne where we might stop briefly for more food. Then we'll head for a small place called Mimizan, where I thought we might have lunch and a swim.. If we make good time we might go for it and try to make Biarritz tonight. I took a good few trips with my folks along the West coast of France when I was a kid. This will be the last motorway we'll take. It'll be just secondary roads from here all the way to the Spanish border."

"Right. Keeping off the grid?"

"So to speak. Anyway, it'll take us about a day or so to get to the border. And then we continue south to Avila where my parents have a small place. No one knows they own it because my Dad bought it using a Spanish company and not his own name."

Dane raised an eyebrow and grinned.

"No. Nothing like that," Beth rushed to explain. "It was just the handiest way to purchase property in Spain at the time. Anyway, we'll stop off in the town of Burgos for a night. I reckon that in five days max we'll reach Avila."

"This is such a good idea, but what about the cops in Ireland and whatever? They'll be looking for us. For me."

"I left a timed email for the guy heading up things, the American guy, Tiberius? I cc'd the other one, Doyle. The grumpy one."

"The grumpy one?"

"Well, grumpy but nice. Anyway Tiberius won't get it until tomorrow and there is no record of us having left the country. Even if they start looking for us, they won't find us until we're ready to contact them."

"And the investors? Rayne?"

"I've asked Tiberius to forward my email to her to explain things. I know I've taken a risk of losing her input and the investment, Dane. But it's a calculated risk. If our platform is as good as we think it is, even if we lose her, there will be others to take her place. Although I must admit I do respect her and I reckon she'd make a good partner."

"To be honest, I think I was getting a bit starstruck or maybe bedazzled by the money," said Dane. "The numbers which were being thrown around. So a bit of space there is probably no bad thing."

"Me too. OK. Let's hit the trail Pardner!"

"Oh God!" Dane complained. "Please don't. I don't think I can survive a road trip if you're going to do that 'lonesome trail' shite."

Beth ignored him, climbed into the Porsche and waited for him to put the debris of their impromptu breakfast into a nearby bin. As soon as he settled in beside her, she yelled "Yippiekiyay!" and pulled out. Dane put his head in his hands.

CHAPTER
FORTY TWO

Ashling slid her arm around and rubbed his chest. "Hey Yank," she whispered mischievously "you awake?"

"Uhhmmm, kinda." He sleepily took her arm and pulled her into his back.

"I've got to go home."

"Yep."

"So talk to me before I go."

Tiberius turned around on the couch and kissed her gently. "About?"

"What are you going to do? You said you had made a decision?"

"Yep."

She slapped his chest. "Stop that! Come on. Enough with the John Wayne impression. I care, you know?"

"I do." He sat up on the couch and turned to her. "My dad has a place in Madrid, so I'm thinking of heading there for a while."

"Oh." Ashling sounded disappointed. "That's a bit far."

"I get it." He smiled, "and we've just gotten a lot closer, and it's early days too. I guess."

"Well no, not that. It's just another country. I don't know how good I am at long distance relationships. Or any bloody relationships, come to think of it."

"Don't do that Ashling. Don't allow past events to undermine how you feel about yourself." Tiberius told her. "Anyway, I was wondering if you had ever seen the Prado?"

"The Prado?" She looked at him wide eyed. "Are you asking me to come with you?"

"Well you and Cian. It's a pretty big apartment. Kinda more like the top floor of a building in the centre of town. And you can come for as long or as short a stay as you feel comfortable with. I'm not sure how long I'll stay myself. I'm playing it by ear at the moment."

"Wow. Can I think about it?"

"Sure."

Ashling stood and headed for the bathroom. Tiberius began straightening out the couch where the two of them had been lying for the past hour or two. *Making out like two teenagers, I guess,* he smiled to himself. *Taking things slowly, which is no bad thing right now.*

He couldn't believe how quickly it had all happened. After he left the coffee shop he and Doyle were in, Tiberius's phone had received a text from Ashling, inviting him to an event called "Outdoor Cinema" in a public park beside the sea. Tiberius had thoroughly enjoyed the evening, sitting with Cian and Ashling on a rug on the ground with lots of other people in front of a large outdoor cinema screen. After running around like a madman with the hordes of other children, Cian had flopped down, ate several sandwiches and drank a small gallon of tea and fizzy orange and then promptly fell asleep during the opening credits of the film.

The film was interesting. A documentary by Sir Richard Attenborough called "Blue Planet". But the best part happened about half-way through when Ashling complained about her back being sore from sitting on the ground and he told her to lean on him. Which after a heart-stopping moment, in which he thought he'd really messed it up, she did. As the film rolled on, twilight passed and darkness fell. She relaxed into him, and finally when the closing credits scrolled up the screen, she turned to him, their faces only inches apart, and kissed him softly on the lips. She pulled back slightly and looked at him, which was when Cian decided to wake up and announce that he felt awful. Ashling jumped up and brought the little boy over behind a low wall where from her movements he could determine that Cian was being sick. He packed everything and went over to where Ashling had seated Cian on the wall. He handed her a packet of moistened wipes and she wiped Cian's face.

"Do you want me to carry him?" Tiberius asked.

"No that's OK. If you don't mind taking the picnic gear. I think it will do him good to walk back to the car," she said in a monotone.

"Don't wanna walk," moaned Cian.

"It will help you feel better, darling," replied Ashling and got him standing. Then she half-carried and half guided the boy slowly back to the car. When they got there, she knelt and asked him "How do you feel now Cian? Do you think you'll be sick again?"

"No. I feel a bit better" and the little lad belched loudly and then giggled. "Sorry Mummy." Then turning to take Tiberius's hand he looked up at him and said, "Sorry Tiberius."

"Don't you worry about it buddy" Tiberius replied kindly. "Let's get you home."

No one said much on the way back to the house. Aoife opened the front door as they walked towards the porch. "Cian got sick," Ashling informed her. Aoife took Cian's hand and said "I'll put him to bed. Nice to see you Tiberius."

Tiberius nodded and smiled. Then he stood awkwardly on the porch and said, "Where do you want me to put this stuff?"

"Oh that's no problem. I'll take it."

"Thanks for inviting me."

"I'm so sorry about Cian. I hope it didn't ruin it for you?"

"On the contrary," he stared at her intently, a slight smile playing on his lips. "Best movie show I've ever been to."

"Oh good," she breathed softly. "Me too." She cupped his cheek and kissed him again softly.

"Goodnight Mr. Frost," she said teasingly.

"Goodnight Ms Clarke," he replied in a mock formal tone.

After that they had met each other two or three more times, always with Cian present, which Tiberius was OK about as he had clicked with the boy and they got on really well.

Today was the first time they had been alone. It was Ashling's suggestion that she call over for a coffee. He had served them on the low table in front of the couch which looked out a massive glass window at a panoramic view of the city and the bay. The coffee was still untouched.

Ashling walked back in. "OK. I would love to come but I need to think about Cian's welfare first and foremost. He's so little and I don't want to confuse him, what with everything that's going on with the divorce. You know?"

"So it's a no?"

"No. It's not a no. It's a maybe. It's an - I'll think about it but know this." She slid back into his arms. "I want to do it. I just need to work it out."

"Great. I'll wait until you do. No pressure either way. OK?"

"Thanks." She kissed him quickly and ducked back inside.

CHAPTER FORTY THREE

Mr Black was sitting still again. He had lost count of how long or how many days he had been in the cottage. He was topping up his batteries. Restoring his energy levels. He was opposite the open door where he could see out to the valley walls and on down below. Yesterday he had hiked down the mountain to a hut he maintained where his land abutted the road. He unlocked it and got into a scruffy Land Rover Defender. The engine started instantly and purred as he drove along. He maintained it carefully, getting it serviced regularly by a local mechanic, always ignoring the man's offers to repaint it and tidy it a bit. He wanted it looking nondescript.

He drove past the nearby village to a further away town with the uniquely Welsh name of Blaenau Ffestiniog. It was larger - just enough to have some supermarkets where he could shop anonymously. He didn't even try pronouncing it.

He made himself dinner that night and this morning commenced meditating at around five. He was coming to the end of his stay.

Now he needed to decide his next steps. Research was needed. He wanted to find out more about the people who had pursued him from Ireland. He needed to find out more about the two targets. He didn't want to be obliged to return any part of the substantial sums he had been given by his employer so he would have to locate the targets again and make a proposal to his employer regarding them – capture and either another attempt at interrogation or termination, he assumed. He was under no illusions about his employer's resources. He had managed to identify him and through a contact had gotten a deep background file on Deng. Mr Black now knew enough to realise that he didn't want a problem with him.

However, it was a lot of money and would just top off his fund sufficiently that he wouldn't have to work again for a very long time or ever. No. He could just do his own thing. A cold smile infected his perfect face.

*   *   *

"Tiberius?" came Doyle's voice.

"Hey Doyle, give me a second. I just want to take the phone off speaker." Tiberius reset his mobile and then said, "How are you doing buddy?"

"Good, thanks. The team are all missing you but they understand the situation, but that's not why I'm ringing."

"Oh?"

"You obviously haven't seen the papers or any online media today, I guess." Doyle sighed heavily.

"Nope."

"Someone in Harcourt street leaked to the press that you were taken off the investigation."

"Great," Tiberius said drily.

"I know. I know," Doyle said sympathetically. "It's the last bloody thing you need right now."

"History repeating itself," Tiberius ground out.

"Not quite, Tiber. In fairness to you, you kept control of this one. But the bottom line is that you need to lie low, maybe get out of Dublin to avoid being door stepped by journalists."

"I'm in the Business Lounge at Dublin Airport. My flight's in twenty minutes."

"Good." Doyle sounded relieved. "Don't tell me where you're going on this call. Just let me know when you get there safely. OK?"

"Will do. Are you making any progress?" Tiberius couldn't resist asking.

"Ahmm, I'll explain when we meet next. OK?"

Tiberius understood Doyle's reluctance to discuss the case over an open phone line so he simply said, "thanks for the heads up man. Much appreciated."

"Always Tiber. Always."

Tiberius ended the call and gathering his bag and coat headed for the departure gate for the flight to Madrid. Doyle sat in his office feeling unhappy and not a little guilty about not being able to explain to his friend that he was now investigating his sister.

Ashling hadn't been in touch with Tiberius since they had discussed her joining him and he was concerned about the total lack of contact, his mind inventing all sorts of silly reasons for her not communicating at all with him, especially as she knew he was flying to Spain today.

I guess she made her decision, he thought ruefully to himself as he walked along. He passed a shop selling books and newspapers and slowed down to check out the newspapers.

There was nothing on the first six papers, but on the last one, a tabloid which had devoted the majority of the front four pages to the aftermath of the Shannon Atrocity, had a small panel on page five with a heading "Bumbling Cop Fired!" Fortunately, the image of him which they had used was pretty old and grainy and could have been anyone. Inside, the hysterical tone described how he had been kicked off the investigating team due to the lack of progress the team had made under his leadership. He replaced the paper and continued on his way to the flight departure desk, thinking as he did so that the Shannon terrorist attack had turned into his saviour as he reckoned if the media hadn't been totally focussed on it then his face would have been plastered all over. Worse, they might have done some digging into his history. It was just a filler piece. *Thank god for lazy journalism,* he thought wryly

He boarded the flight and found his window seat. He turned on his iPad, popped on his headphones and settled in to watch a Netflix movie he had downloaded for the flight which would take about two and a half hours.

The last thing he did was check his phone for any messages from Ashling. Still nothing. He turned it off.

CHAPTER FORTY FOUR

Beth looked out across the sand to where the waves broke against the Landes shoreline. She couldn't see Dane and was a little anxious. Then, like a Greek god, he broke from the water, with his long dark hair drawn back from his face, his muscled torso testament to regular early morning sessions in the University Gymnasium. Two French matrons walked past him, their heads swivelling on their necks as they walked past, appraising the young man.

No one looks at me like that, thought Beth, a little enviously. And then the French waiter brought the drinks she had ordered and nearly spilled them because he was busy checking out her boobs, which, oddly, cheered her up!

"Good swim?" she asked as Dane sat on the adjacent sunbed, draping a towel over his shoulders and putting on his sunglasses.

"Great! Very refreshing. Needed it. Thanks," he added, accepting a glass filled with ice and Orangina, a sparkling orange drink which was in Beth's opinion, quintessentially French. "These beaches are amazing. They seem to go on for ever. I've gotta come back here sometime."

Beth sipped on her coke and said, "I'm going to go for it and try and hit Biarritz this evening, stay there tonight, then we pass to the west of the Pyrenees and into Spain. The most direct route is to go through Burgos and then we arrive in Avila. However, we'll be passing close to Bilbao and I've never seen the Guggenheim Museum in Bilbao. It's supposed to be amazing and it's just forty minutes off our route? What do you think?"

Dane considered her soberly, "I thought we were trying to stay off the grid. A low profile?"

"I know but we can just like nip in and nip out? Wear hats and glasses or hoodies or whatever? No one will know us and we'll be quick. I'd just like to tick it off the list, y'know?"

"Well, you planned all of this out, so I guess it's your decision Beth. If you think it's an acceptable risk. Art isn't my thing though."

"Are you saying you don't want to come?"

"Not to the museum, but if you want to go, I'll be happy to stay in the SUV and sleep for a while. Just be careful you're not picked up on any cameras or whatever."

Beth replied "OK, I'll think more about it. If you're ready we'll finish our drinks, get the bill and head for Biarritz?"

"Sure thing." Dane put his empty glass down and threw on a tee shirt and a baseball cap. Beth slipped a large white man's shirt on over her swimsuit and headed for the bar. The horny French waiter was nowhere to be seen but an elegantly coiffed woman was manning the till and happily took Beth's cash for the overpriced sunbeds, food and drinks they had consumed during their brief stopover in the little town of Mimizan in the heart of the Landes region.

They got into the dark Porsche Cayman and headed inland briefly then turning south for Biarritz. As they drove along, Dane looked out, catching glimpses of the distant sea every time they crested a hill. "This was such a good idea Beth. I needed some down time after everything that happened. I thought I was going insane. And then when I woke up and you were there, it was like it was a bad dream. But it wasn't a dream. It happened and she's gone."

Beth said nothing. She focussed on the road ahead. They hadn't talked about Dane's ordeal. She felt he would do so when he felt able, strong enough. Maybe now was the time.

"Mary had a terrible death. I can't believe that a human

being could do that to someone. Am I being a coward in being grateful that I was out of it?" Dane continued in a low monotone. "I think if I had been awake it would have destroyed me. What I can't understand is why? There was no ransom demands and it was a hell of a long way to bring two people to just bloody torture them. He could have done it in Ireland. So why? What was the point?"

"Guy was a nutcase." Beth said.

"No, Beth. It was more than that. Based on what you told me, he had access to serious resources. Private jets, taxi's, transport to that awful place, and the place itself. It sounds like it was some kind of freaky military facility. And why did the British Army help to get us out? They had to commit a lot of troops and stuff to make it happen? What was in it for them? I've got so many questions running around inside my head and as the days go by they multiply. And all with no bloody answers!" Dane sounded frustrated and angry.

"Take your time Dane," answered Beth. "Think it through and eventually the pieces will fall into place. Just don't be too impatient. I think it's going to be a slow process for you."

"Too bloody slow," Dane grumbled and lapsed into silence for the rest of the journey to Biarritz.

Hours later, and more than a little drunk Beth and Dane made their way through the streets of the seaside town after a great meal in a local restaurant. They were laughing again at Dane's choice of meal. He'd gone for Steak Tartare, not knowing it would be a lump of raw, highly spiced minced beef!

"Shoulda seen your face when they showed up with it! Oh God my sides," Beth sniggered and hiccupped simultaneously, which set the pair off again.

"We're here," Dane announced as they arrived outside the little pension in which they were staying. There was only one room left in the inn, not due to the number of guests but due to the other bedrooms being refurbished. One bed was massive and the other tiny. Dane had tried to be gentlemanly and offered to take the small bed but she told him not to be silly. "Horses for courses" she had told him.

On their way over the border the following morning they decided to divert to Bilbao after all. The plan was that it would take roughly two hours in total. Forty minutes from the E80 Motorway to Bilbao, Beth reckoned she only needed forty minutes inside as she already knew what she wanted to see and then forty minutes back to the Motorway.

"The big thing for me is to experience Richard Serra's works." She told Dane as she drove along. "He exhibited nine sculptures, well more installations really, back in 1999 at the Guggenheim Bilbao and now they're showing some of the pieces from that series again, just for a really brief time so it's just so much good luck that I'm going to manage to see his stuff. His work is huge! Absolutely vast. Long ribbons of weathered steel, kind of twisted into ellipses and curves."

"Doesn't sound like art to me," said Dane.

"Dane it's not what you would call classical art. It's more the experience he creates when people interact with his work. I knew some people from Dublin who went to Bilbao to his first exhibition and said it was mind blowing. What you have to understand is that you walk in and through the sculptures. Each ribbon of steel is lying on its edge and is about thirty or forty feet high. They curve in and out and form a walkway. Some people find them very threatening, some uplifting, some just claustrophobic."

"Enjoy Beth. Rather you than me." Dane remarked casually. "I don't think I could handle an experience like that right now."

"I understand." Beth said quietly.

She managed to find a parking space just past the Guggenheim on the tree lined Campo de Volantín Pasealekua street beside the river. Beth put on a baseball cap, sunglasses and a hoodie and asked Dane "how do I look?"

"Like a terrorist, I reckon," said Dane as he lowered his seat put his cap over his face. He covered himself with his coat and muttered "have fun."

Beth headed off along the road and climbed the six flights of stairs to the bridge over to the opposite side of the river Bilbao where the Museum was situated. The elevated bridge was a great place to see the Museum from as she walked towards it. *It's a symphony in steel,* she thought. *Frank Gehry was some architect. What a legacy.*

The morning sun peeped over the tops of the surrounding hills as she walked along the bridge. It bounced off the giant stainless steel leaves of the building, creating beautiful reflections on the urban landscape surrounding it. Shards of light penetrated down into the murky depths of the Bilbao river below her. Beth was transfixed.

An hour later she returned to the car and pressed the remote control to unlock it, as a gentler way to awaken Dane.

"Ooh God. I'm stiff." Dane stretched, yawning. "Well how did it go? As good as you hoped?"

"Better."

"Good."

After a few moments she added, "just one little problem."

"What problem?" Dane sounded wary.

"I had to pay in using Revolut."

"Why? I thought we were trying to stay off the grid? Cash only. Keeping a low profile and all that. Your words not mine, Beth." He reminded her in a matter of fact tone.

"I know but I left my cash in my other coat. I was so excited to finally get here I forgot to put my cash in. All I had was my mobile phone. So I paid using Revolut."

"We need to get out of Dodge. Right now. And I suggest we continue to stay off the motorway s. Go through the back roads. Maybe not stay in Logrono or Burgos. Bypass them and stay in some little village somewhere. That is if you reckon we won't make Avila tonight?"

"Probably not. I'm an idiot. I should have come back for my cash. But they had just opened and there were very few people around so I felt I could get the maximum out of it by being virtually alone going around the exhibits. In retrospect, it was short sighted."

Beth got out her phone and worked out an alternative route. Then she took off. They headed South West along perfectly adequate secondary roads and then moved South East crossing under the E80 Motorway, which they had been on earlier and up into the Sierra de la Demanda Mountains, just East of Burgos.

"We're heading into hillbilly country, Pardner. Backs to the wall and don't drop the soap!" Beth hummed a few bars from the theme tune to the movie "Deliverance".

"Dear God!" was Danes only comment.

The countryside changed from highly cultivated gently rolling hills, to steeper, heavily wooded mountains.

Eventually they came to a massive dam and passing along one side of the reservoir it had created, they found a little bar just in from the road. Beth managed to communicate sufficiently well in her pidgin Spanish to get two rooms, side by side with a connecting door, dinner and breakfast all for the princely sum of sixty five euro.

After a simple meal, the pair crossed the darkened mountain road to the edge of the reservoir to get some air before dinner.

After some time Beth said, "plan's changed again Dane."

"Oh?" he sounded wary.

"I'm not driving all the way to Avila. We're going to park outside the town in the car park of a cinema on the outskirts and walk in with our bags. I've been thinking about it and the Porsche might have been a mistake. It kind of sticks out. There aren't exactly a lot of Porsche Cayennes knocking around this part of Spain. I can leave it in the car park for as long as I need to. I just prepay for the period of time we need and the machine takes cash. You OK with that?"

Dane was hunched down at the water's edge. Eventually he stood and turning to her said "I'm absolutely fine with it Beth. It's a very sensible idea. We should probably walk separately to your place, within sight of each other but just not together? And," he paused.

"What?"

Dane put his hand on her shoulder and looked down at his diminutive partner with genuine emotion said "I'll never forget what you're doing for me, Beth. The risks you're taking and the trouble you've gone to. Never. I'm so lucky to have you in my life as my best friend." His massive arms enveloped her, lifting her off her feet and hugging her tight.

"Jeez! Dane!" she squeaked. "Love you too but you're killing me."

"Sorry." He plonked her back down.

"No. No." She said. "I really appreciate what you said. You just don't know your own strength pardner." She punched him playfully on the arm.

As they walked back to the Bar, she thought to herself. *There's a million girls would give their left tit to be in a situation like this with Dane. A moonlit night beside a lake, nestled in the middle of the mountains in Northern Spain and I get bloody best friend status!* She sighed and hurried to catch up to him.

*   *   *

"Boss?" Prendergast put down her phone with a stricken look on her face.

"What?" Doyle swivelled his chair around.

"Dane Wilson's disappeared from his hospital room."

"What the hell? Not again! Jesus!" Doyle took a moment to calm himself, then asked more calmly, "OK, what do you know?"

"Well, they had weaned him off his medication a day or so ago but he was still sleeping late each morning. At his request, they had stopped serving him breakfast. When the orderly brought in his lunch the blind was drawn and he could see what he assumed was the patient in the bed, turned on his side asleep, so he left the food on a tray at the end of the bed. No one checked back in until ten minutes ago. That's when they discovered he was gone."

"Do we know if he was grabbed again or left voluntarily?"

"Not yet but there's no sign of a struggle and the window was closed but unlocked."

"Which it wasn't supposed to be."

"Yes."

"Let's go."

Fifteen minutes later Doyle and Prendergast were pulling into the hospital car park. As he got out, Doyle checked his phone and stopped still.

"Boss?" Prendergast called back to him.

"Hang on. Hang on." Doyle said tetchily, reading the contents of Beth's email to him and Tiberius.

Finally he finished, put the phone in his pocket and looked to the skies. "Jesus Christ! Un-believable," he uttered savagely.

"Sarge, what's going on?" asked a bewildered Prendergast. He leaned on the roof of the car and looked over at her, "I know what happened to Dane Wilson."

"OK?" said Prendergast warily.

"He's with Beth. She sent Tiberius and me an email. She persuaded him to leave the hospital with her last night and they are staying together for a while. She thinks it will be safer for him to drop out of sight completely, especially as whoever discovered Dane's whereabouts nearly killed Sweeney. She doesn't want to run the risk of them getting at Dane again."

"She might have a point Sarge," interjected Prendergast diplomatically leaving Tiberius's departure unremarked. Doyle glowered at her nevertheless and said "Oh and they both need to get some headspace. Whatever that's about!"

Before Prendergast could say anything else, he headed towards the entrance. After a quick survey of the room and a few acidic comments to the police officer standing outside, Doyle led Prendergast to Sweeney's hospital room.

Sweeney was sitting up in bed with a laptop on his bed.

"Well, how're you doing?" asked Doyle slumping into an armchair facing the bed. Prendergast went over to the window and leant against the ledge.

"Better each day Sir," answered Sweeney. "Um, Sergeant, if you don't mind me asking? What's going on outside? I can see a lot of unusual activity. Kind of non-medical?" He ventured.

"Dane Wilson has left our protective custody in the company of your little pal Beth."

"Wow! Never saw that coming," said Sweeney.

"None of us did," stated Prendergast from her window perch.

Doyle leaned forward, his hands on his knees. "So what do we do in a situation like this, my little bedridden colleague?"

Prendergast grinned, suddenly figuring out what Doyle was up to.

Sweeney sat back and groaned, " We find them." Then he looked at Doyle's face and added "Or rather, I find them."

Doyle got up, stepped around the bits of medical equipment to the side of Sweeney's bed and patted him on the shoulder. "Yes you do. And fast kid. Discreetly and fast."

"I'm sick, you know." Sweeney called out to Doyle's retreating back.

Doyle called back over his shoulder, "I know. I know, and I think you're great. The bedrock of this team, kid."

Prendergast closed the door behind them and the last thing Sweeney could see was the cheesy grin on her face. As they walked down the corridor Doyle said quietly to her, "I want you to being surveillance of Rayne Frost."

She looked at him surprised.

"And I don't want you to tell anyone, especially Tiber."

CHAPTER
FORTY FIVE

The pair of fugitives were busy in the kitchen of the Frontemont's apartment in Avila. Everything had gone according to plan, with Beth arriving at the front door of the sixteenth century building first, entering and leaving the door ajar for Dane who had followed her at a discreet distance. They had bought lots of groceries in a supermarket just before arriving on the outskirts of Avila. Dane ended up carrying most of them in his larger bag.

Dane had been very impressed with the ancient walled city and loved the eclectically furnished apartment. It was bright and airy and overlooked the Rio Adaja river and along the expanse of the massive medieval city walls.

"Feels very secure inside these walls doesn't it." Said Dane.

"Yes. We'll just take our time and chill out while we figure out what to do. I forgot to tell you I emailed Rayne as well. Just explaining that we had taken some time out and we'd be in touch once we figured out things?"

"I hope she won't be too pissed off."

"She'll be fine," said Beth confidently.

*   *   *

Back in Dublin, Rayne was methodically kicking the stuffing out of a punch bag. Her punches and kicks increasing in ferocity with every strike. The few other hotel residents in the gymnasium glanced over worriedly at the whirling explosion of violence in the corner. Finally, drenched in perspiration, Rayne leant against the railing looking out the plate glass windows and drank deeply from a water bottle.

Stupid little bitch, she thought. *I really want to terminate her with extreme prejudice.*

Taping her hands and using protective gloves and foot pads hadn't quite mitigated the effects of her aggression on her hands and feet. Her knuckles were throbbing with pain and at least one was split.

Now what do I do? she thought. *Gotta tell Deng, I suppose. But what do I say? Oh by the way, our two promoters have disappeared. Taken fright and evaporated! Exit stage left, Deng ol' buddy.*

She stopped as the thought occurred to her whether she needed to tell him anything. She could just continue the negotiations as though she was consulting with the pair. She would hire lawyers herself and get everything to the signing stage, all on the basis that by the time the deal was ready to go ahead, she would have re-established contact with them. The other possibility was to blame Deng's guy, Riga. She could say that what happened had scared the two students so they were taking some time out.

Actually, she thought, *this could be refined further.* She could tell Deng that Riga had scared them off but she had been authorised to continue to bring the deal to fruition. She would get the paperwork to them for signing once everything was ready. She might even be able to parlay this into a situation where she could represent herself as having saved the deal despite Riga's blunder. *Deng needn't know I don't have a monkey's notion as to their whereabouts.* Beth's email was sent from a temporary, self-destructing email address. So she couldn't reply to that, but she could email progress updates to Dane and Beth's normal email addresses. When they finally checked them, they would contact her. Hopefully. It didn't bear thinking about what would happen if they didn't.

She decided to inform Tiberius also. Keep him sweet. In

fact she'd do that first. She returned to her suite, showered, dressed and rang his mobile. It was a foreign tone, not the usual Irish ringtone. That was unexpected. *Where was Tiber?*

An hour later Rayne was sitting in the lobby of the hotel eating a salad, when she noticed a guy at the next table reading one of the less sleazy tabloids. She was about to look away when she saw what looked like a small photo of Tiberius on the bottom right of the page facing her. She called over a waiter and was about to ask him for a copy of the paper when the man got up and left the paper behind him on the table. She jumped up and grabbed it. Returning to her seat, she told the waiter to get her a glass of water and turned her attention to the paper.

Poor Tiber, she thought as she found the small article inside on page seven. *This is a bit of a butt-kicking. Not a lot in it, just that he got canned really. They obviously don't know about the L.A. screw-up.*

She settled back in her seat. *I bet he went to Dad's place in Madrid, and if he didn't, I'm gonna suggest it. Pity I won't have the same access to the progress they're making, or not.* She grinned to herself. *Tiber gave me that guy Doyle's number, so I'll call him and see if I can establish contact. Build a relationship. You never know. Every little helps!*

*   *   *

Sweeney was running a variety of different search routines and had also written some code in an attempt to locate any sign of Beth and Dane. It was as though they'd vanished off the face of the earth.

In another country Mr Black was doing the same.

Deng picked up the phone and rang Kent Gulbenkian. He explained what he wanted and ended the call. In a darkened bedroom in his house Kent put on his underpants, switched the massive screen at the end of the bed from porn to a computer screen. Cracked his knuckles and got to work.

*   *   *

The twin objectives of their various digital hunts were sitting in a quiet corner of a little bar on a narrow side street in the centuries old historical centre of Avila. They had spent the day in Segovia on a double errand. First, they checked out the fairy-tale 12th century castle known as the Alcazar. It was the ancient seat of the Kings of Castile and reputedly the inspiration for Disney's iconic castle. The second reason was to buy some mobile phones and sim cards. They had turned off both of their own phones back in Northern France on the basis that it would be too dangerous to risk using them. They had driven the sixty six kilometre journey from Avila to Segovia in Beth's parent's Smart car. As she said on a few occasions they didn't have it for long journeys, just for getting around the narrow, ancient streets of Avila. Still, they had got there and back and completed both missions and were now tucking into a selection of tapas and a couple of beers.

"I'll set up some email accounts and VPN shielding OK? Take out your sim card from your Irish phone, turn off the location feature and only use Wi-Fi. That way you can access most of your stuff on your phone but you'll use it like a dumb terminal" Dane informed Beth over a mouthful of spicy potato.

"VPN? Dumb terminal?" Beth queried. "Sprechen zie English, Dane?"

He sighed. "Virtual Private Network. Hides your IP address – y'know it hides your physical location when you're online? And a Dumb terminal phone is just that. You can only use it to access whatever is saved on the phone and nothing else."

"Sorry to be such a Luddite. Oh mighty one!" Beth said sarcastically. "Oh these little pygmy sausages are soooo good. Aren't they?"

Dane popped three of the little honey coated morsels into his mouth in response and grinned.

"Have you contacted everyone you needed to?" He asked.

"Yes. Well, just Tiberius and Rayne. Don't think I need to communicate with anyone else. I hope we didn't drop Tiberius in it by disappearing."

"Yeah... Don't care."

"That's a bit harsh."

"We've got to put ourselves first and everyone else second. Taking this time out is a great idea. Give us some perspective. What did you say to Rayne?"

"Same as Tiberius. But I reckon I should have maybe said a bit more, reassured her?"

"You can send her a new email address, which I'll kill off after a few uses. So that way you'll be able to check out where's she's at."

*   *   *

Tiberius stepped out of the shower. He had gone for an early morning run, pounding the Madrid streets, detouring around groups of revellers and municipal workers cleaning the streets. When he got back he worked out hard in the gymnasium which was part of the apartment.

He threw on a tee shirt and pair of shorts and was fixing some eggs in the kitchen when the Intercom rang.

"Yes Carlos?" he said, looking at the very large security guard on the screen.

"Senor this lady wishes to visit?" answered Carlos who then moved his massive frame to reveal Ashling standing behind him.

"I'll be straight down." Within seconds Tiberius was in the elevator, heading to the lobby.

She was standing beside Carlos, who was practicing his English, mixed with a spot of ogling. She looked so cool and calm in blue jeans and a white shirt, beaming at him.

He picked up her bag and shooed Carlos back to his desk. When the elevator doors closed and he turned back to her after pressing the button for the top floor and keying in his code, she was inches away. She flung herself forward, throwing her arms around his neck and kissed him deeply and passionately.

The lift went bing and the doors opened so they moved apart. With her bag in one hand and her hand in his other, he brought her to the front door of the apartment. They still had not spoken. He opened the door with his code and went in. She pulled her bag out of his hand and dragged him towards a couch in the sunken living room.

An hour or so later, she sighed, turned to him and said softly "hi."

"Hi to you too," he smiled.

They had made it as far as the bedroom when he remembered the maid would be coming in shortly, but what she would make of the trail of clothing they had left behind them he didn't know or care about.

"So. You made it." He said

"Yes. Cian's with Aoife and Mum and Dad in their holiday home in the South, which he loves and Aoife said I'd be nuts not to take advantage and so," she paused, "here I am. Is that OK?"

"Absolutely. It's so good. I couldn't happier."

"Sorry I wasn't in touch before now but things moved very suddenly with the divorce."

"Good or bad?"

"Good. In a way. My lawyer, who I mentioned really hates Robert, went to all of our neighbours and interviewed them. Over the years, Robert upset most if not all of them at one point or another. So she felt she might get something to help my case?"

Ashling sat back against the headboard cross-legged.

"An elderly couple who live next door asked Robert to cut back a tree which was shading their garden and conservatory a year or so ago, but he said no. Actually he was very rude and told them to piss off. It was very embarrassing and I had to apologise. Anyway, they gave her a DVD from their CCTV system, which showed Robert and this woman, clearly not me and not even the neighbour he was most recently screwing. They were having sex on a seat at the back of our garden. It's date and time stamped. I was abroad with Cian and Mum at the time."

"Asshole!" Tiberius sounded angry.

"Well. My solicitor has had this for a while and was waiting for Robert's lawyers to lodge their defence with the court and obviously to share it with us. He claimed that his fling with my neighbour was a once off and that I had completely overreacted. It's virtually impossible for him to retract what he's said so she waited until a few days ago to drop a copy of the DVD on them with a list of our requirements. They gave in. Apparently his father went absolutely ballistic because Robert had obviously lied to him too. I got everything we asked for. We signed agreements two days ago and everything has been passed to the judge for approval."

"Must have been quite stressful all the same."

"Yes. However, I wasn't looking forward to going to court or having to meet him. Now I don't have to and I should be able to close that chapter."

"What happens with Cian? Does Robert have visitation or custody rights?"

"No. I was quite disgusted with him really. He didn't even fight for access? He was more interested in the numbers, the money! Bastard!"

"But Cian may want to see his Dad?" Tiberius pressed gently.

"I'll cross that bridge when I come to it. If he does, I'll arrange it. If not, I won't push it. As time passes I can't help but feel the less Cian has to do with him, the better for Cian."

"Wait and see. I guess?"

"Yes." Ashling slid back down on the bed and snuggled close

to him, nose to nose. "So. Now what?"

"Now? Hmmm. Let's see." Tiberius gently pulled her on top of him. "How long have you got?"

In answer she mischievously reached her hand down between them and grinned "oh I'd say that's long enough!"

CHAPTER FORTY SIX

Kent Gulbenkian knew code. Writing programs and routines since a child, he intrinsically understood the fabric on which the tapestry of global computing is embroidered. Deng's Chinese superiors had more than once instructed him to get rid of Kent because they regarded him as a loose cannon. Unpredictable, unreliable and uncontrollable. One particular general had informed Deng that either he eliminated Kent or they would eliminate both of them but would take their time with Deng due to his disobedience.

Deng's response was to contact Kent later that day, a Wednesday. He explained the situation and told Kent to sort the general out. Kent bought lots of Red Bull and some pills from a friend and did not sleep until Sunday morning. On Sunday evening while Kent slumbered, Deng received a call from a senior contact in China informing him General Chang had been arrested on Saturday and questioned. He had confessed to attempting to pressurize Deng into diverting funds into several hidden accounts in Macao and had been executed that morning. Deng was to be congratulated for resisting the General's threats.

No one threatened either of them again. Kent had more than cracked the top levels of security in several systems in China and Macao not to mention Google. He had sliced through them like a knife through butter. In order to protect him further, Deng let it filter out that he had asked his "programming team" to investigate the general in order to get to the truth of the matter, and that during their trawl they had unearthed a great deal of unexpected information.

The threat was inherent in the vagueness of the comment. Any further interference with him or his operation and who knew what damaging evidence might be revealed about the accusers.

Kent rang his boss and friend, well Kent thought so anyway.

"Yes Kent?"

"The girl bought entry to the Guggenheim Museum in Bilbao, Northern Spain. A few days ago."

"And?"

"Just piecing together her movements since then. Shouldn't take long."

"Call me when you're done."

Deng ended the call and rang Rayne.

"Hi Deng, what's up?" She chirped into the phone.

"Your colleagues are in Northern Spain." He tested her with the bald statement.

"Oh. Spain?" She paused. "Cool. I didn't realise they had travelled that far yet." Rayne kicked to touch in an attempt to seem unflustered. "Why did they contact you?" She threw the question at Deng to try and confuse matters a little.

"They didn't." Deng replied.

"So how do you know where they are Deng?"

"My resources are sufficient." Was all she got in reply.

Rayne sighed. "OK. Did you just ring me to tell me this? Or what?"

"When we locate them I suggest you go there and clarify your ability to do a deal with me. Otherwise what is your role here?"

"We have a deal Deng and I expect you to honour your side, as I will mine."

"I always honour my deals as long as everyone delivers. Will you deliver to me Rayne?"

"I always deliver Deng."

"Let's keep it that way. I'll be in touch."

Deng ended the call abruptly. Rayne swore and walked to the window of her suite staring out at the rain battering the trees outside.

"To hell with this. I'm out of here. Need to be where the action is. At least it will be warmer and drier in Spain." She checked her phone and saw there were only Ryanair flights to Bilbao and the nearby airport of Santander. "Aren't they those guys that don't do first class?" She wondered. "Maybe I'll go to Madrid? Meet up with Tiber? Hmm."

*   *   *

Mr Black was sitting in a tiny room high in the tower of Castle House, one of the oldest parts of Aberystwyth University's Old College Building on the Welsh coast. The University had outgrown the iconic 18th Century turreted extravaganza perched on the edge of the sea front and had moved to more modern quarters inland. However, Mr Black had discovered that during the process of moving they had laid temporary data cables between the Old College and the new campus and like many such temporary arrangements in the public sector the cabling was still in place.

Mister Black had patiently combed through the ancient building until he found a connected computer terminal in this dusty old storeroom at the top of one of the Castle House towers. The door was a massive old oak beast with a heavy, cast iron lock, which he removed and had a key made for it. He also oiled the sliding bolts on the inside so that once he was inside and the door bolted even if someone had a key it would seem like the door was irretrievably jammed which would buy him sufficient time to get out.

When you stepped inside you were confronted by what looked like a massive wall of old boxes and piles of documents. However they were actually fixed to a partition which divided the room. To access the window area beyond the partition you opened a narrow section of the barricade at one side and slipped through. Inside was a desk and a docking station, into which Mr Black could slot his laptop.

When he did so he was able to log straight into the University's servers in their main campus and use them to screen his actions. Even if someone tracked him to the University computer systems he was over a mile from the campus proper.

Behind him, a ladder led to a trapdoor in the ceiling and up to the open tower roof, on which he had installed a rope ladder which would allow him to directly access the car park behind in an emergency. Or he could make his way onto the main roof of the building, from which he had mapped out several escape routes.

However, things weren't going well in Mr Black's little lair. He was using the digital skillset he had acquired during his training some years back but he was getting nowhere. He just couldn't locate them.

He stared intently at the screen and thought about what he knew so far. Was there something he had missed about the pair he was tracking which had escaped his notice. Anything? Maybe instead of trying to locate where they were he needed to focus on where they might go and then whittle down the possibilities.

So where would they go? He knew Dane was an orphan, came from reduced circumstances, so was unlikely to have access to anything like a family summer home or second home. What about favourite hotels or holiday destinations?

Mr Black began searching travel patterns of Dane and Beth and their immediate family. Who had gone where and when?

After an hour or two he had created a grid onscreen listing family and friends, their flights and car hires and any trips using public transport which they had taken outside of Ireland.

Interesting how her parents' travel changed about a year or so ago, he thought. *All those trips to Madrid and car hires together and now just single tickets to all sorts of locations. And Daddy is on top of a mountain in Scotland right now, about eight hours' drive away. I wonder is there any merit in grabbing him and stashing him somewhere for leverage?*

He decided against it. However the pattern which stood out most clearly was several trips Beth's parents had made over a lengthy period to somewhere in Spain, via Madrid airport. So he assumed the destination was not too far from Madrid? Say within a two or three hour drive? They were going there so frequently at one point that anything further away would not make sense. He delved deeper into the car rental records and discovered a damage report from a tiny hamlet called San Bartolome de Pinares, about an hour and a half west of Madrid. Then a second one. A year later, someone had driven into the back of their car in a place called Avila, half an hour north west of San Bartolome.

He realised he was gambling and it was fairly long odds but it was all he had to go on at present. So what next? He needed to continue searching and try to cross reference the information. It would be short sighted for them to travel by air as they would be too likely to be spotted and he had already ran a programme checking CCTV footage for any sightings of them at all Irish airports which had yielded no results, nor could he locate any other signs of them in Ireland. Somewhere near those two towns in Spain was his only lead. He needed to narrow it down, find something to corroborate his guesswork.

He sat back and drank from a bottle of water. His IP phone rang. "I require your services again," came the robotic sounding voice.

"Yes?"

"The two targets you were unable to interrogate have resurfaced." Mr Black said nothing, just waited silently.

"They are somewhere in Spain."

Mr Black was relieved. "Yes, near Avila," he responded.

"How do you know this?"

"I have located them in case you required further services."

"I do. Go to Spain, physically locate them in Avila and if I require it, eliminate them. A possible third target may present herself also."

"Is that all?"

"For now." The call was terminated.

Mr Black leaned back, thinking that the timing of the call had been fortunate. If it had come a few hours earlier he would not have been able to prove his worth to his employer again. Also it demonstrated he had resources of his own and was not to be underestimated or more importantly undervalued. There had been no reference to the funds which had been transferred earlier, nor had there been any reference to the funds during their previous call which Mr Black had initiated after escaping from Dungeness.

His employer had evinced mild surprise at the size, scale and identity of the forces which had assaulted Mr Black. Mr Black had said his view was that it was a joint operation between the Irish and UK authorities, but he had left no trail for them to follow and he was in a position to continue his task should it be required. At that point, his employer had instructed him to stand down and await further developments.

Under normal circumstances he would have gone straight to Madrid, however after his recent experiences Mr Black decided to leave the UK via Cardiff Airport on a charter flight to Alicante which was due to leave at two am the following morning. Then he would drive the four and a half hours to Avila, where he would base himself. He went back to his hotel and shaved his bearded face for the first time since Dungeness, leaving a moustache with long sides running down to his chin. The style was known as a horseshoe moustache. Next he went to a tanning salon in Aberystwyth and got an all over dark spray tan which the lady operating the service assured him would take a few hours to darken his skin. He got on a bus which took him to Cardiff after an interminable five hour journey. By the time he got to the airport on another shuttle bus the tanning had kicked in and he looked more like the swarthy character in his passport.

He had managed to secure a window seat on the half empty charter flight to Alicante and even luckier was at the rear of the group which was full of half pissed holidaymakers and families who kept the flight attendants occupied throughout the flight. In Alicante he got through customs quickly and caught another shuttle into the city of Alicante, where he collected a rental car, which he prepaid with cash. He drove out of Alicante and stopped at a roadside services area about an hour later, tilted back the seat and slept.

*   *   *

Sweeney was not a happy puppy. The nurse had forced him to move his laptop so she could give him his breakfast and just as he did so the machine pinged, which meant that one of the search routines he had created had come up with a match. However, the harried looking nurse had told him to close the laptop and eat his breakfast or she'd confiscate it. Sweeney reckoned she couldn't but wasn't one hundred percent sure so he grudgingly complied.

He ate the food so fast; he virtually inhaled the breakfast. He set the tray on the bedside locker to the side just leaving the mug of coffee on the trolley he was using. He opened the laptop again and sure enough one of the search routines which was running a facial recognition search powered by an artificial intelligence based algorithm had come up with a match. It was a massive piece of software which was so resource hungry that he wasn't actually running it on the laptop. It was running on powerful servers he had access to in Dublin City University on the north side of the city.

Anyway, it had found what looked like Beth and Dane walking along a seaside promenade in a French town called Mimizan on street CCTV which had been installed outside a small French police station. As they walked he could see Beth saying something to Dane and they both put on hats. "Trying to be careful," he reckoned, "but not careful enough. The question is are they still there?"

Two hours later he got another hit from the same software. This time they were walking along a well-lit street in Biarritz in the evening time. He could see them turn left and disappear into a side alley. Unfortunately for them, the previous year an English soccer club called Chelsea played a Spanish club called Real Sociedad from San Sebastian, which was just over the border from Biarritz, in a European competition. Most Chelsea supporters had flown to San Sebastian and nearby Bilbao, but, aware that Spanish authorities were on the lookout for football hooligans at the airports, a smaller group had decided to fly into Biarritz and make their way to the match by bus and so avoid being stopped at the airport security teams. It worked. They got to the match and caused mayhem afterwards in San Sebastian and of course, also in Biarritz.

As a result of this the Mayor of Biarritz diverted funds into a state of the art CCTV street monitoring system which worked really well at night also. The response was totally over the top but it meant that the images of Beth and Dane were clear and unambiguous.

Kent's searches had yielded the same information but he had scored the hit on the visit to the Guggenheim in Bilbao and decided the visual hits of them in France just clarified the route they had taken to get to Bilbao and nothing more.

Sweeney lay back on the bed considering their route. He figured it was not a random route. They were heading due south in an almost direct line along the French Coast. The question was would they remain in the South Western corner of France? Would they head east past the Pyrenees Mountain ranges over to the Mediterranean or would they continue south into Spain?

He gambled on Spain as his next step and set to work again. After an hour or two his mobile rang. It was Doyle. "how are you getting on? Any news?"

"Yes Sir. I located them in a couple of places. They are travelling South along the French Atlantic coastline. The last place was in Biarritz."

"Jesus! Why would they do that?"

"Not sure at this point and to be honest, I don't think they have stopped travelling yet Sir, so I am continuing to search, until I find their destination."

"Biarritz? Either they're heading for Spain, or the Pyrenees. Good place to get lost, the Pyrenees. Or they could head East for the Cote d'Azur."

"At this point I'm thinking Spain Sir."

"Why Sweeney?"

"I recall overhearing Beth on the phone to someone mentioning her mother's Spanish boyfriend? I know it's a long-shot."

"Don't ignore the other possibilities, but I'll contact the Spanish Police and get some assistance."

"Anything else?"

"No Sir. I'll get back to it."

"Good man."

Doyle turned off the phone and looked at Prendergast who had been listening in on the call. "What do you reckon?"

"It's progress but we need more."

"You're right." Doyle rubbed his chin feeling the rough spots where his shaving blade had missed. He had been preoccupied that morning. "I'm thinking I might let Tiberius know? He's in Madrid at the moment."

"I thought he was off the case. Harcourt Street won't like you pulling something like that."

"I'd be doing it for his own safety really. Just sort of looking after the security of a brother officer, kind of thing." Doyle said with a smile.

"Up to you. I'd wait until we get more information."

"OK let's wait. In the meantime locate the relevant phone numbers and ring the Spanish police. If it's a case that Beth and Dane are heading their way, there's no harm in getting ahead of the game, for once."

"Will do."

*   *   *

"They're in a place called Avila, Sir." Sweeney sounded exuberant on the phone.

"Where the hell is Avila?"

"West of Madrid Sir. Beth went there a couple of years ago with her parents. I then checked her parents travel patterns and found they have been going in and out of Madrid for years, hiring cars. They have had very few incidents with cars during that time and the only one I found so far was in Avila. So then I checked with the Spanish police and there's an apartment in Avila registered in the name of a company and her Mum resigned as a director of it about a year ago. Thanks for bringing the Spanish in on it Sir. It really speeded things up. Anyway I reckon they went to her Mum's place. It's just a five hour straight drive South West from Biarritz."

"Sounds plausible to me. Well done Sweeney. That's great work."

"Just trying to help Sir."

"No, really. I'm delighted. Just you get better and get back in here. This team needs you fighting fit and raring to go!"

Doyle told Prendergast the news from Sweeney.

"You going to call Tiberius now?."

"No. First I inform Harcourt Street. I know they are aware of his whereabouts. Let them suggest any possible involvement." Doyle stretched and continued "the important thing to consider is that, no disrespect to our resident computer whizz kid Sweeney, if he found them other interested parties might do so also. Like that nutcase we tracked to Dungeness. That bastard got away and is still at large. I'm just stating a concern as to Tiberius's potential safety in the admittedly unlikely event that he encountered one of those parties again. Of course, if one of his colleagues decided to warn him, without my official knowledge, well that wouldn't be the end of the world would it?"

Prendergast realised that despite appearances, Doyle wasn't actually covering his own ass, but he was protecting the investigation and the team. Even though Tiberius's loss had hit them hard, they had recovered swiftly as Doyle continued to drive matters forward in pretty much the same style. The fact that Tiberius and Doyle had collaborated so closely previously worked to their advantage.

"I'm just going to go out for a fag sir," she announced.

"I'd hold off on that cigarette until say four or five-ish if I was you Prendergast. Timing is everything, they say." Doyle continued typing his progress update for his superior on his computer.

CHAPTER FORTY SEVEN

Tiberius and Ashling walked out of the Tourist Information Office and headed to a nearby bar to read the various leaflets they had been given.

"I like the idea of going to the Las Luminarias Festival," Ashling said.

"Me too, as long as the horses aren't harmed." Tiberius replied

"Of course not. It says here they are protected and never harmed as a result of jumping through the flames. That would be too cruel."

"Well this is the country of bullfighting. I mean, tell that to the bulls." Ashling looked up to see the grin on his face. He was teasing her again, which she loved, but would never admit.

"Well it sounds pretty cool to me and it only happens once a year and we happen to be just an hour or so West of the town."

"Sure. I'm happy to see it and we've got transport in the garage."

"It'll be fun."

Tiberius's phone rang. He looked at it and Prendergast's name came up. "It's Prendergast," he told Ashling.

"Who?

"One of my," he paused, "one of the investigating team on that case I was working."

"Take it."

"Thanks." He stood and walked to the edge of the footpath.
"Tiberius?"

"Hi, what's up?"

"Can you hold for a sec?"

"Sure."

After a few moments and some muffled noises, Doyle came on the phone.

"Hi Tiber."

"Hey Doyle. Good to hear from you. Did you forget to pay your phone bill?"

"No but you'll understand in a minute."

"OK"

"Dane Wilson slipped out of hospital with Beth's help."

"Damn"

"Precisely. Anyway, courtesy of your and my colleague and mini-genius Sweeney we have managed to locate them."

"Well done to Sweeney. Where are they?"

"That's why I'm ringing you. They're in Spain. More specifically in a place called Avila."

"Wow. That's weird. We're going to a festival in a little place called San Bartolome de Pinares in a day or two and Ashling was suggesting we stay in Avila overnight."

"Ashling was suggesting?"

"Uh. Yeah. She kinda came to visit."

"I'm delighted Boss! Ye're made for each other."

"Thanks, Keep it to yourself, OK?"

"Will do. So," Doyle moved briskly on, "fancy doing a little snooping around in Avila when you're there? Before I have to fully go down the official Interpol and Spanish Police route?"

"Are they aware of this in Harcourt Street?"

"Why do you think I'm ringing on Prendergast's phone?"

"OK. Let me rephrase. What are they aware of in Harcourt Street?"

"They are fully up to speed. They even know you're in Spain and in a convenient location. I'm hoping they will suggest you take a look."

"So why not wait?"

"I'm concerned we may not be the only people to have located the pair of muppets!" Doyle sounded exasperated.

"Yeah. I get that."

"If they had only talked to us. We could have organised something similar but with better security. As it stands they're out there, hanging in the wind, just waiting for someone to chop them down."

"OK. Well. We're going to Avila and San Bartolome so I'll check on them. Do you want me to identify myself to them or stay covert?"

Doyle was impressed with how easily Tiberius adapted to their new roles. He reckoned Tiberius was trying to make it as easy as possible for him.

"What do you think would be best?" He threw back, trying to show he still regarded Tiberius as his boss or at the very least his equal.

"Covert. That way they won't be spooked and head off to another crazy bolthole."

"OK. Thanks."

"How will I contact you?"

"Just ring me. There's nothing unusual about you keeping in touch, just in me reaching out to you for your assistance, prior to those politicians in Harcourt Street seeing sense."

"OK. I'll call."

"Thanks. Take care, Tiber."

"Bye."

Tiberius ended the call and looked over at Ashling poring over the maps and leaflets. Under normal circumstances he wouldn't tell her, however, he realised he didn't want anything to jeopardise this wonderful relationship he'd just stumbled into and keeping secrets or trying to discreetly find time alone to fulfil Doyle's request would do exactly that. Ashling was no fool and her antennae would be even more sensitive, courtesy of her asshole ex cheating on her.

On the other hand, it was inappropriate for a civilian to be aware of what he was about to do. Tiberius stuffed his hands into the pockets of his jeans and stared at the pavement, aware he really, really needed to get this right.

Wait a second, he suddenly thought. *I'm not operating in an official police capacity. I'm just giving a friend a hand. I'm the civilian around here.*

He looked up to find Ashling staring at him intently and he smiled reassuringly and walked back to the table.

"What's going on Frost?" She said in a mock sharp tone.

"I'm going to share with you what that was about and you can decide what we do next? OK?"

Thoroughly puzzled and a little thrown by Tiberius's serious demeanour and cryptic words, Ashling just nodded and sat back, arms folded.

When Tiberius finished, she was about to speak, but he held his hand up quickly and said "whatever you decide we'll go with. I haven't been this happy in a long time and I don't want anything to screw it up."

"Yes but you already agreed to do it Tiberius, prior to speaking with me. So isn't asking my permission kind of window dressing?"

Tiberius could have shot himself. He had handled this so badly. He stopped for a moment and thought and then said "you're right. I should have said to Doyle I'd think about it and get back to him, but I didn't think. I can easily sort that though because if you are not happy with this, I'll just ring him and say I can't do it. I'm sorry."

His honest response was precisely what Ashling needed to hear. She suggested they continue to plan their trip and have dinner and discuss it some more. Take some time before making any decisions.

Tiberius agreed and they went back to their planning.

*   *   *

Rayne was constructing an email in response to Beth's last communication. She wanted to structure it so Beth and Dane would have no alternative but to give her more authority to use in negotiating a deal. She had come around full circle in regard to the pair's disappearance. It was annoyingly sudden, but it meant that if she could get the authority she needed, she would then have a free hand to move the deal to the final stage without any interference from either of them. It would be much swifter and simpler without having to manage them through the different decisions which would need to be made. She could just present them with a fait accompli and pressure them into signing. She certainly didn't feel bad about it. After all, she was going to make the pair of them fabulously wealthy.

She sent the email from her phone as she walked to the departure gate for the Lufthansa flight to Madrid. She was absolutely not going with those Ryanair guys. *What kind of airline didn't have a first class section? Not even a business class for God's sake!*

Minutes later, Beth and Dane were sitting outside a pop up café situated on top of a section of the massive city walls of Avila. They were having their first argument in ages. Dane was unhappy with granting Rayne carte blanche to proceed as she would be able to do whatever she wanted. Beth finally won the argument by stating that due to the strict privacy cocoon he had constructed to protect them, they were in no position to liaise with Rayne on a regular basis as would normally be needed during negotiations like these. Beth felt that Rayne was just being sensible and had their best interests at heart. The alternative was like asking her to run a race with one leg tied to the other and the big risk was that Rayne could just walk away on the basis that it was too much hassle despite the money she would make. Beth also pointed out that the more money Rayne made, the more they made because they had agreed a performance based deal.

After a lot of wrangling and discussion Dane grumpily conceded and ordered more pastries, intending to indulge in a little childish comfort eating. Beth, meanwhile, sent a quick email to Rayne authorising her to complete negotiations and finish out the deal on their behalf. Although she was a highly intelligent person, due to her lack of experience in the mechanics of Mergers & Acquisitions, Beth did not realise that she had actually given Rayne even more then she had requested and that as a result Rayne no longer needed their signatures to complete the deal.

Twenty three thousand feet above sea level, logged into Lufthansa's Wi-Fi, Rayne was thrilled to receive the email. She had everything she needed to deliver to Deng. Perhaps she should return to Dublin and work on it from there?

No, she thought. *First things first. I'll flip this email onto the lawyers and get an opinion as to how much I can depend on it. If they reckon it's cool then I'll contact Deng. The substantive elements of the deal have been agreed so it's really up to the legal folk to draft the agreements based on that.*

She forwarded the email to the lawyers she had engaged and waited for their opinion. She ordered and finished her lunch and nothing arrived. The plane landed and she went through passport control and customs. She went to a café in the terminal and ordered a coffee, sitting and waiting, her security team clustered around her, in various positions. It had been roughly two hours, which wasn't a long time but she felt it was more than enough for several legal eagles to read, analyse and render an opinion on a short email.

After another half hour, she had had enough. She rang the senior partner in the law firm she was using. "Conrad? Rayne Frost here. Did you get that email?" she queried the man abruptly.

Rayne was always barely civil to people in the legal profession as she figured they were so well paid and still managed to make mistakes which cost their clients money and worse.

"Ah yes, Ms Frost. Hello. Hello there. How are you?"

"I'm waiting for you guys to do your job, Conrad. Can you educate me as to when that might happen Sweetie?" She dripped sarcasm into the phone.

"We have indeed considered the email in question and we are just waiting for one colleague's perspective on it?"

"How long's that gonna take?"

"Well she has it and is looking at it right now."

"Well can you give me a steer as to the opinions expressed before this woman comes back to us?"

"The issue appears to centre around proving that the email did in fact originate from Ms Frontemont and her partner Mr Wilson." He continued in a regretful tone, "unfortunately it is all too easy in this wonderful new digital era to create such electronic communications. The wording is fine, just the provenance, you see?"

"So what do we need?" Rayne was exasperated but acknowledged that this guy was just protecting her ass, and, of course, his own.

"Well if we could get a scan or even a photograph of a similar physical document actually signed by them both. That would be ideal."

"Fine. Have you got something ready?"

"Um. No. Not at present. As I mentioned we were waiting on my esteemed colleague's opinion, you see."

"I do see and here's what I want. Draft a simple document which mirrors the email, send it to me and I'll forward it to them. Hopefully, they can print it and sign it and sent it back."

"Well I really would like to get my colleagues op..."

"Conrad!" Rayne cut across him. "Just do it. Now! I don't care about your buddy. I need to strike while the iron's hot here or this deal will go down the Swannee river along with a good eighty percent of your fees pal!"

"Ah, well if you insist Ms Frost. We will of course do our best to deliver what you have requested." The man still sounded calm, urbane and relaxed.

"Good. I'm waiting." Rayne ended the call abruptly.

She decided to continue to wait where she was until she had received the document. She had nothing better to do and everything hinged on getting this issue resolved. When it finally arrived, she scanned it eagerly and was pleasantly surprised that the wording was quite straightforward with nothing which she felt might scare off Dane or Beth. Rayne attached the document to an email where she explained to Beth that she had sent Beth's email to the lawyers because she wanted to ensure that everyone was protected in case anything went wrong and they were insisting Dane and Beth both sign a printed copy of the document, scan it and send it back to her. She was very apologetic and explained that she felt it was a bit over the top but that was lawyers for you.

Again she waited. She had finished her second coffee and sat drumming her fingers on the table, watching the ebb and flow of humanity as it passed through that section of the Arrivals area in the airport. Sooner than expected, Beth replied saying that she and Dane would return to where they were staying, print the document, sign it, and send an image of the signed document back to her, but it would take about half an hour.

Finally! thought Rayne. She rang Deng.

"Rayne." He answered as unemotionally as always.

"Deng. Good news." Rayne said calmly.

"Go on."

"I have received full authorisation to complete the deal with you from the promoters. I am just waiting on a signed letter which means that I can probably sign any documentation which is required also."

"Good."

"OK so you know who we're using for this. Do you want to fire up your legal guys and get them talking so we can make this happen?"

"Yes. I will instruct them."

"Great! We need to move quickly. I see this as a window of

RUN FROM THE DEVIL

opportunity to get this deal done now in a really efficient, timely manner without interference or hesitating from the promoters or any other parties."

"I agree."

"I'm in Spain at the moment, but plan to return to Dublin as soon as everything is ready for signing."

"That may not be necessary. We can always send the documents for your signature to you, wherever you happen to be."

"OK. I'm cool with that. So when will you send the first payment to my account?"

"I want to see a copy of your authorisation first. Then you will receive the first tranche. Bye." Deng ended the call.

Rayne got up and went with her team to a couple of dark windowed SUVs which headed for Madrid. As they approached her destination she spotted Tiberius walking along the street with his arm around a woman. "Stop." She ordered the driver.

"It's difficult to stop here Ms Frost."

"Won't be for long," she said dismissively.

"Sure but with the Royal Palace just across the way, the Spanish cops ain't gonna let us stay here," the driver persisted.

"Shut up." Rayne ordered, following Tiberius's progress. Sure enough the couple turned and went up the steps to the building where the family's apartment was located.

"OK move on." She told the driver and sat back.

"Yes Ms Frost."

She thought about whether or not she wanted to interrupt the love birds. There was plenty of bedrooms in the apartment but she just wasn't sure.

"Take me to the Palacio de los Duques Hotel. It's nearby."

"Yes Ms Frost."

She booked into the luxurious hotel and headed straight for her suite and a shower. By the time she got out and checked her phone, she had received Beth's email with the signed

443

document attached. She sent it onto Conrad and Deng and decided to celebrate. So she booked a table in a restaurant called Sobrino de Botin, reputedly one of the oldest restaurants in the world and one of Ernest Hemingway's favourites, as her father had informed her when he had brought her and Tiber there as a big treat because she had been accepted to MIT. *It seems like centuries ago,* she thought.

Rayne flung her self-discipline and diet out the window as she sat in a corner table of the small wood panelled first floor dining room. She decided it was as good as when she had been there with her Pop. She finished her main course of roast suckling pig and finished her glass of wine. She enjoyed the glass of rich Rioja wine but its predecessor, a glass of white Albarino had been over-chilled and she had found over the past year or two that anything very cold was like a kick in the kidneys and sent her straight to the john.

There was a queue waiting outside the ladies toilet, so she moseyed on downstairs to the ground floor toilet. As she left the toilet, she bumped into an attractive woman, who apologised to her in an Irish accent. "No problem," she smiled at the woman, feeling a little horny because she was really good looking. Then.

"Rayne?" She heard her name called behind her.

Standing there, with an amazed look on his face was Tiberius.

"Hi Babes!" She stepped towards him and gave him a big hug. "Didn't expect to see you here!" She said quickly. "What are you doing in Madrid?"

He looked a little uncomfortable and glanced over her shoulder. She turned to see the woman she had bumped into watching them.

"Rayne, this is Ashling. Ashling this is my sister Rayne."

The woman offered Rayne her hand and said "Hello there. Nice to meet you Rayne. I'll let you two get reacquainted while I just nip in here to the loo," and she disappeared inside.

Rayne turned back to Tiberius and said with a big grin, "OK Buster. Spill the beans! What's going on?"

Less uncomfortable but still a little sheepish, Tiberius said "I came over for a break after everything that happened with the case. I invited Ashling to join me."

"Go on," Rayne prompted, enjoying herself hugely at her brother's expense.

"Well. She did."

"Did what?"

"Join me. She's staying in the apartment with me." Then Tiberius, stopped and said "Wow. Sorry Raynie, obviously you can stay too. I mean it's no problem."

Rayne decided to take mercy on him and said "no thanks Tiber. I'm already booked into the Palacio de los Duques. I have a series of meetings gonna happen at the hotel so I figured may as well stay there as well. Which is lucky for you, imagine how shocked I might have been if I'd just arrived at Pop's apartment and you two were at it like bunnies!"

"Very funny." Tiberius had enough teasing. "Will you join us? We're in the basement. It's noisy but good fun."

"I'm sitting upstairs at that table we shared with Dad last time we were all here, remember? So why don't you guys join me? Please?" She pleaded with Tiberius as Ashling returned to them.

"What's happening," she said with a smile. "Have you two caught up?"

"Will you and Tiber come and share my table?" Rayne asked Ashling.

"Love to." Ashling replied. So Rayne slipped her arm through Ashling's and cheerfully told Tiberius to sort out things in the dungeon!

An hour and a seriously good bottle of Rioja later, the three of them were chatting away and having great fun. As they left the restaurant Rayne insisted on giving them a lift back to the apartment. Ashling looked at Rayne's security team with great interest.

Outside the building, they decided to meet for lunch the following day.

Rayne's SUV's sped off as Tiberius and Ashling went inside.

"Why does she need all of the bodyguards and stuff," asked Ashling who was a little bit tipsy.

"She's seriously wealthy so basically a target."

"Well looking at our little palacio in the clouds which your Dad owns I reckon all of you Frosts are a tad well off."

"Yeah, but Rayne's very successful in business and equally high profile. Back in California, that means you need good security and she has them."

"OK. Well good for her." They had reached the door of the apartment and Ashling drunkenly grabbed Tiberius by the lapels of his jacket, to kiss him hard "and good for me," she breathed softly. Tiberius opened the door and they slipped inside.

*   *   *

Rayne re-read the email from Conrad. He confirmed that the document signed by Beth and Dane would stand up in court. So now she didn't really need them. She could just make the deal happen and they would have to deal with the outcome, well for as long as they stayed incommunicado with everyone. She would check her account for Deng's twenty million payment tomorrow.

She could just return to Dublin or even L.A. and finish everything off but last night Tiberius and Ashling invited her to accompany them to the Las Luminarias festival, which she hadn't been to since her Pop took her to see it as a young teenager. She loved horses.

It's funny how little we realise quite how random Life is. Turn left along one street and you get knocked down. Turn right along a different street and you meet the love of your life. Stop and have a coffee and while you're sitting there you could get an idea which makes you rich or you could catch a bug from the person sitting next to you which turns into a life changing illness. You just never know. A decision which seems very innocuous and unimportant at the time can have ramifications in your life and that of others far beyond the fabled butterfly effect.

Normally at this point in time Rayne would be heading for the airport, firing out emails and texts to all and sundry, driving the deal forward. But this morning she woke late and, truth be told, a trifle hungover. So she had a really nice leisurely breakfast and lounged around the room in her pyjamas.

She was genuinely pleased for Tiberius. She felt Ashling was a nice person, good fun and with a great sense of humour. She had kept the Frost siblings roaring with laughter as she regaled them with stories about some of her Mom's nutty artistic friends. She hadn't seen Tiberius in such good form for years. Ashling was definitely good for him and she was quite a hottie! She felt a little envious. The thought of spending a little down time was appealing. She had agreed with Conrad an update schedule so she could allow the process to just move forward and keep a watching brief. The icing on the cake came when she checked her account to find that she was twenty million richer!

That morning Rayne Frost could have stuck to her usual hard charging, deal making path in life and as was her wont, simply focussed on the prize, but for no really commanding or major reason, she decided against it. It was a decision she and her doting brother would come to regret.

CHAPTER FORTY EIGHT

Tiberius put his phone in his pocket and asked Ashling in a surprised voice. "Did you invite Rayne to come with us to Las Luminarias?"

"Uhm not really too sure. To be honest, last night's kind of a blur, but it sounds like something I could easily do. Why did she say no? Was she upset or something?" Ashling sounded concerned.

"No. That's just it. She said she'd love to join us." Tiberius sounded amazed.

"Why so surprised. Aren't we lovely company?" Ashling teased, a little relieved. She had really wanted to get on well with Tiberius's only sibling.

"It's just so out of character for her. She mentioned last night that the deal she's been working on is going ahead and they should get it over the line pretty soon, so it's just odd. She's such a go getter that I would have expected a text from the airport saying she was leaving."

"Like I said. We're fun people! So let's organise this a bit more then now that it's for three and not two."

"Sure."

*   *   *

Mr Black was lying on his back. He had slipped out of the bed and put on a pair of boxers to hide the tan lines around his groin because the woman he had met in the bar last night assumed he was Spanish. He had a flair for languages and was fluent in several. He challenged himself to blend in when he was on a mission by trying to seem a native of whatever country he was in. He had a musical ear and could mimic ways of speaking and pronunciation very quickly.

As usual he wasn't horny and didn't find her particularly attractive but he would stay with people overnight whenever possible so as to minimize the trail he left. Women, men, transgenders, couples. He knew a wide cross section of people found him attractive. It didn't matter as long as they were able to invite him back to their place. No need for hotel registration or provision of ID when the hormones were in full flow.

And if the individual or individuals looked like they were going to cause any issues, he would simply kill them and move on. He had been fascinated by a course Lord Jocelyn had sent him on in the good old days when he was his prize asset. It was run by some shadowy intelligence section in the United States, which was exclusively devoted to Accidental Deaths and how to simulate the conditions surrounding them. He had practiced assiduously and developed his repertoire until he was confident he could adapt to any set of circumstances or environment. Covering where the fake tan ended and his pale Ulster skin began was doing her a favour really. She had been quite drunk when they had returned to her apartment so she didn't care when he kept the light off.

Kent had located the apartment owned by Beth's family, which Deng passed onto Mr Black. He would leave the little town of San Bartolome where he was staying that night and continue on to Avila, locate them and shadow them until called upon to act.

He decided to leave at dawn and find somewhere to stay over an indefinite period of time in Avila. His concern was this might leave a trail so while his bed partner snored gently beside him he booked an apartment in the historic centre of Avila on Calle de San Segundo, opposite the cathedral with off street parking for the car. He booked for a month at a cost of two thousand three hundred euro. He paid the owners up front for the month in full and explained he was a botanist from Scotland doing research on the flora in the surrounding mountains which would mean he would be out all day and only returning late at night to write up his work and sleep. He emailed them a copy of a passport he kept on his phone for such situations plus a scan of a fake University ID and asked where he could collect the key? They were happy with everything, especially being paid in full upfront so they arranged to leave the key at a local bodega about thirty metres from the apartment building. He went back to sleep.

*   *   *

Conrad brought the conference call to a close. Everything had been agreed in relation to the transaction and the various pieces of documentation could be generated for signing by the relevant parties. Contracts would be sent to the other side's lawyers to be checked in the next few hours. He was delighted. It was proving to be one of the more problem free deals he had ever been involved with despite the waspish and unpleasant client he was saddled with. Although Rayne had proven to be very much on the ball and useful in error-trapping during the negotiations. It made things so much easier when both parties wanted the same thing, then the transaction tended to move along quickly. Not to mention that the fees were going to be very very juicy. He would finally be able to trade in his yacht for the new sixty five footer he had been lusting after.

Shaylene was sitting at the conference table Deng had used with his lawyers and advisers for the call. He turned to her and said, "chase the lawyers on both sides to deliver the documents faster." Caught off guard she replied, " I didn't realise we were in a hurry on this?"

He stared at her coldly and she thought, *Oh no! I need to be more focussed. He ain't too happy with me. Again.*

"I want signatures as quickly as possible."

"Yes. I'll see to it." She answered quietly. He got up and left the room leaving his executive assistant wondering what the hell was going on.

*   *   *

Ashling, Rayne and Tiberius drove from Madrid the following morning heading west towards Avila. For once, Rayne told her security team not to come. After all she would be with her brother, who was a cop. Dave Gant, her head of security, wasn't happy but she overruled him.

The plan Ashling had cooked up was to stay in the Parador de La Granja, a converted palace which had been built in the eighteenth century for the children of the Spanish King Charles III. They would then drive to San Bartolome de Pinares for the evening portion of the second day of the Las Luminarias Festival when as many as eighty horses would jump over bonfires lit along the cobbled streets of the little town in a purification ritual which went back over two hundred and fifty years. She had wanted to return to the royal town of La Granja for their second night, visit the Royal Palace the following morning and then head back to Madrid afterwards, all going well. However, Tiberius had said he wanted to spend a night or two in Avila, so they booked a second set of rooms at another Parador in the older part of the city.

They had good fun driving along, laughing and chatting. Rayne had decided to be as charming as possible to Ashling. Insofar as she was capable, she loved her older brother and wanted Tiberius to be happy and he certainly seemed happy with Ashling. Tiberius was delighted to see the two most important women in his life getting along so well.

The Parador proved to be a great idea. It was sumptuously decorated and the food they enjoyed in the restaurant was superb. Ashling and Rayne had disappeared into the Health and Wellness Centre for lots of treatments and treats. Tiberius went for a run around the little town and then swam several laps in the pool. Finally he returned to their room and rang Doyle.

"Hey Doyle. How are you doing?"

"Hi. What's up?

"Nothing. We've arrived at our hotel and we're heading to San Bartolome de Pinares tomorrow. We leave there tomorrow evening for Avila, where I'll have about two days to find her Mom's apartment and nose around discreetly."

"That's great. I'll let you know if we want the local police to come in on it."

"Do we?"

"Not sure at this point in time. By the way Harcourt Street asked me to see if you were willing to take a look for our fugitives in Avila."

"Good. That's a bit of a relief."

"I know. I reckon they're just trying to save money. Too fecking mean to send anyone out from Ireland and there's some issue with Interpol at present."

"OK."

"By the way I had an interesting call from John Burke yesterday."

"Oh? That's the security services guy, right?"

"Yep. He wanted me to know Beth and Dane were in Avila."

"What? I wonder how he even knew they were missing."

"He has his claws deep into Harcourt Street and I doubt anything goes through there that he doesn't know about. What's interesting is that he would have known I'm the one who informed Harcourt Street in my weekly update about the location of Bonnie and Clyde."

"Didn't strike me as a guy to waste his breath telling you something you already know."

"Me neither. John is as deep as they come and his right hand never knows what his left hand is up to. Anyway, keep an eye out for him or the other giant who accompanies him, yeah?

For guys in their line of work they're a bloody conspicuous size."

"Sure. Will do."

"OK, Tiber. Look, you be careful, yeah?"

"Absolutely. See you when I get back."

"Good stuff. Bye."

*   *   *

In Avila, the kitchen was busy. Beth was setting the plates and cutlery out on the breakfast bar and Dane was cooking a couple of omelettes. He freely admitted he wasn't a great cook but he reckoned he did a decent omelette. When he moved into Campus accommodation for the first time he did some research and figured that an omelette was the most flexible, quick, easy to prepare and nutritious type of food, especially as you could simply chop up and throw in a wide variety of ingredients.

Over time he had perfected his omelettes and Beth freely admitted that his Hangover Special was one of Life's great treats. Tonight they were sampling his Excellent Evening Eats Number Three. There were three different variations on this Omelette, but this was his own favourite.

An hour later they were sitting on a couple of couches polishing off a couple of beers and taking it easy. After a while Dane asked, "do we know how far Rayne has got with the deal?"

"Nope."

"Uhm, should we check?"

"Nope."

"Why not?"

"Dane, just let her get on with it. Horses for courses and all that." Beth was stretched out on her couch and beginning to doze off.

"Yeah." Dane agreed, "Actually, it will be a relief not to have to worry about it all anymore. Might do something completely different with my dosh. What about you? Have you thought about what you might do?"

"Visit Japan."

"Japan? Okay, so just go on a holiday then and after that?"

"No. more than a holiday. I'd love to go there for like six months. You can get this boat which travels all around the coasts, and you just get off and stay wherever you want. Really get under the skin of the place. It's always fascinated me."

"Not really my thing but go for it."

"You know we'll have to work with the new investors initially. We won't be able to just bugger off to wherever we fancy for a while."

"No. I get that. We have to do a knowledge transfer to whoever comes on board. I've prepared for it."

"Oh?"

"When Rayne first got involved, I realised it was all much more real so I restructured everything and created a pile of documents and rewrote the code so pretty much anyone can understand it."

"Wow. When did you find the time to do that?"

"Between the night in the Tapas place back in Dublin with Rayne and the day before I was kidnapped. I worked every hour I could. I had been thinking along those lines anyway. I figured if either of us was, you know, run over by a bus, like, a random event blindsiding us, we would need to have all of our work in an accessible format."

"So, what you're saying is that a handover or whatever, shouldn't take too long?"

"Nope. It's good to go right now and it's all really easy to understand, well for programmers anyway."

"I should let Rayne know. It might help with the negotiations."

"Sure. If you want."

Beth picked up her phone and using the short term email system Dane had created, dashed off an email to Rayne.

*   *   *

Rayne saw the email while relaxing after a nice massage at the Spa in the Parador they were staying in. Delighted, she sent a carefully worded email to Deng. Explaining that Dane had complied with her request to prepare a data dump for the new company majority shareholder. It wasn't true but, she felt it was worthwhile as it underlined her value to Deng and would help to secure her second payment.

When Deng saw the email, it had the opposite effect of what Rayne intended. He decided that once the documents were signed and the data dump triggered, he wouldn't need Rayne, Beth or Dane anymore, so if they could be eliminated prior to funds actually transferring then he would save himself a vast sum of money and still get the technology for Kent and his team to work on. Furthermore, no one other than the solicitors would be aware that he had it which was a further advantage going forward. He could keep it from the solicitors if the data dump looked like it was only going to be triggered after completion. He felt that Rayne would comply if he asked to have it done on signing but prior to funds transfer, especially if he sent her the second payment of twenty one million, or maybe he didn't need to pay that either if she simply wasn't around to collect it.

However, Deng considered further, because Dane was so talented and downright brilliant, he was possibly worth keeping alive. Who knows what else he might come up with in the future, so eliminating him might be like killing the goose laying the golden eggs? But then, what would his motivation be like if his partners were both dead? Once Deng had the software it was a game changer as long as it could do everything it was purported to. He had never seen Kent so excited as when he had checked out some data Dane had sent to Rayne prior to his being taken to Dungeness. Kent said it was a phenomenal piece of coding. So Deng spent the rest of the day mulling over whether or not to kill this particular goose.

*   *   *

Mr Black sat on the roof of an office building which offered a clear line of sight into the apartment Beth and Dane were in. He still felt a little odd about the girl. He still hadn't come to terms with it. He wasn't sure he would be comfortable killing her. He felt that he could overcome it but it puzzled him that he had any feeling about it at all. Definitely a first.

He could see them lying on couches in a living area after eating some food. They looked very comfortable with each other, but something in their body language or lack of it suggested to him that they were not intimate with each other. He had a natural ability to interpret people's body language and analyse them. It was very useful, especially when he needed a bed for the night. He could work out quickly who was most likely to be receptive to him.

In this case he was pretty sure they were friendly but not sexually or romantically entangled. The two processes were utterly separate for Mr Black insofar as the latter was real and the former fictional, in his opinion, which was probably why he was having difficulty understanding his feelings about Beth and the fact that he had any at all.

Once he communicated to his employer he had located them, his latest set of instructions had been the same as previously, to continue to monitor and shadow them. He had purchased a handgun with a silencer, a sniper rifle and some knives from a contact in Madrid on his way to Avila in case he was instructed to kill some or all of the targets. So all he had to do now was to sit and wait. His mind came back to dwell on the Taig policeman and the Yank who had messed everything up for him in England and nearly gotten him captured or killed. The way he considered it; the scales needed balancing. He owed them a little pain.

*　　　　*　　　　*

"See you tomorrow guys. Goodnight." Rayne called to Tiberius and Ashling as the lift doors began to close.

"Goodnight. Sleep well cos' we've a surprise for you tomorrow." Ashling called back.

Rayne smiled at her, continued to the next floor and got out. She had wanted dinner to end so she could get back to her room and check out Conrad's latest communication about the deal. Things had moved forward faster than she could have imagined. It looked like things were almost ready for signature. She had already forgotten about Ashling's 'surprise'.

The next morning they had an early breakfast and left the Parador at around ten am. An hour later they arrived at a Yeguada or stud farm near San Bartolome de Pinares. Tiberius had shared with Ashling the story about how Rayne and he had spent long hot Californian summers on horseback at his father's property, so she had arranged for them to take some horses out for a trek into the nearby hills with a guide. They had a great time and after a couple of hours arrived back to the stud farm for lunch. Rayne's horse had been spooked by something moving in the brush nearby and she had expertly brought it under control which had impressed their otherwise taciturn guide Manuel.

The owner of the stud, Diego, joined them for a coffee after lunch and remarked about Rayne's skill with a horse, to which Tiberius replied that she was an expert horsewoman. Diego asked would she like a little race against Manuel? Before Tiberius could backtrack, Rayne agreed to the challenge. Then she smiled sweetly at Diego and asked if his horses took part in the Las Luminarias festival? Diego said he always put a few horses in. Rayne then moved on and asked what the wager would be?"

"Wager?" asked Diego.

"Sure. If your guy Manuel wins?" She was still smiling. Tiberius was watching this with growing concern. He knew when Rayne was suckering someone into something. She had done it to him often enough, growing up.

"If my rider wins, you must give me a kiss, beautiful lady!" proclaimed Diego.

Rayne laughed and said, "if your guy wins I'll even kiss the horse, buddy!" Everyone laughed.

Then Rayne said, "what if I win?" Diego looked at her.

"What do I get if I win?"

"Name your prize," said Diego gallantly.

Rayne looked as though she was considering this carefully, but Tiberius knew better. She had this all worked out.

"OK." She said finally. "If I win, you give me a horse to ride in the Las Luminarias."

Diego looked very uncomfortable. So Tiberius jumped in and said, "she's just joking, Diego." Turning to Rayne and glaring at her, he said, "aren't you Raynie."

She looked crestfallen but agreed. "Sure. Sure. Just joking."

Diego looked relieved and bustled off to arrange the race. After fifteen minutes he returned and invited them to follow him outside. Manuel was waiting with two stallions.

Diego gestured at the horses and said to Rayne, "pick one. Manuel will ride the other."

Rayne was a good judge of horseflesh and quickly selected the better of the two. It was somewhat shorter but very powerful in the shoulders and broad. The horse looked as though he could run all day.

The course Diego had selected involved circumnavigating the horse farm twice. To make things fair, the two riders mounted and gently cantered around the course. On their return, Diego, Tiberius, Ashling and some other members of Diego's family were sitting on the front veranda overlooking the roadway leading to the main entrance, which the two riders were to ride straight up at the end. A light plastic tape had been run across the entrance to the large courtyard.

Diego's youngest daughter stood near the horses with a flag held high. After a few moments Diego nodded to her, she dropped the flag and they were off. Manuel spurred into an immediate lead and they disappeared off through a different exit from the courtyard. After eight or nine minutes they saw the two riders in the distance passing the main gates, with Manuel still in front and Rayne's horse about fifteen metres behind him.

Ashling leaned over to Tiberius and whispered, "he's still in the lead."

"Don't worry. She's like this, just waiting for the right moment. She'll hold back her horse until she's ready."

Sure enough a little while later the two horses approached the main gate for the second time. They could hear shouting and cheering from some staff at the gate who had blocked the road so the horses would turn right and along the roadway to the courtyard. Rayne was right behind Manuel and Tiberius could see her body language change as she began to push the horse harder, increasing the tempo and waving the whip she carried. She surged past Manuel's horse and tore through the tape about two lengths in front. Rayne pulled him up sharply and jumped off. She hugged the horse. As Manuel dismounted she went over and kissed him, then she walked over to Diego and kissed him. Everyone laughed. Diego said, "Senorita Frost, it would be an honour to have you represent Yeguada de Cervera in the Las Luminarias this evening!" Everyone applauded and they all went inside for a celebratory drink.

Ashling dragged Tiberius and Rayne away from the impromptu party and back to their car to head into San Bartolome and check out the town and the preparations for Las Luminarias. Diego had told them that his riders would only go to certain parts of the town and they would attend the same street party as in previous years. Ashling also wanted to look for some gifts to bring home.

It was fascinating to wander around the old cobbled streets

of the town and see massive bundles of wood all laid out. Tiberius told them food would be cooked in the ashes of the bonfires after the horses had run and jumped through them in the centuries old purification ritual. "It's gonna be very smoky because the idea was that the smoke and flames would purify and protect the animals from pests and diseases throughout the year ahead. They prepare the horses carefully and they are not harmed in any way."

"It's cool. I'm really looking forward to it." Rayne said casually.

"When Tiberius said you were into horses, I never realised just how good you were. You were great!" Ashling smiled.

"Thanks." Rayne replied.

"I'm just going to pop in here," Ashling pointed to a shop with a window display of stuffed rearing horses and other souvenirs.

Tiberius turned to Rayne and said, "I'm proud of you sis," and he folded her into a hug, kissing her forehead before releasing her.

About a hundred yards further along the street, Mr Black watched Rayne and Tiberius hugging from a doorway. He smiled.

After an hour or two wandering around, Tiberius, Rayne and Ashling made their way out of the town and back to Diego's stud farm, unaware that a nondescript grey Seat car was following them. When they entered the stud, the grey Seat continued thirty metres past and parked in a layby. Mr Black got out and quickly climbed over the wall. He then climbed a tall old oak tree until he found a good vantage point which let him look out over the main stud buildings. He arrived in time to see Tiberius walking in the front door of the main house through his binoculars. After a while Rayne appeared adjusting riding clothes she had changed into and carrying what looked like heavy coats and a hat. Pleased, Mr Black descended, climbed back over the wall and got into his car. He headed back into San Bartolome. He had planted a bug on the Smart car Beth was driving and it had been activated. He wanted to check where they were going to park and base themselves as he had overheard them planning to visit the Las Luminarias festival the previous day over lunch while he had sat at a nearby table.

He found them quickly enough. Although San Bartolome de Pinares had a year round population about six hundred people, it increased during the festival to about two thousand, mostly people from the surrounding countryside and nearby Avila. Fortunately, it hadn't made it to the list of must-do tourist trails yet. Still it was a small town and Dane was pretty tall, so it wasn't difficult to spot them. They were just wandering around. After some time, they went into a small restaurant and he felt happy gambling that they would be there for a while.

He walked to a liquor store and purchased two bottles of an American liquor called Everclear 190. It was 95% alcohol. He then went back to his car and took out a soft plastic bottle with a spout, into which he decanted the clear, odourless liquid. Then he put it into the boot and headed back out to the stud farm, just outside the town. He resumed his perch in the tree until he spotted a small convoy consisting of two four wheel drives vehicles towing horseboxes and a car with Tiberius, Ashling and Rayne inside, leaving the courtyard. He returned to his car and drove back towards the main gates. He waited a moment or two until the group of three vehicles turned onto the road and headed for San Bartolome. They stopped outside the town in a large open space where about sixty or seventy vans and horse boxes were located. The area was a hive of activity.

Mr Black parked near the entrance and strolled in casually, carrying a plastic carrier bag. He located his quarry again after a few moments. He noted an elderly man dressing Rayne in a bright red overcoat. She had on a hat which covered her hair, ears and lower neck. She sported a pair of goggles on top of her head and what looked like a face mask was hanging below her chin.

Satisfied, he walked back to the entrance and strolled towards the town. He knew that at around seven thirty or eight pm, the horses and riders would all head to the church first and after some religious Taig mumbo jumbo would then leave to begin the fire ceremony in the streets. So he analysed the route carefully.

Tiberius and Ashling walked into the town with Diego who wanted them to join him in the church, while Rayne stayed with the other riders.

As they approached the church, Tiberius spotted Dane and Beth sitting in the window of a tiny restaurant they were about to pass.

"You go on ahead." He said to Ashling and Diego. "I'll join you in a minute. Call of nature," he nodded towards the restaurant entrance. He turned and walked into the restaurant and then swivelling quickly, moved to the table the pair were at and sat in front of them. They were stunned.

"Jesus!" said Dane.

"Tiberius, how the hell did you?" Beth trailed off.

"Find you?" He finished for her. "I didn't. I'm here for the festival. I just saw you guys in here as we were passing by."

"Oh my God!" Beth groaned. "I suppose you're really pissed off with us." Then she stopped. "Wait a minute. What do you mean you're here for the festival? Are you on holiday or what?"

Tiberius sat back and regarded the guilty looking pair evenly.

"OK." He said eventually. "I'm gonna level with you. I'm no longer working the case, so I came to Spain to stay in our family place in Madrid with my friend."

"Oh. OK" Beth relaxed slightly. Dane still stared at him intently, waiting.

"However. This isn't quite a coincidence. Sweeney tracked you guys to Avila and then I got a call from his boss to see if you were OK. Seeing as I was just down the road, as it were."

"Sweeney tracked us?" Beth sounded surprised and a little annoyed.

"Yes," answered Tiberius, "and if he found you, you can be sure other parties may have also." He paused. "Get the picture?"

"Yes. This changes things." Dane growled.

"You guys need to tell the Spanish police who you are and where you are. Then you need to either allow them to protect you or return to Ireland where we can do it."

"The reason we left was because you weren't able to protect Dane," Beth protested. "A guy nearly got into his hospital room."

"Also we needed time to work things out." Dane added.

"We were unaware there was more than one party interested in you. Now we know we can take appropriate precautions." Tiberius argued.

"Not so sure about that." Beth said.

"Sweeney found you very quickly, and while he's good, you can be sure he's not the only one."

"Bugger it." Dane grumbled. "He's right. Now what?" he looked at Beth.

"Look, why don't we meet in Avila tomorrow?" Tiberius suggested. "I'm staying in the local Parador in the town and we can have a chat there? Say eleven am? By the way, I'm with my friend and my sister."

"Rayne is here?" Now Beth looked truly dumbfounded.

"Yes. She's doing some deal on behalf of you guys, right?"

"That's right."

"Well. I think it's nearly completed, so she's spending some time with us."

"That's good news. I think," added Dane.

"Sorry for the dumb question. But is Rayne here in San Bartolome or in Madrid?"

"San Bartolome. Actually she's riding in the Festival."

"She is amazing!" Beth sounded impressed.

"That's Rayne." Tiberius grinned. "So are we agreed? We

will meet tomorrow at my hotel and figure out the next steps?"

Beth and Dane looked at each other and after a brief moment Dane nodded, so Beth said, "Sure We'll meet you tomorrow."

"Thanks." Tiberius got up to leave and then placed his hands on the table and said quietly "please don't disappear again. I don't want to have to go actively looking for you and it'll screw up my vacation. OK?"

"I promise." Beth answered.

Tiberius looked at Dane. "Me too," Dane answered.

"Thanks guys. Enjoy the festival. I hear it's really cool and keep an eye out for Rayne. She's in a bright red overcoat, riding a big grey horse."

Mr Black stood in the crowd near the horses, outside the church. As the priest ended his blessing the horses began to move off in procession. The smoke from the bonfires filled the air and it was becoming difficult to see through the billowing clouds. The crowd was singing and chanting and some musicians were playing lively tunes along the streets. It was noisy and smoky and chaotic.

Diego's horses, including the one Rayne was riding, were at the rear of the procession and Mr Black was shadowing them closely. Like many others, he had a scarf wound around his face. Up ahead people were cheering and shouting as riders began jumping and riding their mounts through the bonfires. A group of riders just ahead turned right and headed along a narrow street. Mr Black hadn't expected this. So he moved closer to Diego's group. He was jostled from behind and the man apologised in Spanish and again in American accented English. He glanced back to see Tiberius standing right behind him.

"De nada," he said. It's nothing. He moved quickly to his right, melting into the crowd. He stopped and allowed the crowd to flow past him until he was just behind the group again. Then he moved to the other side of the horses to keep the animals between him and Tiberius. He hadn't noticed Ashling beside Tiberius.

The group moved along the smoky street to a fork in the road where the junction created an open space. Mr Black noticed Tiberius and a small group move forward following an older man to stop a few metres beyond a large bonfire blazing across one side of the street. The first of Diego's riders, pulled on his reins and his horse reared briefly on his hind legs. Then he rushed towards the wall of fire and he and his horse leapt through the flames, disappearing through to great cheers from the gathered crowd. There were two horses in front of Rayne and Mr Black moved to the rear and side of her horse. Another cheer as a second horse jumped through the flames. Two young women were holding the bridles of Rayne's horse and the one in front. As the horse in front was released and headed for the flames Mr Black pulled out the soft plastic bottle and, having previously satisfied himself that no one could see him due to the billowing smoke. He swiftly covered the body of the horse and the back of Rayne's coat with the clear, odourless fluid. It took seconds.

Mr Black turned and quickly walked away with the bottle back in his carrier bag.

He stopped and turned to watch briefly. He could barely see Rayne's horse as it surged towards the massive bonfire. He saw it leap towards the flames and then there was a loud noise. Whoomph! The horse and rider were engulfed in a massive fireball exploding out from the centre of the bonfire. He smiled and continued to walk in the opposite direction. He threw the bag into a smouldering bonfire as he passed. He jettisoned the gloves he had been wearing into another bonfire as he made his way back to his car, humming a cheerful ditty. He got in and drove straight to Avila. He decided he would check in on Dane and Beth's apartment to ensure they were there in a few hours' time. But first he would shower and have something to eat. It felt like order had been restored. Things were more balanced. It had been a productive day.

CHAPTER
FORTY NINE

Ashling and Tiberius looked up as the door to the Hospital waiting room opened. Diego was standing at the window and turned. A doctor came in wearing operating theatre scrubs. He looked grim. He squatted down in front of Tiberius and said softly " Lo siento mucho, señor Frost. Ella no sobrevivió. Sus pulmones estaban demasiado dañados y las quemaduras que sufrió fueron demasiado extensas y graves."

"Sorry? I don't speak Spanish." replied Ashling.

"She didn't survive. Her lungs were too damaged and the burns she suffered were too extensive and severe." Tiberius said in a low monotone. "She's dead."

The doctor stood and walked outside with Diego. Ashling could hear them speaking in soft voices outside the door.

Tiberius was staring at the floor, unmoving. Ashling was sitting beside him with her arm around his shoulders, saying nothing. Just being there. Supporting him. Her instincts told her that there would be a time to talk but now was not that time. Diego returned and Tiberius stirred to look up at him. Diego put his hand on Tiberius's shoulder and he and Ashling stood.

"I am so sorry Tiberius. I feel if I hadn't invited her to take part then this terrible accident would not have happened. It is my fault."

Tiberius said "No. Diego. It was not your fault. I just don't understand how it actually happened."

"Sorry?" Diego looked confused.

"Has it ever happened before? To anyone? In the history of the Luminarias?" Tiberius continued.

"No. No. It is a terrible thing and I would know about such a thing if it had happened before, Senor. In fact the Las Luminarias might not continue as a result of this. That is what my daughters have told me on the phone. There is a lot of talk in San Bartolome of stopping the festival right now."

"It was just a terrible, terrible accident," said Ashling, sounding very shaken and close to tears.

Tiberius persisted as though she had said nothing, "so how could it happen? I saw the extent of the flames around her. She exploded in a fireball. What could have caused it. You guys gave her all of the protection she would have needed, I know. She was wearing the exact same as the rest of the riders." He walked to the window staring out but seeing nothing, his mind reverting to familiar patterns in the face of this overwhelming, heart breaking tragedy. Ashling had a vague sense of what was happening and was unsure of what to do, however when Diego started forward about to speak and possibly disagree with Tiberius, she laid her hand on his arm and shook her head.

After a long moment, Tiberius turned back to them, his face set in a resolute grim manner. "Something doesn't add up. Why was she the only one this happened to? And what was it that caused the fireball?" He paused, "the explosion."

Ashling felt that if this analysis helped him to deal with the shocking death of his sister in such a bizarre manner then she wouldn't stop him.

"Go on," she prompted.

"How could such an explosion happen? I can only see a few possibilities. One, the bonfire was boobytrapped somehow. Two, there was some kind of gas leak in the vicinity of the bonfire or Three the horse was boobytrapped in some way."

"Senor, if you are suggesting," Diego sounded outraged.

"No Diego. I am not suggesting you or any of your people

had anything to do with it." Tiberius answered quickly. "I'm trying to understand how this happened and the more I think on it the more I feel that someone, some person caused this, somehow. I think that option one is unlikely. How could you set up some kind of incendiary device inside a bonfire that wouldn't detonate until a rider was at the precise point of no return. Very difficult to do and if it is the case I'm sure the police will locate some evidence of the device, assuming they have the area cordoned off."

"Yes, my daughter Inez says the street is cordoned off. No one allowed in or out."

"OK, so if they find a device well and good. If not then we have the possibility of a gas leak but surely that would have been a far greater and less localised explosion. Also it would more likely have taken the form of a jet of flame at least initially and we would have noticed it? We were looking right at the bonfire."

"And we did not. At least I didn't. Did you?" Ashling asked Diego.

"No. I saw nothing like that. Everything looked normal until she jumped."

"So that leaves us with option three and if you think it through it is the most likely scenario. I think what happened was that something was on the horse and possibly on Rayne which ignited when she entered the flames. Something highly volatile, highly flammable. The street was full of smoke and noise and people. There was a lot going on in a small enough space. It would have been easy for someone to douse her and the horse with a liquid."

"Hijo de puta!" Diego exclaimed. He sounded enraged. "You have opened my eyes, Senor. We need to find this sonofabitch."

Ashling looked horrified. She was pale. "Oh God." She said and rushed from the room. After a little while she returned looking even paler. "Sorry." She said.

"You feel better?" asked Diego solicitously.

"Yes thanks," she replied. Tiberius just looked at her, or rather through her as though she didn't exist.

Another knock on the door and two Spanish police officers entered. One in uniform and one wearing a suit with a badge hanging from his breast pocket.

"We are sorry to intrude, but we need to talk with you please." The plain clothes police officer said. "I am Detective Gonzales and this is my colleague Capitan Ruiz. I am to translate as my colleague does not speak English."

"We would like to speak with each of you in turn. We have a room set aside for this. Can you join us first Diego?" asked Gonzales, dropping his formal tone and showing he was acquainted with Diego.

"Si. Si." Diego went out with the two policemen.

Still unsure of what to say or do, Ashling sat, perched awkwardly on the uncomfortable plastic sofa while Tiberius quietly paced the room.

After a while, she ventured timidly, "I've never spoken to the police before. I'm not sure what to say." Tiberius stopped pacing as though suddenly remembering she was with him. It occurred to him for the first time how traumatised Ashling must be and possibly how she might be blaming herself as Diego had tried to do. So he moved over and sat beside her, gently taking her hand.

"Just tell 'em the truth. Answer their questions as best you can. Don't venture any opinions. Stick to the facts of what you know," he said softly. In answer she turned into him, throwing her arms around him and sobbed, her entire frame convulsing with grief.

A few moments later Detective Gonzales stuck his head around the door and was about to speak when he noticed Ashling crying in Tiberius's arms. Tiberius shook his head at him and Gonzales tactfully disappeared.

In a little while her sobs slowed and softened. Ashling pulled back slightly, and he reached and tenderly brushed her tear streaked face with the back of his index finger. She took a deep breath and seemed to physically pull herself together. "I'm so sorry Tiberius. I'm useless to you right now. I'm such a wuss."

"No. It's OK. You're here and I know you care. That matters." He comforted her. "The police want to speak to us. That Gonzales guy stuck his head in a few minutes ago. I'll see where he is."

Ashling stood up and said firmly "no. You stay. I'll find him and if it's my turn I'll speak with him and if not I'll be straight back for you. OK?"

"OK." Tiberius walked to the door with her. She went out and shortly after Diego re-entered.

"Do you feel up to talking with them?" He asked Tiberius carefully.

"Yes."

"OK. Good. I mentioned to them our conversation about the circumstances surrounding the accident and they seemed very interested. They asked me a lot of questions about the preparations for the Luminarias and I explained we did the exact same as we have done for the past thirty or forty years since I took over from my papa."

"OK"

"Then Gonzales - I know his mother and father quite well and he worked for me when he was a kid. He is extremely smart. – he says the only difference is the rider. So I get angry and say are you suggesting she did this herself? No one would do this to themselves, but he stops me and he says that the only part of this which is different is the identity of the rider."

"You're right." Tiberius interjected.

"Sorry?" Diego sounded perplexed.

"He is smart. Her identity is a key part of this."

Tiberius looked hard at Diego and said, "I think someone killed Rayne, and your horse," he added as an afterthought, remembering that Diego had lost a valuable piece of horseflesh in addition to the tragedy which had taken Rayne's life.

"Si, my best, but it is of no consequence compared to the tragedy we have all suffered." Diego replied politely.

The two men lapsed into silence, each preoccupied by their own thoughts.

Suddenly, Tiberius sat up and took out his mobile phone then dialled a number.

"Hello Dave? Dave Gant?" he asked when the phone was answered.

"Yes Tiberius. What's up?"

"Dave, I've some bad news." He paused, steeling himself. "Dave, Rayne's dead."

"What?"

Even Diego could hear Rayne's head of security. Then after a pause Dave asked, "how?"

"It was a bizarre incident. We met some folk who lent her a horse and she rode in the Las Luminarias festival in San Bartolome de Pinares earlier today. It's where…"

"I know about it. I got her itinerary and checked it out when she told me her plans. Go on." Said Dave, a slight tone of impatience entering his normally even tones.

Tiberius took a deep breath and said in a measured tone "when it came to her turn to jump her horse through the flames. There was an explosion, like an incendiary. She was burnt to death."

"Damn, I'm sorry."

"Thanks"

"No. No. Thank you for ringing me to let me know. Where are you now?"

"The hospital in Avila."

"We can be there in under two hours if you need us."

"No, we're good here."

"You reckon it was an accident?" Dave left the insinuation unsaid.

"Nope."

"No? I should have just ignored her. I should have trusted my instincts and come anyway!" Dave snarled.

"Dave, I reckon it was deliberate. It was a massive fireball which ignited the instant she jumped through the flames. One of the local cops said that the only thing which was a variation from the norm was the fact that Rayne was riding instead of a local. Everything else was as normal. I saw the precautions they took. She was treated the same as the other riders, one of whom was the stud owner's daughter. He's here with me right now."

"I think you should let me bring the team Tiberius. It won't cost. It's the least we can do. The guys are going to be gutted, even though she decided against our advice and didn't let us come. You never know we might be able to come up with something. Two of us are ex-military police."

"OK. Why not. Thanks. We're all staying in the…"

"The Parador in Avila. I know. We'll meet you there or at the hospital shortly. Bye." Dave ended the call abruptly before Tiberius could change his mind.

*   *   *

Dane and Beth had finally returned to the apartment in Avila. They had been about to leave the restaurant when people had flooded into the entrance and blocked them. After a while they discovered there had been some sort of accident with a horse and rider and the police had blocked off the street. It was another forty five minutes before the Padron of the restaurant agreed with the large policeman standing outside the entrance on the street that he could allow people to exit via the rear entrance onto the street behind.

The pair made their way to their car and tried to leave the town. However, they were soon caught in a traffic jam which seemed to just stay static for ages. Another hour passed before a police officer walked past them and headed towards the front of the traffic jam. They couldn't see what was going on but after about half an hour more the cars in front of them began to move slowly forward. When they got back to Avila it was dark and they were so tired that they opted for comfort food and grabbed some hamburgers in a place called Soul Food, which was reputed to have the best burgers in Avila and was on their way to the apartment.

When they got back to the apartment, Beth sent a text from her Spanish phone to Tiberius telling him that they were tired and would call to the hotel in the morning. An evening of Netflix and relaxing on the couch followed and the pair of them went to bed early. Beth was surprised Tiberius hadn't replied to her message but Dane said he had probably gotten delayed by whatever had happened, just like them.

*   *   *

Ashling woke as dawn peeped in through the large windows of their bedroom in the Parador in Avila. She turned to find that Tiberius's side of the bed was empty. There had been no lovemaking last night. She told Tiberius to turn on his side and she put her arm around him and snuggled in, the comforting warmth of her body against his back, and that was how they had fallen asleep. Or she had, at least. He had obviously gotten out of bed at some point.

She put on a dressing gown and went into the living area of the suite to find him sitting in a chair with his feet on another looking out at the sunrise. She moved around to see if he was awake or asleep and her heart broke to see his red rimmed eyes. He had clearly been crying.

"Sorry. I couldn't sleep and I didn't want to wake you, but every time I closed my eyes..." his voice, hoarsened with grief, trailed off.

"You kept seeing it? Me too." She murmured sympathetically.

"It's always just after the fireball. It's not her anymore just a dark shadow inside the flames. Burning. Screaming. I didn't even know which of them was screaming at that point, her

474

or the horse. I couldn't distinguish it. Both of them. Or maybe it was me? I keep seeing it over and over again when I close my eyes. And I couldn't do a thing. Nothing to help her. Nothing to save her. First Goddy, then Alexa and now Rayne. I'm bad news to women, Ashling. You should get away from me."

Ashling moved around and knelt on the ground behind him, resting her head on his shoulders and cradling him with his arms. "You're stuck with me, Mr Frost." She whispered in his ear. "I'm not going anywhere."

*   *   *

Sometime later Tiberius and Ashling were sitting in the dining room trying to eat some breakfast when Dave Gant came in. Tiberius invited him to join them. Ashling ordered him some food and more coffee for all of them. No one spoke much. Tiberius because he didn't want to, Ashling because she was trying to gauge Tiberius's mood and Gant because he was one of those rare creatures, comfortable to be silent in the company of others.

"Hi!" They heard a young female's voice at the far side of the room and Beth arrived in, followed by Dane.

The pair sat themselves at the table and Beth reached across to Ashling to shake hands saying. "Hi. I'm Beth. That's Dane?"

"I'm Ashling, Tiberius's friend and this is Dave."

"Hi," Beth smiled at Dave. "Why so glum guys?" she asked, quickly picking up on the mood of the table.

"Rayne's dead." Tiberius said quietly.

"What? Oh No!" Beth was dumbfounded. Dane just sat there. Eyes wide.

"She was killed yesterday in an incident at the festival in San Bartolome." Dave added.

"We wondered what had happened. We never got out of the restaurant we were in." Beth said to Tiberius. "After ages, they let us out the back door and we just came back to Avila.

Oh I'm so sorry Tiberius." She looked at him with sadness and eyes brimming with sudden tears.

"Thanks." Tiberius said then stood. "I'll be back in a moment," and left the table.

Ashling watched after him, deciding to let him go, to give him space.

Just outside the window a gardener was trimming one of the ornate hedge sculptures in the formal gardens. If you looked closely enough though, you would see the clippers never actually touched the foliage.

Mr Black was fascinated by the gathering inside the breakfast room. He was also annoyed with himself that he hadn't placed a bug on the window so he could hear the conversation. He recognised Dave Gant though. He had encountered Dave some years before when he was working for Sir Jocelyn. He also knew that Dave now worked as the boss of a small security outfit of British ex-military guys, based out of California, though he wasn't sure where. He was curious to know what Dave was doing here. He hadn't realised that Tiberius Frost had hooked up with his pair of targets. It was a complication he could have done without. He bent back to his task of not trimming hedges when he saw Tiberius re-enter the room.

"Sorry." Tiberius said. He looked at Ashling and asked "Did you tell them what happened?

"Yes." She answered.

"We were all interviewed by the police last night at the hospital." He said to Dane and Beth. "They are coming around to the idea that it was too extreme and unusual to be an accident. I reckon and they agree, well Detective Gonzales agrees that it looks like someone deliberately killed her."

There was silence around the table.

"That's terrible," said Dane softly.

"This has implications for all of us. Right here. Right now." Tiberius continued as though Dane hadn't spoken. "We don't know the reason why this happened. Whoever did it had to have a good reason to kill her. Right now the only one I can think of is the deal she was involved in with you two." He stared hard at Dane and Beth.

"Tiberius. God! We don't know what or who would have done this?" Beth said, in a defensive tone.

"You misunderstand me," he said evenly. "What I'm getting at here is that you're in danger. The common thread here is your deal. It's massive. Multi-million dollar right? So first Dane is kidnapped and now Rayne is killed. To me, this huge deal IS the common thread. Massive amounts of money is one of the most powerful motivators there is."

"OK. But why kill her. What would they gain?" Dane asked patiently.

"Scupper the deal?" Dave Gant suggested.

"A competitor? That's a distinct possibility," said Tiberius. "What else?" Then he thought for a second. "Who's your investor?"

Dane looked at Beth and she quickly said, "Deng Holman Lee."

"Seriously rich. Seriously ruthless." Said Dave quietly.

"Ruthless?" queried Beth in a worried voice.

"I encountered him in the past in L.A. and again in San Francisco. He'd shoot your mother if he thought it would help him in a deal." Dave said in a conversational tone of voice then added "and his own, come to think of it."

"He may already have done," Dane replied quietly.

"No! Dane! You don't mean that?" Beth expostulated.

"It's a possibility." He turned to Dave and said "My foster mum was killed when I was kidnapped a while back. So you see, you're not so far from the truth."

"Hang on. What could this Deng character have to gain from killing Dane's foster mother and Rayne? Especially if Rayne was the person who was delivering the deal he wanted to him." Ashling interjected. "It doesn't make sense."

"True." Tiberius said thoughtfully. A waiter approached the table and said "Senor Frost? There is a telephone call for you?"

Tiberius looked up and the waiter said, "at Reception, Senor. Gracias" Tiberius stood and walked out.

Shortly afterwards he returned and sat. "That was Doyle. I rang him last night from the hospital. They don't have anything new at their end, but I was able to run everything past him and he's going to discuss it with the team and some of his contacts and get back to me."

Mr Black had had enough of watching the group. There was nothing to be gained from remaining there any longer. He dropped his shears under the bush and walked away removing his gloves and putting them in his pocket, unaware that Tiberius had looked out at him walking across the gardens to the exit.

After the breakfast, Tiberius and Ashling left the others to get some air and aimlessly wandered around the garden talking quietly. As they did Ashling banged her foot against the handle of a pair of shears on the ground under a bush. Tiberius looked down at it and turning around, he realised he had a perfect view of the other three still sitting at the table, eating. He figured he was being a little paranoid, as a result of everything which had happened but he still filed away the thought. The feeling.

*   *   *

Mr Black was back in his apartment, on the balcony on the IP phone to his employer.

"The female target you requested me to monitor – she died in an accident yesterday," he informed his employer.

"Did you do it?"

"No."

"How did she die?"

"She was taking part in a local festival involving jumping horses through bonfires. She got burnt."

"I know it. Las Luminarias."

"Yes."

"That is inconvenient."

"What are your instructions?"

"If we are unable to secure signatures on the deal, then I want you to extract both targets. I will send some staff to relocate them to a suitable location where we will question them ourselves."

Mr Black was annoyed at this development as he had been hoping to get back to having some fun with the young man Wilson. However, money talked and that was what mattered right now. "I'll make preparations," he said.

"Good. I'll inform you if we decide to follow this course of action."

"Very well." Mr Black waited for the other party to end the call as usual, but he didn't. So Mr Black asked, "was there anything else you require?"

"Not at this point." Normally his employer ended each call abruptly, however on this occasion he did not. He just went silent. Mr Black wondered if his employer was waiting for him to end the call or was there something else. He pressed the end button.

Mr Black looked at the phone, puzzled and wondered why the delay? He was fairly certain this particular type of phone was pretty untraceable. The only IP information either party had was the country location. Still, he had survived this long by never assuming anything. No technology was fully secure, un-hackable. He put the phone into a bag and resolved to get rid of it later that day.

In Dublin, Deng looked at Kent on his monitor. "Well?" he asked.

"Give me a minute." Kent didn't look up from his own screen.

A minute passed and then another. Kent sighed and leaned back in his chair; his fingers interlaced behind his head. "No go. Sorry."

"That is disappointing." Deng said in a chilly voice.

"You needed to keep him on for longer. I told you I needed at least another forty seconds to a minute. Just sitting there saying nothing might a spooked him."

"That is valid."

"So just try to get him to stay on for longer next time." Said Kent. "Oh and hope he doesn't change his phone."

"Why?"

"If he does I have to start all over again and this ain't simple stuff. It's supposed to be un-hackable."

"Very well." Deng ended the video call.

*   *   *

Mr Black was strolling along an old Romanesque stone bridge across the Rio Adaja river, just outside the imposing Avila city walls. There had been an unusually heavy rainfall in the mountains south of the city which had prompted grumblings about climate change amongst the Avila worthies. The swollen river swirled and gurgled around the old stone pillars of the bridge. He stopped halfway across and threw his dismantled, cleaned IP phone into the water and then continued across to a café with a balcony overlooking the river and the city walls where he sat with a coffee and contemplated his next move.

He had definitely balanced the scales somewhat, however, he hadn't realised the value Rayne Frost had to his employer. Having said that his employer hadn't fully explained her value to him during any of his briefings. He had only described her as a possible ally and possible target. Still, on the bright side, it narrowed down the potential tasks he might be required to perform. Now, it was just a case of will they or won't they? And if they won't then he would have to perform a simple snatch and grab. Bit more difficult with two but not impossible. However, he needed to know what Gant's role was in all of this. It would certainly complicate matters having a full security team in place around his targets.

And then there was Frost. The man had a talent for making his life difficult. It was entirely possible he had brought in the Security team. Although his employer had informed him that Rayne Frost had a security team on her payroll when he had briefed him about her. Why would they hang around now that she was dead? He knew enough to know they would normally just move on to their next assignment. And his research had indicated she was not particularly well liked. So why stay around? Unless her brother had requested it.

Frost again. He needed to do more than balance the scales really. A more permanent solution was required, preferably prior to the requirement for him to secure the targets for his employer. Once that was achieved he would give further consideration about how he felt about securing both targets or just the man, Wilson. He was still confused as to why he was loth to do anything to damage her. It was weird. Like he had some odd flu bug or something.

In the meantime he would figure out how to deal with Tiberius Frost.

CHAPTER FIFTY

"Beth, Mofo, I've been thinking."

Beth had been leaning over the castellated city walls at Avila looking at the river flowing past. Now she swivelled and leant back with eyes fixed on her best friend.

"Thing is. I've been thinking about everything. I mean. If we hadn't come up with this software, would any of this happened? Would I have been kidnapped? Would any of these people died?" Anguish poured out of Dane.

"Dane." Beth replied firmly. "This is not your fault. Don't take that on yourself as well. You've enough to deal with right now."

"I know. I know. But this needs to stop? I mean, how much is it worth if we made all that money and someone else dies? I can't help thinking, I just wouldn't cope if it was you."

Beth was silent. She had been devastated when they found out about Rayne and was very upset for Tiberius. She could see how deeply he was affected by the terrible tragedy. She hadn't considered how it might affect Dane. She looked at Dane and encouraged him to continue. "Go on," she said.

"Well. The thing is. I wondered what would happen if I got rid of it?"

"The Software? The tech?"

"Yes. I have a failsafe routine built into it and if I initiated it everything will be destroyed."

"Oh. Wow!" Beth sounded stunned, then asked "but hang on, isn't it all in your head? I mean if it's gone can't you still reconstruct it?" She paused and shuddered, adding "or God forbid, be forced to reconstruct it?"

"No. That's the point. I used several different mathematical algorithms to create the core of the software. Not all of them are mine. Three were specially created by Professor Savage in MIT in the US. He guaranteed me they were one-offs, no copies. He owed me big time and he died last year of a brain haemorrhage. So, as we have the only copy, they're irretrievable once our tech is gone. I got a pile of information and six or seven algorithms from a girl in Shannon, who worked in Shannon Airport and used a bunch of servers she had access to in the building. So…?"

"You're not going to tell me those servers were damaged in the Terrorist attack? Seriously?

"A partition wall separated them by about six inches from the site of one of the explosions. They were literally obliterated. And guess what? She didn't keep copies elsewhere. She had massive amounts of storage on the servers so she felt she didn't need to, and like they were in the middle of an airport that's not exactly a major aviation hub." Dane sighed then added. "It gets worse."

"Jesus! I never realised our tech was so fragile! Anyway go on!" Beth sounded exasperated.

"She was caught in the attack, got shot in the arm. Not fatal or anything but I rang her Mum cos I was worried about her and her Mum said she has had a complete mental breakdown. Severe post-traumatic stress disorder. Doctors say she'll never work as a programmer again. Be lucky not to end up on a lifetime diet of Valium or whatever.

So, when I say if I erase everything. Well. It's gone." Dane looked at her anxiously. "Don't hate me?"

"God! Dane don't be stupid. I'm just thinking about it. I mean we need to discuss this. It's a huge decision. And I don't mean about the money. Like that would be amazing but I'm on the same track as you - just no longer sure it's worth it." She slipped her arm through his and pulled him to walk with her along the top of the battlements.

*   *   *

Several hours later Dane and Beth called back to the Parador to meet Tiberius and Ashling for dinner. Dave Gant had requested they eat in the hotel dining room so they did. Dave declined to join them.

It was a subdued meal despite Ashling and Beth's best efforts. When they finished, they had some coffee in a corner of one of the lounges.

Finally Beth announced, "we've got something to tell you." Tiberius and Ashling looked at her, waiting.

"Dane and I have decided to get rid of the software."

Ashling let out a low whistle and sat back into the sofa. "Wow!" she said.

"I know it seems extreme," Beth rushed on and put her hand up to forestall Tiberius's reaction. "Just hear us out?"

Tiberius smiled briefly, saying nothing.

"We decided if it's gone and we are pretty sure the process we'll use means that it can't be resurrected or replicated and before you ask , it's not possible for Dane to do it either so there's no benefit to anyone in trying to force him to." She paused and looked around. Dane nodded at her, encouraging her. "We'll communicate with the buyers and explain everything and we'll announce it on Social Media explaining that we felt it was too dangerous and that we had ethical issues with its potential misuse. We will explain fully why it simply cannot be resurrected also." Beth took a deep breath and finished with "That's it. That's everything. What do you think?"

"You're walking away from possibly hundreds of millions of dollars," said Tiberius in his quiet way.

"We know, but we won't be able to forgive ourselves if anyone else dies because of this bloody software." Dane said a little aggressively.

"No." Tiberius replied thoughtfully. "I get it. It's very admirable. But will it work?"

"Why not?" Dane said.

"Well. What if people don't believe you?"

"We'll make it crystal clear. And we'll video Dane deleting it on his screen."

"I think we should let Dave know you're about to do this."

"Why Dave?" asked Beth

"He deserves to know. He and his guys are protecting us. They're not charging a dime and they ain't cheap. Also he may have some suggestions," Tiberius replied.

"Fair enough." Dane said before Beth could argue the point any further.

Tiberius texted Dave who arrived a few minutes later. Tiberius asked him to join them and explained what Dane and Beth were proposing.

Dave said, "I think you're nuts!"

"Why?" Beth sounded hurt.

"No one will believe you. No one will believe that anyone would walk away from this kind of money. You've got to remember I was with Rayne throughout her negotiations on your behalf. I know how much is at stake here and believe me there is no one in the world will accept that you guys would do what you're proposing here." He scratched his closely shaven head and added in a sarcastic tone, "I'm not sure I do either. Are you hoping it will protect you in some way? I think you're being a bit naïve, to be honest. Having the ability to spend millions on your personal security would be a better protection than hoping all the nasty people will believe you have destroyed the software and then leave you alone."

There's an ethical issue also." Dane added defensively. "We are concerned about people misusing the software. Everything that's happened has made us think through the ramifications of the effect this software could have globally. Before we were just focussed on the concept and could we built it? Now that we have successfully done that, we need to think about whether or not it's too dangerous to simply let someone with lots of money buy it and use it in whatever way suits them. Including governments."

"OK well that's a more credible and valid rationale then the concept of you two as the tech version of Saint Greta bloody Thunberg!" Dave replied, "but assuming that the world will leave you alone is a bit unrealistic. No matter what you do next, people will still assume it can be recreated."

"Which means disappearing as well as deleting the software." Tiberius interjected. "And this time, you need to do a better job. New ID's, relocation, new life really."

"Oh," Beth was getting more upset.

"It's really me though isn't it." Dane said quietly. Beth turned to stare at him.

"Yep. She can't make it work without you but at this point you could probably make it work without her, which is what people will assume." Tiberius replied. "So explaining how the deletion process works on a video and videoing you doing it will be useful but not totally persuasive."

"I'll open my servers for public scrutiny?" Dane suggested.

"Nah, you could have stuck it on a flash drive first. It could all be for show." Dave replied caustically.

"We've already done it." Beth said quickly.

"Wow." Tiberius sat back.

"We've videoed it and Dane has written an accompanying explanation of what happens and why it's not recoverable. Anyone who understands cyber security will get what he's saying."

"Doesn't matter. People won't believe it." Dave argued.

"We've sent the video and information to Mr Holman Lee's lawyers." Dane said.

"We've explained that after Rayne's death we can't risk anyone else getting hurt in any way." Beth added. "We hope he'll understand. But at least he won't have paid us any money and nothing has been signed so he won't be out of pocket."

"Just out of sorts," Dave grinned.

"Sorry?" Dane queried.

"He's gonna be very pissed off." Tiberius answered. "He just lost out on an incredible deal where he had the inside track, exclusivity and it would have made his wealth explode, plus he would have become one of the most influential and powerful men on the planet. I'd say that's a bit of an under-statement."

"I don't care. It was the right thing to do." Dane sounded obstinate and looked at Beth, who nodded. "We know it was the right thing to do," she backed him.

"Fortunately for you, you've got Tiberius and Dave here to advise you on your next steps." Ashling, who had been sit-ting silently observing, stated. "And you're going to need all the advice and help you can get."

"We need to work out a plan." Dave said, looking over at Tiberius.

"Yep." Tiberius replied. "Guys, I'm gonna head to the bar with Dave for a drink. When we've worked out something we'll talk to you. Don't know how long it's gonna take though." He grimaced.

"We'll head back to the apartment and…" Beth began but Dave interrupted with "And pack. You could be leaving in a hurry." He stood and walked out with Tiberius.

"Is there anything I can do to help you?" Ashling asked the two students, kindly.

"No thanks. We appreciate the offer though," Dane smiled.

"We'd better get back and get organised," Beth said stand-ing.

They left and after a few minutes Ashling headed upstairs to the bedroom for a lie down. She was exhausted.

*   *   *

Mr Black finally moved. He was dressed as a waiter and had been standing inside a glass door which led to the now darkened restaurant. Softly he detached a tiny clear plastic sucker from the pane of glass and popped it into his pocket. It amplified the sounds on the other side of the glass and clarified them, then played them in his earphone. It had worked perfectly. Finally he was ahead of the game and had the necessary information he needed.

Based on what he had just heard, he could expect his employer to ring soon with fresh instructions, so he needed to be out of the Parador and somewhere convenient to take the call. He picked up the tray of dirty crockery which he had placed beside his hiding space and carried it across the dining room and into the kitchen area beyond. He laid it down near the sink area and checked his watch. If he hurried he would be able to leave by the staff entrance with the rest of the kitchen staff. He moved quickly and managed to catch a group of young Spaniards just about to walk out the rear entrance of the building onto the street. One of Gant's men was standing across the road watching them leave so he kept the group between him and the security guard. At the end of the street he moved with the group as they walked through the ancient alleyways winding their way around the medieval heart of Avila. After about five minutes he ducked into a darkened street and began moving faster.

He climbed a stone stair onto the city walls and moved to a corner above a buttress tower. He dropped down and sat quietly waiting. After an hour or so his IP phone buzzed.

"Yes?" he answered it.

"I no longer require you to extricate the targets."

"Oh?" he said trying to inject a note of surprise into his voice, forgetting for once that it would have any emotion stripped from it when replayed at the other end.

"You will leave Avila. The contract is ended."

"You have already paid me for a service." He had decided to raise the issue of the money in this manner. There was a pause while his employer was considering his comments.

"Why did you change your phone?" came back the question.

He thought quickly and answered "I do it regularly. It is more secure that way."

"I see." More silence, then, " I expect you are unwilling to return the money I have paid you."

"You paid me for a service and you have decided for your own good reasons not to have me perform it. It was your decision, not mine. If it were as a result of my decision I would return the funds in full."

"Go on."

"I would be happy to work for you in the future, so as a token of good will, I am willing to return fifty per cent of the fee. Is this acceptable?"

"Unexpected and acceptable."

"Good. I take it you will contact me again should you require my services?"

"Yes. Goodbye."

The phone went dead. Mr Black remained sitting on the ground, his back against the sun warmed stone of the battlements, thinking. He could simply leave now and that would be that. However, his decision about Tiberius Frost required implementing before he left.

So how to kill him? How indeed?

*　　　　*　　　　*

The phone beside the bed rang and Tiberius reached over and grabbed it. "Yes?" he answered.

"Senor Frost, so sorry to disturb you but we have a call from the United States for you? Will you take it?" came the receptionists voice. He glanced at the time on the clock beside the bed. It was six am and he'd only gotten to bed at three am having spent a long time with Dave chatting and working out different scenarios until they just gave up from tiredness.

"OK, put them through" he said sleepily.

"Hi, am I speaking to a Mr Tiberius Frost?" said a man with a nasal East Coast accent.

"Yes."

"Sorry to get you so early Mr Frost. My name is Neil Oppenheimer? I work for Mr Holman Lee. Are you aware of Mr Holman Lee's recent negotiations with your late sister?"

"Yes. I am."

"Mr Holman Lee's right hand person ah, Ms Foster has flown to Spain to meet with all of the parties involved in the transaction. However, in light of your sister's unfortunate demise, my deepest sympathies by the way, in addition to the unfortunate decision just announced by the creators of the software Mr Holman Lee had agreed to acquire, we have had to re-organise just a tad."

This guy had already annoyed Tiberius by waking him early for what didn't seem like an urgent call, but the callous, uncaring expression of sympathy had gotten under his skin. "Gee. I'm sorry if y'all have been inconvenienced by what's happened here in Spain," he replied through gritted teeth.

"No. no. It's fine," the annoying WASP type lawyer carried on blithely. "So anyway, Ms Foster would like to meet with Mr Wilson and she is mindful of what has happened to Mr Wilson in the past so she felt you might like to suggest where and when and also perhaps to accompany him or whatever measures you wanted to take?"

"I see."

"Yeah. She's a tremendously nice person. Very thoughtful," Oppenheimer oozed faux sincerity into the phone. Tiberius thought fast.

"There's a café on Bajada la Losa, just off the main bridge running west from the old city walls. It's called Gloria Bendita. We'll meet her there, on the roof terrace at three pm Ok?"

"No problem. She should have reached Avila by then. Thank you for taking the call."

"OK. Goodbye." Tiberius ended the call abruptly and a little rudely but the man had bugged him. He would discuss it with Dave and Dane later on. They didn't have to show up but it might help to draw a line under this whole mess which would help Beth and Dane to move on and they could always stand her up and not appear, if they felt anything was off.

*   *   *

Mr Black put down the phone. He was delighted. It couldn't have gone better. His talent for languages and accents had served him well. He had already visited the cafe and knew it well. As a result he knew precisely what to do. He wouldn't even have to meet them. *Happy Days!*

*   *   *

"Explain to me again why you are meeting her? Especially when we just spent hours packing?" Beth was annoyed. She was put out not to have been invited along and also worried for Dane and Tiberius.

"Look it's an opportunity to put all this behind us." Dane answered wearily. "If I can convince her the software is gone and there is no way of getting it back, then she might put the word out on our behalf."

"I still don't like it." Beth insisted obstinately.

"Dave and his guys will be there." Tiberius said.

"We will, but I think it's a bad move too. This pair should be busy putting miles between them and Avila like we planned last night." Said Dave.

Tiberius said "well, all I'm doing here is replaying the conversation for you guys and letting you decide what to do. I'm not going to comment one way or the other on how smart it is or not." He sat back and then added. "For what it's worth. I didn't like the guy, but that was just a personal thing, I guess."

"My team will head over there immediately and scope it out, if you decide to go." Dave stood. "Just let me know, OK?"

"Well I vote yes." Dane said raising his hand.

"I'm abstaining on this one." Tiberius said to Dane's mild annoyance.

"I do not expect to have a vote, so I'll stay quiet." Ashling added smiling.

"Oh God! I know I'm going to regret this, but on the basis that it just might help us set things up better going forward, I suppose we could delay leaving for a few hours until you see what she has to say Dane?" Grumbled Beth

"OK. Decision made." Dane answered.

*   *   *

Back in Dublin Deng stared at an email on his screen. "So you don't know who sent this?" He asked Kent.

"Nope. It's UK originated but beyond that nothing. It could have been rerouted several times before there."

"It appears our primary operative in Avila is playing a double game."

"If you believe this email."

"Nevertheless, activate Riga."

"OK."

CHAPTER FIFTY ONE

A few hours later with his wristwatch showing two forty five pm Tiberius sat next to Dane with a coffee and a Coke on the table in front of them on the open terrace of the little café overlooking the river. They had sat at a table in a corner which Dave had selected for the meeting. Dave himself was sitting nearby at a table wearing sunglasses with an untouched glass of sparkling water in front of him. Tiberius could see the slight movement of Dave's head as he scanned the area. Dave had requested they change the location as he felt it was too open and exposed but Dane had insisted on continuing as it would be too late to contact Holman Lee's representative.

Time crawled. Everyone was on edge.

*　　　　　*　　　　　*

Mr Black couldn't see them properly. The table was too far back and Gant was sitting smack in the middle of his line of sight. He would have to wait. Hopefully when they realised no one was coming they would stand up and move into his sightlines. *Patience is a virtue,* he sighed to himself. *It will be a trophy shot though. Over one hundred and fifty metres, between the trees on either side of the river and across the river. Pity no one will know. Well. Except for Mr Annoying Frost!* He smiled happily. *It'll be the last thought going through his mind, closely pursued by my bullet.*

*　　　　　*　　　　　*

It was now three thirty and Dane was getting anxious. He

rang Beth to check she was still with Ashling and was OK. Tiberius was sitting calmly to his left sipping on a coffee. "It's three thirty," Dane went, "I don't suppose she's coming? Or perhaps she's been delayed?"

"If she'd been delayed she would have contacted us or Oppenheimer would have." Tiberius replied

"So what's going on?"

"That's what I've been considering. I reckon she was never coming, so the call I got was to get us here. And either someone will try something here or they wanted to get us away from the girls." Tiberius spoke loud enough for Dave to hear and as no one else was sitting on the terrace, he couldn't be overheard. Dave imperceptibly nodded his head and spoke softly into his earpiece.

Eventually he sat up and turned towards Tiberius. "The other half of the team are with the girls and they are secure. I suspect your first instinct is the right one. Someone has lured you and Dane here."

"Me and Tiberius or just me?" Dane asked.

"Dunno, but I reckon it involves Tiberius and possibly Beth." Dave replied.

"Bloody hell! We need to get back to Beth!" Dane stood up.

"Get down for God's sake!" Dave hissed, moving from his seat. At the same time Tiberius stood up and moved towards Dane, who turned angrily to face him. Dane's head exploded. Dave dived sideways, cannoning into Tiberius and tackling him to the ground below the parapet. Dane's body toppled slowly sideways and for a horrible moment Tiberius was lying on his side looking at Dane's ruined face. Dave rolled off Tiberius and began crawling into the interior of the building while speaking rapidly into his earpiece. "Client down! Check for sniper. Possibly on city wall. Report!" He looked back at Tiberius who was still lying on the ground and ordered him to follow, which after a moment, Tiberius did. Once they were inside. Dave asked "Are you OK? I reckon it was just one shot, but?"

"I'm fine. Where's the shooter?" Tiberius asked. Dave scanned the wall facing the Terrace and finally said "OK there's the bullet hole in the wall so based on the angle and Dane's height I reckon the shooter is on the battlements across the river." Tiberius realised Dave was still communicating with his team and not with him.

*　　　*　　　*

That stupid boy got in the way at the last minute, Mr Black thought angrily as he rapidly broke down his rifle, popped it into the carry bag and then slung it over his shoulder. He sprinted across the small tower he was on and down the stairway to the walkway on top of the ramparts. Turned and began walking swiftly. He glanced to his left and saw a dark SUV racing across the bridge towards him, which prompted him to move faster, almost jogging. He would slow down once he had gained a little distance.

*　　　*　　　*

Tiberius followed Dave downstairs and into an SUV, which the driver drove across the bridge at high speed. They jumped out at the entrance stair leading to the walls, which Dave and two of his team took two at a time with Tiberius following. By the time he caught them on the wall top they had fanned out and were moving steadily along the walls. Tiberius noticed a door to their left was ajar. It seemed to lead to a higher floor in the buttress they were approaching. Dave tried the door and it opened easily. He slipped inside and the rest of them followed. Tiberius was about to enter when he noticed a tall man about two or three hundred yards further along the battlement, walking away from them. The man had some kind of long bag slung over his shoulder, like for carrying fishing rods, "or guns," Tiberius thought. He began to walk briskly and then to run, his long legs beginning to eat up the distance between them.

When he was about a hundred metres from the man, he turned and looked back. He locked eyes with Tiberius, turned away and began to sprint rapidly. They passed one tower and then a second. Suddenly the man darted to his right and disappeared. When Tiberius arrived at the place he had disappeared, he could see a stone stair leading down to the street level. He was about to race downwards when his arm was caught from behind. He whirled and saw Dave and his two guys, one of whom had grabbed him. "He's gone that way! C'mon."

"Hang on. Let the boys go first. They've experience of this." Dave motioned to his two men who began to move down the stairs.

"We found a cartridge back at the tower." Dave said as they waited to follow. "We must have arrived faster than the bastard expected."

"Show me." Tiberius said. Dave held it out in a clear plastic Ziploc bag.

"High Calibre round." Tiberius studied it briefly. "A sniper's bullet."

"Yeah." Dave replied. "Let's go," and he moved swiftly down the stairs with Tiberius close on his heels. Dave's men hadn't waited and they could see them moving fast along the street ahead.

"They see him." Dave told Tiberius. "He's stopped sprinting. Just moving at a fast pace. We'll track him and see where he goes."

The man walked fast through the maze of streets. He stopped once on a busy thoroughfare in front of a shop, but Dave and his team were careful and kept well back, out of sight from the man looking at the reflection in the window. He moved on again quickly, turning into one alley first and then another. Often one or both of Dave's men would silently sprint off along a parallel street and wait at the next junction.

"They like bloodhounds," Tiberius marvelled to Dave at

one point.

"We're lucky. These two are brilliant at tracking in an urban environment. It was just dumb luck I picked them to accompany us. Not a skillset I thought we'd need on this job," Dave remarked in a matter of fact tone.

They turned a corner and came onto a wide road.

"He went into that building," Dave pointed at an apartment building opposite. "Rear and side. I've got the front," he barked into his earpiece. One of the team disappeared around one side of the building and the other around the other side.

"Number three where are you with the vehicle?" Dave said. He turned to Tiberius and pointed. The SUV was heading towards them. It stopped and they got in. A second SUV arrived which prompted Tiberius to ask. "who's watching Beth and Ashling?"

"I've three guys on them. I wanted a second vehicle here for us." Dave said absently as he watched the building. Without taking his eyes off the target he handed Tiberius a handkerchief. Tiberius looked at his reflection in the driver's and was shocked to discover his face spotted with blood. His pale grey jacket also bore the evidence of Dane's death. He took it off and cleaned his face, while they waited. Then began scanning up and down the road, just in case the man reappeared. After a few short minutes, the driver of their SUV said "Boss? See the grey car? Coming out from the building next door. What do you reckon?"

Tiberius glanced at the car and then looked up at the building. Right up at the top. He thought he could see something connecting the roof of the apartment building to the one across the alley, from which the car their driver had noticed, was emerging.

"Dave. Is that a ladder running from one roof to the other?" he asked pointing over Dave's shoulder.

Dave glanced up, "yeah. Smart bastard," he commented as he watched the car waiting while the gates slowly moved apart and the driver drove the final few feet to the edge of the street. It turned right and slipped into the traffic.

Dave glanced at Tiberius, then said to the driver. "We'll take the chance. Follow him." Then he spoke into his earpiece telling the rest of the team to wait and watch the building for a further ten or fifteen minutes and if nothing happened to follow them.

Their driver was good. He stayed well back, allowing lots of cars between them and their quarry.

As they moved through the traffic. Dave put a call into the Spanish police. He explained who he was and what had happened. He told whoever he was speaking to that they were in pursuit of a man who had fled the scene and now looked to be heading out of Avila in a grey Seat Leon car.

Tiberius wasn't listening. He didn't care about the Spanish police. He was just staring intently through the windscreen at the car they were pursuing.

Dave ended the call and said "Thank God. We caught a break. The guy in charge of the investigation trained in London on a counter terrorism course I gave. He remembered me. He's agreed to allow us to continue pursuit until he can bring some unmarked vehicles into play. Max here, will give him updates on our position, so they can move into position and take over from us. They are going to set up roadblocks one we've clarified the direction he's taking."

"If he continues on this road Boss, he will either end up on the N502 or the N110" said the driver.

"Where will they take him?"

"the N110 heads west through the Gredos mountains and across the border into Portugal, which ain't far. The N502 goes south and joins the A5 motorway which goes to Toledo and Madrid."

"Thanks Max." Dave replied.

The car headed out of the city and after about ten minutes turned onto the N110. At the same time Dave's phone rang and he told their driver to slow down and pull to the right.

As he did so a shiny new charcoal coloured Seat Tarraco moved smoothly past them taking their place. Dave gestured and Max pulled back behind the sleek looking SUV.

"They took the engines out of those and put 'em on steroids," said Max. "That thing has a monster under the hood."

"I don't care as long as they don't spook him." Dave remarked.

Now they were finally sitting still in the vehicle speeding along in pursuit, Tiberius had time to think and the full horror of Dane's death hit him. He looked down. He still had Dave's bloody handkerchief in his hand. He just dropped it on the floor. He felt nauseous and weak. He had seen death before, but this was different. It was truly horrible and so sudden. They were passing through a small town called El Barco de Avila when suddenly the thought struck him. *Did Beth know?*

"Do Beth and Ashling know about Dane?" he asked Dave.

"I'll check," he answered and began speaking into his earpiece. After a few moments Dave said, "no."

"I'd better ring them. It may be better coming from me."

"Probably."

Tiberius dug out his phone and dialled Ashling's number.

"Hi. It's me. Are you OK?" He asked when she picked up.

"We're fine. What has happened? The Parador is swarming with Spanish police? Three of Dave's guys are with us also."

"Is Beth with you?"

"Yes. We're both safe. Tiberius. What happened?"

"It's bad news and I need to tell Beth myself, OK?" He took a deep breath. "Dane was shot. He's dead."

"Oh God! Are you sure?"

"Unfortunately. Can you give the phone to Beth?"

"Sure," Ashling went silent and there were some muffled noises as she handed the phone over to Beth, who immediately asked in a frantic tone, "what's wrong? Tiberius?"

"Beth, I'm sorry. Dane got shot and he died at the scene. We're in pursuit of the guy who shot him."

"Oh No! No!" She screamed. He heard a bang and sobbing, then he heard Ashling say. "Tiberius, I need to deal with Beth. Let's talk later. Please! Please be careful!"

"I will. Look after her," he said grimly. As he ended the call they left the town and went over a bridge then took a sharp left and continued along the N-110 motorway. After some minutes, another unmarked police vehicle swept past them and took over the point position in pursuit of their quarry. The SUV which had been in front slowed, edging slightly to the right of the lane in an invitation to overtake him, which Max did.

"Jesus. These guys are being too obvious," Dave said in an annoyed tone. "He's gonna spot the pursuit."

Mr Black had indeed worked out he was being followed, but much earlier than Dave thought. As always he had more than one escape route and realised that the one he had intended to pursue was not going to work out. *Time to change to plan B.* he decided.

Suddenly the car they were following swerved off the main road and onto a side road, signposted Umbrias - seven kilometres. It accelerated away from them along the narrow road.

"He's made us! Damn these guys. Too eager. No patience," Dave was really pissed off. Max swerved off the main road just behind the lead Spanish police car. They were gaining a little when the road turned sharply left and the car they were following pulled away again. They raced down another long straight section of road when the driver turned left onto an even narrower road. They tore through a sleepy little village, twisting and turning through the, thankfully empty, streets.

"This guy is good Boss. Trained," whistled Max admiringly. "He pulls away every time there's any bends. Damn good!"

"Just give the Spanish wheel jockey in front plenty of room, Max. We don't want to rear end him or hit him if he loses control."

"Yeah." Max said absently as he concentrated on following the vehicle in front as it hurtled out of the town. After a straight stretch where they gained on the fugitive vehicle, the road curved and they shot past an elderly couple walking a pram, mouths open in shock at the speeding vehicles so close to them.

They raced through another hamlet and Tiberius was conscious they had begun to climb, the road becoming more twisty and the bends more acute. Looking ahead, he could see the mountaintops obscured in clouds, which seemed to be rolling towards them. As they headed further into the hills the road turned into a nightmare. The corners were often one hundred and eighty degrees. At times they could see the Seat they were pursuing above them heading in the opposite direction and the road surface was increasingly poor and bumpy. Then the Seat whipped off the tarmacadam road and onto a dirt track. They turned swiftly and fishtailed as Max fought for control on the gritty surface. The track rose steeply now and they were thrown about with every bump and rut they cannoned over.

Mr Black breasted a rise and noticed two people in the distance ahead. They were standing just off the road to the side. He opened the window and shouted at them as he approached, "¡Atención! ¡Baja por la montaña ahora! ¡El bosque está en llamas! ¡Baja por la montaña!

All the young couple saw was a man in uniform yelling at them to get down the mountain because the forest was on fire. After he sped past, they turned to look and all they could see was massive clouds shrouding the mountain range behind them. So they turned and began to walk briskly along the road.

Suddenly the police car in front swerved hard right to avoid the young couple in the middle of the road. There was a massive bang as the police vehicle hit a large boulder beside the road. Max pulled the car hard left, then right just missing the couple. Tiberius glanced through the back window to see

the couple heading for the police car. The second car coming over the rise fortunately missed them. In the meantime
Max gunned the engine, trying to catch the Seat they were
pursuing.

Mr Black drove into the mist. *It's silver lining time!* He
thought as he drove along, glancing in his rear view mirror,
pleased that he could see nothing behind him. *And if I can't
see them…?*

His painstaking research was proving its worth as he knew
the road ended soon and there was a track to the right leading to a mountain hut called a Refugio and a large lake,
Laguna del Barco. More importantly he also knew there was
a steep drop coming up on the left hand side just before the
turn off. As he approached he slowed just a little and opened
the driver's window. He threw out a rucksack and unlocked
the door. Wrenching the steering wheel to the left, he dived
out. He rolled and tumbled as he hit the rutted track at
speed.

He could hear the car banging and clattering as it fell down
the precipice and then a loud noise and a whoomph as it
impacted on the bottom and exploded into flame. Getting
up gingerly, he felt pain and a wetness at his shoulder. The
recently healed bullet wound had re-opened and was bleeding. It felt like something was wrong inside too. Somewhere
in the muscle. He ran to where the rucksack had fallen and
threw it on his back, grimacing as the straps dug into the
bleeding wound. He turned and was about to head off when
he noticed a goat standing at the head of the trail to the lake.
He took out a handgun from his pocket and shot it in the
head. The goat dropped like a stone. He dragged it into the
middle of the track, in the hope his pursuers would think
he had swerved to avoid it and waste valuable time locating
the car at the bottom of the ravine.

He jogged past the turn off, heading left along a barely rec-
ognisable trail and into the thickening mist. He had a fifteen
mile hike ahead over the Corral del Diablo mountain to get

to the tiny hamlet of Guijo de Santa Bárbara where he had a motorbike stashed. From there it was an hour and fifteen minutes to the Portuguese border and a different police jurisdiction which should mean some bureaucratic delay with the handover of his pursuit, allowing him to continue the further three hours and forty five minutes to Porto Airport. However, moving along the track another thought struck him and he pondered it as he jogged along.

Max had slowed and put on his beams. It didn't make much difference. The mist was thickening. Suddenly he braked hard and the car ground to a halt. He put on the hazards.

"Body in the road." Dave said, taking a gun out of his pocket as he got out. Tiberius followed him around to the front of the car. They could hear the other car roar up and Max sounded the horn. One short. One long. Repeating it over and over. The other driver slowed and stopped. Tiberius and Dave regarded the body realising that it was a dead goat. It looked like it had been hit in the head.

"He hit the goat. Where's the car? Gone over the side?" asked Dave. He walked back around the vehicle. Tiberius stayed hunkered down, examining the dead goat.

"Tiberius?" Dave called. He made his way over to him. "You can see where his vehicle swerved. Look down there." Tiberius could see a dim flickering at the bottom of the defile.

"You reckon he swerved to avoid the goat? Coming too fast?" Tiberius prompted.

"Looks like it."

"Or looks like he wants us to think it. Come over here." He led Dave back to the where the dead goat lay. "You can see the head is pretty smashed which looks like it could have come from an impact with a vehicle."

"Looks like it."

"So how come there's an entry wound at the other side of the head?" Tiberius moved the head with his foot and it flopped over with a sickening squelch.

"Sneaky bastard."

"Yes he is. Fast thinker too. Question is. Which way did he go? He could have gone in any direction in this mist."

"Hola Dave." A deep Spanish accented voice came from behind them.

"Carlos." Dave turned and shook hands with a dapper Spanish policeman.

"You hear all that?" Dave asked

"Si. I think he can either go one of three ways," replied Carlos.

"OK?" Dave replied.

"He can double back. He can go to the right down the track past the Refugio at the Lago del Barco and over the mountains but there are landslide problems recently. The track is blocked. Or he can go straight on and over the Corral del Diablo. About ten or fifteen kilometres beyond it are many little towns which lead to the A1 motorway which goes to Portugal."

"Which do you reckon?" asked Dave.

"Not sure amigo. The passes around Lago del Barco are very dangerous and blocked in places. If he doubles back, he's heading into a lot of angry Policia Espanol searching for him." Carlos smiled grimly. "I think he heads up and over the Corral del Diablo, but it's dangerous too."

"He's been trained to operate in the mountains apparently," Tiberius said quietly, "by British Special Forces."

"Merda! A dangerous man," said Carlos.

"Yep. He just took out my friend with a single shot from over a hundred yards, maybe further. He's a trained killer," said Tiberius who knew in his gut who they were pursuing.

"You know him?" quizzed Carlos.

"I'm involved in a case in Ireland where he killed at least two people in Dublin, one in Nice, Southern France, one in England and two here in Spain. So yeah. I know him and yeah, he's dangerous." Tiberius replied.

"We follow him. Ahora! Now!" Carlos turned and walked back to the second vehicle. Dave reached into the boot and discreetly handed Tiberius a pistol.

When Carlos re-joined them, Max handed him and Tiberius earpieces and the four men headed around the SUV, along the track leading towards the Corral del Diablo. The Devil's Lair.

CHAPTER FIFTY TWO

Mr Black was a predator. He could no more change his ways than a leopard change its spots. He had made his decision. He switched the rucksack around to the front and took out a dark handle. As he walked along he fitted different pieces to it, getting one of his favourite toys ready. *Time for some more fun.*

His four pursuers walked quickly and in single file. Carlos was in the lead with Max just behind him, then Tiberius. Dave brought up the rear.

After some minutes, Tiberius could hear Carlos' voice in his ear "He knows we are on his ass, so maybe he lays a trap or something, No?"

"He could try to just outrun us." Max whispered.

"Not sure." He could hear Dave. "Not his style. He likes carnage, this boy."

As they walked, the mist deadened all sound. Tiberius's mind went back to the day in the car park when Sweeney had been knocked down and almost killed. Only this was different. The fog in Dublin had been a sea fog. Heavy and almost solid. You could taste it. This was different. More insubstantial. The winds blowing wisps around and creating eddies and whirls. He wasn't sure but he felt they might climb out of it.

The ground underfoot became more treacherous and the track seemed to have disappeared. Carlos moved ahead in a constant crouch checking the ground in front. Often they found themselves scrambling over loose rocks and scree. Tiberius reckoned the mist was definitely lightening and he could see a little ahead.

Then, at the top of a rise, Carlos stood quickly and turning towards them, fell backwards. They rushed towards him. To Tiberius's horror there was an arrow sticking out of Carlos' eye.

"An arrow? A fucking arrow?" Max swore viciously. "Who is this guy? Paddy Rambo?"

"Get down! You muppet!" Dave ordered. They all ducked.

"Seriously boss. I didn't sign on for this crap." Max complained.

"Fine. Go back down if you want. Once you get back to base I'll settle up with you, but you'll never work for me again." Dave said in an annoyed tone.

Tiberius wondered at how Dave held it together. He was one of the coolest characters he'd ever met. Tiberius was seriously shocked by Carlos' death. He felt himself shaking.

"Make your mind up Max. We can't stay here. We're sitting ducks." Dave shouldered past them and crawled up and over the ridge staying well to the side of the path they were on.

Tiberius glanced at Max, patted him on the shoulder sympathetically and followed Dave.

After a few moments, he heard Max curse "ah to hell with it. Who needs a pension plan?" Then he heard him following behind them.

"The mist is lightening, which means if he's waiting for us he's got all of the advantages." Dave said softly. "He'll see us before we see him." Dave had stopped, hunkered down behind a large boulder.

As Tiberius crouched beside him he said, "we need to change things. Stop playing things his way. If we continue in single file he can just pick us off."

"If we split up he can take us out one by one," Max sounded worried, "what do you reckon Boss?"

"I think Tiberius's right. I'll continue on up this way, maybe draw his fire. You keep to the left of me, Max. Watch out for the edge. Tiberius, you try moving out to the right. Bit of a climb but maybe he won't expect it. Don't move forward until I say."

"OK Boss. Worth a try," Max moved off to the left, feeling his way along carefully.

"One change," said Tiberius to Dave instead of moving. "I go in the middle. You're fitter than me and if he gets me you're more likely to spot him."

Dave was impressed with Tiberius's courage, but simply said "fine," and moved up the slope to the right.

After a moment he could hear Dave's voice whisper "move out."

They crept forward slowly, as silently as possible. It was hardly a path, more a goat track, but as he moved along Tiberius felt horribly exposed. It felt like a massive motorway and he was creeping up the middle with no cover whatsoever. *Sometimes, I'm a real dumbass!* He thought to himself. He kept moving forward.

Then through the mist he heard a scream. He froze. And immediately a second one. This time longer, ending in a muffled thump.

"Check in." came Dave's voice in his ear.

"Tiberius. Check" he replied.

There was silence.

"Max?" came Dave's voice again.

Silence.

"Bastard!" said Dave viciously. Then quietly, "Tiberius stay on the path. Stick to the plan."

"OK."

They crept forward again. For a few moments, the mist was blew away to reveal that they had been climbing around the rim of a gigantic bowl with a deep, dark, circular lake at the bottom and smooth snow covered slopes descending sharply to the water's edge. If he wasn't so scared Tiberius would have stunned by the beauty of the place.

"Gotcha," came Dave's voice. "Look up towards the summit. See him?"

Tiberius scanned up ahead and then was relieved to pick out a dark figure against the snow, climbing upwards. He began to move quicker, watching the figure all the time. He glanced right to see Dave moving fast and beginning to advance well ahead of him. He picked up his pace, not wanting to let Dave out of his sight, but the guy moved like a mountain goat.

Tiberius looked back towards where he had seen the figure last and was dismayed to find he could no longer see him. He stumbled, his foot slipping on the compacted snow beneath him. He cursed. Getting back up, he realised that he needed to focus on his footing as much as where his quarry was heading. As he moved off he could just about see Dave, haring along up the slope to his right.

There was a massive knob of rock at the summit, sitting dourly on the broad shoulder of the mountain encircling the lake below. Tiberius thought he could see movement to the left just below the summit. He continued to scramble upwards, legs aching and lungs gasping for air, aiming for the collar below the summit.

Further ahead, Dave continued his rapid ascent. He was unsure where their quarry was, only that he was ahead of him and it looked like he was now trying to escape rather than trying to kill them. He swung down around a large boulder and dropped to the ground at the other side. There was a figure about twenty metres ahead pointing a weapon at him. Dave tried to duck but there was a searing pain in his skull and white lights and then nothing.

Tiberius heard a gunshot ahead and called out, "Dave, check in?"

Silence.

"Dave?" Then casting all caution to the winds he raced towards where he had heard the shot. His own weapon in hand. He skidded to a halt when he saw a body on the ground. It was Dave. He knelt beside Dave's body, still scanning ahead. He reached down to feel Dave's neck for a pulse. It was there.

He was alive. Tiberius noticed a long wound to the side of his head. The bullet had knocked him backwards and from the look of it he had knocked himself out.

Tiberius got to his feet and grimly moved forward.

Mr Black was running out of arrows, which was why he had used his gun on Dave. The blood loss from his wound was definitely slowing him also. *Time to finish this? Yes. Time to finish it and Mr Bloody Frost!*

He moved back to the track and straightening up, walked quickly towards the summit, turning off the path just before the massive cap of rock. It was easier going here as the steep cliff face turned into a gentle slope like a shelf running below the summit and above the steeper snowy slopes to the lake below. *Hopefully, my frosty friend will see me and follow like the good little lamb that he is.*

*   *   *

The mist swirled. Thickening and then lightening as Tiberius trudged doggedly upwards. He keep checking ahead, expecting an attack to come at any moment. Then he saw him. He had turned off the track ahead and opted to walk around the collar below the summit, where there little or no cover.

He could see the figure clearly. He was slowing. *Good,* Tiberius thought to himself. *Time for payback.*

At last he got to the area where he had seen Black move off the track. Unfortunately as he followed, the massive rock above him sheltered the area from the wind so the mist thickened again. As the wind quietened, he could hear much further than before, but then so could Black. He carefully picked his steps as he moved along, conscious to keep close to the rock face. It felt like an eternity as he inched his way silently along. He could hear the snow crunching underfoot and the soft murmur of the wind somewhere above his head.

Then! An agonising pain in his arm. An arrow transfixed his forearm. He dropped to one leg, the gun falling from his nerveless hand.

Another searing pain in his shoulder, as another arrow slammed into him, knocking him backwards onto his back. He could feel himself sliding headfirst down the gentle sloping shelf. Panicking, he scrabbled with his good arm for anything to grab onto to slow his descent. The arrow in his forearm snagged on a rock, tearing the flesh and making him nearly pass out. It was excruciating and he roared with the pain, but it slowed him down and turned him, so that his feet were below him and he was able to dig his heels in, slowing himself further. Finally he stopped sliding.

The wind picked up and the mist cleared again. Lying on his side he could see the edge of the slope some four or five feet away. Then he heard the most unexpected sound. Whistling. Someone was whistling the melody to the Sound of Music! Groaning, Tiberius raised his head and managed to get up on his good elbow. He could see a figure walking towards him along the edge, whistling. He tried frantically to get to his feet and managed to get to one knee when it was whipped away from under him as another arrow tore into his leg.

"Aaaah!" he cried out.

"Aaaah! Indeed. Mr Tiberius Frost," came a soft well-spoken voice with a faint Northern lilt. He could see him now. Mr Black stopped six or seven feet away. Ignoring Tiberius, he dismantled the bow and put it into his rucksack. He took out a gun. "Time to die. Say goodbye." He raised the gun and pointed it at Tiberius.

Tiberius, despairing, tensed, waiting for the impact. A shot rang out.

Mr Black whirled, punched by the impact of a high velocity bullet and fell to his knees. Tiberius couldn't believe it. He wasn't sure who had shot his tormentor or whether or not they were going to shoot him but he didn't care. Ignoring the agonising pain from his wounds, Tiberius got to his hands and knees and crawled towards his adversary. Black too, was on his hands and knees, his head was down and he groaned.

Slowly he raised himself and looked at Tiberius, bleeding heavily from a hole in his upper chest, near his shoulder. Tiberius gritted his teeth and swung a punch with his good arm, connecting solidly with Black's face. Tiberius cried out from the pain the effort had caused him and fell sideways. With a superhuman strength, Black taken the punch but hadn't fallen over the edge. He was swaying, still kneeling with the precipice to his back. Slowly, painfully, shaking his head. Trying to clear it.

"I don't think I like you, Mr Tiberius Frost," he said and reached slowly into his pocket, pulling out a knife with a black blade and handle. He began to climb to his feet and his rear foot slipped as the soft earth on which he was standing crumbled. His foot dropped suddenly and he fell. Tiberius could see the black knife stabbed into the earth; Black's hands wrapped around it. He dragged himself painfully forward to the edge and looked down. Black looked up at him, expressionless. Tiberius thought for a second and then slammed his open palm into the hands holding onto the knife. Black fell. He could see him sliding faster and faster down the smooth icy slope. Tiberius watched until he could see the figure hit the water far below. It didn't surface. Satisfied, he rolled away from the edge onto his back, staring at the sky above. He could see two planes, way up high, cross over each other. Their contrails creating a massive X in the sky. *X marks the spot* he thought. Then he passed out.

*   *   *

About five kilometres west of Corral del Diablo, Riga Wong got into his car. He picked up the IP phone he had left in the glove compartment. He punched in a code and waited.

"Yes?" a metallic voice answered.

"Done."

"Good."

"Anything else?"

"No. Meet me in Los Angeles." The call was ended.

Riga put the bag containing his rifle on the floor in front of the passenger's seat and drove away.

CHAPTER FIFTY THREE

Tiberius woke to the Sun. It streamed in the window and warmed his face. Somewhere he could hear a voice arguing. It was an English accent.

Then he felt soft lips on his and opened his eyes to find Ashling smiling down at him.

"Hi Yank, welcome back."

"Ohh Hi."

"How are you feeling?"

"Everything feels numb."

"Well you have a serious amount of drugs in you and you had lots of holes in you."

"Like Swiss cheese." He laughed and then coughed as the pain spasmed. "Damn that hurt."

"No more jokes, Frost. I don't think you can survive your own sense of humour," she said teasing. Then she leant forward again, her breasts pressed against him, her hand on his forehead and kissed him long and deeply. She pulled back slightly, "I thought you were dead when they brought you back last night."

"How did I?" He paused then continued "what happened after I passed out.?"

"Doyle happened. He flew in from Ireland with the rest of your team yesterday morning. When we got to the road, he was waiting with the Mountain Rescue guys and some very scary looking Spanish military types. They went up and came back down with you and Dave. We were so scared you were both going to die."

"Dave's OK?"

"Yes. Thank God."

"What about Carlos and Max? Are they dead?"

"I'm afraid so," came Dave's voice from the hallway. "Max took an arrow and we reckon Black threw him over the side. Carlos died instantly."

"I'm glad you're OK." Tiberius said to Dave whose head was covered in a bandage which looked like a turban.

"Just a bad headache. The knock to the head from the fall did more damage than the bullet. So what happened up there?"

Tiberius swallowed, remembering.

"He had me Dave. He was going to kill me. Then, from what I can figure, someone else shot him. I hit him and the edge crumbled. He fell over the side and into the lake. That's where they'll find his body."

"Great! Back in a sec." Dave went out. A few minutes later he returned with two Spanish policemen and Doyle.

"Good to see you in one piece, Tiber." Doyle grinned at him.

"Thanks buddy," Tiberius said quietly. Doyle just nodded and stepped back.

"Tell them what you told me." Dave said.

So Tiberius recounted what had happened again, in more detail, but left out the bit where he banged Black's hands on the knife and sent him down the slope. He stopped every now and then to answer questions of detail posed by the Spanish police officers. Finally, they stood and one said "Gracias Senor. We thought he had escaped so were searching the surrounding terrain. Now we organise divers to search the lake." They left the room.

Seconds later, the door burst open and a tearful Beth rushed into the room. "Is he? I mean, I can see you're awake and that and oh God! Tiberius! I'm so glad you're OK!" Ashling smiled and moved to one side to allow Beth to hug Tiberius, a little too energetically as he groaned. Horrified Beth jumped back.

"I'm so sorry Tiberius. I didn't mean to hurt you! Sorry!"

"It's cool. I'm fine."

"Me too, not that anyone's asking," said Dave grumpily. Beth turned and gave the surprised man a big hug and he smiled.

Tiberius reckoned it was the first time he had seen Dave smile.

"Oh Tiberius. Poor Dane!" Beth began sobbing. Ashling stood up and walked to Beth, putting her arm around the young woman. "We're going to get a coffee," Ashling said as she ushered Beth and Dave out. "We'll be back shortly."

Doyle sat at the end of the bed and patted him on the leg asking quietly, "you OK, Boss?"

Tiberius glanced down at where Doyle's hand had touched his legs. He said nothing. Then he stared at Doyle wide eyed, a look of horror on his face.

"Tiber? What's wrong?" Doyle asked, worried.

"My legs! I can't feel my legs!"

The End.

LIST OF CHARACTERS

Aika Sato – American/Japanese TV Chef, serial killer.

Alexandra Hilton – Tiberius's fiancé, deceased.

Ashling Clarke Brady - Tiberius's Girlfriend.

Assistant Commissioner Kane – Tiberius's Superior.

Beth Frontemont – Student and Software Developer.

Cian Clarke Brady – Ashling's and Robert's Son.

Colonel Peter Carmichael - UK Special Forces Commander.

Dane Wilson - Student and Software Developer.

Dave Gant – Head of Rayne Frost's Personal Security Team.

DCI Tiberius Frost – American ex-policeman, now with the Irish Police.

Deng Holman Lee – Chinese American Billionaire.

Detective Inspector Maurice N'Dour – French Police Officer.

Detective Prendergast- member of Tiberius's Investigation team.

DS Freya Grimstad - Tiberius's L.A. partner.

DI Aoife Kellett - Irish police officer. Ashling's Sister.

Diego de Cervera – Owner of a Stud Farm near San Bartolome de Pinares in Spain.

DS Tiernan Doyle – Irish police officer and Tiberius's partner.

Garda Sweeney - member Tiberius's investigation team.

George Black – Mister Black's Father.

Gillian MacAllister – Roger's wife, deceased.

Godiva Frost – Tiberius's sister, deceased.

Ingrid Campbell Clarke – Ashling and Aoife's Mother. Sculptor.

James Plenderleith – Lecturer, deceased.

Jamie Wilson - George Black's best friend. Loyalist paramilitary leader.

Jessica Plenderleith – James's wife, deceased.

Jo Anne Sutherland – Student, deceased.

Joe Clarke – Ashling and Aoife's Father.

John Burke – Irish Intelligence office. Tiernan Doyle's oldest friend.

Kent Gulbenkian – Deng's Head of Technology.

Lady Gwendoline Stubbs - Sir Bartholomew's Wife.

Lord Jocelyn Fanthwaite-Gibson (Joss), Earl of Lansbury, Viscount Baskerville - British Intelligence Senior Officer.

Marsala (Sylvia) Frost – Tiberius's Mother. Artist.

Mary Gill – Dane Wilson's foster mother.

Mister Black – Psychopath, Assassin.

Moira Wilson – Jamie's wife.

Morag Black – Mister Black's Mother.

Rayne Frost – Tiberius's sister. Internet entrepreneur.

Robert Clarke Brady – Ashling's soon to be ex-husband.

Roger MacAllister – RUC Police Officer, deceased.

Sir Bartholomew Stubbs (Barty). British Intelligence Senior Officer.

Whitaker Frost – Tiberius's Father.

FAMILY TREES

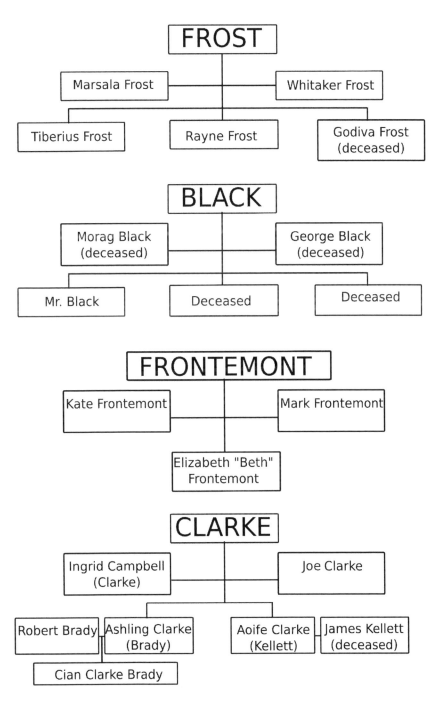

FROST

Marsala Frost — Whitaker Frost

Tiberius Frost | Rayne Frost | Godiva Frost (deceased)

BLACK

Morag Black (deceased) — George Black (deceased)

Mr. Black | Deceased | Deceased

FRONTEMONT

Kate Frontemont — Mark Frontemont

Elizabeth "Beth" Frontemont

CLARKE

Ingrid Campbell (Clarke) — Joe Clarke

Robert Brady | Ashling Clarke (Brady) | Aoife Clarke (Kellett) | James Kellett (deceased)

Cian Clarke Brady

MAPS - UCD CAMPUS

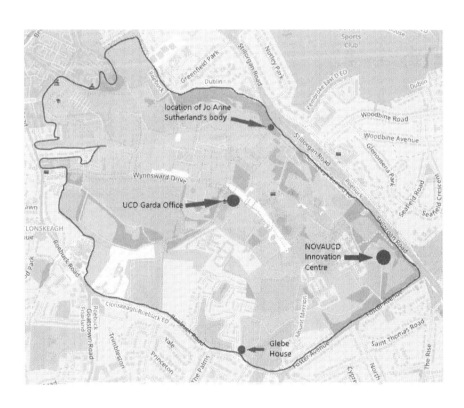

MAPS - DUBLIN

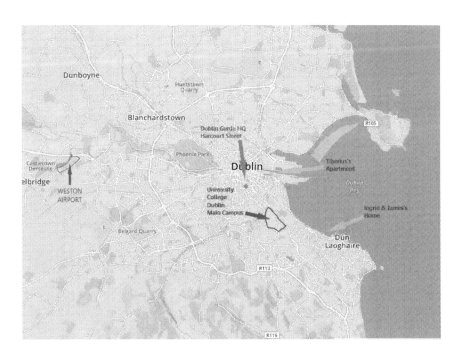

MAPS - SPAIN

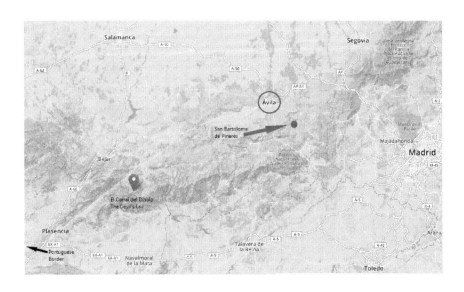

MAPS - FRANCE/ITALY

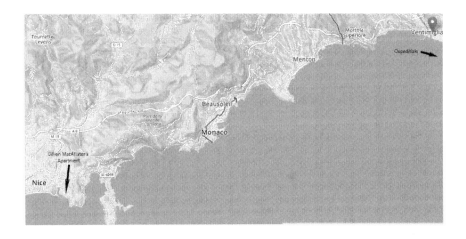

ACKNOWLEDGEMENT

To my old friend Denis Lane, thank you very much for your hard work and honesty. I wouldn't have gotten here without you.

To my Beta Readers, Eddie Rowley and Graham & Lisa Tolhurst, thank you for your encouragement and support.

A special thank you to Rita de Bruen, for your honest appraisal and kind words.

To John Burke, you have always been there for me and I can never thank you enough.

To Paula, Jack and Clare - you make it all worth while.

ABOUT THE AUTHOR

John Whelan

John worked as a publisher for twenty odd years, then as a consultant and currently works with an auction business in Dublin.

He has no need for a door bell as he shares his house with a psycho chihua-hua.

Printed in Poland
by Amazon Fulfillment
Poland Sp. z o.o., Wrocław

61972009R10319